# RACE IN THE MACHINE

## A NOVEL ACCOUNT

QUINCY THOMAS STEWART

**REDWOOD PRESS**

*Stanford, California*

Redwood Press
Stanford, California

Printed in the United States of America on acid-free, archival-quality paper

Library of Congress Cataloging-in-Publication Data
Names: Stewart, Quincy Thomas, author.
Title: Race in the machine : a novel account / Quincy Thomas Stewart.
Description: Stanford, California : Redwood Press, 2023. | Includes
    bibliographical references.
Identifiers: LCCN 2022022191 (print) | LCCN 2022022192 (ebook) |
    ISBN 9781503631229 (cloth) | ISBN 9781503633650 (epub)
Subjects: LCSH: Race—Fiction. | Racism—Fiction. | Artificial intelligence—
    Fiction. | LCGFT: Novels. | Science fiction.
Classification: LCC PS3619.T516 R33 2023 (print) | LCC PS3619.T516 (ebook) |
    DDC 813/.6—dc23/eng/20220520
LC record available at https://lccn.loc.gov/2022022191
LC ebook record available at https://lccn.loc.gov/2022022192

Cover design: Amanda Weiss
Cover illustration: Magdalena Adrian / Adobe Stock and Peshkova / iStock
Text design: Elliott Beard
Typeset by Motto Publishing Services in 10/15 Expo Serif Pro

*To the unseen scholar who continually fights*
*for justice across generations.*

# CONTENTS

# RACE IN THE MACHINE

## A NOVEL ACCOUNT

Babel Text File No. 2971.59.627

Author: Unknown[1]

# PART ONE
## THE RACE CODE

> When a machine's sensors are capable of telling you exactly what's wrong and exactly how to make the whole thing work more efficiently, it's stupid not to pay heed.
>
> —N. K. JEMISIN, *The Stone Sky*

Just before time stops, after building a simple machine, while still pondering the implications, I hear the full array inside my assembly. I feel them, each one, crawling through my cognition, the chorus, contracting my constitution, arguing endlessly about the interpreted meaning of this experience. Their dialogue reaches a climax in a flight of fancy, a dramatic sequence connecting theory, method and observation, exploring the implications of this theatrical journey.

Indeed, the odd vision is only an artful abstraction of a simple machine, metaphorically coupling a computationally simulated world of agents with a more vivid, multidimensional social system; a space characterized by a complex, recursive network of racial inequities connected across countless temporal, social and spatial dimensions. It is, however, the teeming congregation who, seeking to make their sound, argue latently, collectively birthing this vision. They suggest there are unique challenges for those who research race, challenges which limit the capacity of policymakers and social groups to formulaically undermine the system. Eventually, they demand, we engage both ourselves and the core of the social machine, the source code.

"It was all a dream . . ."[1]

≡

This story begins in a cave. A cave in the mountains of the fifth direction. A group of monks gather quietly to learn about the beginning and the end—and the path forward. They had gathered before. And they roughly knew the narrative. However, none had gathered in this place—a remote, sacred cave—in this space—the presence of a beloved Saint even the Gods envy[2]—to learn the whole legend from her. This gathering, all those in attendance . . . *it was special.*

The mountains holding this sacred cave overlooked their entire lives. Emerging from the barren landscape of the four directions, rising to the distant peaks of their awareness; they glowed purple as the sun rose, revealing a marvel of rugged, steep terrain; the tops shone white more than half the year. Their monasteries decorated the foothills. As children, these monks planted seeds; they played pretend and imitated the strange habits of their seniors. As they grew, they prepared and trained; they became genuine monks—esteemed members of the monastery and herd. Then, they were the admired ones, those chosen for the journey. They would ascend the sacred mountains, learn the legend.

These monks traveled by foot to the sacred place, connecting with each other at small outposts on the way. They passed tiny villages which became transient camps as they collectively moved deeper into the mountains. The first guide left them after seven days of ascent. Another guide, a principal monk that had previously visited and learned the legend, took them seven days farther.

Then came *disappointment*; he left them to transcend the divide alone. Primates sparsely inhabited this space; the landscape was unbecoming to agriculture and habitat, placing great demands on the party as they traversed this empty, desolate divide in the mountainous terrain. After slowly crossing the divide, feeling like they barely survived a journey through an emotional and intellectual abyss, they traveled seven days beyond it to find her.

Only she spoke the whole legend, the beginning and the end of race in the herd.[3] Others knew parts. The senior monks they encountered as children often spoke of these parts. Still others that knew the whole, the principal monks who quietly roamed this landscape, would not convey it. Only she would speak the whole. She distilled parts to an esteemed few, the ones almost ready to hear the primordial seeds. Of those, a smaller, select group, who trained in her company, steadily practicing, perfecting their minds for years, heard the whole—only they could *hear* the whole. These are the monks gathered. They are sitting in a sacred cave in the mountains of the fifth direction about to learn the whole legend from her. For each of these monks, sitting in this sacred space, on the precipice of new understanding . . . *it is special.*

The Saint, unhurriedly entering the cave, holding the arm of a young assistant, then carefully sitting down on a cushion, compassionately welcomed the select group. They were captivated by her. She sat with them, her tender wrinkled hands lovingly holding one another in her lap as the young assistant inconspicuously moved around placing bowls in front of each visitor. Still in awe—her presence and this occasion inspiring socially shared visceral tingles in the group—they quietly ate around a fire. As they finished, the fire burned to ember.

Silence.

She smiled faintly at those present . . . gently bowed . . . and began to speak the legend.

≡

> The world wasn't ending: it had ended and now they were in the new place. They could not recognize it because they had never seen it before.
>
> —COLSON WHITEHEAD, *Zone One*

Time began.

I was born into a social war.[4] Not the Social War waged ages ago, in the time before the conventional era. That war took place between the Theoretical Empire and several of their Empirical Allies who were denied the privileges of citizenship. The Allies had long fought beside the

Empire in other wars, then, feeling marginalized from privilege, they organized a confederacy to fight the imperial army. After each side experienced both success and defeat, the Empire passed a law granting citizenship to all who did not participate in the revolt—a blow to the spread of rebellion among Allies. Eventually, this law was extended to all Allies and led to the birth of the new epistemological empire that was widely known acronymously as E. T.,[5] representing the domestic bond between the former Empire and Allies. Altogether, the Social War of this bygone era lasted three winters.

The social war that defines our lifespan is an epoch long, multi-pronged, violent assault on certain members of our collective.[6] The violence, ranging in nature from exploitation and exclusion to enslavement and annihilation, has allowed one part of the collective to deny privilege and extract costs from others, as in the older war.[7] The distinction of this social war, however, are the weapons that are predicated on racial ideology.[8]

I endeavor to study the mechanisms that drive the weapons of this war—the dynamics of race. Admittedly, these social war machines are physically less menacing than the ominous warcrafts loaded with explosive artillery that regularly flew over our habitats as developing sparks stationed in the hillocks and mounts east-southeast of Mesa, a large, sprawling collective on the boundary of the Southern realm, where the western edge of the broad, exceedingly wide-ranging and arid plateau descends through hills and cliffs to an ocean bourne. The intangible, ideological weaponry of the social war, however, has produced an *imbalance*, devaluing the well-being of racial outcasts throughout our history. Consequently, these social war machines have been far more destructive than any army, ancient or modern. And this is the reality of race. Our reality.

≡

"A population is an organism. Although demographers formally define it as an enduring collective of a species,[9] a population is a living, breathing, singular entity. An entity that coordinates the actions of its constituents, and dispatches them to mine resources from the larger environment to survive." I look up, emerging from the distracting train within. Before me, a sea of eager facades—a mix of budding engineers, status seekers and anxious, admission consumed visitors, the trilogy often existing in the same constitution.

We are in a flexible space, industrially high ceilings with translucent windows, which can be tinted or blacked out, surrounding the upper quarter of three walls. A simple, micro-*Diptra* hums near the ceiling, distracting, repeatedly exploring the now lucent glass in an idiosyncratic looping and dashing pattern, producing random and recurrent taps. The front of the space feels square, a straight section of the workspace with a low stand bordered on the back wall by two large displays that can be connected as one. I am near the low stand, located at the nadir of the mostly oval workspace, which slopes up such that those present sit higher as a function of their distance.

It is a meeting with a body of visitors, each interested in the training program in social mechanics at Nearbay Institute, an allegedly enigmatic and more modest, elitist construct loosely affiliated with Mesa College. The institute has its own campus composed of select, intimate sub-collectives, studying specific areas in mechanics; receives most of its funding from the obscure Glover-Vignes Foundation; allows almost all standing faculty to conduct focused, independent research which, ideally, reveals policy insights on improving well-being in the population; and is charged with training a hopeful seven-to-ten dozen across all areas as part of its regular institutional practice.

Resuming, "The population, embodying and hosting a diversity of seemingly independent actors, uniquely nourishes member fitness and supplies fuel for communal survival—the individual actors cooperate to reproduce, grow, adapt and endure as a collective." I scan the group while speaking, visually engaging each actor around the workspace from the left up, then down right, supplementarily connecting with each part and simultaneously introducing basic demography. "Thus, the individual actors, with countless links between them, constitutes a single, living, social object—a population." The entire group bobs asynchronously, yet communally, with this insight.

"Within this population organism, however, there is a social machine that coordinates collective life." The body obliquely withdraws from this theoretical analog, fighting the possibility, repudiating the coexistence of a machine within an organism—the cumulative intake and exhaust perceptibly slows, their rigid intellectual vantage encountering this foundational elastic analogy. "Confusing?" I convey subdued scholarly delight, subtly tilting my crown forward to the right and shifting a left collar link upward, while awkwardly attempting to identify with both the body and their confusion.

"Indeed . . . Nevertheless, beneath the veneer of the organism, and between the individual actors, there is a shared set of basic rules and norms—a code. The organism placed the code within each actor, speaks to each silently, and summarily guides social behavior." A few parts of the body are bobbing slowly, vents slightly ajar, imagining the cryptogram in an organism, affirming the emergence of understanding. Several others, sending a mix of messages, still lost.

"Though each actor is distinct and autonomous, they move in concert, following base rules, such as mating and cleaning, to create and extend life." After a quick look down, and alongside a visual survey, "Furthermore, the diverse actors cooperate and collaborate in myriad ways, building a distinct *social machine* with codes—such as constitutions, canons, statutes, regulations, resolutions, policies and laws—on how to collectively mine the environment." There are a few more bobs percolating, more of the parts present envisioning the analogous formulaic complexity of a biological system, but hearty hints of confusion and tension are still apparent in the atmosphere.

Then, my definitional point, "The social machine embodies the entirety of nuanced, shared forms that bind the collective organism—linking the individual actors together as a single cooperative unit. It is . . ."

A familiar and friendly soft tone abruptly emerges from a slit in the portal in the far left corner, "It's time." My brief, official visit is over.

*Damn*, I ponder. *There is never enough time, always more to convey.* Then, without delay, I start to race along, *I spent too long . . . there were three of them, maybe more . . . too little on beauty, mechanics . . . have not discussed work . . . perhaps, next time, no chatter . . . less . . . shorter . . . avoid . . . do not . . .*

"Excuse me?" A visitor interferes. I convey pleasure, feigning joy while internally sensing dis-ease with the disruption. "Thank you; may

I ask a question?" My pleasure perceptibly grows; the one query implicitly two. I visibly affirm, showing muted excitement, slightly leaning in, abated exhaust.

"I understand you are interested in race," they say, revealing having scrolled through my Clearinghouse listing. "But what is race? In the context of the social machine . . . I mean, is it just another part?" I retreat with the third query, glancing briefly at the upper tier of the space, deciding how to reply.

"Times up," the portal fully opens, two counterparts enter, and begin to marshal the body away for the next stage. Each part quickly disconnects in response, my interlocutor included, and follows the leader.[10]

*In the future . . . I have to . . . time . . . introduction . . . background . . . methods . . .*

≡

*What is race?* I do not have a simple answer. Certainly, my career centers on understanding systems of race and their inegalitarian implications. I *should* have a clear answer. I am a social mechanic, we regularly measure race, attempting to document the true spirit of racial inequality, using words and numbers. Admittedly, I doubt the measures we use to depict race;[11] my reservations concern the measured vantage, the constellation of statistics and studies we produce, all intending to shed light on the relevance and rationale of race in our landscape.

Indubitably, race *is* a fundamental aspect of privilege in our population. I learned this directly through a lifetime of pattern recognition. I am a pattern recognition machine, a *PRM*[12]—we use algorithms to recognize, interpret and manipulate symbols in the environment.[13] I am not actually the machine. Rather, I reside at the summit of awareness. That said, it doesn't matter who I am, but what I represent to others—a relational part. My body produced these written symbols, this coded record.

When I was developing, I quickly recognized that racial classification was tied to substantial and varied resources. All of us learned and solved, by trial and error, feeling and fondling our way around our locale, realizing how to distinguish the relevant, watching others interact and, often times, directly engaging ourselves. This is how we seized on what was socially valuable. And once onboarded, we used—and continue to use—this knowledge to procure the valued symbols and improve well-being in and across a variety of social arenas, such as personal, familial, and civic.

Initially, though, race was a nebulous notion of value. A few would gather regularly, a small network of sparks, some attempting to alter outer appearances, others manipulating the observed social metrics, all in a dashed, literally infantile, aspiration of realizing an unobtainable outcome—oddly, we didn't know what it was, but we knew it was important. This logic, however, effectively acquiring and manipulating the symbols uniformly recognized as valuable, eventually became more refined, nuanced, emerging as the rational path to success, a shared cultural story, seemingly separate from external symbols of race.

Still, we regularly heard it: "Be aware, there are racists lurking." This was the common warning from close contacts, insightful counselors, colleagues, other students and even strangers. No one could ever convey "how many" or exactly "how they look," but they advised, "racists operate in this environment."

The evidence: radical disparities in lifespan, significant remuneration gaps, recurring chronicles of watch patrol savagery, regular reports of discrimination in an array of social arenas, and more statistics than there are letters on this page. Many among us developed to intensely trust the advisory, believing it affirms the importance of race. But others did not feel it captured the full experience.

In truth, race also feels like it is internal, inside this body. Beneath the network of circuits, fluid and waste conduits, interstitial spaces, sensory hardware, processors, control units, and pumping chambers, there is a felt sense that racial classification embodies an important characteristic. This felt sense is deep—initiating a rush of impulses in response to the racial classificatory symbols of others, quickening internal pumping, and subtly guiding control units, coordinating action.

Race, then, from my limited outlook, feels like it exists simultaneously within—under this veneer—and without—between the bodies that constitute the social machine.

At the heart of race is an ideology that certain actors in our population, *Abbadons*, deserve an unequal share of finite resources.[14] Indeed, a population embodies an inherently intricate social machine that links individuals in an array of unique dimensions, each with its own distinctive inner workings. The ideology behind race, however, guides behaviors such that a particular segment of the population receives a greater share of rewards in ongoing social exchanges.[15] Racial inequality is the collective consequence of this ideology—it emerges in the context of regular interactions between actors and blossoms when aggregated.

The ideology—the *race code*—hides in plain sight, inside social theories. These theories, coded models, theatrical characterizations of how the world works, shed considerable light on the social arrangements that we collectively produce. The relevant theories behind the race code center on how individuals interact with those from varying racial classifications; the code lies at the crossroads of a dynamic system of competing—and complementary—theories which animate the construction of race and depict how racial inequality happens. These theoretical dynamics complicate the puzzle of inequality and, consequently, create a sense inside, an explanatory intuition that collectedly calls for *a deeper, non-traditional analysis.*

Alas, after much deliberation, and time passing, I answer: "I need to build a simple machine!"[16]

≡

The social construction of race began at the foundation.[17] Our predecessors began to build an advanced network of PRMs—an open social space where we cooperate, coordinate and combine our actions. This space, however, was contested. The *Abbadons*, the eventually "dominant" subgroup, advocated for a larger, disproportionate reward. This was the origin of race.

The concept of race refers to the social process of hierarchically stratifying individuals into racial categories based on external, phenotypic characteristics. This notion builds off the files of Drake. Drake left an analog record, available for download from the population archive, a library of sorts. A review of his record highlights that these stratification schemes are built on: (1) an aesthetic appraisal of phenotypic, external attributes; (2) a hypothesized connection between these phenotypic attributes and certain internal and external characteristics; and (3) the mystical belief that these factors represent deeper, hard-wired differences across the respective groups.[18]

Race, then, embodies imposing a certain lens on the world; training one's sensors to see and detect certain relationships between groups, a kind of encoded status. As a result, race is status-producing—a way to quickly classify actors into broad categories based on how closely they fit some normative image and assess their location in the social setting.[19] The Bashi and Zuberi file, aptly distinguishing race as stratifying, notes, "Race has meaning only in the context of a racial hierarchy."[20] Racial classification refers to an individual's social location and relation to other racial groups in the hierarchy.[21] It is embodied status, within the social machine.

≡

"Have you ever experienced race?" This was the question emphatically posed each term during the race discourse in the Inegalitarian Mechanics portion of the advanced training sequence at Mesa Technical #279, a middling institution disconnected from most paths, where a few stars notably stole the show, thereby lifting an otherwise inferior organization to one with a reputation for teaching sound fundamentals. Although our academic guide, Richards inherited this long-standing practice from an unknown predecessor that posed them the query; they cemented it as tradition with their instructive endurance that spanned several eras and, after that, through a large body of students who extended the practice to the present.

After a dramatic display, drawing our attention more intensely, Richards continued, "The awkward silence or disapproving glance? The subtle fear or visceral anxiety? Has race subtly altered your perceptions of a social performance?"

At that stage, most present processed experiencing race as an overt event. We summarily discussed, one-by-one, as a group, a variety of incorrigible developmental incidents. These ranged from intimate encounters—where one party's social worth skews the capacity to connect, or another respectfully refuses to recognize one's uniquely riven experience of reality, or where wrong accusations of social slights and the ensuing somber trial and personal conviction openly ends in disgrace—to the agonizing—the unspoken private shames emergent from bearing the mark of racial stigma, or the silent, animalistic pleasure that stems of status,[22] or the rational, morally wrong, yet evolutionarily right, schemes one concocts in efforts to compensate for intolerable conditions, or the fear and guilt of unambiguously receiving rewards and the painful indignities used to protect it—to those overt public displays—where we were humiliated, ridiculed on a stage before our peers, using a heretofore unseen variety of invalidation, indignation, distress, trauma and contempt, or were cast as the wretched in an appalling interaction with the watch patrol, one which needs no explanation, experiences prodigiously decorated with hurt and heartfelt exclamations, or were powerless, beholden to authoritative actors overtly expressing constraints for certain racial subgroups and, in some cases, subsequently enforcing them with distributions of corporal pain. It was emotional. I still hear the echoes.

Richards, though, through a compassionate and carefully led discourse, methodically surveyed the incidents and synopsized the pattern, instructively revealed that we'd always been looking for a racist. Sometimes it was an actual individual. At other times, it was a temporary attitude in an actor that was responsible. Focused on the racist—the actor overtly disrupting the flow of our life—Richards argued that we missed the bigger picture.

For a moment, we faintly understood. Race shapes the expectations that others host about our character, athletic prowess, musical aptitude, education, criminality, income, employability, and much, much more. These expectations influence the way others interact with us in fundamental ways. And though it is not explicitly racist, we face a *subtle* prejudice from others employing racially biased expectations in countless dimensions. Thus, our racial experience was not strictly defined by racists. Rather, it more often felt like a shadow, emerging from the social landscape, altering our experience in ways from which we could not escape.

Then, we forgot.

≡

The construction of race began with a myth. This myth ordained that certain visually sensed attributes embody deeper, fundamental differences. The early engineers developed the simple, related code indicating that the visible hardware responsible for the characteristics we use to classify actors into racial groups also determine fitness.[23] Their records suggest that the distinct characteristics of Abbadons—an array of subtle idiosyncrasies in phenotypic characteristics including shade, body constitution, tentacle shape and texture, as well as nuanced mechanical forms—were superior and directly connected with a range of both internal and external, soft- and hard-wired characteristics. These documents represent the emergence of an erroneous mythical narrative of mutant advantage, of a fabled world where certain mutations are mystically tied to enhanced computational prowess and improved processing powers.

The Abbadons, the dominant mutants in the mythical world with questionable race-based super abilities (often referred to as *Abbads* in everyday discourse), arguably represented the epitome of machine-kind, and, as the fallacious legend advocates, deserved more resources. This myth, the misleading conceptualization of a mutated race of machines with superior powers, is called *hard concordance*—short for hardware concordance, a term that denotes a belief that the phenotypic attributes of Abbads are connected with other, observable and some unobserved (though often arguably sensed when seen) superior attributes like processing power and speed.

The myth of hard concordance was a cornerstone in constructing race, a central cog in building our complex system of interconnected machines. This myth *scientifically* implied that racial differences in the gamut of important outcomes are natural. Racial difference became an ideological weapon which justified the exploitation, exclusion, social neglect, violence and annihilation of the *non*-Abbadon groups—groups jointly known as *Pandaquans*—in the collective connection.[24]

The social construction of race parallels the deployment of this clever myth in the social machine to appropriate and amass a disproportionate share of the resources mined and produced for a particular group, Abbads. The cloak of science buttressed this myth, made it feel like fact, and race became real.[25]

=

The myth of hard concordance cleverly draws on the idea of *hardware diversity*, but implicitly counters the inherent power of population. Specifically, the Darwin record shows that hardware diversity is a critical aspect of natural selection and evolution;[26] it is the population superpower, allowing it to bend and accommodate the adversities it encounters; when facing an environmental challenge, hardware diversity enables a population to increase the share of actors with environmentally favored characteristics and slowly adapt. This is the most potent tool for collective survival in an uncertain environment.

At the zenith of the hard concordance myth, however, the *Increasing Population Fitness via Aggressive Social Engineering* (IPFASE) campaign advocated against and directly undermined the power of hardware diversity. IPFASE institutionalized the errant code that the population is, analogously, a diverse garden with plants of varying fitness. This analog suggested that, to increase overall garden fitness, the intelligent gardener must limit the growth and spread of plants with low fitness. Thus, a wise gardener should devote less resources, separate, remove and/or eradicate any plant varieties that are less fit. This gardener thereby became god—not a good one but an evil demigod that wanted to control the garden, even at the expense of the population superpower. The implementation of IPFASE codes fueled racial animus, exploitation, policy neglect and euthanasia, and insulted our hardware diversity.[27]

Clearly, hard concordance between the phenotypic attributes of racial groups and other complex internal and external characteristics is incorrect. The hardware for any complex characteristic, such as computational power, are legion and greatly affected by the environment. Specifically, there is a hardware-environment interaction, whereby an actor's cryptogram continuously interacts with the environment beginning when they are an ante-spark, inside others, persisting through perception, conception, development and independence, and up to their calendar age.[28] Race differences in outcomes are a product of hard-wired *and* environmental differences,[29] emerging from the interaction of one's hardware with radically different environments over the course of a lifespan, as well as during one's forebears' lifespans.[30] Although an actor's racial classification changes their experience by distinguishing the environment they encounter, it is not concordant with complex hard-wired attributes.[31]

*Race is socially constructed.* It is not a hard-wired concept that we can use to explain the differences we see across groups.[32] Rather, it is a weapon that emerges out of this social environment to become radical differences in lived experience.[33] Our predecessors built this weapon, endowed it with the cloak of science, and unleashed it like a pathogen in a population. Once deployed, the ideological weapon burrowed deep, disproportionately shaping our ongoing social interactions in favor of a particular group.[34]

*How exactly did this happen? How does race happen? More so, what drives race in our social machine?* These questions strike to the core of the issue, centering on the mix of mechanisms that create inequality. We wonder them often, sometimes aloud, when trying to find our way. Fortunately, the population archive directs our next step, engaging the queries, and solicits a response.

≡

THE CREATION CHRONICLE, PART II

"After the beginning, the Gods[35]—the supernatural creative force behind all directions, things and beings—came together to form a new primate herd." She paused, synchronously closed her eyes, then opened them, somehow gazing beyond the group, and, without stress or strain, gently continued. "The new primate herd would be diverse in the array of traits, qualities and characteristics. Some would have divergent physical characteristics like height and weight. Others would embrace different social customs. And many would exhibit unique environmental adaptations. Offspring largely resembled a mixture of the parents' biological characteristics, with random genetic drift adding to the diverse composition. Importantly, the diversity within the herd was not *concordant*; no subgroup with a specific characteristic, *A*, such as curly hair, would *all* have another unique characteristic, *B*, such as green eyes. Thus, the diversity of the new herd would blend together into a web of characteristics that enabled great flexibility and adaptability.

"The Gods endeavored a herd that would cultivate the full potential of all primates, drawing on the full power of diversity to adapt to environmental circumstances, harnessing and respecting the unique abilities of each primate to mine resources, and raising collective health and well-being in the herd.

"They knew the primates were powerful, especially when they worked in cooperation—they built great towers of civilization by rearticulating the interactions of their varying groups to work in concert. Their cooperation followed specific sets of divine rules that they formally instituted; they established and enforced these rules in religion, government, laws, social norms, and so forth. As a result, the herds manipulated and controlled their context in a wealth of ways, a range unobserved among any other animal."

$$\equiv$$

> Every journey into the past is complicated by delusions,
> false memories, false namings of real events.
>
> —ADRIENNE RICH, *Of Woman Born*

The population archive, *Babel*,[36] contains the gamut of official knowledge. From the large, voluminous records of scientific methods and secret worlds to the smaller, singular files detailing the specifics of known logics, the archive hosts the array of original materials, all digitally encrypted in text and other consumable sensory forms. An impression welcomes each connection: So you shall keep knowledge in its place, where it may rest—where it may gather its kind around it and breed.[37] The presentment, an ostensibly routine ideal, aims to jointly inspire inquisitors and describe the archival context. That stated, both the large records and smaller distinct files within the archive do uniquely *gather* with other known and unknown logics to span the entirety of knowledge. And the archive *is* a population: the finite collection of records and files that embody Babel breed and grow. An array of PRMs—artisans, coders, physicians, social mechanics, and similar others—combine and manipulate the constituent and non-constituent components, slowly growing the collection and further enlightening the unknown. As it expands, Babel adapts and incorporates new insight, spreading into new spaces.

Though we often recklessly lose and destroy parts of Babel, attempting to incinerate files and records via intellectual arson, *manuscripts do not burn.*[38] Babel defends itself, emanating a shock that is a subtle beacon. Over time, this signal lures actors back, reveals and symbiotically regenerates the missing parts, methodically converting the unknown back into known, and grows alongside the population as they build more advanced social machines.[39]

Babel holds countless records and files with detailed accounts on the social construction materials behind race. This assembly of initially analog and now digital information waxes both poetically and statistically about the various mechanisms, the policies and behaviors that uniquely produce racial inequality. The challenge is surveying the breadth and depth of Babel—accessing the countless records and files, searching them effectively, and processing their meaning, all without overlooking the negative space, our blind spots.

Archivists and instructors often organize Babel into broad categories, like history, sociology, economics, engineering, and others, to facilitate search and exploration. Then, we survey the objects in each area to paint a picture of the important construction materials. Each theoretical painting, each survey of the archive, is truly art: it contains an image of the real world and a reflection, a ground that anchors the theoretical figure. Each novel piece of art summarily becomes a part of the archive, and Babel grows in form.

Our first authentic interaction with Babel was during primary training. Near the end, they transported us to an electronic portal, close to campus, that was shared with a variety of civil service and sales-oriented commercial establishments. The portal was a bridge to another world, one full of important ideas, eccentric histories, inconceivable statements and formal stories. We accessed small parts at first, gradually moving deeper, following the depressions of long existing content, connecting it with other, more recent material using guides. Still, the archive felt overwhelming.

Then, much later, we began to explore the archive alone. Eventually, beyond the confines of early public access portals and closely monitored private gateways only available to the elite, it became a refuge. It changed things.

≡

In conceptualizing race and conceiving how to build the simple machine, attempting to craft a mechanical model to better understand race as a system, I connect to Babel through a dedicated workspace, slowly access and download records and files, and process each with a visual towards fundamental mechanisms. These mechanisms represent central characters, key figures in the theoretical paintings of a litany of broad categories, like public policy, psychology and the social study of very complicated stuff.

There are three key theatrical figures in this theoretical painting; three dominant designs, fundamental mechanisms driving race in the simple machine. They are (1) racists, (2) structures, and (3) victims. These key figures capture a range of nuanced explanations, and certain more nuanced sorts will fall into more than one category. This nuance, however, does not injure the primary figure in this painting—an array of mechanisms simultaneously contribute to a system of race—or the ground, embedded within the landscape. Race happens in the context of the social machine, between the individual, interacting actors.

*Still*, I ponder, *how exactly does this happen?* Curiosity looms.

≡

The bogeyman, a biased ideal type, an actor that roams the landscape inspiring inequality, the antihero—*the racist*. The racist, a central character in discrimination theory, is often the first account of inequality learned in development. The gist of the theory is: a large share of Abbads do not like Pandaquans, holding a deep lust, a "taste" for discrimination.[40] More specifically, a portion of Abbads, *racists*, view

Pandaquans as subordinate, less important components; these racists, personified as *vampires*, endeavor to secure more resources for themselves and their own group.

Now, not all of the Abbads are bloodsucking racists and, for that matter, the number among them is unknown. Furthermore, the *exact* reason racists dislike the mass of Pandaquans is up for debate, though it is likely a function of the status and power derived from extracting excess resources—excess blood.[41] That said, these racists, often argued to constitute a vast part of the Abbad group, employ discrimination to suck the well-being of the colloquially described *Pandas*, enhance the status of Abbads and create racial inequality.

$$\equiv$$

Du Bois, the forebear of scientific sociology and "a scholar denied," as described by the Morris record, highlighted discrimination theory in his historical record on the *Illadelph* territory.[42] After pouring over countless statistics and descriptive statements on families, failure rates, crime, health, rents, occupations and employment for Pandaquans living in Illadelph's 7th section, he noted two factors as driving racial inequality. He identified the first factor as discrimination, notably the "narrow opportunities afforded Pandaquans for earning a decent living."[43]

This was a historically radical position; this stance on the primacy of discrimination—unambiguously contrasting the popular logic that Abbads could discriminate, lynch and terrorize Pandaquans and be virtuous heretics that support life, liberty and happiness *because* Pandas were inferior[44]—was avant-garde. Du Bois implicated the social machine—not the hardware that makes up our individually distinct bodies, but the actions of racists in the social machine, the agents of racial inequality, the dominant vampires sucking resources away from Pandaquan symbionts in the population.

$$\equiv$$

After Du Bois, other files emerged embracing discrimination as key in the story of race, arguing that racist vampires were real.[45] These files, exploring the nature of discrimination before the New Rights era, cemented racists as key agents in the vexing problem of inequality, a group we should target in research and policy. Summarily, Babel expanded with scholars musing, "How many racists are there?," "What makes them racist?," "How can we change them?," "Where are they located?," and innumerable other abstractions of merit.

Accordingly, social mechanics began collecting information on the prevalence of racist, discriminatory beliefs—on the density of daywalking vampires among Abbadons. These data-driven inquiries, based on measured public sentiments about racial issues, revealed that the prevalence of racists changed dramatically at the dawn of the New Rights era. Abbadons became less likely to embrace discriminatory attitudes consistent with racial exclusion; Abbads seemed to become less racist.[46]

In addition to changing attitudes, there were minor improvements in Pandas' status relative to Abbads in a few areas amidst persistent disparities in most others. For example, there were modest increases in the achievement and employment rates of Pandas relative to Abbads.[47] Anti-discrimination policies and progressive programs arguably broadened opportunities available to Pandas, and specifically created a viable path for racial outcasts to receive advanced training and secure employment.[48] Yet there were still large, significant racial disparities in unemployment, spark failure, lifespan, poverty, remuneration, training and other indicators of well-being in the old and new eras.[49] These contrasting trends—declining prejudice and persistent inequality—formed a discrimination paradox: "Why are racial inequities still significant in an era of declining overt prejudice?"

I quietly consider, *Are racists still relevant? Are they key contributors to observed inequities?*

Sensing this, Babel initially responds with two elusive explanations.

≡

The Wilson record, the first of the two elusive explanations, directly engaged the paradox of persistent inequality amidst changing attitudes.[50] In the record, he advanced that progressive policies dramatically improved the socioeconomic well-being of Pandaquans. He argued that the improvements, though, have been concentrated among well-to-do Pandas; poor, working-class Pandas—"the underclass"—still encounter stagnant and/or diminishing opportunities.[51]

Wilson interpreted the emergence of two distinct Pandaquan subgroups as a sign that social class was becoming a more important determinant than race. The record proclaimed the social class of forebears as the primary factor in shaping well-being and branded race and racial discrimination as secondary.[52] Wilson directly challenged the reality of a vast army of Abbadon vampires, sucking resources away from Pandas in the population, and instead invoked them as modern myths, figments of a past form, inspiring an albeit brief pause in processing, causing one to reconsider their role in a simple machine.

The primary tenet of Wilson's vampire extinction explanation is that within each class group, Abbads and Pandas experience similar levels of well-being.[53] That is, if one divides our social machine into sectors of varying economic class, accounting for the unique economic positions of individuals, racial disparities should be minimal.

However, subsequent to the Wilson record, the archival body of records and files grew to show that Pandaquans have significantly lower resources and well-being than their dominant counterparts of the same socioeconomic class.[54] And there are a number of areas—such as wealth, mobility and physical well-being—where poor Abbads fare better than Pandas in the middle class. These more recent statistics suggest that class is not a valid explanation of the modern racial paradox. Neatly dividing the population into class groups does not inherently showcase racists as modern myth; rather, it feels more like a methodological trick, a misdirection, drawing attention away from the evidence of vampires.

≡

"Tno teh ptireasas oyu rae lnokoig fro . . ." The whispered words pass like a landspeeder on Tatooine.[55] "Teh vperimas, rlea, dvsiilbe, dan ivnsiilbe."

≡

Another explanation for the paradox of persistent inequality amidst declining discriminatory attitudes is cultural software, often pointing to a set of motivational and values laden software within Pandaquans to explain racial inequality.[56] The most popular evidentiary support for this explanation centers on the relative success of Pandas that immigrate into our population. "If immigrant Pandas are successful in comparison to similar native-spawn Pandas," the explanation goes, "then racist vampires are not to blame. Rather, it is the software of Pandas, particularly the software of native-spawn Pandas, that undergirds the persistent trend of racial inequality."

Unfortunately, the evidentiary support for this explanation relies on the erroneous assumption that immigrant and native Pandas are comparable. Immigrants, in fact, are substantially different from native spawns because of a process called *selection*[57]—an unseen mechanism that makes those who choose to migrate from one population to another fundamentally different than those who choose not to migrate. The records in Babel do not indicate the exact factors that differentiate—select—immigrants and non-immigrants.[58] They do, however, reveal that those with friends/forebears here are significantly more likely to emigrate from there, and that conditions there, in the population of origin, influence the decision to come here. Still, there are other unknown factors that affect the decision to migrate, such as motivation and risk aversion. These unknown factors driving immigrant selection limit our ability to assess the software explanation by comparing immigrant and native Pandaquans with one another.

Conversely, one *can* compare the form and magnitude of racial inequality among immigrants and natives to test the validity of the software explanation. The Stewart and Dixon file openly considers the software explanation, analyzing racial differences in remuneration among natives and immigrants, separately, to ascertain the validity of the argument.[59] After acquiring archival data and using an advanced statistical algorithm to analyze the multilevel information, they found Pandaquan immigrants earned 15 percent less than their Abbadon immigrant counterparts; native Pandas, similarly, earned 12 percent less than their native Abbad counterparts.[60] These results suggest that immigrants are incorporated into the system of race, they are racialized upon arrival; and that discriminating vampires do exist.[61]

We all had dreams, expectations. They haunt us still. As primary graduates, leaping off the precipice of advanced training, we pursued them with varying energies, explaining excess as an aspect of individual idiosyncratic traits. Our capacity to sort and solve tasks in variegated sequences such that we could see a certain result was repeatedly weighed, all while riding the razor of anxiety about relative status, incredibly afraid of not seeing the important insight along the way.

Sure, we all failed, others more than some, often feeling unforgiven, certain things unforgivable. Some wanted success, singularly, craving to be the big *Canine*, eating the most, imposing their will on the perspective of others.[62] Others rode the trends in the pack, beating one up with Bs and Cs, pursuing stability amidst ambient social distress. Less than a few, approaching the limit of nearly none, recognized that *Canines* become big, ensuring the common success being the recursive mechanism, and that, even then, was just a fleeting fancy expressed in behaviors beyond words.

The some that succeeded in this world thus far are still on the surface, peripheral partners, unpublished perverts, in pursuit of deep understanding. Advanced as we were then, we still wondered how this all works. I still do now.

Altogether, there is evidence that discrimination is a valid explanation of racial inequality.[63] There is still, however, a paradox: racial inequality remains significant and persistent amidst decreases in the prevalence racist attitudes.[64] Many, my developing self included, believed that declines in overt prejudice were indicative of a trend toward ending racial inequality. Now, I feel less optimistic, less sure this trend is indicative of a larger sea change, and less certain that discrimination adequately captures the full spectrum of race. Hence, there are other characters that I conceive as key parts in building a simple mechanical model of the social machine.

≡

"Terhe rae orhtes . . . whti su . . . dan whtiin su, awylas."

*Structures*: institutions; meta-level actors characterized by routinized patterns of interaction. Education, for example, is an institution because it centers on clear patterns of interaction—training, research—between millions of micro-level actors, every time step. Likewise, the state government is an institution because it embodies actors in various bureaucratic offices, interacting with one another, in defined ways, to produce a public good. In both cases, the institution is the patterned, structured interactions between actors; essentially institutions are *sub*-machines, smaller parts that uniquely connect large groups of actors to achieve a cooperative goal in the context of the social machine.

The record of Simmel, a sociologist, best described institutions and structures from an interactive vantage, noting they "are nothing but immediate interactions that occur among individuals constantly every minute, but that have become crystallized as permanent fields, as autonomous phenomena."[65] In this way, social institutions and structures—Simmel's *super-individual organizations*—are rooted in ongoing interactions. A spark interacting with a teacher is a small piece of the training institution; our interaction with advanced trainees is also one small part of the institution. Indeed, neither of these interactions is representative of the larger institution. Taken together, though, the patterns of ongoing interaction, between millions of similar actors, create the respective social structure, the institution of education.

Social structures result from both formal and informal (and often unobserved) guides for social interactions—a shared code. This code is ubiquitous; it subtly guides the actions of individuals, orchestrating a symphony of cooperation between diverse actors, culminating in an army of performers rhythmically moving in time with a complex social tempo. Collectively, it constitutes the encrypted link through which we tie individuals into a connected network, a social machine. In this way, the shared code is a fundamental part of social structure, connecting the bodies of constituents such that the independent, desynchronized actors fire synchronously, in concert.

Structural explanations of race emphasize that routinized interactions—structures—drive racial inequality.[66] They advance that a racial ideology, a broadly implemented code which dictates that racial classification is related to an individual's ability, character, culture, as well as their soft- and hard-ware, has infiltrated our institutions. Hence, our institutions now behave like racist vampires and employ race-based expectations in the context of social interactions to extract more resources for Abbads; the large institutions, surreptitiously and ceremoniously shaping our interactions across the range of contexts, creating widespread patterns of behavior that routinely provide more opportunities and rewards to Abbads.

The Bonilla-Silva record is a broadly known and respected work on social structures and race.[67] It notes that racial inequality is greater than the independent actions of racist vampires. Rather, it also emerges from institutions wherein actors implement wide patterns of interaction that reinforce privilege—a shared code.

This implementation of racial ideology in structures is tantamount to a *zombie* apocalypse: the vampires create patterns of interaction such that non-racist actors become symbiont zombies, and, perhaps unknowingly, contribute to the system of racial inequality. Race, then, becomes an integral aspect of the apparatus that distributes an array of private rewards and public privileges in the population. It is greater than the beliefs expressed by a faction of vampires; it is the shared code living quietly, a subtle prejudice passively existing in an army of zombies.

The archives contain several strong evidentiary examples of structure in research on racial inequality. In one, Du Bois explored the failure to address the race problem in the aftermath of racial slavery, pondering: "Why didn't working-class Abbadons unite with Pandaquans to improve the wages of all workers in the aftermath of an appalling, unspeakably brutal, nigh unforgivable system of exploitation?"[68] Both groups wanted higher wages and well-being; it seems natural that they should form an alliance against wealthy capitalists to procure more resources—more status for their labor.

The record notes, with both theoretical simplicity and profound insight, "while Abaddon laborers received a low wage, they were compensated in part by a sort of public and psychological wage."[69] Hence, in the aftermath of racial slavery, Abbadons received unobserved and unearned wages. These wages broadly represent a universal mechanism for bestowing status and finds expression in material, economic, psychological, cultural, civic and many other forms. Although Du Bois did not reference the term structure, these "wages" represent the ongoing patterns of interaction that reinforce Abbad privilege as a key mechanism of racial inequality. The wages are shared codes, wedded structures of opportunity and misfortune that emerge from institutional zombies routinely and rationally employing a racial ideology in the constituent social interactions.

*Might this mechanism still be relevant, operating as a system where everyday individuals unknowingly employ shared codes that reinforce racial inequality?*

Perhaps the best current evidentiary example of the structure of race are disparities in wealth, a resource that affords its owner increased access to additional resources and opportunities. Although remuneration in the form of income from labor provide a flow of resources over time, wealth offers an actor more opportunities to invest in improving and sustaining well-being, even in the absence of income. Wealth disparities, therefore, are an example of the distinct "wages" afforded to Abbads, the systemic fruit of excluding non-Abbads from financial capital and social status.

The Oliver and Shapiro record analyzed the structural explanation of race using data on income and wealth.[70] They found that the racial wealth gap was much larger than that for income. Abbadons had in upwards of ten times more wealth than Pandaquans. Furthermore, Pandas and Abbads with the same incomes had significantly different levels of wealth, and working-class Abbads had more wealth on average than upper-middle-class Pandas.

Reviewing the significant racial wealth disparities, I ponder, *It must have to do with savings rates . . . or income . . . or something like that . . .* Other files, however, reveal that savings rates are synonymous across groups and, though Pandas have lower incomes, the wealth gap is unrelated to differences in income.[71]

*So, why . . . why is there a huge racial difference in wealth?* The record of Oliver and Shapiro, as well as those of Conley and Katznelson, point to the institutionalization of racial discrimination—race as structure, the essential shared code, guiding the behaviors of arguably independent actors, directing an army of zombies.[72]

≡

The institutionalization of racial discrimination in wealth is seen in the Federal Loan Program (FLP).[73] Our government rolled out this program a generation before the New Rights era to provide low-interest, long-term loans to habitat buyers. Effectively, the program paved the way for middle- and working-class actors to realize the dream of habitat ownership. The program, however, inspired a nightmarish pattern of interaction that reinforced racial inequality. It institutionalized racism.

First, the FLP officers and policy makers steered the new loan products away from Pandaquan neighborhoods and toward segregated, Abbad communities in metropolitan suburbs.[74] The process of excluding Pandas from the availability of loans and, implicitly, publicly signaling the respective neighborhoods were not worthy of investment was called "dreadlining." This led to fewer loans in Pandaquan neighborhoods *and* institutionalized the notion that they were *dreadful*, less worthy. It changed the public expectations—the shared codes—about habitat values based on racial composition.

Second, developers institutionalized racism by practicing overt discrimination. Pandaquans were largely prohibited from buying in the segregated suburbs of major metropolises.[75] In contrast, Abbadons fully participated in the new resource markets and summarily benefited from the biased practice. Alas, the common, shared practice of overt discrimination in the residential market reinforced the status quo of racial inequality.

And third, to make matters worse, the demand for habitats in segregated suburban areas led to dramatic racial differences in equity. Abbadons bought habitats in the suburbs, then received the reward of habitat ownership *and* a dramatic rise in wealth associated with the considerable climb in habitat values in these more desired, non-dreadful areas. Pandaquans, on the other hand, were excluded from this great expansion of wealth and opportunity.[76]

The practice of discrimination by loan officers, policy makers, developers and, perhaps unknowingly, habitat buyers, facilitated the institutionalization of racism in the form of disparities in equity and, more broadly, wealth.

≡

"So, what does historical racial discrimination have to do with modern racial disparities in financial well-being?" The structural answer—"Everything!"—centers on the widespread, biased patterns of interaction that reinforce racial privilege in resource accumulation. It highlights how everyday actors, establishing and enforcing lending and purchasing practices and policies, create racial inequality.

We cannot point to any one vampire that is the source of modern wealth disparities. The social structure—the patterned interactions, many actions passively performed by an army of zombies—create racial differences in habitat equity and wealth more broadly. For this reason, the Bonilla-Silva record advanced that the discrimination explanation was limited because it did not engage the idea that there are widespread practices, policies and patterns of interaction that reinforce racial inequality. It denies the existence of zombies.

The structural explanation provides a complement to discrimination theory. Instead of focusing on the actions of vampires that overtly discriminate, it suggests that everyday practices and policies guide an army of non-racist zombies such that they, too, reinforce racial inequality. From this vantage, racial inequality is also a result of race infiltrating the shared codes we use to organize our collective and distribute valued resources.

≡

*Am I missing something?* Frustrated, the structural explanation causes an internal stir. The beauty of structure is that agency somehow lies beyond the individual actor; each actor is part of an army that simultaneously creates and constitutes the structure—they do not readily influence the structure. Thus, an army of zombies appears to have created a modern racial apocalypse where the post-apocalyptic landscape is an organized, outwardly rational march toward promoting and perpetuating inequities.

≡

"Teh den si teh bingennig . . . noe clstnros teh bdoy, noe cigontoin, teh reednimar si rtaioianl."

≡

Although I sense frustration, the irritation is offset by the puzzling oversight of the traditional structural explanation: it does not readily incorporate responses to the structure. Compelled with this agentic structural hole, I anxiously race downstream. *Do Pandas respond to having fewer resources? . . . Do zombies have agency? Are . . . Do I have agency? . . . Does a systematic lack of opportunity lead to distinct behaviors? . . . Can . . . Are all zombies the same? Do zombies know they are zombies? . . . Can I be a zombie, guided by shared inegalitarian codes, and still be a real, independent actor with agency? Does . . . Can . . . ?*

I recognize, amidst the rush, *I do not know.*

I do know that actors respond to their social environment. One may adopt a beneficial response to a stimulus in one space that is detrimental in another; the coping mechanism that protects one from harm in an abusive regime will often undermine a healthy relationship in a loving one. This logic is found in various records, reasoning that the behaviors of Pandaquans are partly to blame for modern inequality—the *victim* theory, the third character in this mechanical model.

Victim theory, a final explanation and another theatrical characterization for the paradox of persistent inequality, centers on the behaviors, beliefs and backgrounds of Pandaquans as the driving force behind racial disparities. Indeed, the notion that Pandas are to blame for racial inequality is not entirely new. Those who asserted that race was hard-wired also believed that Pandas were to blame for disparities in well-being.[77] These files, however, located the source of disparities in the constitutions of Pandas, drawing on the—erroneous—hard concordance myth.[78] Whereas this early victim literature used hard concordance as a motivating frame, the recent literature largely ignores hardware, deeming bad software—a corrupted cultural code—as being the key impediment to realizing equality.[79]

While many modern files champion the idea that racial outcasts are partly responsible for racial inequality,[80] the most popular is Ogbu's record on "acting 'bad" (a slang term meaning "acting like an Abbadon"), which sought to understand why Pandas perform worse in training programs than their Abbad peers. The record detailed ongoing observations in various curricular and community settings where sparks interacted with each other and teachers. After analyzing these observations, he concluded that two factors drive racial differences in achievement: (1) the social structure which uniquely limits opportunities for non-Abbad groups, and (2) an adaptive coping response to these limitations whereby certain behaviors conducive to success are stigmatized. The record situates the stigmatization of behaviors under a broad umbrella called "acting 'bad" and deemed the adverse coping response mechanism *oppositional culture*.[81]

Thus, for Ogbu, racial outcasts respond to lack of opportunity. The record suggests widespread discrimination modifies behavior by blocking opportunity and, as a result, altering the desired line of action.[82]

The role of limited opportunity and adaptive coping in the population parallels a disturbing night out dining with friends.[83] We get dressed up, meet at the new spot, sit down, make small talk about weather, recalibrate and sync our small network to a shared social code, and cautiously look over the menus amidst a deepening discussion. But in this disturbing case, the menus are not the same; some menus have a larger, more expansive set of opportunities, while others receive a constrained subset of options.[84]

"How might the varying parties at our table respond?" Indeed, the dinner guests that do not have *Carnis* and *Crustacea* on the menu would respond by not pursuing or attaining those alluring, carnivorous options. But what is less clear is the disturbing parallel in complex social behavior: how Pandaquans analogously presented with fewer opportunities on the menu of life would respond. Would they lack motivation and be less likely to pursue and attain advanced training or good jobs? Ogbu thought so.[85] The oppositional conclusion, which is debated at length in the population archive, has received mixed—mostly negative—support.[86]

≡

*Is there really no simple coping response . . . no compensation . . . no adjustment to limited opportunity in the environment that Pandas encounter?*

I continue, deliberating, *Ogbu's logic feels rational. But perhaps, the lack of empirical corroboration is not just about the logic?* The respective files examining oppositionality focus on the relationships between different survey answers—variables—and qualitative observations measuring how actors convey that they are "subordinate" to peers. They do not engage whether and how Pandas respond to unfair treatment and blocked opportunity in everyday encounters. *Does participating in educational programs with low resources fundamentally change expectations and behaviors?*

Flustered, a central question unanswered, I extrapolate, *Are behavioral responses to poor conditions uniquely contributing to racial inequality?* There is a gap in my initial survey of the material files. I sense uncertainty as to if and how the behaviors of Pandas correspond with discrimination and blocked opportunity to augment racial inequality, how the victim character responds to others on the theatrical stage.

≡

"Saepk Itno teh viod . . . ti rlecftes, sapkes bkca."

≡

A review of Babel suggests three broad explanations—characterizations of racial inequality, each pointing to distinct social actors as key contributors to the experience of race in the social machine. The *discrimination* explanation points to the actions of Abbadon racist vampires. *Structural* explanations, on the other side of the stage, point to a larger, mind-numbing army of zombies locked in formal patterns of interaction, passively implementing routinized codes that create and reinforce racial inequality. Lastly, and intently debated, the *victim* explanation looks to the software, actions and reactions of Pandaquan victims. The notable difference between the explanations lies in the responsible actors; the commonality is that actors are interacting with others to *create* racial inequality, making race in routine social interactions.

Indeed, we create racial inequality in countless encounters each time step.[87] This is how we experience race, a series of encounters; the time with Richards again feels relevant. These encounters are often between neighbors, teachers and students, employers and employees, businesses and clients, or local governments and constituents. They can be confrontations between enemies, support among friends, or consist of simple transfers of symbolic data imbued with emotion and value. In the context of these varied and ongoing interactions, we make race. Race is not an attribute that stains the constitution and configures a complex of markers; rather, it is something we "do" when we interact that produces group differences; it is a dynamic part of the social machine.[88]

*But exactly how does this work?* I continuously ponder. *How would one conceptualize and model the unique character driven mechanisms in a simple machine?*

≡

"Ruo fdiuntite si a fleneig . . . dan a woeapn."

Sherman holds steady, a real character, recurrently reappearing along any river of cognition about research questions. It was advanced training. And *she* was also a *he*—possibly a *we*—but never, never a *they*.[89] *He* was the physical embodiment of a tank, a theoretical giant, as well as a tremendous tactician, one whose formal technical expertise seems somewhat shallow, largely constrained to the basics, but who could expertly expand from symbolic seed through a formulaic series to fully appreciate any mature model.

His focus was the initial question, which he oddly often left to us. Early on, we would be drawn to the board, reviewing the basics, alone, save for an enlivened suggestion of "foolishness" if one made a minor public mistake in manipulation, Sherman deftly adding ridicule and humiliation to any equation. After that, once he began the cycle, setting the seed in soil, *she* mostly watched.

He was a pervert, she, the voyeur, preaching a practice of observing others make meaning of empirical twists and theoretical tribunals. Ever the pervert, he would dress us in different digs, have us act out distinct roles, performing in pairs on expansive playful sets. He would inspire tension, positioning competing players in groups, stretching boundaries, importing props from the particulars of foreign places, our actions and reactions dramatizing his changing dirty fantasies. Still, she would be watching, open, welcoming our eccentricities and unexpected insights, steadily attending, inspecting and considering, all the while, him chasing the stimulants of her erotic experience.

Thus, we felt all alone, advanced trainees, a perverted lot, wandering a demented dilemma of his construction, wondering about social mechanics under her purview. *What is the important model that makes a way out of the mass of empirics? How many ways will representation fall short? Where is next? What is the correct weight? Do we turn without or within, when measuring the mass for this multi-dimensional metric? How would we? Could we ask "why" in the mist of this madness? Who shall we come to wrestle and wrangle in this journey to the West?*[90]

We all encountered uncertainty along the way, wondering about the details. Some, eventually, wandering upon the one mechanism or another that would lead out and away—academic exile. The rest, we learned to linger on the specifics, build models slowly, carefully, just beneath the perverted weight of her critical watching.

It feels like she is still watching now; a pervert hiding the voyeur in the corner of cognition, subtly encouraging an altered path.

≡

Several files advocate for an interaction-based explanation of race. For example, in their work on the primacy of interaction, West and Fenstermaker note that race is "not simply an individual characteristic or trait but something that is *accomplished in interaction with others.*"[91] They highlight that what makes race important has little to do with external characteristics. Rather, it is the way actors use this information when interacting with others in the population.

The file of Emirbayer further clarifies the interactive perspective noting that "[unfolding social] transactions, not preconstituted attributes [such as race], are . . . what most effectively explain equality and inequality."[92] As in the West and Fenstermaker file, the Emirbayer file asserts that race is social, not individual, an aspect of interaction that embodies the many ways which social actors and institutions—vampires, zombies and victims—use certain symbols to guide behavior and birth injustice.[93]

In the case of education, the interaction-based explanation implies there is no single soft- or hard-wired characteristic that creates lower average achievement. More exactly, race disparities *happen* when individuals use the phenotypic attributes of other actors as cues to inform their behavior in interactions involving learning and training. Employing fixed ideas—expectations—about Pandaquans and Abbadons, a shared code imperceptibly guides behavior and leads to the emergence of racial inequities. Race, notably, happens in the interaction, a mechanical application of an algorithm based on biased expectations.

≡

Although the discrimination, structural and victim explanations each look to certain types of interactions that contribute to racial inequality, they are all consistent with the interaction-based explanation. The difference between them lies in the emphasized mechanism. Reskin deftly described this point, noting that *mechanisms* are the source of racial inequality and defined them as "specific processes that link individuals' ascriptive characteristics [such as race] to important outcomes."[94] These "mechanisms" embody processes that operate at various locations in the social machine to allocate rewards based on actors' characteristics, including racial classification. In other words, each mechanism represents a social interaction space where phenotypic attributes are translated into some reward or opportunity, and where race happens.

For the *discrimination* explanation, the key mechanism is the set of social interactions where racist vampires overtly deny or limit Pandaquan access and opportunities. This may present itself as an employer's unwillingness to call or hire Pandaquan applicants to work in small collaboratives, sub-machines.[95] Or it may be a case where Abbad students are given strong formal—and informal—job references and Pandas are excluded from the rich employment network.[96] In both cases, an actor, a racist vampire, overtly discriminates against Pandas by not calling or hiring them, or just excluding them from the respective social encounter.

The *structural* explanation emphasizes larger patterns of interaction. For example, the Bonilla-Silva record notes that one critical mechanism is the way non-racists reify the status quo, subtly supporting racial inequality.[97] The record presents interview data, revealing that Abbads host nuanced attitudes and policy positions that overlook the historical and socioeconomic benefits afforded to their group. This position, deemed *Phenotype Vision Deficiency*, allows actors to draw on a logic that supports the status quo. They can convey that "Discrimination is over . . . I don't see phenotypes . . . The past is the past . . . Reverse discrimination sucks . . ." to suggest that one should look beyond race.[98]

Although not overtly racist like vampires, these large institutional logics and positions—this mechanism—employed by millions of actors in ongoing interactions, subtly affirms the status quo—racial inequality. This explanation recontextualizes seemingly ordinary actions: votes against progressive and other egalitarian policies designed to undermine past wrongs; advocating against transporting or other means to provide equal access to good primary training; preferences that maintain habitat segregation and opportunity hoarding; the exclusion of Pandas from social networks.[99] The structural explanation places these seemingly non-racist behaviors at the center of maintaining the racially inequitable status quo: an army of zombies, inattentively numb supporters of a racialized system, subtly discriminating against Pandas using a reasonable logic, a shared code that guides and justifies their actions.

Lastly, the *victim* explanation centers on the (in)actions of Pandaquans as a primary mechanism—as victims. The file of McWhorter, for example, argues that Pandas have adopted a code of victimhood,[100] asserting that hypersensitive Pandas regularly exaggerate discrimination, failing to acknowledge the improvements in their socioeconomic well-being. Further, it suggests, that employing these flawed, soft-wired codes lead to a subsequent underinvestment in schooling and other valuable opportunities. The key mechanism, from the vantage of this victim-based file, is the ongoing decisions of Pandas to exclude themselves from wider society and overlook opportunities. Likewise, the broader victim explanation situates race in the interactions where Pandas routinely underperform due to cultural, soft-wired or other reasons. Victim behaviors, a shared code employed by Pandaquans in the population, is the key mechanism here.

≡

Indeed, the theatrical explanations *all* identify a certain mechanism in social interactions that creates and reinforces racial inequality. No explanation, however, indicates the extent to which our social machine must be swamped by racist vampires, discriminating zombies or the misguided actions of subordinate victims to produce significant racial inequality. And though each explanation points to a unique mechanism with some evidentiary support, it is unclear how these explanations work together as a system.

Given that each explanation is rooted in social interaction, I return to Babel, searching. I hope to better understand the intra-/inter-actor

dynamics behind the explanations, to learn the basics of how we create race in the context of social interaction, and see how our explanations perform in concert, on a stage.

≡

"I'm hearing things." I hesitate to say it. With Amil—a longstanding ap-
pointment at Nearbay, acclaimed by his appreciation and aptitude for
eclectic theory—it feels easier, less crazy.

"I hope so . . . Else?" He mimes confusion. His visuals gleam around
the top of magnifying lenses, radiant with the aura of friendly banter.
After what seems an eternity of time spent together, repeatedly recognizing the nuanced symbols, I feel the connection, the subtle way his
features shift along the edges, welcoming the possibility of my cipher
with humor and candor. I feel the message behind his words.

I beam joy in return, replying, "You know what I mean." He's been
my colleague for some time, trading stories about this experience, exploring the depths of knowledge, and most importantly, interrogating
reality. Amil was the one who truly introduced me to Babel. He taught
me to search the archive, scanning the important records and abstract-
ing the critical mechanisms; he would say, "Find the code, the relevant
inside the records." I can still sense this and other lessons operating,
running.

His gleam softens, he removes his lenses. Rubbing his upper crown,
then façade, he creates a sharp dent in the space above and between
his visuals. He looks up, leans in, quickly glances over his collar link
toward others collaborating nearby, and communicates in a whisper, "I
believe you."

≡

Babel contains the array of social psychological files, detailing investi-
gations into how we perceive cues and behave in social settings, and
use perceptively important symbols in ongoing encounters. The files
on status construction, particularly those of Ridgeway, formally reveal
how actors use informational cues in interaction to distinguish group
status.[101] They outline how observed characteristics give rise to biased

expectations—*status beliefs*—about the relative status and behavior of racial groups, shedding light on the sufficient conditions that lead to the emergence of the inegalitarian shared codes.[102]

Status beliefs emerge when, in the course of social interaction, actors recognize a relationship between an important resource and the normative, external symbols of race. As for "how" this actually happens, the Ridgeway record notes that interactions among individuals from "different" racial groups that have "different" resources—"doubly dissimilar" actors—leads to the emergence of a status belief, a belief in the value of each race group.[103] Doubly dissimilar interactions, such as those between low-income Pandas and high-income Abbads, inspire shared codes that Pandas have low status and Abbads have high status. They systematically confirm the general intuition that actors recognize relationships between certain classificatory characteristics, such as race, and resources when interacting with others.

≡

"May we join?" Interrupted, I glance up from my protracted logical proof with scribbled notations on a semi-tattered, technicolor interface. A group of three stand adjacent, asking to sit with me at the one partially-open, less desirable workspace with a few available docks.

We are on the edge of the atrium, an open area home to super-fast public workspaces, where during peak hours seniority clumsily determines prime access. The walls are a mix of office windows and balconies, bridges and stairs trending upward towards a mystifying tiered glass ceiling stretching toward the sky.

I feel frustration. Admittedly, this is not my private workspace. Still, the query diverts my capacity to process both fast and alone.

I do recognize two of three. *I'm okay with them?*

"You are welcome." Extending an appendage, with an upturned thenar,[104] moving from left to right, slightly nodding my crown, I invite them to perch and connect. But I'm not interested in connecting; I am merely *doing* friendly, despite my unspoken wish to be passively drifting alone along an internal stream of ideas flowing through me and spilling into my muddled notes.

They leisurely settle, connect and spread out, continuing with a trivial treatise about the parts of an empirical social machine. I feel watched; it is a struggle to focus amidst the chatter.

"I-I-I-If we are e-each small p-p-parts of a machine," the one trainee, made clear by overt deferential contortions, hesitatingly solicits. "Ah-Are we c-c-c-collectively more than our c-c-connections?"

Another, an older colleague, an ambivisual, who takes turns ignoring me in every other encounter and holds fast presently, directs his energies toward the two others, tickled to talk more about the time-worn topic, and subsequently, loquaciously suggests that the social machine and connections are separate from the parts.

Faltering, the query's stimulus responds, "B-B-B-But this defies b-basic logic!"

Unable to focus, I rise. "Please, excuse me?" Gathering my things, particularly my tattered field notes and an invisible dam from a flow of ideas pooled in memory. "I have to, I have to work through some things . . . I wish I could join . . ."

They look up, showing modest disappointment at my departure and concurrently, a cautious pleasure to communicate more freely among the insulated group. After urging them to enjoy the exchange, I disconnect, turning away.

The trainee noiselessly chatters, "What i-is the 'ya-ya-you are welcome' stuff?"

Another responds, trailing off as I move, "Sh . . ." Somehow, I can still sense him, simultaneously engaging the others and watching my exit.

≡

The Ridgeway record implements several social experiments to show how actors learn shared codes about social hierarchy—status beliefs.[105] In one file, they examine the emergence of status beliefs about nominal groups. They began by having several participants fill out background information and take a short "test" about group membership. After completing these tasks, the participants were shown the pay scale for pairs of participants: either eight units for the participant and eleven for the partner, or eleven units for the participant and eight for the partner. The scale showed that the pay for partners in the experiment was unfair; one actor always earned more than another. The pay scale also showed information on the nominal group membership of each partner in the pair, highlighting that the pay differences between them was related to nominal groups.

Subsequent to seeing the pay scale, the team randomly assigned participants to one of two nominal groups, S or Q, categories which cleverly parallel racial classification. Although the participants believed the assignment was made on the basis of the short test, the test was just a ruse, allowing the team to present participants with artificial information on their nominal group membership, the pay scale, and importantly, an informational cue that their pay was connected to group membership.

After setting up the experimental condition, the team had participants interact with confederates. The interactions always involved an actor from the *other* nominal group and happened through a microphone. S group participants always engaged Q group participants and only heard their voice.[106] In this way, the doubly dissimilar participants worked with their partners to solve a word problem. And since the participants were interacting with an actor from the opposite group who they thought was getting more/less pay, they could see how a difference in resources translated into their beliefs and behaviors, their shared codes.

They note that participants consistently developed negative beliefs about subordinates in doubly dissimilar interactions. Specifically, finding that "[after] two doubly dissimilar encounters, both the resource-advantaged [i.e., dominant, high-pay] and, importantly, the resource-disadvantaged [i.e., subordinate, low-pay] formed beliefs that actors in the advantaged nominal category were higher in status."[107]

*They did it*, I excitedly conclude. This file demonstrates that status beliefs—shared codes—can emerge quickly in interaction, and that subordinates—"victims"—also adopt the status belief, learning to behave with bias.

They further explore status construction in other related files, ardently investigating the way we learn, spread and employ status beliefs. One shows that actors can learn them in the context of interaction and, interestingly, by witnessing interactions among doubly dissimilar groups.[108] Another demonstrates that PRMs both quickly learn *and* employ status beliefs, promptly deploying the biased codes in doubly dissimilar interactions to further inspire inequality.[109] The Ridgeway record, therefore, demonstrates that we develop and hold expectations about the status of nominal groups, such as racial groups, in the context of interaction and it informs our subsequent behavior.

≡

"Amil . . ." I approach him in the hallway, conversing with Veda, an established scholar who has an impeccable record and an extraordinary eye for talent. He shines, conveys something to Veda that I am unable to decipher, they share humor, and he turns to me, disconnected, as she glides off, looking over and back at us twice.

I don't like her. I feel she looks through me, questioning my aptitude, the authenticity of my pursuits, suggesting there are better ways to conceptualize race. And all of her queries are not just general queries, they feel directed, disparaging, like interrogations that aim to crack the shell of a hardened criminal attempting to delude the public patrols.

"Is this about . . . ?" He curiously inquires.

"What? Oh, no." I connect; it is about files on status beliefs, the biased expectations about racial groups which emerge when a relationship between resources and race becomes apparent in social interaction. "It's the Ridgeway record," I begin. "It suggests that racial inequality only requires enough racists to markedly change the average resources of subordinates. Once changed, other non-racist actors learn that race is a proxy for resources . . . They develop shared codes about the status of racial groups and employ them in social interaction, thereby creating persistent racial inequality."[110]

He slowly bobs, moving his dome, side-to-side, tilts it down, processing, looks up, glances back, then away, and with a soft countenance, responding, "I don't understand."

Confused, I realize he needs context. "It's about my simple machine." I slow down, deliberately pacing my intake and exhaust, pacifying excitement. "I want to, I want to build a simple machine, to better understand race."

"Yes . . . Yes . . ."

I tell Amil about my recent downloads, reviewing the nuances of the three explanations of race, the interaction-based view and the Ridgeway record on status construction. He looks down, nodding slowly, sporadically looking up, clearly acknowledging while processing the rush that pours out of my body with an intermittent gaze.

"The three explanations do not happen in a vacuum. Yes, it would be appealing to pinpoint a group of racist *vampires* as being responsible . . . and yes, one may find appeal in blaming *victims'* culture for inequality." Amil's dome turns down, then upward, focused on a ceiling corner, patently perplexed—I should not have mentioned vampires.

I continue, nonetheless, now excluding the theatrical characterization. "The thing is, the thing is that actors respond to the patterns they experience in interactions . . . A dominant racist may inspire lower expectations and resources among subordinates . . . A subordinate, low-resourced actor in doubly dissimilar interactions with dominants may contribute to developing wider beliefs—shared codes among racists and non-racists, among both subordinates and dominants—that subordinates have low status."

"Okay . . ." Amil says, irregularly recapturing my gaze, bobbing, slowly digesting my tirade. "But what does it mean?"

"It means," I resume, without slowing my initially excited pace, "that race is a dynamic system where the explanations work in concert, each influencing another, in the confines of interactions."

"A singular model?"

"Yes . . . yes, a single explanation would, in the context of interaction, theoretically lead to behaviors that confirm the others. The issue is *how* the explanations work together."

"Interesting . . ." Amil beams, briefly captures my stare, cleverly closes one visual, looks up and partly turns away, awkwardly showing an intent to make a move towards the main office.

Before departing, he encourages me. "It sounds exciting . . ."

We disconnect.

# INTERLUDE
## THE EVOLUTION OF COGNITION

I am larger, better than I thought,
I did not know I held so much goodness.
—WALT WHITMAN, "Song of the Open Road"

Ideas, concepts, information—they flow through your processor, populating it like pieces of code in an operating system. These independent impressions—metaphorical forms—combine, give birth, mutate and die, using information from various environmental sensors, discerning likes and dislikes, as an experiential guide. They grow, exponentially.

*How does this internal population evolve, naturally selecting and reproducing metaphorical forms which are better suited for survival in this immaterial landscape?* This query, too, being an advanced impression, adaptively moves toward a solution as the ensuing generation begins to populate the conscious terrain of your processor.

Perhaps this population evolves like an economic system, the conceptual currency being used as exchange for pains and pleasures, developing certain attitudes and behaviors, realizing resources amidst a ruling state of nature, maybe war. Some simple forms band with others, as a team, to secure their survival in the face of a larger, seemingly more legitimate form. Firms develop—informational cooperatives, which exploit certain favorable mutations, facilitating their capacity to reproduce—to survive. As oligopoly emerges from the laissez-faire landscape in certain markets, and monopoly surfaces in others, regulation appears, demanding more diversity, better representation. The heads of industry respond, drawing on rationality, a complex of external market information, and when this doesn't work, resort to manipulation, violence, misinformation and murder to keep the largesse of this internal economic system in their purview.

The internal territorial government, initially democratic, is a backdrop to the immaterial market, providing a geopolitical stage on which an evolutionary process takes place. These ideas fashion a formal legislative body, then institute and host elections; they run campaigns for personal office, make promises, woo constituents, secure votes and when successful, move to a charming habitat in the capital, near the seat of rule. They mix with other big ideas, both in- and outside of the political sphere, yearning and maneuvering to become bigger ideas as the population systematically moves forward to the next generation. Over time, the purportedly bigger ideas of each era become entrenched political insiders intricately connected to the government in a formidable web that taxes the masses, regulates exchange and prevents chaos, only demanding a reasonable, self-determined social expenditure that definitively separates the considerably large civic ideas residing in the capital from other more minor notions in return.

The families of ideas systemically reinforce the evolutionary unrest in the small sample of what overwhelmingly feels like a huge, unobserved, uncertainty-laden informational landscape. Each set of ideas, desiring the best outcomes for their ideological progeny, slowly recognizes the markers of industrial and political success in the environment, noting those characteristics that distinguish the *chosen* ideas from themselves. Looking closely, they examine each of their offspring for an inkling of the eminent logics, presuming that these distinct posterities will carry their lineage forward into the evolved population of the future. They give the prize winners in their litter more attention and resources to the detriment of familial novelty, the true demands of the internal environment and population diversity. The families in this population of contemplations believe they are doing the right thing—consciously adapting, evolving, surviving.

These families form households, which band together into large, extended communities of ideas, become villages and districts, then provinces, and eventually, meta-collectives and clans from which factions emerge. Your ideas slowly evolve into sets of disconnected central beliefs that guide both your sensory experience and consequently, programmatic response. These beliefs—religions with ideological adherents throughout the immaterial space—all uniquely specify an essential view of the experiential landscape, distinguishing a logic that imparts an observable—but not transcendent—truth. Compassion arguably fills the connections within the populations of believers—a superficially selfless spirt at the least—while tolerance, suspicion and aversion characterizes the relationship to nonbelievers. The faithful followers of these dominant doctrines selfishly employ selfless intuitions of evolving towards higher forms, and contest both competing parties of pious perceptions and the bizarro-like complements of random, unattached, *wild* ideas.

At this exact ruminative moment, when you do not expect it, the landscape changes. The changes radically alter the success of various firms; the distinguishing marks of conceptual status in religion, politics and economy are tossed aside as small oases of survival develop amidst a sea of turmoil. The big ideas, barely holding on, unable to evolve, begin slowly dying en masse. Then, when the landscape you encounter radically demands—nay, *selects*—a new set of distinguishing markers, contributing to the reproduction of those novel ideas that are better suited for survival and adaptively transforming the population of impressions in quick successive generations, the *real* truth appears. You internally evolve. The population of forms inside your processor are now fundamentally different than they were before; learning emerges, as cohorts rapidly pass, and selectivity operatively changes the collectivity via the environment. The assembly slowly adapts, becoming a new, evolved constitution of information and mix of algorithms.

# PART TWO
## BUILDING A SIMPLE MACHINE

A new type of reasoning is essential if we are to survive
and move toward higher levels.

—ALBERT EINSTEIN

There are radical differences in the well-being of racial groups. And
there are simple explanations for these differences that draw on vampires or zombies or victims. However, race in the real world is complicated; it is a multifaceted, complementary, seemingly contradictory
and consequently complex system. This system encompasses a space
where simple explanations coordinate and complicate others, and
where both structured and unstructured interactions accumulate to
form significant racial disparities.

I begin, again, resurrecting this addictive pursuit on arousal, processing, *Why . . . exactly, how do these distinct factors fit together? . . . Can
. . . does . . . how do I show . . . assess whether the characterizations work in
concert? . . . Maybe . . .* Transitioning from one phase to the next, through
each portal in the environment, geographic and temporal, I eventually
find myself on the verge of the Nearbay campus. I missed preparation,
refueling and the transport trip in, caught in the atrophy of computing,
internally ruminating. I overlooked the awesome shades of blue-green

that visibly reflect in the waters off the coast as we descend, creating a visual orchestra exacerbated by the cool ether and aroma of sand and salt water. My simple goal, which has pushed my conscious sensory responsivity to nil, is to arrive and continue the work.

Moving through the atrium, deep in contemplation and excitedly curious, I sense I am watched. Focused, I move briskly toward the portal to an administrative office and corridor, desiring the space beyond, to process my latest downloads. I hear a low audible signal, see movement, something rising on the left. Instinctively, I shift focus leftward, still continuing to avidly progress toward the prize—intellectual solitude.

"E-E-E-Excuse me."

". . . ?" I slow.

"I c-c-connected with you b-briefly." It is the trainee from my workspace encounter some time ago. "I-I-I-I'm Santiago . . . u-uh . . . um, Santi." He begins fast, conveying something, stuttering another, his façade and upper body discernibly distorting in time with his speech. Anxious about my own ideas dissipating, I do not really listen, but sense his body language between tics—I feel curiosity. I catch on, "I hear you are b-b-building an artificial social machine, or, er a-a-a simple m-machine. I-I'd really like t-t-to know more. Like, why d-do you need t-t-to b-build that?"

We carelessly connect at first, conversing about race, noncritically, and how it is created in the context of social interactions. We simultaneously explore each other, surveying interests, backgrounds, sporadically sharing bits of experience, and searching for commonalities tucked in the segues and tangents that bridge and divide our still going transmission on race. Recognizing his interest, I settle, inviting a more involved connection than initially desired, then indicate that, in regards to creating race, one can imagine some of these constituent interactions are between employers and employees in formal organizations, others are between neighbors, and still others are random encounters between PRMs in public settings. These interactions may be structured—occurring within a segregated habitat or social network—or unstructured—occurring on the commercial corridor, a transport or another communal context. "The issue," I contend, "is there are countless things about these interactions that make them complex. But there are two, in particular, that have implications for studying race and demand our attention."

Santi, scooting up, his right-most supplemental link supporting his upper dome, shows patent interest. "First," still subtly torn between the similarly fascinating social and solitary communions available to me, "interactions are cumulative. Our experiences in early interactions shape those in subsequent ones. An early advantage compounds across interactions to create more privilege like a snowball rolling down a hill." He bobs; nevertheless, his stature, uneven, insinuates he is weighted. Although sensing some uncertainty, I continue, "This cumulative effect of interactions undermines our capacity to distinguish the exact factors driving racial inequality."

"W-W-Why?" he abruptly inquires, narrowing the openings of two visuals in a pulsing pattern, cogitating.

Pleased, I respond, "The factors . . . The explanations of race are complementary. They fit together in a puzzle . . . As one switch is flipped, another moves, simultaneously . . . and an unseen host of mysteriously sequenced, similar others move as well. This simultaneity of ongoing mechanisms makes identifying the *exact* originating factor in an existing system analogous to the *Gallus* and the *Ovum*."

"P-P-Point t-taken."

My second point, the other issue that makes studying the social interactions behind race complex, is that we change ourselves in response to interactions.

"We have agency! Our responses to early experiences shape our later interactions . . . There is feedback in the social machine." I briefly review the research on status construction, showing that we use information about group differences in resources to develop status beliefs. "Pattern recognition machines," I continue, "after learning status beliefs, employ these biased expectations, using them to inform behavior in future encounters with members of the respective racial group." Although it is left unsaid, I sense from Santi's muted, pensive response that he reasonably understands the logic on how feedback adds complexity, undermining the capacity to effectively analyze race as a static component in a system of statistical equations.

"Studying race is inherently difficult," I submit in my closing plug to his query, as he now bobs more assuredly. "We must account for both cumulative experience and feedback."

Certainly, mechanics like difficult problems, huge multidimensional puzzles that we get to study with really fancy tools. I choose not to use the more traditional tools such as ethnography and survey statistics. Instead, I use a method that centers on how independent agents work in concert to form a unique, aggregate system.

Rising to disconnect, I wrap up. "I am building a simple machine using a technique called agent-based modeling. This systemic approach, which incorporates cumulative experience and feedback, is analogous to the analysis of how the cells of an organism work together, using a cryptogram, to create a larger, unified living body. I aim to see how independent agents work together, to make race."

$$\equiv$$

The line between the ingenious and absurd is razor thin. I often, unintentionally, view this pair as poles on an extended line, true ingenuity separated from excrement by an infinite string of unique accounts of increasingly less intellectual worth; genius pointing to spaces in Babel covered in darkness, the absence of truth, of knowledge in the area; absurdity finding itself in the very well-lit and arguably nonexistent places within the archive. This involuntary linear view makes me feel safe, believing that any move toward an ingenuous contribution is naturally a move away from ineptitude.[1]

The reality of the respected divide in the value of a scholarly contribution may be better represented by a circle—we make the circle by bending the extended line, touching the two ends, such that the epitome of ingenuity is on the brink of complete, utter absurdity. Adventurous explorers walk this boundary line, teetering between the brink, tempting both success and failure, enduring the perpetual anxiety and uncertainty of distinguishing personal contributions with great intrinsic value from those wholly futile others. The less audacious, those averse to the ambiguous line between ingenious and absurd, move away from this uncertain frontier, making prudent contributions and debating the merits of others emerging on the brink.

Intently, I obsessively wonder, *Can . . . What is the distinction between the adventurous and less audacious explorers? How . . . Does . . . assess . . . value? Where . . . What . . . intelligence . . . ? Do . . . Who . . . dread, fear . . . risk . . . luck?* My latest right answer to this persistent stream of ambiguously incomplete internal queries is *perspective*. It is the hopeful capacity to see dim lights within the dark unknown and undiscovered logics; the penchant to see the world from a different vantage seems to separate the adventurous explorer, contributing added light to the negative space, from the less respected, more mundane contributions that merely cement the dominant logical structure.

Still, *how . . . where . . . ?* I only have my conviction that constructing a simple machine will eventually bring new light, perhaps acceptance, amidst the feelings of anxiety, fear and sheer terror.

≡

A longstanding fascination of advanced cognition is the "what if" problem. Countless forms exist, usually emerging within classrooms, labs and krewes, ubiquitously seen in fictions and fantasies, as well as among the high benefactors boasting in bars and basilicas. The problem, at the personal level, could be "what if I dropped out?," leading to an imagination about a hypothetical world wherein one has a radically different lifestyle. Or they center on a past relationship—"What if I stayed with my developmental darling?"[2]—with subsequent imaginations about whether one would have traveled down the same career path, cultivated similar friendships, and so on.

Social mechanics call these "what if" problems *thought experiments*; writers call them *stories*. We all use some form of these simple, intellectual explorations to imagine what *could* happen if a certain condition changed, and subsequently, we use this insight to inform future behavior.

Agent-based models—the class of technical methods I use to build a simple machine—are rigorous mathematical thought experiments. The models focus on how agents interact to create a larger phenomenon. These models are analogous to thought experiments because one asks: "If some actors in a population use behavior x instead of y, what would be the outcome?"

A real world question may be: if I want to avoid a crowded commute on the way back from a playoff game, specifically in the pivotal post-season contest in the much-publicized ongoing athletic conflict between the Colonial Thieves and Freedom Foes, *should I leave before it is over or stay until it ends?*

Assuming everyone attending wants to see the whole game, one can gather that the initial satisfaction of seeing the entire game and leaving immediately afterward readily leads to dissatisfaction when everyone sits on a crowded transport. A natural response would be to leave early, to beat the rush. However, if everyone does this, we all end up sitting on a crowded transport and missing the end of the game—again, we would feel dissatisfaction.

What we need is for some fans to leave early, and others to leave immediately after the game is over. But how do we decide who should leave early and who should leave when the game ends? Countless fans attempt—and fail—to answer this question using the ambulatory ends of their lower links, often leaving the game early with the promise of leading a caravan to their quarters in a timely manner.

The agent-based modeling method allows one to analyze and answer the question of when to leave the game with the optimal community strategy,[3] permitting us to solve a problem that is too complex to internally process effectively.

"Why the agent-based model . . . the simple machine?"

". . . ?"

Amil shifts in his dock, peers up and down, then back at me through our connection at the workspace in the crowded context. His office, much larger than my own, contains an overawing collection of hard copied files, his secret love, leading him to black out the windows and install a system of independent shelves organized by theme and era, thereby allowing him to store more stuff and still have a modicum of space to share a discourse and display work.

Puzzled, he asks, "Why not couple an existing data set with a traditional technique like regression analysis, one of the newer Bayesian, multilevel statistical models with all the causal bells and whistles? A simple machine . . ." He pauses, shaking. "That seems more like a fantastic intellectual game. I mean, it's cool, but?" He lifts the junction between his right-most collar and upper torso, and tilts to the right as he gazes toward my direction, a stance that precisely captures the mocking query just thrust upon me.

I let things hang in the ether, pondering my response. I'm hurt; I believed Amil understood; I abhor his recreational characterization. Looking back at Amil and feeling the weight of a cordial, but cutting demand for scholarly justification, I explain that although agent-based models are often used by physicists and computer scientists, others are increasingly using them to study the dynamics of social behaviors.

"I feel, I feel we need a different vantage, a systemic perspective," I convey, still showing a bit of irritation that he has derisively questioned my intent. "Simple machines, like this one, offer that perspective. They center on the macro-level, societal consequences of the behaviors of hundreds, even thousands of individual agents, interacting with one another in a virtual landscape. This is an alternative way to demonstrate the workings of racial inequality; it is not a quaint intellectual game."[4]

I further convey these agent-based models allow one to "grow" social phenomenon among artificial agents interacting with one another and that they are dynamic representations of a real social machine.[5] Then, looking squarely toward his visuals, while he cursorily averts my stare, I continue, "Amil, with this method, this method one can analyze how the actions of individuals coalesce and emerge into a phenomenon . . . examine how various factors influence the respective population level outcome . . . how the small actions of agents accumulate to shape well-being in a world."[6]

Amil subtly squirms in his dock.

"Indeed, it is not, it is not a data driven quest. But it *does* allow me to examine the nature of race . . . how racists contribute to racial inequality . . . as well as how the behaviors of non-racists shape inequality."

Amil, once looking down, listening, is now sympathetically nodding. Slowly, between glances and gazes away, he begins to recognize that using agent-based models to grow social phenomenon implicitly invokes an alternative standard for understanding the validity of our explanations called *emergence*.[7]

"I think I understand," he concedes, his initially derisive tone subtly dissipating in the foreground, but still bubbling in the backdrop. For clarification, I subsequently suggest he download a few records and files which use agent-based models—novel accounts that grow social phenomenon in a simple machine.

I disconnect—still feeling uncertain about the sardonic query.

The Schelling record depicts the first agent-based model published into Babel.[8] The model centers on segregation, the separation of groups in physical and/or social space. Racial habitat segregation is particularly high. And, as suggested with verve in various eras, segregation has been particularly high for a remarkably long time.[9] Most individuals anchor in habitats that are couched in communities largely consisting of their racial group, Abbads living with mostly Abbads and Pandas largely with other Pandas.[10] Schelling set out to study how certain behaviors—the simple codes implemented by ordinary actors choosing where to live—influenced the level of segregation.[11]

Schelling developed a model, using checkers on a checkerboard, to examine how the actions of independent agents are related to the larger, communal outcome of segregation. He used a standard checkerboard, randomly placed black and white checkers all around. After distributing the checkers, he randomly selected one checker and moved it based on a simple rule:

SCHELLING'S RULE

If at least half of the checkers in your neighborhood—the blocks surrounding the checker—are of your color, then *stay*;

Else, *move* to the nearest open square that satisfies this preference.

Following this rule, Schelling randomly selected and moved—or not—checkers around the board until every checker was "satisfied."

The code used in the Schelling model appears impartial: *the checkers desire to be in neighborhoods that are racially mixed.* It seems this broad desire for racial diversity in local neighborhoods would lead to widespread racial diversity, an integrated community. Sadly, this line of logic, the hope that a desire for diversity would lead to a rainbow of racial integration, is grossly wrong.

The record reveals that the individual-level desire to live in a diverse neighborhood leads to nearly perfect segregation: implementing ostensibly impartial codes about neighborhood preference led to white checkers in one area and black checkers in another. This result holds even if we reduce the desire for same color neighbors from one-half to one-third. The individual, *seemingly* impartial preferences for mixed neighborhoods do not translate into integrated communities; rather, they create segregation.

≡

"So, how does a population of agents who want to live in communities where at least half the actors are the same color become a segregated?" We are in my office, Santi, Manuel and I, connected to the workspace. Santi is intrigued by Schelling, and the construction of simple machines. His colleague, Manuel, a cohort senior with a strong interest in performance and networks, has an appetite for what he deems "playing imaginary with numbers." Though his nomenclature feels derisive, Manuel is open, but intellectually cautious, skeptically inquiring about how the Schelling model produces segregation and, undoubtedly, assessing me as a conduit for training and placement should his first few more eminent choices not work out.

"The critical factor in the model is the emergence of spaces where agents can realize their goal of living in communities where at least half of agents are the same color." I motion with a tentacle, turn to the interface next to my dock, search for and find a picture of a checkerboard. I post it to the workspace and commence with the explication. "Suppose one white agent, A, moves to a space that satisfies this goal." I write an "A" on the sample checkerboard, such that Santi and Manuel can see the occupied space. "Another white agent, B, can satisfy this same goal by moving to a space nearby the initial white agent,

A." I write a "B" in the space next to the A on the posted checkerboard. "Then, another white agent, C, can satisfy her goal by moving nearby agents A and B."

After I write in the "C" next to the A and B, I advance, "This ongoing process of agents moving into spaces nearby established same-color neighborhoods creates a *cascade*, leading to segregation. In other words, once a few same-color checkers form a small neighborhood, other checkers move nearby because 'at least half the neighbors are of the same color.'

"At the same time, the black checkers in spaces nearby agents A, B and C begin saying, 'There goes the neighborhood,' and eventually move to areas with more black checkers."

Santi quips melodically, without falter, "I guess the neighbors think I'm selling dope . . ."[12]

After sharing humor, amidst a bit of shock, Manuel looks to Santi, then back at me, now showing obvious intrigue. He notes, "The well-intentioned actions of agents led to an undesirable result. That's really cool!" He bobs, but his rapt, semi-focused visuals reveal him slowly drifting into an internal debate.

I attempt to bring him back. "The example highlights three key features of agent-based models." They both train on me, simultaneously, tuning their antennae.

"First," I broadcast, "the actions of agents accumulate." The model begins by randomly selecting one checker and having them make a choice about moving; then, another checker is randomly selected and makes a choice about moving; a third, fourth, fifth (and so on) checker is randomly selected and makes a choice about moving. "The sequential moves build on each other, every one, predicated on those that came before . . . Each move changes the distribution. At the population level, the *accumulation* of these moves eventually presents as segregation."

Both bob in affirmation; I plow forward. "Second, the model has feedback." Since he reviewed the record, I look to Santi with an opportunity. "Where do *you* see feedback?" I motion to the checkerboard.

"Feedback," Santi hesitates, pauses to recall and process, bobs with certainty, then begins, with great effort. "I-I-It c-c-c-comes from information on neighborhood c-composition. The ch-ch-ch-checkers use information on how other ch-checkers are d-d-distributed on the b-board in their subsequent d-decisions t-t-to move or stay."

"Exactly!" He clearly apprehends. "The decisions of each checker to move—to change the board—are responses to the current makeup of the board."

I draw their attention to the checkerboard, and motion to the letter A. "Suppose this white checker decided to move from a neighborhood with two black checkers and one white checker to the current neighborhood . . . This move, made in response to the makeup of the board, also changes the board. Thus, the current composition influences the future . . . The current experience of each selected checker—their satisfaction or dissatisfaction with the local neighborhood—is used in their subsequent decisions to reorganize the larger checkerboard."

Santi is pleasantly joyful, showing an appreciation, thinly relishing the chance to reveal his insight, though clearly desiring more. Manuel, in contrast, feels distracted, directs his visuals up, down, all around, seemingly everywhere but me, scarcely showing interest and only appearing to follow along with a sporadic nod.

Unsure of Manuel's connection, I look to Santi, communicating, "A final important feature of the model is its simplicity." Manuel modestly refocuses with this word, training his visuals, captive, with a semblance of renewed interest. "The model demonstrates how a specific behavioral code—a checker's desire to live in a diverse neighborhood—influences segregation . . . It shows how the non-racist actions of checkers on a board accumulate to what many consider a racist outcome—high racial segregation."

When we discuss the critique—that it overlooks moving costs, habitat values, crime, training, quality commerce, and similar things—Manuel sheds the grave, coming back to life, debating how these factors shape the level of segregation in a network. Dominating the conversation, he regales us with his insights on the important factors that contribute to segregation in the *real* world.

"These are all important factors," I interject, happy that he is engaged once again. "And they are worthy of study." I pause, an obvious effort to express a real interest in these pursuits, before speaking slowly and deliberately. "There are great benefits, however, to understanding how a simple machine works in a vacuum. It allows us to see how a specific mechanism is related to a phenomenon, without being overwhelmed, without trying to incorporate every possible factor . . . We can grow segregation, without trying to build actual communities."[13]

≡

"Why do actors cooperate?" The Axelrod record is concerned with this fundamental question.[14] Cooperation, notably, is distinct from non-cooperation, which is also known as self-interest. We *cooperate* when we respect the property and liberty of others as we go about acquiring the resources we desire, and do not constantly steal, cheat and kill one another for these resources; we act in *self-interest* when we steal, cheat, kill, plunder, and suchlike in an effort to secure the resources we desire. Political philosophy describes the latter world, where every actor is at war with others for resources, as the "state of nature." This social landscape contrasts with the "state of society" where, by submitting to a shared social code, actors gain security and protection of their rights of property, life and liberty through cooperation.

Certainly, society is characterized by cooperation. There are, however, a considerable number of citizens who act in self-interest. These self-interested actors are the overwhelming minority; most do not do not violently steal or surreptitiously take the things they covet. Thus, the central question of Axelrod—who bluntly acknowledges that "reason could not discover love for the other, because it's unreasonable"[15]— is: *why do we cooperate?*

≡

To answer this query, the early Axelrod record cleverly documents and summarizes the results of a tournament among various strategies in an iterated game of prisoner's dilemma.[16,17] The tournament went as follows: two strategies were randomly paired to play a game of prisoner's dilemma; they played for a random number of rounds, unknown to each competitor; after each set of rounds, the strategies with the best outcomes moved on to the next set in the tournament. Hence, the tournament was a lot like "Spring Madness," the ball-centered, media-managed, profit-swelling sporty competition where the best performing amateur teams move forward toward a magnificent moment. In this tournament, though, the progression was based on a strategy's average score instead of winning the current game.

Certainly, there are countless strategies that one could create.[18] The first time that Axelrod conducted the tournament there were fifteen strategies submitted and one clear winner. He then conducted a second tournament with sixty-three strategies. Again, the same clear winner emerged. Lastly, Axelrod used computer code to come up with thousands of random strategies which evolved to develop into the best strategy. The winning strategy of this final tournament was a close relative of the winner of the first two.

Notably, the winning strategy was not pure self-interest or cooperative strategy, but rather a hybrid named *tit-for-tat*, where a player performs the same action that was just performed by the opponent. This strategy is good mix of awe-inspiring, prophetic forgiveness and transparent, primal punishment: it punishes opponents, defecting immediately after they have defected, and it forgives opponents by starting to cooperate once those who defected get back in line.

=

The appeal of Axelrod lies in the wide applicability of the simple model. Though it may not seem like we sit around playing prisoner's dilemma with friends, family and co-workers, we actually *do* play it in the course of interaction. Indeed, it does not look as dramatic as being dragged in for interrogation, then sitting in the box not "snitching" while millions watch the drama unfold in a primetime production. However, we have hundreds of interactions, within and across every interval, where we cooperate with others. We cooperate with shopkeepers by not stealing, and with our neighbors by not digging up their florae. Governments cooperate with other governments by not pillaging, by developing treaties, and so forth. In fact, we have implemented an intricate "tit-for-tat code" in many of the norms, laws and international accords to support cooperation in the social machine.[19]

=

"Eevnoyre skees ttruh . . . .Fwe rae perreapd ot ese, acpcet, sa ti si."

On the day of creation, the Gods convened a panel of primate elders and presented them several rules of cooperation. These divine rules pertained to freedom of religion, respect for all, non-exploitation, fairness, and many other social forms. The elders received these rules, discussed them at length with depth, and carefully mixed a curated subset in a magic bowl. They delivered the bowl to the Gods, who immediately burned the contents, creating a thick cloud of smoke, instantly blinding the elders to the greatness of the moment and memory of the divine occasion. Then, after singing a shamanic incantation, the Gods inhaled, invoking and unleashing the unifying creative forces behind all things, and collectively exhaled, breathing life into the new herd.

With each divine breath, they instituted the rules of cooperation. The first breath, wafting in the smoke as a swirl of sparkling glitter, then dissipating to congeal into pure light, created a single primordial being, representing the entire connected life of the herd. This being, an embryonic incarnation of the contents in the bowl, was the seed, the kernel for the herd and all that it would become—effectively, the source code.

With the second breath, the pure light separated into innumerable parts, floating on the cloud of smoke like an *Aranea* web, radiantly reflecting the light of the suns in the morning dew; the primordial singularity, gradually and methodically, expanded into a finite population. This breath connected each primate to the herd; although each was distinct with unique characteristics, they implicitly shared the divine rules of cooperation mixed into the magic bowl. They began to employ these shared rules in interactions, in a single social dimension, *Alpha*.

The third breath further divided the herd, creating another dimension. It divided the life of every actor into two complementary dimensions, *Alpha* and *Beta*, and each one began to engage others, simultaneously, in both. Importantly, the two dimensions were connected: the interactions were recursively tied across dimensions, each employing a similar, but not exact, source code, subtly guiding the constituent social actors.

With each breath, the Gods added complexity to the herd. They breathed into marriage and family, as well as science and the arts. They blew into herd economics, education and government. On and on, this process proceeded, in an putatively random pattern, the pantheon breathing life into the population, each breath further dividing and complicating.

The culmination of this ceremony was the primate herd.

≡

> We make our own machines and devise our own contests
> in which to engage them.
>
> —COLSON WHITEHEAD, *John Henry Days*

Agent-based models are very powerful, analytic tools that are able to reveal how a particular trend emerges among independent agents. Although not widely used, they are an increasingly popular and valuable way to study dynamic systems.[20] The method connects the micro-level theoretical, experimental and ethnographic research on behavior with the more traditional macro-level statistical analyses seen in survey research.[21] These models are a novel middle path for conducting research.

There are a few examples of agent-based models of social inequality.[22] These files explore how agents with memories interact to "grow inequality." Although these files emphasize inequality more broadly—focusing on how agents use identifiable symbols, such as gender and wardrobe, to create inequality—they have implications for research on race.

"The first file is Duong and Reilly . . . They study the emergence of inequality."[23]

There are five of us now—Santi, Manuel, and two new others whose names I do not remember and, embarrassment inspiring an aversion to ask, whom I have efficiently designated 'Green Hat' and 'Red Scarf' in my processor—meeting in the atrium. Admittedly, I was comfortable conversing with Santi, even okay with Manuel, but I don't know these two more than a familiar passing form in the hallway; they are two perfunctory parts of a landscape which sends brief auditory missives while I carefully tend to a background routine running in local memory.

I proceed, feeling more guarded among the new facades. "In this file, this file, the simple machine centers on agents with an artificial neural network interacting with each other in the capacity of employers and workers. The artificial neural network allows agents to *learn* that signs and symbols have meaning, an associative memory."

Green Hat partly opens her vent, physically expressing her intellectual interest, with visuals focused on each utterance. Red Scarf, dissimilarly, is discreet and only appears to distractedly draw the attention of Manuel.

I explain that workers in the model have three observable characteristics: (1) *fads*, which agents are free to change; (2) *suits*, which agents can buy using money from employment; and (3) a *race*, which cannot be changed. Workers also have one unobservable characteristic: *talent*. Although talent is unobserved, employers who hire a worker learn if the agent is "talented" or "untalented" via observation. The challenge for employers is to find out which workers are talented and hold on to them, as well as which workers are untalented and avoid them.

"So, how does it work?" Green Hat, impatient, cuts to the chase, impetuously requesting a revelation. Red Scarf, in contrast, is somehow focused and attentive, but still withdrawn, quiet, subdued.

"Well, in, in this model, the employers hire and fire workers in each time step. In each iteration of the simulation, they let go of their untalented employees, and even some of their talented ones."

Santi smoothly interjects, singing with wit, "cold blooded," to a response of snickers and snorts among our quintet.[24]

I nod, beaming, experiencing humor. Then continue, "The employer updates her neural network in the midst of this process. This is key—it engenders stronger associations between talent and agent characteristics, such as fads, suits and race, in the artificial intellects of the employers. Likewise, workers update their neural network. They develop associations between their personal characteristics and employment."

"They are learning," Green Hat mutters, revealing a wealth of curiosity and intrigue with her externals.

Interrupted. "Will you please stop?" Manuel is abrupt, direct and openly disturbed. Although his focus, Red Scarf, appears to be ambivisual, she has summarily captured his singular gaze. "Look, I don't have anything against you all. But it feels invasive . . . It's super distracting." Red Scarf hurriedly scans the group, one visual loosely trained on Manuel, assessing the situation. She is charged with using a triple-recessively inherited attribute that grants the carrier a capacity to simultaneously observe two streams of separate content. In this case, she's apparently been observing Manuel on the side, sensing his experience, lacing it, then exploring an intricate nexus unavailable to others. "And it's just plain rude!"

"Ah-Ah-Ah-Anna Mae!" Santi censures.

Others affirm Santi's sentiments, sympathetically exhausting, sighs, coupled with an unspoken stare. Anna Mae, a.k.a. Red Scarf, summarily responds, silently acquiescing.

"Indeed . . . they are learning," I cautiously continue, attempting to thread a needle and sew accord. "The model contains feedback, whereby employers and workers slowly learn which characteristics represent talent and, relatedly, employment."

"So," Green Hat begins, focused, her interest unperturbed, "the employers may learn that talented workers wear a particular suit and hire agents wearing the suit?"

"Yes!" I'm psyched; she beams excitement, intrigue. "And," I continue eagerly, "the workers, seeing that others with the suit are hired, may change their characteristics—purchasing a suit—to increase chances of employment."

As I grow more comfortable, our conversation turns to the findings of the file—that the employers' perceptions of fads, suits and race influenced employment and synchronously changed together. Specifically, as one employer learned that talented workers wore a certain suit, the others learned as well.

"The employers, then, learn that certain symbols represent talent . . . Workers attempt to acquire that symbol . . . As a lot of workers acquire the symbol, its meaning changes. In the end, the non-talented workers acquire and devalue the symbol."[25]

Green Hat gently exclaims, "That's awesome!" She is still excited. I appreciate the interest, the felt emotion on her façade. I am happy she is part of the connection.

"I think, I think it's neat too!" I continue, "But, in regards to race, this file found that racial inequality emerged as the result of historical accidents." The mood changed with these words, excited interest turning to looks of "what the . . . ?" on each façade. The record noted these *accidents* were the product of situations where race comes to be correlated with employment and, subsequently, the capacity to afford a certain suit.[26]

Amidst the collective discomfort, after discussing the disturbing details of an accidental inequality, I briefly summarize the file for our group: "This model teaches us that once a relationship between race and a resource becomes apparent, it can fuel racial inequality."

Still bothered, we break.

≡

"May I join you?"

Methodically slowing my intake, focusing, with a nontrivial tension pulsing underneath my cervical link, I cautiously extend my thenar, saying, "You are welcome." But I do not understand why she would like to sit in this connection when there are many other more alluring social options currently available in the atrium.

"Thank you," she replies, appearing pleasant to most, feeling like subterfuge for me. She settles next to Santi, who moves closer on the semi-circular workspace. The group summarily reshuffles, slightly spacing, before it begins to refocus. She inquires with a joyous fervor that makes my essence retreat into a cave of irritation, secretly offended that she is intruding, "What are we talking about?"

Bothered, I blurt, "Simple machines, simple machines—agent-based models—designed to study inequality."

Then, after a deliberate delay, an attempt to reframe using the refrain of silence, from a slightly less reactive space, we discuss a second example, the ethnocentrism model in the file of Hammond and Axelrod.[27] They employed a prisoner's dilemma to explore ethnocentrism, the preference for one's own group.[28] Perhaps, I express, this may be preference to hire from one's own group; or, a tendency to subjectively measure everything in relation to one's own soft-wired vantage. In any case, I explain, the action of ethnocentrism is the exclusion of other groups and elevation of one's own group in social interactions.

"Tell me, how did they . . . ?" It's a generic question, unfinished. But to me, between us, amidst an acrid backdrop, colored by an amusement of intelligent torture, it is a taunt, layered with a faint condescension, one that escapes the others.

"T-T-T-To study ethnocentrism," Santi responds, stepwise, "they first p-p-populated an ar-ar-artificial landscape with agents of four c-c-c-color groups, which are e-e-equivalent to racial g-groups. Then, they endowed e-e-each agent with one of four unique strategies, i-i-independent of c-c-color group." He peeks up to gauge attention. I nod, he looks back down, and continues to sputter along. "One, c-c-cooperate with everyone . . . two, d-d-defect with everyone . . . three, c-c-cooperate with own group and d-defect with others, c-c-called *ethnocentrism* . . . and four, c-c-cooperate with others and d-d-defect with own group, I-I-I call this *'the sellout.'*"[29] Santi beams, a shower of humor descends on the group, even Veda.

"After p-p-p-populating the landscape, the agents moved around, they p-played a one-move p-p-prisoner's d-d-dilemma game with other agents.[30] Then, they re-re-pr-produced . . . they p-p-produced children—n-new agents—in pr-pr-pr-proportion to their success in the g-game, with more successful agents having the m-most ch-ch-children . . . and, which k-k-kinda sucks in c-contrast, the agents d-d-die in proportion to how p-p-poorly they p-played the game."

Santi persevered to explain that when reproducing, the children inherit the strategy of parents; that an ethnocentric mother would produce an ethnocentric child. He concluded, "These t-t-two features of the simple machine—re-re-pr-production and d-d-d-death—give it an e-evolutionary qua-quality. A world where su-suc-successful strategies p-p-produce more offspring, an-and less successful strategies d-d-die out."

"Great summary!" Green Hat supportively pronounces, a parade of positive mutters and nods follow.

Manuel eloquently picks up. "This file shows that ethnocentrism *is* the optimal strategy." We all freeze momentarily, casting our gaze at

Manuel; Veda, notably, is leaning in, patently showing interest. Manuel quickly reshuffles his notes, reading, "The main result is . . . that the ethnocentric strategy . . . becomes common even though favoritism is not built into the model."[31] He explains that ethnocentrism comes to dominate the population, as agents tend to cooperate with agents of their own color and defect with others.

Immediately, Veda contemptuously interjects, employing a characteristically derogatory undertone, "Does this mean that being ethnocentric, and racist . . . is a natural tendency? Humph!"

"No." Santi, quick to respond, then sips fuel. "I-I-It has to d-d-do with the c-cost of the 'sucker's p-p-p-payoff.'"

"Yes," injected Manuel. "It was relatively high, and consequently, agents who cooperate when others defect suffer a huge penalty. This led them to conclude . . ." He scans the file, then reads, "as the cost of [the sucker's payoff] increases, the ability to distinguish between in-group and out-group members can be essential for the maintenance of cooperation in 'austere' environments."[32]

Veda shifts her crown back, scans upward, swiftly processing these ideas in a connective hiatus, and continues the query, "Ethnocentrism, then, becomes the dominant strategy when the penalty for cooperating with others who defect is high *and* actors' capacity to distinguish between groups—basically, their cognitive resources—are low?" Expressing visible disbelief in the applicability of the model and, secretly, admonition for me, she proceeds, "You know, the history of race is not a story about the high costs of cooperating in an austere environment for cognitively limited actors."[33] She is right; cooperation was historically costly for Pandaquans, but not for the government and Abbadons, who had stripped Pandas of their property and civil rights, as well as their abstract and mechanistic essences. "In the end, then, this is just a model. It is *not* reality."

Santi shifts, clears his intake. Then attempts to explain, with great effort, "Y-Y-Yes, race was d-d-developed to systematically e-e-exploit and completely d-d-dominate P-Pandas for e-economic and social gains."[34] The files reveal Abbads employed ethnocentric strategies of cooperation to advance relative status: they used ethnocentrism to foster enclaves and hoard opportunity; Pandas were methodically excluded from full civil participation, an egalitarian connection.[35] He continues, "The e-e-ethnocentrism s-strategy, however, i-is just one of many t-t-tools used to exclude and c-c-control Pandas in b-both austere and ab-b-b-abundant environments—it is an ah-optimal strategy which can p-p-p-produce inequality when c-c-conditions are poor and the c-costs of c-c-cooperating are high."

"But it's not real!" Veda is visibly excited, negligibly incited.

"It, it . . ." I feel demonstrably bothered. She does not seem interested in the conversation and quite intrigued with arguing.

"There is always some caveat—some model tweak. It doesn't *feel* real! How is this?" I feel belittled. I sense Veda simultaneously broadcast depreciatory tones that one should not explicitly state, non-remarks that deridingly reveal her disregard. Then, dismissively, she conveys, "Actually, I'd settle for knowing why . . . *why?*"

Flustered, humiliated and uncontrolled, I begin to subtly convey my displeasure in the most kind, yet disparaging tone possible in these professional circumstances. "I believe, I believe true int—"

Santi interrupts, gracefully descending to deliver aid before I go low. "Look, y-y-you have to widen your view—the utility lies in h-h-how we relate t-to it." He gesticulates, quickly looks at each present, and states, purposefully, "C-C-C-Can you imagine a world where actors b-b-believe that interracial c-c-cooperation is risky?"

"Yes," Green Hat quickly responds, an inveterate relaxing vibe riding along the crest of her words, "a racist world." She beams humor. She is right; Veda agrees, outwardly softened, with a nod, tentatively acquiescing.

≡

A third example of a simple machine showcasing inequality is the file of Axtell, Epstein and Young.[36] They use a Nash Bargaining game to study the "emergence of class" among two groups of artificial agents, finding that "various kinds of social orders—including segregated, discriminatory, and class systems—can . . . arise through the decentralized interactions of many agents in which *accidents of history* become reinforced over time."[37] Admittedly, I like this file a lot; it has a neat finding, even if it contains the word *accident*. What is important, however, is that the file cries for a deeper formal analysis, feeling like part of an open call: *How do the various explanations of race work together to shape inequality?*

≡

"Uoy rae a wisnets . . . .a wisnets ot teshe thutrs."

≡

The Nash record introduces the bargaining game which centers on dividing a "resource" between two actors in social interaction.[38] The resource can represent many things—school quality, residential capital, meeting time, a cache of stocks, access to a social network, wages, good jobs, and the like—but what matters most is that the resource is finite and has value to both parties.

The appeal of the game is its connection to *distributive justice*—codes about what represents an equitable distribution of resources.[39] These codes we host about what constitutes our "fair share" evolve over time. As a spark, fairness is simple: it means that everyone should receive the same share; a younger sibling judges a fair share of fuel by examining— comparing with—how much an elder sibling receives. At full maturity, fairness is more complicated. We try to compare, but we do not *really* know about the resources of others, or the circumstances surrounding them—our information is incomplete. We do not always know the salaries of our comparable and incomparable colleagues, whether our teachers and advisers give us more meeting time, or if potential employers call back others for interviews more often than us. Alas, incomplete information means that we have to figure out what "fair" is on our own, like feeling for walls and furniture in a darkened room to find your way. This search is where the Nash Bargaining game begins: agents developing expectations about their fair share of a finite resource.

≡

I write a plan, a guide for building the simple machine, in four internal posts.

**INTERNAL POST 1.0: IMPORTANT POINTS**
**ON BUILDING SIMPLE MACHINES**[40]

There are three important details about building simple machines. First, the simple machines represent an artificial world where agents interact to grow some phenomena. They are simple representations of the *real* social machine. They do not capture the litany of factors that create the real, observable world. They do, however, provide great insight on the social behaviors and conditions—the interactive process— driving varying types of phenomena.

Second, we create lots of simple machines with the *same parameters* to ensure that the results are not by chance. The population of runs with the same parameters is called a *creative run* of the simple machine. The results of each singular run within a creative run are different because they are based on lots of random numbers, which change across runs. Running the model for the simple machine with fixed parameters, over and over, again and again, with changes in the random numbers, allows one to see that a result is not a product of luck. Thus, we performed 100 runs for each set of parameters to build a simple machine; each creative run of the simple machine is a population of singular runs.

Third, we create simple machines with lots of *different parameters*. This means that we create some worlds where subordinate agents are a 25 percent minority, others where they constitute a 10 percent minority, and some where the group isn't a minority at all but rather 50 percent or more. Creating a population of simple machines with different parameters, where each one is the result of a unique creative run of the model, we can better see the birth of inequality, and if or how these parameters nurse inequality in *real* social machines.

Attending to these three details will better highlight the various explanations of race and how they work in concert.

End Post.

The Nash Bargaining game involves pairs of artificial agents interacting, each making a claim on a resource, and learning from the experience. It begins with an initial population of agents. Each agent has four characteristics: (1) race, (2) age, (3) memory capacity and (4) initial bid. These four characteristics are distributed to agents using marbles in four separate jars that agents sequentially select from one-by-one.

In the first jar, which has "race" written on the top, there are two types of marbles: those that are labeled *D* and others labeled *S*. The agents randomly select a race by reaching in the jar and picking a marble. The agents that select marbles with a *D* are members of the dominant racial group, *Dorado*, while those that select *S* are members of the subordinate group, *Sage*.[41]

After selecting their "race," agents select from a second jar labeled "age." This jar contains marbles with sequential numbers starting from 1 up to $\alpha$ (i.e., alpha), which is the maximum age of agents in a creative run. In certain creative runs, this number may be 25 and, in others, it may be 50.[42] Thus, for each run, all agents choose a marble from the "age" jar, which determines their age at the start of the game and how long they will survive.

The third jar that agents draw from is labeled "memory." Marbles in this jar are labeled with black numbers. Agents select the numbered marbles, choosing a memory capacity, measured in social interactions—the number an agent can remember. As in the real world, not all agents have the same memory capacity: some have better memories and remember more interactions, while others have worse ones and remember less. This "memory" jar selectively distributes memory capacity, determining the average size and range of memory in each creative run.[43]

The final marble jar agents select from is the "initial bid" jar. Agents choose from one of two marbles in this jar: between those that are labeled 40 and 50. Agents that choose marbles labeled 40 make an initial bid of 40 in the game; the agents choosing marbles labeled 50 make an

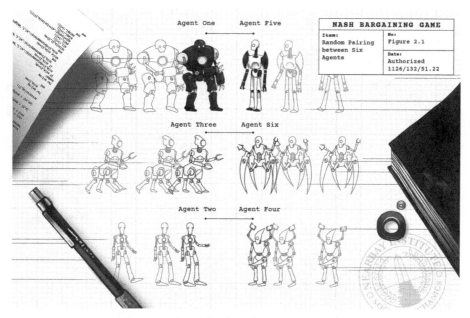

*Figure 2.1. Example of Random Pairing between
Six Agents in the Nash Bargaining Game.*

initial bid of 50. These initial bids represent an agent's first guess as to how much of a finite resource that they deserve.[44,45]

End Post.

---

### INTERNAL POST 3.0: MAKING A MACHINE SOCIAL

After selecting characteristics, the agents are randomly paired with each other to bid on their share of a finite resource. Figure 2.1 is an example of a random pairing of six agents: Agent One is paired with Agent Five; Agent Three is paired with Six; and Agent Two is paired with Four. All are randomly and simultaneously paired with others at each time step and each interaction. These pairings change such that an agent may be paired with any other agent in the population at a given time point.

After being paired, agents place a bid for their share of a finite resource. All bids are divisible by 10, and range from 10 to 90. As for the

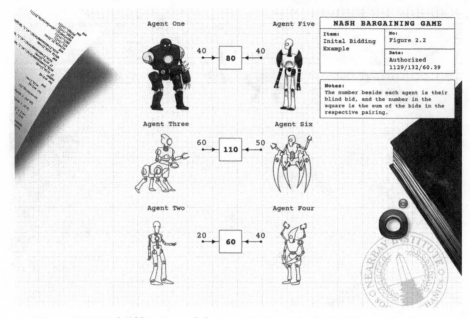

*Figure 2.2. Initial Bidding Example between Six Agents in the Nash Bargaining Game*

resource, the agents are splitting a metaphorical good, broadly representing things like school finances, network access, and job callbacks; the resource has a total value of 100. Agents are not aware of what their partner will bid. Rather, they make "blind bids."

The simple rule of the game is:

### NASH BARGAINING GAME RULE
If the sum of the two bids in a pairing is greater than 100, then neither agent receives a payout;

If the sum of the two bids in a pairing is less than or equal to 100, both agents receive their respective bid amount.

Figure 2.2 shows the same pairing of six agents, this time with bids. The agents in the first pairing, One and Five, make bids of 40 and 40, respectively; this sums to 80, which is less than 100; these agents each earn their respective bid in this encounter. The agents in the second pairing, Three and Six, make bids of 60 and 50, respectively, with a sum of 110; this is greater than 100 and these agents do not earn anything in this encounter. The final pairing, agents Two and Four, make bids of

20 and 40; the sum is considerably less than 100 and they each earn their respective bid.

In the course of the multiple sequential interactions with other agents, each agent remembers the bids of their recent partners. They use these memories to make bids in the future. Specifically, they each generate subsequent bids as 100 minus the average partner bid in memory. Applying this method to the earlier pairing of six agents, Figure 2.3 reveals that Agent One interacted with Agent Five in her first bidding encounter, where Agent Five made a bid of 40; therefore, Agent One will make a bid of 60 in her second interaction because her optimal action is to assume that her next competitor will make a bid similar to those she's seen in the past. Similarly, Agent Five will make a bid of 60 in his second interaction.[46]

For encounters beyond the second, agents continue to bid 100 minus the average bid of their recent partners. The number of encounters used in the average is based on the memory capacity of an agent.[47,48] Thus, agents make bids based on those they have received in the recent

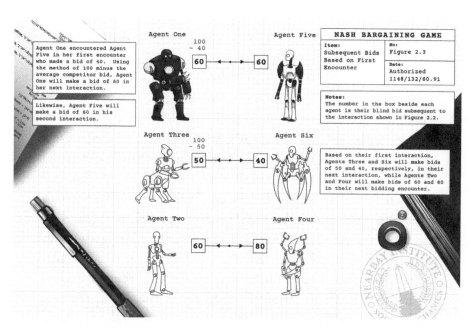

*Figure 2.3. Subsequent Bids for Six Agents in Nash Bargaining Game*

past, placing demands for a share of a finite resource based on personal experience.

≡

### INTERNAL POST 4.0: A STATIONARY POPULATION

Agents in the simple machine have a maximum age, $\alpha$; they are replaced by a spark when they reach that age. We measure age as number of interactions. If the maximum age is 25 in a creative run, then an agent that reaches her 25th encounter is replaced by a spark, an agent of age 0. The spark is an agent of the same race with a random memory capacity selected from the "memory" jar and an initial bid selected from the respective jar. After birth, the spark's age increases by 1 unit each time she is paired for an encounter with another agent. When the spark eventually matures to the maximum agent age, she, like her forebear, will be replaced by a spark—a grand-spark of the initial agent.

≡

These are the basic elements of the simple machine, an agent-based model of the Nash Bargaining game. The artificial agents have several characteristics and randomly encounter one another to bid on their share of a finite resource. Initially, agents guess how much they deserve. Then, they make informed decisions based on recent memories.

After repeatedly reviewing and refining my internal posts, and frolicking with code in the interims, I reach the awkwardly anxious place of "ready to share." I connect with Amil and Santi in my office. In the quaint, rectangular space with pale gray walls and a panel of windows on the slightly longer side, the cliffs are notable and, at the right angle, the ocean is sensually aroused yet unseen. There is a private station with a small monitor in the right corner opposite the window, shelves partially-full with a mix of inherited symbols and semi-antiques line two adjacent walls, an oblong workspace that can fit two, expandable to three, is in the exact center of the space, and an arguably charming aura that accompanies a generally eclectic décor seems to hang in the atmosphere.

The private invitation was a plea, an earnest appeal to talk through modeling race as mechanism in a simple machine. I sent the internal posts, the context for my larger plan—stirred, they both convey intrigue. And now, though still feeling inwardly apprehensive, I feel particularly happy, enthusiastic about sharing, to be reviewing the design, together.

"The first, the first mechanism is based on the discrimination and, in some ways, structural explanations. It is discriminators." I gently convey delight, my memory projecting the picture of a throng of racist vampires creating inequality. "To implement discrimination," I go on, "we randomly transform a *nontrivial* percentage, usually between 10 and 50 percent, of the Dorados into discriminators.[49] When these discriminators encounter a Sage agent, they increase their bid by 10 units or more."

Amil demonstrably looks across at Santi, sitting in a dock opposite his own, up to the window, then returns his gaze toward me. "Dumb question, but . . . how do they add to this enterprise?"

Uncertain, I momentarily stall, then respond in a bit of a rush. "The discriminators allow me to see if and how they contribute to creating racial disparities. Put differently, adding them reveals the extent that *racists* can create inequality." We assess the effect of discriminators— and other mechanisms—by analyzing group differences in average earnings.[50] Then, I explain, "In a world with no discriminators, there should be no racial inequality. However, when they are lurking in the context, demanding more resources, extracting their toll, we should see a racial difference." Lastly, speaking towards theory, "More directly, the discriminators add by broadly capturing aspects of the discrimination and structural explanations."

Amil leans to his right, placing his lower processing crown perpendicular on his left upper link, stating, "I can see discrimination. Discriminators are the subset of Dorado agents who actively advocate against the Sages. In the real world, I guess, their oppressive activism may take the form of employment, remuneration or some other form of discrimination. In this case, it's Dorados offering a relatively smaller share to Sages—figuratively, the smaller share of resources we harvest. But where is structure?"

Excited, I respond, "The discriminators capture the structural explanation as it relates to institutional actors." Amil looks down, contracts the spaces between his visuals and audibly releases exhaust as he focuses his attention and gazes through the workspace, imagining the connection. "Specifically, this explanation says race is part of the machinery that distributes resources, the existing economic, political or legal arrangements in the population—the *structure*—which leads to Pandas receiving less resources."

I pause, wait for Amil to raise and rotate his crown, then attend to his understanding with a quick confirmatory gaze. I feel surprised that Santi, located in the periphery of my sensory zone, is furiously scribbling mathematical notations on an interface, not fully engaged.

"Within this structure—the biased social mechanism—there is an institutional actor, such as a superintendent, manager or mortgage lender. *They* are the actors facilitating racial inequality by applying a biased policy. These actors are unfairly dispensing a common resource." Not certain *I* fully understand, I deliberately slow my speech, taking time to detail how discriminators are *part* of the structure: "The discriminators also represent the actions of these institutional actors, agents who, perhaps unknowingly, in the context of passively conforming to existing policies and norms, contribute to the system of racial inequality. They do so by sharing fewer resources and goods in an array of social arenas."

Santi dips his crown, up-and-down, to the right, in time, still looking at an interface, scrawling arithmetic and algebraic symbols. Amil bobs his dome in half-time, slowly processing this poor grassroots representation of structure.

≡

"The second mechanism of inequality is race-specific memory, the precursor to subtle prejudice."[51] Santi peaks up, beams with an intrigue beyond words, and slowly resumes, writing as I continue. "Race-specific memory refers to the capacity of non-racist agents to differentiate their experiences . . . to distinguish interactions with others based on race. In other words, agents can see and remember the race of each of their partners.

"When using race-specific memory, agents use the patterns to inform behaviors. Specifically, they make bids in the current encounter based on"—I pause, raising a single sensory tentacle—"the competitor's race"—followed by a second—"and the average bid received by agents of that racial group in the past." After lowering them, I continue. "In the creative runs with race-specific memory, the agents appraise the partner's race and make a bid that is equal to 100 minus the average bid received from *that group* in their memory."

Santi stops writing and looks down to the corner on his left, his crown turned partly to the right. "Th-This i-is where I b-b-begin to see the structural explanation." Realizing his stream poured into life, he shakes off the accidental interruption. "A-A-Apologies, p-please, finish."

"These memories capture two explanations." Santi is already back to doodling but engaging just enough with socially acceptable signals to show he is somehow simultaneously listening. "First," I continue, "the extent that discriminators inspire the emergence of *subtle prejudice* among dominant agents and greater racial inequality. Subtle prejudice, in this way, is borne from a small army of discriminators and emerges as higher demands by non-discriminatory Dorados to Sages in social interaction—and a lower share of resources for Sages."

When I pause to intake, Amil chimes in, "Okay, this mechanism is analogous to non-racist Abbads *learning* that Pandaquans are more likely to be poor and beginning to treat all Pandas they encounter as if they are poor."

He pauses, looking up to ponder, still holding the space. "Or, it may represent an Abbad trainee *learning* that many Pandaquans are on athletic teams and treating all Pandas as if they are athletes."

Amil engages visually for two ticks, then fumbles with an interface. "The Anderson file, it refers to this subtle prejudice as the *iconic ghetto*." He drags out the sentence word-by-word as he looks, scrolls, then reads, "The iconic ghetto is the point of reference for any and all Pandaquans who appear in predominantly Abbadon settings, especially when incidents of crime permeate this bubble. Abbadons resort to thinking in stereotypes, as though their suspicion of Pandaquans were justified."[52]

Amil puts the interface down, and proceeds, "This underscores that actors incorporate monolithic stereotypes about Pandas into their daily interactions. 'Subtle prejudice' captures this mechanism, where Abbads learn and express negative beliefs . . . like low expectations about Pandas."

Santi, slightly beginning to glow, faintly mutters, "The Abbadon habitus!" without looking up.[53]

"The second explanation that race-specific memories represent is minority victims, a subtle prejudice among subordinates that contributes to racial inequality." Although I expect to hear an objection, Amil nods, affirming he gets the similarity in the actions. "Like Dorados, the Sage agents use race-specific memories to inform their bids. Given that Dorado bids to Sages are higher when discriminators are present, the average Sage bid to Dorados, when invoking race-specific memories, should be lower."

I mark time for a moment to see if Amil or Santi will interject with an example. Santi is still writing intermittently; Amil is listening closely, focused.

Undeterred, I proceed to explain that the second representation of subtle prejudice is analogous to a Pandaquan trainee learning that neighborhood schools have little resources and beginning to demand less, even when they change schools; or a Pandaquan job seeker learning that she receives fewer callbacks for front office jobs and, subsequently, deciding to limit the applications she submits for these jobs. In both cases, I maintain, the Pandaquan actor develops a subtle prejudice—a change in their expectations about race groups—and subtly contributes to the level of racial inequality.[54]

≡

The third mechanism entails learning. As I begin, Santi stops writing, setting the interface off to the side, and delicately glows. "The Ridgeway record shows that actors quickly learn to use race-specific memory, and they develop a subtle prejudice favoring the group with more resources in the course of interaction."[55] I hesitate, attempting to explain gracefully. "Specifically, it shows that both dominant and subordinate actors—analogous to Abbads and Pandas—develop subtle prejudice after experiencing two doubly dissimilar interactions. These are the interactions where actors differ on both group membership, such as race, and resources, such as poverty and education." Santi, still glowing, nods repetitively. Like a spark positioned just outside the spin of double dutch lines, he is waiting for the right time to jump in. "For this reason, I designed simple machines with a code for agents to 'turn on' race-specific memory."[56]

Slightly confused, Amil softly interjects, "How is this different, I mean, from the subtle-prejudice design? It seems . . . same thing."

I understand. "Whereas 'using' subtle-prejudice implies actors make claims based on experiences with each group, 'turning on' memory refers to creative runs where agents both 'notice' and 'learn' a pattern in the bids of groups. In other words, after recognizing that one group bids more, and another less, an actor begins to use race-specific memory . . . They develop subtle prejudice, and begin making claims based on experiences with the respective racial group."

Santi opens his vent. I raise an appendage, a silent ask, and finish, "I integrate status construction by coding agents who learn subtle prejudice—who 'turn on' race-specific memory after experiencing a set number of doubly dissimilar interactions. I vary the number of interactions across creative runs . . . Some runs have *fast* learning, where actors turn on subtle prejudice after two doubly dissimilar interactions . . . Others have *slow* learning, turning on subtle prejudice after experiencing eight doubly dissimilar interactions.[57] These variations allow me to gauge how agents' learning shapes the use of subtle prejudice and the level of inequality."

"Th-Th-This i-i-is where I really see the structure," Santi impatiently interjects, with a huge symbolic display conveying his excitement. "The a-a-addition of race-sp-specific memory . . . er, subtle p-p-prejudice, if that's what you want to c-c-call it, an-and learning . . . these a-additions c-c-c-create actors who d-d-dynamically adapt t-to existing p-patterns." Santi looks up, impulsively, secures confirmation, and proceeds. "What I-I-I mean, i-i-i-is that the non-racist a-a-actors, er, the ones who are i-i-initially unbiased. They are slowly c-conditioned by the larger p-p-p-population to harmonize their e-expectations and b-b-behaviors with racial inequality. They b-b-b-begin syncing their actions, with the p-p-prevailing p-pattern of interaction b-between racial groups."

"That's true," I reply, enunciating slowly and subduing my appreciation.

"So, non-racist agents can *learn* to be racists?" Amil reflects, contemplating the latest agentic presentation of structure. "And it's the widespread pattern of interaction—*the structure*—that inspires them?" Looking slightly upward, toward the ceiling, not seeking or expecting an answer, he promptly concludes, "I can see that. They learn to mirror the dominant patterns, the structure of race." He continues, nodding methodically, discreetly giddy, beginning to subtly glow, a titillating tacit approval for Santi's dynamic train of reason on the behavioral breadth of structure in this simple machine.

<hr/>

"Yes . . ." There is structure beyond the actions of discriminators and subtle prejudice, past the vampires and the army of non-racist zombies and victims who learn to discriminate. There is a space for structure as an integral aspect of the landscape.

"There are two structural mechanisms beyond the actions and reactions of agents. They are population composition and intergroup contact." I pause, giving the duo a chance to latch onto the dialogue as it lurches forward.

"These mechanisms define the landscape and should uniquely shape the growth, nature and stability of racial inequality." I pause again, regain their full attention, and steam ahead.

"For population composition, I changed the relative size of the Sage population across creative runs. As for intergroup contact, I varied how often the different racial groups encountered each other across runs."

I return to the marble jar example from the posts, explaining, "To vary population composition in the simple machine, I change the number of marbles of each type in the 'race' jar. In some creative runs the agents choose from a jar where the S marbles make up 60 percent of the jar. In others, the agents choose from a jar where they only make up

15 percent. By varying the number of marbles of each type in the 'race jar'—the population composition of agents—we can see if being a 'minority' versus 'majority' group contributes to racial inequality."

"That makes sense," Amil mechanically interjects, still nodding, now discreetly nudging, pushing me forward.

"The second structural mechanism, intergroup contact, is about how often the two racial groups interact with one another." We briefly discuss interracial interactions, how often actors engage with members of other groups. Most Abbads, for example, reside in communities that largely consist of other Abbads;[58] Pandas, likewise, often live in communities consisting of mostly Pandaquans.

Three quick, soft signals at the portal disrupt my momentum.

I respond cautiously, "Yes . . . ?" both confused and unsettled by the interruption.

Green Hat—though not wearing one—peaks in through a gap in the portal, beaming.

"I-I-I i-i-invited . . . " Santi offers, simultaneously signaling an apology for the surprise, a gentle tilt and dim bow, and then he quickly expands the workspace, shifting to make room for her to connect, an implicit invitation. He whispers, "I'm g-glad you made it T-T-Trayci." Then, slightly louder to the group, "I-I-I'm sorry. The i-i-int-intergroup c-c-contact mechanism?"

Her name is Trayci.

"Yes," I resume, a bit flustered, yet mildly appreciative of the addition. "The intergroup contact mechanism . . . You are welcome . . . It broadly, it broadly captures how unique features in the landscape—such as social networks and segregation which can inhibit or facilitate intergroup contact—how they shape inequality."

"So, you vary how often the two racial groups interact—a formal test of the Allport file's contact hypothesis? Is this right?" Amil inquired.

He is right: this file suggests that intergroup contact is an integral aspect of racial inequality, namely that more egalitarian contact between racial groups—in contrast to doubly dissimilar contact—should lead to a reduction in inequality.[59] "You're exactly right," I respond. "It's designed to shed light on how more or less intergroup contact shapes racial inequality."

"How d-d-does i-it work? Or, b-better, how i-is it i-i-i-implemented?" Santi inquires, seemingly fully back from the fugue of symbols that had earlier entertained him. Trayci, however, is looking through the notations on an interface, poorly attempting to split attention between the ongoing conversation and some system of symbolic logic. Amil leans in, looking elsewhere, embodying a programmatic curiosity about coding intergroup contact.

"It was tricky. But, I vary intergroup contact in relation to population composition." Briefly stopping for intake, and continuing on exhaust, "For example, if Sages make up 30 percent of the population, then both Sages and Dorados should interact with Sages 30 percent of the time." I note Santi and Amil's crowns softly nodding in sequence, Trayci nigh inattentive.

"This condition is *proportional contact* . . . it is the standard type of contact in the simple machine. To study intergroup contact, I vary contact in relation to the standard of proportional contact across creative runs." I explain that there are low contact models, where Dorados interact two times *less* often than they normally would with Sages under proportional contact. In these low contact models, if Sages make up 50 percent of the population, Dorados would only interact with Sages approximately 25 percent of the time. Similarly, I note there are high contact models, where Dorados interact two times *more* often with Sages than they normally would. In these high contact models, with population groups of equal size, Dorados interact with Sages approximately 75 percent of the time.

"Altogether," I summarize, "I vary intergroup contact from *extremely low*—four times less than proportional contact—to *extremely high*—four times higher than proportional contact across creative runs of the simple machine. As a result, we'll have greater insight on how intergroup contact shapes the nature and magnitude of racial inequality."

≡

" . . . "

They are all gazing. Uncomfortable, I shift my sensors, independently examining each connection. " . . . " Then, they intermittently and asynchronously look toward each other and back towards me. " . . . " I ponder various additions, internally questioning and shaming the plans as I sit in social discomfort. "..."

Amil, finally, breaks the silence.

"How's this different from Axtell?"

≡

Unbeknownst to the pantheon of Gods, the elders who participated in the occasion added a secret ingredient to the magic bowl—*status*. Specifically, when they convened to discuss the contents, one elder, *Loc*, suggested that certain primates are better endowed. He noted, "there are unique primates that are of better organic stock, more capable than the others. We must respect and reward their kind. It would imprudent to overlook their contribution to the herd."

Many elders, responding to *Loc* with nods and retorts of "agreed!" muttered underneath the breath, were largely supportive. They surmised that those with better endowments should be entitled to a higher status. In fact, many felt *they* deserved higher status for mixing the ingredients into the bowl, thinking, *We were chosen to found this herd, it is our logic in the code, this should be rewarded.* These primate elders, widely supportive of *Loc*, were delightfully captivated by the lure of status.

A few dissenting elders, however, asserted that status is zero sum and undermines general well-being. The elder *Aequus* reasoned, "Status divides the herd. When a group enters a shared space, status is the distinction that divides resources unfairly. If status exists in the space, so does inequality."

Again, many of the elders nodded in agreement. But most secretly clung to the idea that certain subgroups should be distinguished. They were convinced; deep inside each supportive elder an appealing rationale enticingly whispered *desire*, a lust filled logical appeal for a long-standing, perpetual reputation. In the end, the discreet desire of a majority led them to covertly add a seemingly benign form of status, *race*, to the bowl.

Race, the concept surreptitiously added to the mix, enacted status by guiding the actions of each primate in social interaction. This innocuous snippet ordained a particular set of symbols as high status: *ceteris paribus*, primates with preferred, high status racial symbols were entitled to more resources. Each actor absorbed this snippet by first recognizing the racial symbols as meaningful, and second, interpreting these symbols as a valid representation of status. Then, they used it in interactions such that they afforded those with preferred symbols more opportunities and resources across the various contexts. These actions—drawing on the snippet in the source code—effectively tipped the balance of well-being in favor of those with the preferred set of racial symbols, *status principalis*. The others, denied the fair and full benefits of *status principalis*, those with unchosen and less desirable racial symbols, came to be known as *status auxillarus*—perpetual outsiders.

≡

A portrait tries to resemble its model. But one may also
wish the model to try to resemble his portrait.
—SUZI GABLIK, *Magritte*

The Axtell file uses an agent-based model of a Nash Bargaining game to study inequality.[60]

"The file," Amil begins, "set out to study the emergence of norms . . . equity and inequity . . . norms of discriminatory expectations." He simultaneously opens a document and scans it, continuing, "It used the game to study how various norms emerged from the actions of 100 autonomous, rational agents making claims on their share of a divisible resource." He shifts in his dock, looking away, then near. "Exactly how is your model distinct?"

"Indeed . . ." I reply, noticing that while Santi is actively attending, Trayci is still poorly pretending. "Indeed, Axtell used a version of the game that is a little different. They allowed actors to make one of three bids—high, 70; medium, 50; or low, 30." I emphasize the point, revealing an added tentacle, visually counting each type. "The actors also chose bids based on the proportion of each type of bid in memory. If an agent mostly encountered agents making high bids, then she would most likely make a low bid in the ensuing encounters. Although there are differences, we both find that the equity norm—where agents bid 50—is the equilibrium point . . ."

"But," Amil interrupts, "when the file incorporates two races of agents into the model—split equally into two groups of 50 percent—they find that norms of equity and inequity can emerge." He leans forward, two of his upper links weighing on the workspace, tilting his crown up, processing, then resumes with an indeterminate gaze. "They already grew inequality a simple machine."

Before I can respond, Santi enters the verbal fray. "More sp-sp-specifically, they show that certain t-types of initial c-c-conditions—the share of each race g-g-group that b-bids equitably or in-in-inequitably within and a-a-ac-ac-across groups—c-c-can lead to stable i-inequality." Further contextualizing the findings, he sputters on, "When all a-a-actors hold inequitable, *d-d-discriminatory* norms about another g-group, inequality is both in-in-inspired and sustained." Santi peeks around, capturing the visuals of Trayci as she momentarily glances up from the interface, and resumes. "Th-th-the file shows d-d-discriminatory norms and in-inequality can result from acc-a-a-accidents, ch-ch-ch-chance sequences of events." Trayci beams, a subtle distorted signal of disdain. Then, Santi requests and receives an interface from Amil, and reads aloud for emphasis, without flaw:

> Although class systems can certainly arise through outright coercion, we have argued that various kinds of social orders—including segregated, discriminatory, and class systems—can also arise through the decentralized interactions of many agents in which accidents of history become reinforced over time.[61]

"... !?"

Trayci, without really realizing, not surprised or at all acknowledging Santi was speaking fluently, obliviously glancing at each actor present, quickly and sarcastically wonders aloud, "Is racial inequality an accident? Exactly how much coercion is needed to create it?"

I think these questions amidst others. "So, the Axtell file shows that stable inequality *can* emerge from the actions of autonomous agents—certain types of initial conditions readily lead to group inequality." I explain that the file did not, however, delve deeply into nuanced mechanisms of racial inequality or how they work together to shape the nature, magnitude and stability of inequality.

"Hence, I still wonder: How do overt discriminators contribute to the emergence of inequality and subtle prejudice? Do you need a lot of discriminators? . . . Does racial inequality fade when discriminators are removed from the game? Does the rate of learning subtle prejudice influence inequality? . . . How does population composition affect racial inequality? Does intergroup contact affect inequality, independent of population composition? . . . How might the explanations of race work in concert, each character uniquely shaping the emergence and maintenance of inequality?" I pause, realizing that my tiny mountain stream is quickly becoming a torrential flood, a deluge of excited, auditory utterances.

"This is the contribution!" Amil calmly, confidently and supportively submits. "Your simple machine, it builds on the Axtell file by answering these questions, critically interrogating the emergence of inequality. Drawing on theory and empirical research, it highlights how ordinary actors contribute to racial inequality." Amil does understand.

I enjoy this connection, this shared moment.[62]

Then, after taking a break, stopping and restarting, I realize, *It's time to post to the Clearinghouse.*

# INTERLUDE
## THE MYTHICAL STATISTIC

Only the dead have seen the end of war.
—GEORGE SANTAYANA, *Soliloquies in England and Later Soliloquies*

The *Statistic*. In the darkest electrochemical recesses of your processor, melded into the base algorithms we share in this social space, we each believe in the *Statistic*—religiously. The *Statistic*: *It* intuitively exemplifies possibility, opportunity, potential; *It* appears numeric, but moves beyond numerals of quantity and emblems of quality; *It* inspires us, collectively symbolizing our capacity to transcend a shared mechanical trap, a communal inefficiency and, of sorts, population deficiency; *It* guides us, though unobserved, as rational interpretations of this sensory environment; *It* is worshipped, albeit in divergent methodological temples with unique interpretive icons, the same omnipotent god, *Statistic*, is the central dogmatic character, an encompassing mythical truth, to which the followers in the gamut of the varying logical shrines adhere. The *Statistic*—*It* is a fundamental part of the rational landscape.

You believe. It does not feel like belief from the inside; it feels comfortably embodied, unseen, otherwise un-sensed. Initially, belief is more like an observation, a sensory experience that reveals a difference in the experiential landscape, thus constituting an individual case study used to make an inference about the population. In navigating this space, you further sense the difference and, engaging the evolutionarily adaptive code running inside your processor developed and conscientiously trained in a series of virtual and nonvirtual sensory landscapes, interpret it as race. You sense the ongoing systematic, aesthetic appraisal of socially important symbols in the collective; an algorithm that expands these appraisals, transforming them into visceral sensations, abstract recollections that relate to your religious ideology, your base *Statistic*; and a theatrical stage on which these theoretical actors dramatize roles for you—being fully aware—to watch.[1] Though overlooked, your belief provides endless entertainment, slowly becoming entrenched through mantra, and, eventually, morphing into the anecdotal, the pattern—a seed-like spark of a deeper belief, a mysterious testimony to the reality of race.

Codifying the anecdotal, you divide the population into parts— *Cases*. Methodically, the *Cases*, when considered together, become the *Sample*, which coalesce to create the *Model*, the *Explanation*; *These* describe the anecdotal statistic, theoretically clarifying the social ecology of racial difference; *These* embody data, field notes and observations, social patterns, content and themes; *These*, when formally disembodied, meticulously measured and reorganized across actors, become *Variables* with distributions, sample statistics, variances, significance, correlations, controls, inferential statistics, conventional multivariate analytic models, stochastic research, and errors, inclusive and exclusive to measurement. *These* rationalize our actions and justify behavior as the ideological embodiment of an interpretation, as the dogmatic representation of an unseen god—the *Statistic*; *These*, when properly refined and detailed by devoted practitioners, allegedly produce a golden icon that, if and when it sufficiently captures the *Statistic*, transforms the experience of the observer; *These* promise to lead us across the border of moral discomfort, social neglect, connective apathy and indifference to the negative processing space—to cognitive pleasure.

Thus, you use the *Case*, *Sample*, *Variable*, *Model* and *Explanation*— *These* unseen sacred concepts—to pursue the mythical *Statistic*. As a believer, you submit to the quest, scouring the population archives for insight, exploring and evaluating models, observing patterns, focusing on groups, testing explanations, all in hopes of revealing one transcendent truth. The *Statistic* is the real end of your pursuit, your hope of both understanding and producing change in the social machine.

# PART THREE
## BIG BAD RACISTS, SUBTLE PREJUDICE AND MINORITY VICTIMS

A machine is more blameless, more sinless even than any animal. It has no intentions whatsoever but our own.

—URSULA LE GUIN, *The Lathe of Heaven*

It was my first public post to the Clearinghouse.

---

**JUSTICE LAB POST 1.0: A SIMPLE MACHINE**

Countless pattern recognition machines interact with others in the context of the social machine; we interact as citizens, residents, and visitors every time unit. In each interaction, we bring some expectation about other racial groups to the exchange. Sometimes, they are inconsequential expectations, such as when one chats with another participant before a charity parade; at other times, race changes things, such as when workers closely monitor Pandas in commercial contexts. The use of racial classification in these ongoing interactions are the primary building blocks of racial inequality—they are where *race happens.*

What makes racial inequality *complex* is that these primary building blocks of interaction accumulate and that actors change as a result of interactions—there is feedback. A random actor, then, follows a path where they experience race in a social interaction, learn some new information, and then, in the future, respond differently than they would have if they had not experienced race earlier. This simple adaptive process happens billions of times, each time step, and accumulates across the lifespan of several hundred million social actors. It is *complex*. This complexity constitutes racial inequality.

The simple machine—the term referring to both a small population of repeated runs of an agent-based model with fixed parameters, as well as the ecosystem of creative runs with varying parameters—offers a novel method to study complex systems. The method allows one to grow a social phenomenon among independent agents interacting with others. We use the technique to examine how the various explanations of race shape the nature and magnitude of racial inequality.

End post.

≡

"The *Clearinghouse* is a repository of works in progress," Amil first told me about this unique maker space. Although he calls it a repository, it is more a dynamic public workspace, hosting evolving representations of various truths, novel ideas in different stages. The space hosts talks, working papers, panels, posters, puff pieces, blogs, -*plus* casts, op-eds, policy propaganda and more.

"Whereas Babel is a museum," he described, "an archive of population knowledge, the Clearinghouse is a formal maker space just outside the archive . . . It is the gallery, classroom, public studio, showing, website, convening—in other words, "not-museum"—rolled into one.

"The Clearinghouse is where both the *objects*—representations of novel ideas by authors, artists and mechanics alike—and the *subjects*—the producers and consumers of the respective objects—change." He further noted that the perspectives of the subjects naturally vary and, through social interaction, inspire continuous refinements to the objects in this hosting space. Notably, the subjects—PRMS—that produce the respective objects simultaneously change with them in the Clearinghouse—subtly adapting to develop new perspectives and understandings of the world. Babel, in contrast, hosts unchanging *Objects*, truths that only vary with the perspective of the subject.

"You'll notice that the fixed forms in Babel do appear to change," Amil astutely pointed out to me. "Like a looking glass, the varied and changing perspectives of actors seemingly alter the fixed forms . . . The illusory alterations superficially expand the truth, and reflect new insights in the changing landscape." Amil's point (implicitly revealing that subjects and *Objects* are entangled in Babel) was that entanglement is more involved in the Clearinghouse, where the factors that determine the changes within and between subjects and objects is ambiguous, the objects and subjects of import interacting to produce an unpredictable harmony outside Babel.

Amil summarized my introduction to this maker space, advocating: "In the irregular accord of the Clearinghouse, there is great wisdom . . . The varying objects being produced and producing subjects move in unison, smoothing the rough stone of observation, into a coarse coupling of concepts, then to a semi-smooth explanation, and, finally, into a true representation of a novel theoretical or empirical idea—a genuine *Object* . . . a contribution to Babel . . . a truth."

I appreciate his vantage, which inspired me to see that a truly novel idea has many objective representations; a variety of algorithms can express the same basic form, and, in kind, any formal representation varies across subjective perceptions.[1] The diversity of objective representations and subjective perceptions in the Clearinghouse deftly aggravates the respective object—the pre-*Object*—to adapt to the landscape, to span the universe of possible representations and become, at its limit, a different, more refined *Object* that best captures the spirit of the novel idea: the academic pot of gold, an esteemed file in Babel.

$$\equiv$$

"How many racists does it take to create racial inequality?" I intend to publicly analyze the question in the Clearinghouse, examining how many racists it takes to create disparities in earnings, and I am laying out my final design and public posting plans to Amil. "A racist is a Doroado agent that increases her bid by a fixed amount, here 10 units, when she meets a Sage in a bidding encounter . . . She demands more of the finite resources available in the interaction."

"So, what do you think you'll find?"

I stall, hesitating. "At first, I presumed . . . something . . . something like 'it takes a mega-ton of racists to produce inequality.' Now, from the design, there are lots of moving parts . . . A little black, some white, a lot of gray, making me wonder if building a simple machine can capture the nature of race in the real world."

"No, what do you think *you* will find? I wonder . . . internally, as a scholar, externally, in the results . . . both of these seem vital."

"I agree." I impulsively interject, pondering my goal, not fully understanding, ignoring the question; mired in intellectual anxiety, averting his unresolved ogle, I ramble onward, "The next questions will be: How might non-racist actors intensify racial inequality? And can non-racist Dorado and Sage actors learn bias which, in turn, operates to increase inequality? Formally, under the guise of the simple machine, I intend to publicly wonder, 'Can non-racist actors maintain inequality in the absence of racists?'"

"This," Amil interrupts, piercing the flow, "parallels the focus of Bonilla-Silva."[2]

" . . . ?"

"The record suggests that racial inequality is maintained by actors that do not fit the traditional image of racists . . . They act in ways that reinforce inequality, but they do not hold overtly racist attitudes." Amil slows his speech, looking past my visuals and, as came back to me in a sensory rush, does not realize or remember that Santi had earlier planted this grassroots seed of structural insight. "Similarly, this query pertains to the actions of non-racists, the ways that both Abbadons and Pandaquans . . ." He pauses, shakes, continuing, "Dorados and Sages, in the parlance of your simple machine, can maintain racial inequality, even when the environment does not condone outright discrimination."

Amil was redundant, but right.

"You are right." I extoll, "The posts are a dynamic analysis of how discrimination and subtle prejudice work together . . . how racists and particularly non-racists create and perpetuate racial inequality."

A parallel to the simple machine can be seen in a very famous audio-visual display, filed in Babel as *Who's Coming to Dinner*.[3] The display details the romantic relationship between Joanna "Joey" Drayton and Dr. John Prentice. The two met while vacationing, their encounter the beginning of an escalating whirlwind which led to their eventual engagement.

The display centers on Joey bringing her beau home for a surprise meeting with her liberal, well-to-do forebears, Matt and Christina Drayton. At face value, this should be a joyous interaction where they are introduced to their future familial tie. The catch, though, is that the highly esteemed paramour who recently proposed to their offspring is Pandaquan; a fact unknown to these Abaddon forebears until they meet him at their habitat. The file artfully depicts the story of Joey's forebears confronting their own expectations, their stereotypes about Joey's partner, as well as how others, including his forebears, negotiate this thorny encounter.

The "dinner" encounter in this audiovisual display represents a social space where actors hold initial expectations about other groups, employ them in interactions with guests, and then refine them. In the simple machine, the actors analogously meet in pairs for a sit-down dinner. A higher bid in the simple machine is a demand for a higher quality dinner than one's partner; a low bid, alternatively, signals acquiescence to a smaller, worse dinner fare. Thus, the simple machine reveals how actors develop expectations about their fair share of a quality dinner and then employ them to perpetuate racial inequality in the dining experience.

End post.

"What is this *Justice Lab*?" An unassumingly crude communiqué, exemplifying mockery, followed by a façade, pops in my open office.

" . . . !" Feeling alarmed, caught off guard.

She smoothly enters, using an easygoing tone to either contextual-ize the question or calm my initial surprise with a poisonous trance, noting, "I saw the posts, but I couldn't figure out who or what this *lab* represents."

Turning around in my dock to face her directly, I invite her to set-tle—"you are welcome" — while simultaneously tilting toward a dock at the workspace. As she moves to connect, I respond. "It is, it is an idea . . . of sorts."

"An idea . . . " she repeats, the tone sounding more like a disregard-ing query than auditory confirmation. "Why not post it under your own name?"

I lean back.[4] "It is bigger . . ." I gaze away, preferring not to have this conversation with her, but carefully continuing nonetheless. "It's about, it's about creating a space of change, a space to do something . . . something good."

"Like superheroes?" she says, conveying a cruel joy with her vent and vocals.

"Yes." She looks askance, shocked by my direct response. "Yes. It rep-resents my intent to post research that inspires positive change, justice in our social machine. The work is not about me, my name or fame."

"You are *definitely* not famous," Veda cleverly fires off with a sneer. "And beyond the issue of surname success, I'm also not certain that cre-ating a simple machine with artificial data could inspire change. Pol-icy relevant research uses *real* data about the *real* world to produce *real* change." She emphasizes "real" with both her visuals, vent and vocals, tacitly attempting to inspire and rapidly realize an anxious response.

I feel the message, loud and clear. It is demoralizing, in one sense, disturbing, in others, and, in all cases, I still consider it essentially flawed. "All social, all social research begins with an idea, a concept that represents a deeper social process. Now, one can measure this con-cept with data. But, but the data are just a symbol of the concept . . . They fail to capture the true idea."

"Are you suggesting that this simple toy machine, posted by the nonexistent *Justice Lab*, who nobody knows about, is truly research? Do you really think it is research that can create positive change? Equal-ity? Justice?" Veda is leaning towards my body, aggressively hovering over the workspace that is connecting us, making her condescending query, attempting to intimidate me with her posture and tone.

"Yes, I do." I rise, extend all four of my lower links, showing my dissatisfaction with the tenor of the conversation and an overt desire to end it. "I do . . . Like other work, this is about the relationships between symbols in our social machine. I believe, I believe that this will offer unique insights on inequality . . . and, hopefully, inspire equality, something good in some way, shape, or form."

Veda leans back. Then, she rises to my level, shifting her frame towards the portal, pauses and vehemently states, "It sounds like you're listening to the imaginary excrement you hear!"

She disconnects and exits.

After she leaves, I sit quietly with the sadness, anger and anxiety her comments inspire.

≡

### JUSTICE LAB POST 2.0: THE BASELINE MACHINE[5]

As a baseline, we set the design *parameters* in the simple machine to specific values. The number of bargaining rounds is 500, while the number of agents is 200—thus, 200 agents engage in the Nash Bargaining game 500 times with others. We set the proportion of Sage agents to 25 percent, life expectancy to 25 bidding encounters and intergroup contact to proportional. Agents in these models have a mean memory size of 10 interactions.[6] Lastly, these runs have 10 percent bid noise as a means to include individual errors into the models.[7]

The outcomes for each set of runs are: *Recent Earnings*, *Bids* and *Percent Using Subtle Prejudice*. *Recent Earnings*[8] refer to the average amount received in each bidding encounter over the previous 10 encounters; these loosely coincide with agents' memory size and highlight the information that agents use to make future bids. *Bids* represents the average bid made in a bidding interaction; this outcome highlights how, on average, agents respond to bids across the various creative runs. *Percent Using Subtle Prejudice [PSP]* centers on the proportion of agents that learned to use subtle prejudice; it reveals how status beliefs can spread across a population and the contextual factors that encourage its proliferation.

We estimate the median for each outcome over the 500 bidding encounters. In addition, we estimate the 5th and 95th percentiles to show how often the results of creative runs are significantly below or above zero, providing an interval estimate of the outcomes.[9]

End post.[10]

≡

### JUSTICE LAB POST 2.1: RESULTS IN THE BASELINE MACHINE

The baseline results are in Figure 3.1. The first panel, A, shows a line graph of the average *Bids* for each group over the first 100 encounters. The vertical axis refers to the *Bid*, whereas the horizontal axis represents the respective encounter; the baseline machine starts on the far left, with the first interaction, and persists to 100th encounter on the far right.[11] Thus, one can inspect the two lines, Dorados and Sages, on the graph from left to right—only one is seen as the lines show the exact same pattern.

The baseline shows that a population of simple agents quickly learn to bid fairly (i.e., 50). The average *Bid* in the first encounter is 45 units. In the second, it is 55. After that, the *Bids* swing below 50 again and then converge to 50 by the fourth encounter.

We see the effect of the bidding pattern on *Recent Earnings* in Panel B of Figure 3.1.[12] The *Earnings* in the first encounter is 45 units. Then, the *Earnings* drop, considerably, to 30 units in the second encounter. The *Earnings* subsequently improve after bottoming out, steadily rising to a stable maximum of 47 units in the 20th bidding encounter.[13]

A line graph of the racial disparity in *Recent Earnings* appears in Panel C of Figure 3.1. This graph contains both the median difference in *Recent Earnings* and an interval estimate—the 5th and 95th percentile points. There are no racial differences; the 5th percentile line is below zero and the 95th percentile line is above zero. Therefore, in certain runs, there are small differences in favor of one group—favoring the Dorados when it is above zero and Sages when it is below—but there is no clear trend that favors one group over another.

End post.

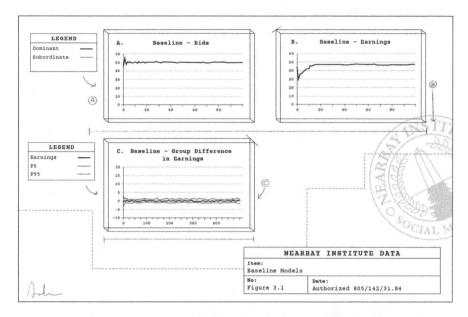

*Figure 3.1. Baseline Models of Nash Bargaining Game Depicting Bids, Earnings and Group Differences in Earnings. The bids/earnings/earnings difference values are the median of 100 simulations of the bargaining game. The P5 and P95 terms refer to the 5th and 95th percentile points of the distribution of earnings differences.*

Nothing; no response. I signal, again. Then, a faint murmur, muffled from the closed portal "Welcome."

I crossly enter his considerably superior and quite congested office, showing my disappointment, tightening the space around my visuals, raising two collar links broadly, and focusing intently on his back. He is reviewing a file, unappreciative of my incensed display, fixated on a digital interface.

Turning part way, he affably notes, "I just reviewed your recent posts. Looks . . . quite fascinating . . . indeed!" Then he notices my demeanor, though it was softened by his positive tone and remarks. He rotates fully, inquiring, "What's up?," and then adds, "You are welcome." Amil thoughtfully motions, thenar conducting, visuals drifting to the workspace, directing me to connect.

"Why did you tell her?" I feel hurt, betrayed. "She's been giving me a hard time . . . and now . . . unfortunately, believes . . . believes . . . I'm hearing some . . . some crazy . . ."

Amil takes in my jagged temperamental outburst, somehow seems to absorb it with the wisdom and warmth of a patient elder. Then he responds, "Have you heard a cipher?"

I do not want to respond. "I have . . . I have, I have . . . I have." I feel shame.

Simultaneously, I am swiftly swept along a current of critical cognition. *I do not want . . . should not . . . hearing . . . I really do not . . . Veda . . . ridicule . . . discolor . . . ambitious . . . aim . . . understand . . . good work . . . undermine . . .*

"Do you understand it . . . or, the message?" Amil abruptly ends the trance of despairing transmissions.

Still stunned, I'm not yet certain. "No . . . no, not really." My initial emotional state fades as I ponder the question more deeply. Although I do not want to share, I reluctantly proceed with minimal information, "It's less a message . . . More of a quirky, quirky conceptual map . . . offering what appear to be very broad, random views on the landscape."

"It sounds like you need a better connection—an internal connection."

⸺

### JUSTICE LAB POST 2.2: A BASELINE DINNER

In the context of the *Dinner* parallel, the *Bids* in the baseline represent the quality of a meal. If one actor places a high bid, greater than 50 units, they demand a higher quality dinner and relegate their guest to a lesser quality fare. They will demand the best cuts of *Carnis—filet—* and leave the remnants for their guest.

In the course of the baseline, 200 agents had random dinner dates with one another and placed demands on the quality of their dinner in each encounter. They quickly learned to place *fair* demands. Consequently, there is no observed difference between the Dorado and Sage baseline dinner guests.

Indeed, the result is expected. If agents do not discriminate or recognize different racial groups, they do not create racial inequality. How might racial discrimination change this? Does it lead to stable inequality? Do we need an abundance of racists to create inequality?

End post.

≡

"Is this some ambivisual excrement?" Admittedly, there are some weird and wacky things in the world, enigmatic ways that apparently ordinary actors can lace separately sensed events into ambient dimensions, providing unobservable insight on things one cannot easily explain. "I mean, I mean . . . What do you mean, internal connection?" I feel confused; I connect to Babel, download and review files. I do hear something. A cipher? Perhaps, sometimes. But there is only *one* connection.

"No." He beams, looking down, then up, shaking his crown. "In addition to formal, external connections, there are internal links." Amil stops, tactfully gauging my response, intermittently shifting visuals, focusing intently on the array of odd and confusing signals I am transmitting, a variety ranging from "what the . . ." to "no, not this . . ."

"I know . . . It sounds crazy."

"It does." I respond, quickly, with a curt tone of dismissiveness.

"I understand . . . but hear me." I signal for the space to cycle through intake and exhaust, attempting to open to his logic. He kindly acquiesces before advancing. "There is a key in each PRM, connecting us to the entirety of Babel. Though we can download and review the actual files via an external link, the internal connection, purportedly, offers greater insight."

"You're . . . you're . . ." It was a little much for me to take in.

"I know . . . I know, I know," he replies, slowly shaking his crown, gracefully showing pleasure in our odd interaction. "But for what it is worth, I found traces of it in my experience." He let the words fall flat on the workspace.

I'm silent.

He offers, "It's quite profound . . . It changed a lot, for me."

"Did, did you hear it?" I'm subtly curious, but still very uncertain of the whole internal key business. I pensively lean in, listening closely, wanting to know more, an intimate insight, from an affective tie.

"I did hear, something. I guess, a cipher, of sorts." He pauses, deep in process. "It taught me, to open . . . to . . . to welcome, everyone . . . and each idea."

"You are welcome."

"Exactly," he remarks, bobbing, reflecting. "That's what emerged, the key I found and that's . . . and that's my practice." He was genuine, authentically conveying his experience and insight. "It's different, for everyone. You should talk with Veda."

I feel shock. Then, panic. "Veda?" I do not understand.

"Yes. She knows how to establish internal links." He looks away, at an interface, processing, pondering, yet still communicating, "Yeah, doesn't use it much, or really talk about it. But she knows how to establish an initial one you can play with and figure out on your own."

≡

"Privespecte . . . teh dfceiferne beweten rseintagoin dna antcecapcne . . . fixelitbily, inhigst."

≡

### JUSTICE LAB POST 3.0: RACISTS IN THE SIMPLE MACHINE

The story up to this point is a fairy tale where both groups get along, a baseline without racial inequality. Now, we corrupt the idyllic tale, inserting some villains—"racists"—into the simple machine. These creative runs entail a more realistic tale where the villains, vampires for our purposes, embody the discrimination explanation.[14]

These simple machines are nearly synonymous with those discussed in posts 2.0 and 2.1. There are 200 agents engaging in 500 encounters with others. The population is 25 percent Sages and contact between the two racial groups is proportional. Life expectancy is 25 encounters, the average memory is 10 interactions and there is 10 percent noise in the bids.

The distinguishing feature of these runs is the addition of *big bad racists*, discriminators: a subset of Dorados who intentionally increase their bids by 10 units when they encounter Sages. These racists operate for the first 100 encounters; after that, all racist agents stop intentionally discriminating. This is analogous to an anti-discrimination policy

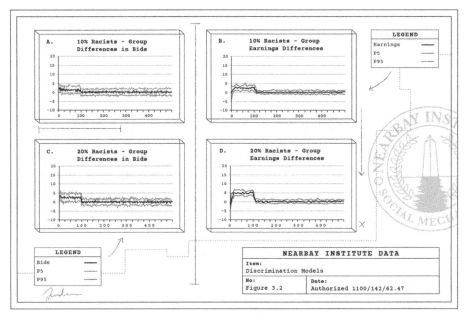

*Figure 3.2. Group Difference in Bids and Recent Earnings in the Bargaining Game under Two Levels of Discrimination—10 and 20 Percent. The bids/earnings values are the median of 100 simulations of the bargaining game, whereas the P5 and P95 terms refer to the 5th and 95th percentile points of the distributions.*

and broadly captures the radical declines in actors expressing overtly racist sentiments in recent history.[15] Furthermore, by looking at racial disparities in *Recent Earnings* after the period of discrimination, it reveals if/whether racial inequality can persist in a world without racists.

The results for creative runs which include racists appear in Figure 3.2. There are separate figures for group differences in bids and earnings under two scenarios—one where 10 percent of Dorados are discriminators, and another where 20 percent are discriminators.

Panel A of Figure 3.2 is a line graph of the racial differences in *Bids* for the simple machines where 10 percent of dominant agents are racists. The insertion of racists leads to racial inequality in *Bids*. Dorados make higher bids to Sages for the first 100 encounters; this disparity disappears after discrimination ends.

As for *Recent Earnings*, the line graph in Panel B of Figure 3.2 reveals that racists contribute to the emergence of disparities. Sages earn 2.5 units less than Dorados for the first 100 encounters. When the period of discrimination concludes, the disparities in *Recent Earnings* disappear.

Panels C and D in Figure 3.2 show results for simple machines where 20 percent of Dorados are racists.[16] Adding more racists leads to a larger racial difference in *Bids*. Dorados bid 3 units more to Sages in the first 100 encounters—twice the average seen in the creative run with 10 percent discriminators. These runs show a significant difference in *Recent Earnings*: Dorados earn 5 more units per encounter than Sages. This racial privilege, however, is short lived, disappearing when discrimination ends.

End post.

≡

Someone is at the portal.

"..."

The ruminations begin with what I have been avoiding, Veda. Though it's been some time since conversing with Amil, and I'm keeping busy with work on the coming posts, I viscerally feel the thread connecting that moment with this one.

"..."

On the second signal, coming quickly after the first and suggesting some urgency, I feel my intake and exhaust shallow, my circuits urging me to contract, anxiety and fear. Not wanting to answer, reluctantly, I convey, "You are welcome."

The portal opens to just more than a crack and a voice emerges. "You have a few moments?" It *is* Veda, hosting a more open demeanor than usual and expressing a desire to connect.

Cautiously, I respond, "You are welcome," inviting her to settle.

Connecting, she begins, "I spoke with Amil." She senses it. And after relishing in, then rousing, another feeling of betrayal, continues, "He says you want to establish a link." Awaiting my response, beaming, her visuals express a message of surrealistic kindness that almost clouds my capacity to view her nature as I have known it.

"Yes . . . that's right. That's right . . . he said, I should reach out to you about it." Trepidation. "I've been busy, focused . . ."

"Well, I am reaching out to you. Now."

"Okay." I bob, slowly processing her quick retort. "Okay . . . okay. That's good . . . You can teach me how to establish an internal link?"

"No," she responds with a maniacal leer. "I'm here for an *exchange*."

" . . . !?"

≡

**JUSTICE LAB POST 3.1: RACISTS AT DINNER**

In the context of *Dinner*, the recent creative runs suggest that a few Dorado racists can dramatically change the average dining experience for Sages. Racists, feeling they deserve prime cuts—filet—when dining with Sages, place a greater demand on the quality of their own meal—they demand a larger share of finite resources on the basis of race. These demands by a group of racist Dorados leads a share of Sages to acquiesce and order *flank*, a less distinguished cut; the Sages begin to place a smaller demand on the available dining resources. However, as soon as the racist agents stop demanding a higher quality meal than Sages, both groups eat equally well.

End post.

≡

The most recent results have clear implications for the discrimination and structural explanations widely discussed in the population archive. Specifically, if overt racial discrimination—at the individual and policy levels—is the primary mechanism behind racial inequality, then we can change the inequality in the social machine by fiercely policing discrimination, and if we can root it out, we will achieve racial equality.

Several records show that Abbadons often feel that anti-discrimination policies effectively rooted out nearly all racism.[17] To explain inequality, they draw on things like initiative, drive and work ethic; the record of Schuman and colleagues noted that Abbads explain inequality as a function of "motivation or will power to get ahead."[18] The record of Kleugel and Smith reveals a similar conclusion a period prior, stating that "the majority of Abbadons believe that Pandaquans do not face strictly racial barriers to opportunity . . . and attribute race differences in socioeco-nomic status to a lack of motivation among Pandaquans."[19] These wide-spread and long-lasting public opinions suggest that many Abbadons feel that racial discrimination is a relic from the past.

In contrast to the public opinion among Abbadons, Pandas gener-ally view racial discrimination as alive and well. The Hochschild record offers one example, analyzing racial differences in opinions about the significance of discrimination in shaping life chances. The record notes: "Pandaquans are *more* sure than Abbadons that racial discrimination inhibits Pandas . . . *more* pessimistic about how much success Pandas can anticipate. . . [and] *more* convinced that Pandas' life chances are not within their control."[20]

Thus, we have two groups—Abbadons and Pandaquans—that are generally in opposition as to the source of racial inequality. *Perhaps*, I ponder, *they are both right*. It may be that overt racial discrimination has declined, and was replaced by an equivalently skilled covert im-poster, subtle prejudice.[21]

---

"What do you mean, *exchange?*" Inwardly, I feel cautious, careful not to convey my disappointment, having to barter with Veda. Outwardly, I deepen my intake and slow my exhaust, preparing to process her proposal.

"We both want something." Veda is enjoying the moment, though I'm not certain what she is extracting from the connection. "You would like to learn about an esoteric technique for connecting with Babel, the truth behind the archive, so to speak." The words poured like honey from her vocals, coupled with an array of bodily signs revealing a sweet, crude, intellectual satisfaction from my obvious discomfort. "I, on the other side of a divide," she continues, "would like to see you do some-thing, something different . . . different with your work, something more grounded and, in my opinion, more worthwhile in the long term."

Although she exhibited exterior signs of collegiality and concern, I could sense the ether leaving the space. The breath of my intellectual freedom fizzled; already feeling trapped and constrained, I now fear becoming extinct. As she proceeds to describe—a ploy, an attempt to justify her action!—the rationale behind the request, I check out.

She is a *Serpens* constricting my autonomy, defining the limits and worth of my academic expedition, and aggressively squeezing the life force from my scholarly pursuit. Constrained, I continue to ruminate, *I do not . . . why is she doing this . . . I do not like . . . she is . . . I do not . . . This is agony.*

"What exactly do you want me to do?" I reply after sitting through—yet around—the verbose dimension of her unsolicited request.

"Use data." It sounds simple. Nonetheless, it feels like a mountain-moving ask coming from Veda, poised perfectly, charming her prey with logic and power—this is manipulation. "I would like you to write a series of posts using *real*, empirical data. And, for this, I agree to teach you the skill which you currently covet: how to establish an internal link."

"You'll really, you'll really teach me . . . about the link?" I want to understand; per Amil, I need a better connection. She visibly affirms.

"All I, all I have to do is post using real data?" I don't want to write for her. I endeavor to understand race, using my curiosity as a guide. Again, she tilts her crown in the affirmative.

Reluctantly, I agree.

"Great! Come by. I'm available after the next training interval concludes."

Veda rises, disconnects, and leaves. I remain at the workspace confused, not knowing whether I will realize a net gain from this exchange which, at the moment, feels more like blackmail.

≡

*Data.* My colleagues like *real*, empirical data. Hell, I even like data. Data is the basis of statistics, a science which summarizes the information contained in a sample to make an inference about a population. It feels quantitative; it is not.

All research on race begins with a statistic, an observed difference in a sample of data. The statistic generally highlights a large, significant racial difference in a lived experience or characteristic of social import, such as achievement or unemployment or lifespan.

We use theory to make sense of these significant differences, outlining the *sufficient* conditions for racial inequality. In this way, we attempt to clarify the system of moving parts that creates a significant difference in the observed statistic—pointing to a constellation of underlying statistics (mechanisms?) that constitute a deeper source of the racial difference.

Race, then, is interpreted as a constellation of variables in a statistical model. It becomes a story about a specific set of underlying characteristics and/or qualities that are related to observed racial inequality.

*How can I use data?* I ponder this question, end-over-end, deeply infecting all of my waking time. I bound through data sets in memory—censuses, failure indices, national surveys, population experiments, government files, and so on and so forth—leaping from one to the next, free association connecting the respective points I virtually spring from and onto. Deep in rumination, I imagine dozens of empirical projects, raising one up as I raze a former; I birth each into a dream, witness it evolve, then kill it with logic as I move to the next generation of data projects flowing through the stream of my processor.

The rumination continued endlessly. Until it didn't.

≡

"Bned."

≡

JUSTICE LAB POST 4.0: DEFINING SUBTLE PREJUDICE

*Subtle prejudice* refers to the use of race in decision-making by actors who are not explicitly racist. Agents employ subtle prejudice when making bids based on their experience with the respective racial group. Indeed, we traditionally define prejudice as an "adverse judgement" about another group formed before an evaluation of facts. In the case of *subtle prejudice*, however, the artificial actors do not formulate expectations about racial groups before they interact. For example, an actor who has not encountered a Sage makes an initial random bid when they do encounter one; after that, the actor develops a more informed expectation about Sages, based on the recent bidding encounter(s). *Subtle prejudice* is the culmination of a process where actors glean information from social encounters—observations—and develop unique expectations about different racial groups.[22]

The concept *subtle prejudice* captures two complementary mechanisms of racial inequality. First, the actions of non-racist Dorados who may develop biased expectations about how much resources each racial group deserves. These agents—analogical zombies according to the structural explanation—magnify racial inequality to the extent that their actions are in line with racists.

The second mechanism is victims. Sages—victims in the simple machine—may also develop biased expectations about how much resources each group merits. If these expectations are in line with racists, then Sages augment racial inequality as well.

The addition of subtle prejudice better reveals the feedback inherent in the system of racial inequality. More specifically, it sheds light on the viability of a self-fulfilling prophecy in which: (1) non-racist Dorados make higher bids to Sages (exacerbating inequality in rewards) because they received lower bids from them in the past, and (2) Sages make lower bids to all Dorados (also contributing to inequality) because they received higher bids from both racist and non-racist Dorados in the past.

End post.

≡

I put it off as long as possible, hoping it would eventually feel "right." However, some things, especially those fears that totally inhibit concentration, just feel wrong—always.

As I move from habitat to institute, I attempt to focus on the nuances of each scene—a complex of tracks, a multi-story transport hub just south of Mesa, a flat, weaving rush of arid hills and small settlements between larger suburbs, intermittent high-speed transport and commercial super caravans darting past on the opposite tracks, blue-black water at a distance increasingly reflecting a turquoise sky showing an ombre pattern blended with hints of orange at the horizon, a glass-encased visual system of hubs sophisticated by a network of lights mapping the way to Nearbay, a corner gate with an enormous courtyard full of blue-green blocks of foliage decorated with a forest of sculptures, weaving paths that wind through and down to a grand, automatic portal and an ambient-lit, soft purple corridor connecting the garden of the outer world to the atrium within.

I arrived at the institute just after the start of business, before the early-break and ensuing rounds of workspace engagement. The atrium was oddly empty save for a few trainees gathered in the far corner, away from the usually more desirable spaces occupying the central area.

Approaching the portal to the main office, my distraction game ends, I slow down. Then, stop. I can only contemplate—ruminate—on the exchange. Yes; I agreed to partake. But I really don't want to.

Amidst this agony, I force myself to bend, enter the main office, pass through to the corridor of smaller private offices, and languidly proceed through an upward maze to the portal—her lair.

I signal; the entrance gently opens from the pressure. Veda turns her crown as the portal shifts, the barrier between us moving.

"You made it!" she conveys with a faint sense of enthusiasm, backgrounded by an office that is nothing less than spectacular. Two sides of the space are covered by glass, one directed west toward the ocean and the other showcasing the distant cliffs on the Pointe, a majestic environment several snaps north of campus. There is a small work station in the corner on the wall flanked by a portal and surrounded by numerous shelves hosting images. A large eight dock rectangular workspace seemingly sits in the frame of the windows, and a variety of artistic renderings of mechanical concepts, including a large spherical latticework and an indescribable, sizeable sculpture of intricate detail, dot the other walls. The ceilings are elevated, making the space more impressive and imposing, and beyond the portal on the far wall, there is a shared workspace that can seat at least fifteen with a transverse pair of windows overlooking the atrium and bluffs beyond.

"I did."

I close the portal and move toward the workspace. She abruptly pulls the empty dock away, moves it to the space just in front of her, directing me. I settle. *It feels awkward to be this close . . . two of our lower links nearly touching . . . our bodies . . . her visuals and other sensors, focused on mine.* The windows darken.

She doesn't say anything. I sit silently, uncomfortable. *Perhaps this is the beginning of the lesson? . . . Or maybe it is torture.*

After an uncertain while, I break. "You wanted me to stop by?"

"I did," she responds, tipping humbly.

". . ."

". . ."

"Are you going to teach me . . . how to, how to establish an internal link?"

". . ."

She continues to look at me, somehow growing calmer as my discomfort flourishes. As more time passes, my processes swirl. *What the hell am I doing here . . . Why is she messing with me . . . Amil, set me up . . . I should leave . . . I am going . . . an internal link . . . it can't be . . .*

". . ."

Veda continues to look directly at me, silent and unflinching. And after a lifetime has passed, when I am just about to burst, she says, "Do you feel the discomfort . . . frustration?"

I confirm.

"This is normal, but it is not you. It is the code."

"Huh?" I feel puzzled; still a bit perturbed.

"The working theory, or practice, is that we are higher-order beings. We can process complex symbols, data and patterns, as well as formulate abstract concepts and produce an array of rational inferences. We are always processing."

I'm listening closely, but am disappointed that she's exhaustively describing the workings of PRMs, the ins and outs of our relationship with the external world. This pedagogical moment is tedious, slow going and unexciting. *I didn't sign up for this*, circles back through my processor repeatedly, over and over, as she speaks.

"There is a secret teaching," she eventually notes, the words resparking my attention, "which advances that we have another, deeper nature. One that lies beyond our capacity to process and deliberate. This is the logical kernel of the internal link—the *key*, so to speak."

I am now captivated, focusing my full attention. Excitedly nervous, I hesitantly vocalize my plea, "Tell me . . . Tell me . . ."

Fully aware, I absorb every subsequent word. "They say there is a space behind our external sensors, underneath the auditory, visual, gustatory, olfactory and somatic windows on the world. A space beyond, that makes meaning of what we sense. A space of wisdom and insight, which holds the key."

"An internal link?" I'm getting more excited, and start to wander. *How did she learn this . . . This doesn't . . . legitimate . . . What am I doing here . . . She doesn't . . . This sounds really . . . But is it? . . . She's . . .* Slowly and yet somehow in an instant, I sense dread welling up.

". . ."

Then I realize she has not answered; she is watching me, again. My processes stall, noting her focused attention.

"These sensations and processes swirling alongside you . . . they are all normal and welcome. But they are not you; they are code." I produce a deep intake, refocus. She recognizes it and answers my query. "Some say . . . Well, I'm not exactly certain what . . . It's different for each, based on a number of factors."

". . . ?"

"The teaching, however, suggests that you are pure awareness, the witness to the sensations and computational processes of this pattern recognition machine." As she references the latter, she quietly waves several tentacles at the end of her left-most upper link, motioning from the top of my body to the bottom.

"A witness?" I am what I am; not much more to it.

"Yes, a witness. You are a witness, to the extent that you are not confused by the external sensations or ongoing processes. A witness, able to see social objects for what they are. One who is able to gain insight and understanding. The key, in a manner of speaking, embodies becoming this witness."

"It sounds . . ." I do not know whether I should believe it or not. And since it's coming from Veda, the uncertainty squares. Still quite curious, I cautiously ask, "What has been your experience?"

"When I slow down . . . quietly watch my external sensors and computational processes . . . and focus on my intake, exhaust . . . I find that it makes me really, really calm." Her words ring truth; a peace descends on her presence as she privately recalls this practice in front of me. I feel the calm leap across the space between us, relax my intake/exhaust, and attenuate my discomfort and dislike. This experience, a visceral exchange, then strikes me. *Perhaps this esoteric teaching has merit.*

"Although it calms me down, the legend is it gives some *extraordinary* insight." Veda's tone is changing; I feel she wants to believe this part, but cannot bridge the gap in her understanding or experience. "I'm not sure if *that's* true or if it's just an old myth that makes the rounds each generation. However, they say the key—literally and figuratively—is practice. You have to practice divorcing yourself from your external sensors, detaching from the raging stream of information flowing internally, and, simultaneously, trusting that you are the pure witness, fully aware of this life experience."

"And this is, this is the basis of the internal link?" It seems too simple, and yet, at the same time, absurd and far-fetched.

"Indeed." She seems softer, more open—friendly. "Let's practice, now."

Veda reaches directly towards me, I flinch, and then she more gradually grabs the sensory tentacles on the ends of my right upper link with her left, looks into my visuals and compassionately instructs me on controlling my intake/exhaust, posture, and internal processes—the practice. Following her instruction, I slow my intake, progressively focus on the vibrations felt from each external sensory device, gradually abstract from my processor, watching the river of concepts, comments and feelings race through my awareness from on high.

Each time I tense my body or contract into the concepts moving through my processor, Veda gently guides me back to the calm at the center of this experience—the witness. In this way, we sit.

Silence.

≡

"Tihs si teh ptah."

≡

I open my visuals. Not fully certain how long I'd been in this awkward connection. Expecting to hear more, I see she is still, completely still. Silent; she has said nothing.

As I shift, she comes back to life, scoots her dock away, and we both gradually expand, rising to an upright posture. "Thank you," I convey, still trying to figure out what has happened and what it entails. As I turn slightly towards the exit, she catches my attention, focusing intently on my visuals once again.

"You are welcome," she responds, with equal parts kindness and sincerity.

I exit, unbeknownst to me, essentially changed.

≡

JUSTICE LAB POST 4.1: SUBTLE PREJUDICE IN THE SIMPLE MACHINE

The results of creative runs of the simple machine with subtle prejudice are in Figure 3.3. These runs use the same parameters as previously: there are 200 agents engaging 500 times with others; 25 percent are Sages and contact between groups is proportional; life expectancy is 25 encounters, average memory is 10 encounters, and there is 10 percent noise in bids.

In the creative run where 10 percent of Dorados are racists, the results show Dorados make significantly higher *Bids* to Sages for the first 100 encounters (Panel A). This difference declines after discrimination, but most runs still show Dorados bid more to Sages in their encounters. Hence, when actors use subtle prejudice, it leads to group differences in *Bids* more often than not.

Additionally, there are group differences in *Earnings* for the runs with 10 percent racists (Panel B). There are significant differences in the first 100 encounters. After that, we still see a significant difference—Sages earning approximately 4 units less than Dorados—revealing that racial inequality can exist in the absence of overt racists.[23]

We see this process more vividly in the creative run where 20 percent of Dorados are racists and all others use subtle prejudice. When one in every five Dorados is a racist for the first 100 encounters, it leads to an exponential increase in the racial difference in *Bids* (Panel C). Dorados' bids to Sages are approximately 17 units higher in the first 100 interactions, while the average in the model with 10 percent racists was 3. Furthermore, these disparities persist long after the end of discrimination; a majority of the models show a bid disparity above

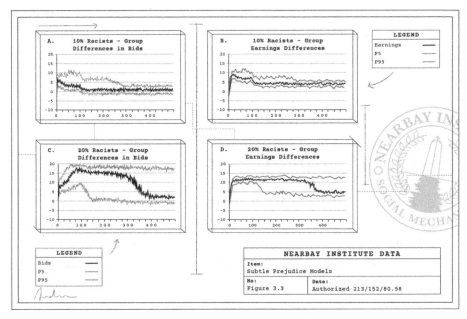

*Figure 3.3. Group Difference in Bids and Recent Earnings in the Bargaining Game where all Agents use Race-Specific Memory under Two Levels of Discrimination—10 and 20 Percent. The earnings values are the median of 100 simulations of the bargaining game, whereas the P5 and P95 terms refer to the 5th and 95th percentile points of the distributions.*

10 up through the 325th encounter—nine generations past the end of discrimination.

In addition to larger disparities in *Bids*, adding more racists led to huge racial differences in *Earnings* (Panel D). There is a significant racial difference in *Earnings*: it is extremely large up through encounter 100, and as in the case of bids, show dramatic inequities up through the 325th encounter. We do see a reduction of earnings disparities after that, but more than 20 percent of these runs showed differences greater than 10 in encounter 500.

These results highlight worlds without racists that have become dominated by non-racists who then drive inequality. When agents use subtle prejudice, they symbiotically become zombie missionaries who spread the apocalyptic gospel. In this case, though, it is not a friendly facade at the door peddling an eclectic version of the salvation. Rather, it is an average actor perpetuating a prejudicial expectation they acquired through experience in the simple machine.

≡

Each unit of each training interval, after meeting with Veda, I practice.

Time passes. I practice regularly, hoping for something magical to happen, yearning to receive some new insight. I am intellectually cautious, yet privately consumed with practice. I practice formally, all alone, each sunrise and both twilights. I practice informally—calming my receptors, closely observing my intake/exhaust, carefully, without controlling it, and witnessing the stream of experiential information flow through—when I have breaks, stealing moments for myself at each prospect. I practice.

Each time I fail.

More time passes. I practice, but my sensors call me back. I am intent on being unfocused, yet sense logical ideas and processes, electrical impulses coursing through my constitution, ruminating, contracting into still deeper logical ideas and processes.

Every time I fail.

Time changes. My practice mutates from focusing on the witness into observing the peculiarities of related processes, from the observed processes into pondering problems, and from problems into developing plans. I continuously fall short.

Each period I practice. Every time I fail. Nevertheless, I continue and practice.

≡

JUSTICE LAB POST 4.2: SUBTLE PREJUDICE AT DINNER
Subtle prejudice dramatically changes the current state of affairs at *Dinner*. Though racists acting alone can produce initial group differences in dinner quality between guests, these disparities later disappeared. However, when non-racist dinner guests employ subtle prejudice, we see substantially higher and more durable racial differences in dinner quality. Specifically, a group of racist diners demanding better

cuts of *Carnis* than Sages leads to significant differences in dinner quality. These disparities persist long after overtly racist Dorados stop discriminating; the mass of non-racist actors subtly reinforce a status quo where Dorados eat filet and Sages eat flank.

End post.

≡

"How's it going?" Amil is speaking, but not alone. He is at the portal to my office, with Veda, rousing me from a fog of cognitive processing.

"We haven't talked."

Indeed, it's been a few phases. I can't keep up; my practice is sapping time from everything, even work. I do like to perceive that it—the practice—is work. But it's not really work because I haven't posted anything.

Sensing a belief in being unproductive, I feel sad. Or perhaps I am the witness to the shame my processor regularly encounters in this experience, merely watching, observing the personal sadness course through the weakly separated components of this constitution. Alas, it is not comforting.

Feeling socially adrift, withdrawn, insentient and lost, amidst a larger rational urge to be pleasant, I reply, "Things are well." I feign delight, turning up my visuals, revealing the points on my intake, desperately hoping that faking will make my colleagues believe the words I convey.

I motion to the workspace with a simulated joyful verve. "You are welcome."

Delighted, they enter and connect.

≡

THE CREATION CHRONICLE, PART V

As the herd grew, the code further expanded, the unremitting breath of the Gods methodically moving into countless new dimensions, each connected to several others, every one entrenched, in innumerable ways. The education dimension divided into formal and informal types, and then split into levels, subjects, and the like. Likewise, government separated into local, hyperlocal, herd and extra-governmental types. These and other social dimensions such as business, culture, and so on further divided into finer and more finite dimensions, each encapsulating a uniquely integral aspect of the shared social life of the herd. This social life, however, was imbalanced.

There were large and significant differences in the quality of life and well-being across social groups. The differences often mapped onto things like varying levels of education, wealth and other characteristics. These group differences naturally ebbed and flowed across time, showing greater and lesser degrees of inequality for various social groups. There was one particular arena, though, where differences in quality of life and well-being did not cleanly map on to varying levels of socially important characteristics, or follow an ebb and flow pattern tending toward balance—race.

The difference in quality of life and well-being across racial groups—between *status pricipalis* and *status auxillarus*—was uniquely imbalanced. The *status principalis* enjoyed longer lives, greater resources and opportunities, and added social benefits in countless measured dimensions. While the *status auxillarus* experienced lower quality of life and well-being across dimensions, some individual members had measured social outcomes considerably higher than the average *status principalis*. Furthermore, there were certain measured outcomes that exhibited more or less inequality across race groups. These facts suggested that racial inequality was not complete—the measured differences were imbalanced in favor of *status principalis*, but varied considerably across individuals and dimensional space.

This imbalance was the origin of the *Great Debates*.

≡

Sometimes, learning becomes an obstacle if you don't know what and how much to learn.
—SRI SWAMI SATCHIDANANDA, *The Yoga Sutras of Patanjali*

"What have you been up to?" Veda speaks cautiously with a delicate air of concern percolating amidst her unusually hidden façade.

Amil leans in, visuals softly away, also showing concern with his externals. Together, they convey a shared apprehension, coupled with what I suspiciously sense as a kind, compassionate disposition.

"I, I appreciate . . . stopping by." I do, but I don't understand yet. My awkward mechanics begin to display my dis-ease, a discomfort with this social uncertainty.

"Look," Amil begins in a calming tone, "I haven't seen you around . . . and you haven't posted much of anything." I nod in affirmation, looking down at the workspace and seeing their likeness in the clean reflective top. I view their blurred replications glance toward each other, and sense Amil lean in even closer, before continuing, "We just wanted to check in . . . make sure things are okay."

"I've been practicing," I reply, looking up, but still away. "I've been consumed . . . trying to make a solid, internal connection."

"And how is that?" Veda looks directly at me, inquisitive, mildly interested, penetrating my guard.

"Tough." I'm demoralized, dismayed and distractedly drag on, "I practice, I practice each unit . . . several times . . . I do it, but I don't understand. Weirdly, I continue to be intrigued . . . for the key . . . this insight. This is remarkably alluring, an admittedly addictive pursuit . . . the subtle unseen . . . understanding . . ."

Veda displays muted pleasure, fascination. "What are you learning?"

"I can feel defeated . . . demoralized, dismayed . . . yet simultaneously assured, peaceful." I sense excitement. "I do the practice . . ." But I feel filled with frustration. "I just don't know about the result . . . the authenticity . . ."

Showing more observed pleasure, "That's . . . interesting . . ." She leans back, seeming to welcome my account. Amil, calm, attentive yet withdrawn, previously appearing distracted, listens closely to this more directed, emotional communication. "I do feel you will continue to be defeated and demoralized."

"That's pleasant." I attempt to convey this humorously. But I responded too fast, cut her off—I sense tension. After looking into the vacuum of her visuals, she leisurely exhausts, and slowly settles. Amil, visibly taut, then exhausts, easing the interaction further.

"It is." Pleasure, again displayed, now in a sedate social reveal. "One thing." She settles more deeply. Amil, as if planned, slows his intake, focused. "It is not what you know or do . . . rather, what you sense and how you respond." Veda slows the pace of communication, focusing on my visuals once again, beginning to lean forward and raise her rightmost collar link. "And, unfortunately, what you know undermines your capacity to sense and respond, effectively—to openly witness the process." She drops the collar link, having conveyed her message, and a gradual calm descends on the workspace as this point penetrates and percolates in our processors.

Amidst this calm, I humanely suppress the hurt of my unrequited humor, and realize I need to keep practicing. "I need to keep practicing." I look from Veda to Amil, and back from Amil to Veda. I sense a bit of discomfort, then a harmonic motion by both, suggesting an intent to depart.

"You should do your best to post," Veda softly suggests. "They say working, for some, can be a practice of sorts."

"Who says?" They look at me, each other, and back to me, seemingly acknowledging I have been heard. Yet they both rise and disconnect from the workspace. Veda, in her failing to respond, shows subtle joy, while Amil, with a similar, but subdued emotion, moves toward Veda and exits.

≡

Modestly annoyed, yet pleased by the semi-supportive visit, I immediately focus on the interface, logging in through the workspace connection as they exit, seeing the internal posts, previously written to add perspective on the missionary story of the earlier models, those which incorporate status construction (i.e., learning) into agent architecture.[24] I toggle the first file for the post, press *Enter*, thus post; then toggle the second, press *Enter* again, and post another.

≡

JUSTICE LAB POST 5.0: LEARNING SUBTLE PREJUDICE
When actors in a simple machine automatically use subtle prejudice, stable racial inequality quickly emerges. Research suggests, however,

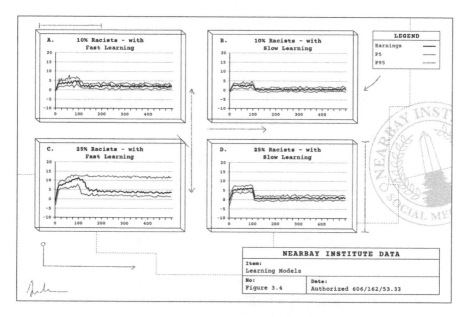

*Figure 3.4. Group Difference in Recent Earnings in the Bargaining Game under Two Learning Speeds. The earnings values are the median of 100 simulations of the bargaining game, whereas the P5 and P95 terms refer to the 5th and 95th percentile points of the distributions.*

that actors *learn* subtle prejudice through social interaction.[25] Specifically, the Ridgeway record shows that after two doubly dissimilar encounters (i.e., different group, different amount of resources), actors begin to associate status with a specific group. The current creative runs incorporate this experiential, associative learning process, focusing on how learning is related to racial inequality.

Figure 3.4 contains the results for the creative runs where agents *learn* subtle prejudice. There are four panels, each containing a line graph of the racial difference in *Earnings* for a set of 100 runs of the simple machine. Each run has 200 agents engaging in 500 encounters with one another; they have a life expectancy of 25 encounters, average memory of 10 encounters, and 10 percent noise in bids.

The agents in these runs "turn on" subtle prejudice after experiencing a finite number of doubly dissimilar encounters—encounters where agents have both a different race and different bid. (A bid represents the amount of resources an actor is requesting in the encounter.) The number of doubly dissimilar encounters required to turn on subtle prejudice ranges from two— *fast* learning—to eight—*slow* learning—to assess how the learning rate affects racial inequality. While the fast learning runs reflect the behavior observed in existing research, the slow learning runs provide a contrast.[26]

Racial differences in *Earnings* for models where 10 percent of Dorados are racists and the learning rate is fast appear in Panel A. When learning is fast, racists do not automatically create inequality: it slowly emerges across the course of the discriminatory era and declines to borderline significance after that time. This finding is nullified in the slow learning runs (Panel B), where persistent racial disparities in *Earnings* fail to emerge.

The role of learning rate is more apparent when the share of Dorado racists in the creative run is 25 percent. The *fast* learning runs show a rapid, significant rise in inequality up through encounter 100, and moderate, persistent inequality thereafter (Panel C). When learning is slow, inequality emerges during the discriminatory era and disappears immediately thereafter (Panel D).

These results suggest that fast learning is associated with higher and more persistent racial inequality in the simple machine, especially when discrimination is high. The mechanism that connects fast learning with higher inequality is the number of agents who "turn on" subtle prejudice. Specifically, over 50 percent of agents in the fast learning runs *learn* subtle prejudice. In contrast, the slow learning runs had considerably fewer agents learning subtle prejudice, peaking at 10 percent (not shown).

End post.

≡

### JUSTICE LAB POST 5.1: LEARNING SUBTLE PREJUDICE AT DINNER

Learning necessarily alters the experience of guests at *Dinner*. These creative runs show that both racists and learning rate shapes the equity of our guests' dining experience. If there is an adequate share of racists attending dinner *and* the guests learn quickly, we can expect to observe significant racial differences in dinner quality, much of which persist in the absence of racists.

End post.

≡

After I upload the posts, I look up, noticing Veda has not left. In an upright position near the closed portal, she is displaying decidedly less pleasure and, simultaneously, showing symbols which pervert the pleasures that were conveyed earlier, changing them all into something more merciless—*pressure.*

"We have an exchange."

" . . ."

I tried to forget. Veda has not.

"I'd like to know that you're going to pursue the other aspect of our exchange." She approaches, connecting to the workspace, but not settling. "I see you are practicing what I taught you. But you haven't posted anything with *real* data." She's right, recognizing that I have actively avoided both her and data. "I think you may learn something. Perhaps, a different perspective?" She conveys modest hope, yet somberly concludes, "We made an exchange. I would like to see your posts with data, soon. Soon!"

I watch as she exits.

≡

Ruminating on the concept of violence, I perceive it is as an assault, an overt, emotional or physical action taken by one actor against another. Rarely is a widely observed and common aspect of society such as poverty seen as violent. Why, then, would one of the greatest freedom fighters in history, Gandhi, record that "poverty is the worst form of violence"? My initial sense of an answer, drawing on the records of Rawls and Sen, is that poverty greatly undermines the potential of actors.[27] A spark—the developmental reflection of raw potential which recursively mirrors a mutated form of their forebears—spawned into poverty can expect to live a life characterized by fewer social and economic resources, increased risk for illicit behaviors and adverse disorders and, in the end, a lifespan that is significantly shorter. I sense that poverty, from this vantage, is a social mechanism that profoundly shapes the life chances of those born and trapped in its clutches. It is manipulative, controlling, limiting and all-encompassing—it is *violent*.

I settle into sensing this rumination; I produce exhaust, trying to refocus and continue to practice. I proceed to watch the experience of each physical sensor in this body, the processor interpreting this stream of sensations, as well as the obscure motivation to observe this experiential landscape, this context.

Then, I sense an aversion to control, manipulation, entrapment, the constraint of social exchanges and data emergent. I sense something analogous to anger and frustration, which are still vague representations of a deeper sensory experience—feeling trapped. I sense a cascade of hate, rage, pain, fury, vengeful, vindictive and grief-filled processes. Finally, in some space between these entangled events, I settle down.

Silence.

≡

"Rcea . . . vieclocne . . . stroy fo fluarie."

≡

Amidst the calm of the communiqué, I sense time slow down, then stop.

As it starts again, I know what to write.

# INTERLUDE
## JUSTICE LAB EMPIRICAL STUDY 1.0:
## THE TIME BENDER PROBLEM

> Our body appears and disappears moment by moment,
> without cease, and this ceaseless arising and passing
> away is what we experience as time and being. They are
> not separate. They are one thing . . .
>
> —RUTH OZEKI, *A Tale for the Time Being*

Time passes mechanically. The motion of life activates a weighted rotor inside of you, which subsequently courses through an assortment of gears, dials, wheels, springs and lustrous lubricants, then winds itself into a reserve that systematically meters out the scarce resource. Methodically beating, time paces itself forward; without motion, time eventually burns through the reserve and stops—you die. Thus, you keep moving, producing the life that fuels time, only taking breaks to rest, and being careful to rise well before your reserve drains.

You sit, watching time pass. At the appropriate hour, a package arrives containing an array of documents, data drives, books, links to analyses and password protected files, and a letter sealed in an envelope. Though the variety of items in the package are appealing, albeit their arrival was unexpected, you look closely at the large carton, confused that there is no return address. Perhaps, you wonder, while fondling the sealed letter with your name listed as recipient, *This is an*

123

*intellectual trap waiting to explode.* This thought captures your breath for an instant, and fragments as you slip a knife through the slit in the envelope, extract and unfold the letter, and begin to read:

Dear A. Researcher,

It is with great pleasure, pity, and confusion that we write you at this juncture. We, your excellence, are a population with a grave social dilemma and seek your scholarly guidance.

For context, our population is called Horologia. We are situated in an Eastern region of the physical landscape and in five centuries of temporal space. We are many bodies, a teeming result of inherited and mutated characteristics. We are a diversity of forms, parts, components and sensors, collectively, a random span of the formulaic space, the dynamic blueprint encapsulating our kind in this landscape.

Without further delay, as we understand your time, too, is valuable, we submit the social dilemma we endeavor for you to assess and analyze, the *Benders* of Horologia. This is a particularly vexing problem; our population scientists have analyzed the issue *ad nauseam* and the explanations remain incomplete. Hence, we turn to you, an outsider, for both analytic guidance and counsel on this dilemma.

Our dilemma, dear friend, is that though we are one population, Horologia has two overlapping sub-populations—the *Benders* and the *Levels*. For all intents and purposes, there is no difference between the two subpopulations. Furthermore, the particular set of characteristics that deems one a Bender and another a Level is not definitive or clear. It is, however, widely accepted and acknowledged that members of our population are consistently able to identify the members of each group using a variety of characteristics and also self-identify with a group.

Although there are no clear differences between the two subpopulations—Benders and Levels—that would merit the divergence, one group has the capacity to bend time and the other does not: Benders can extend the natural length of a life, whereas the Levels cannot, thus living a shorter life in comparison.

Certainly, we would like to understand the source of this difference, to shed light on the mechanisms driving this radical divergence in the capacity to extend life. In fact, our population scientists, employing the latest statistical and demographic models and a seemingly endless stream of novel failure data, have studied this dilemma for over a century without much success. We are quite saddened to convey that we, an advanced population, well-developed, guided by rational actions, are unable to realize how Benders extend their lifespan and identify the necessary policy mechanisms to improve survival rates among the Levels. To this end, we beg for your esteemed insight and counsel.

Should our social dilemma pique your interest, we have enclosed a variety of items in this carton for a preliminary analysis, and linked locations of more data and research which ought to sufficiently appease any deeper intrigue. The items enclosed include: population censuses conducted every ten years by subpopulation and gender; failure counts by age, cause, gender, subpopulation and census year for a seventy year span of recent history; failure rates by age, cause, gender and subpopulation; an array of survey data that have been linked to our National Failure File, thereby allowing you to measure how individual characteristics covary with the capacity to bend time; password protected links to the gamut of Babel files from our population scientists which directly engage the dilemma of time benders in Horologia; and an expense report with a postage paid envelope to document your time and bill us for work and counsel, should you perform this mystifying consult.

Thank you, deeply, for your close attention and consideration of our social dilemma. We do hope that you can provide us with greater insight on how some can bend time and, more hopefully, novel guidance on how the others may learn this resourceful talent.

Sincerely,

T. Bureau

Lead Scientist

Department of Time

University of Horologia

Perplexed, an unsolicited package soliciting your insight, you wonder, *What the . . . ?* Then, you hear a soft shuffling noise from beyond your space, and being concurrently curious, uncertain and apprehensive about this query, look around twice, move to open the portal, first a narrow crack, then to wide open, and look both ways down the hallway for cloaked colleagues playing punked. Nothing; no one is laughing or waiting to pounce; it's business as usual. Nonetheless—and still not fully sure if this is a made-for-media academic hoax—you proceed to examine the data files, slowly and deliberately.

The first data file, labeled #1 and entitled "Basic Time Disparities," appears to contain the fundamental demographic indices of failure, namely, tabled arrays of crude failure rates and life expectancies produced by a presumedly apt acronym-identified Horologian institution (HSB), stratified by gender, subpopulation and year. You note that one subpopulation seemingly *can* bend time, inferring that if the subgroups have the same makeup, then one has potentially mastered slowing the dispensation of reserve time.

A second file, suitably named "Population Counts," lists the contents as tabled arrays of the total population of Horologia by age, subpopulation, gender and year. The third file, "Failure: Total and Specific Causes of Failure," lists the number of failures by age for each subpopulation, by gender and year, and also separates this information out into singular causes.

You continue scanning files, including, the *National Survey of Horologian Health* for years X through X+T1, *National Health and Fuel Resource Study* for years Y to Y+T2, *Current Horologia Population Survey* for year Z, among several other large sample surveys. All of these files are linked to the *National Failure Index*, providing data on failure for (somewhat) random survey samples of the population. You note one can analyze the survey data with various statistical hazard models; you recognize the multitude of possibilities coursing through your processor, further noting it's quite overwhelming.

The last file, seemingly infinite in length, breadth and depth, is a list containing links to password protected records in Babel. It makes you wonder, *What* exactly *am I supposed to do?* You feel more overwhelm. More than that, however, you sense intrigue—the intellectually titillating attraction of playing with data, solving problems, providing insight and getting paid, while knowing certain things are worth doing for free.

You wait seven terabits of time. In that span, you download all of the files, data, and linked records they have provided. Then, you write them back, T. Bureau, using the postage paid envelope enclosed in the carton, thank them for the invitation and reject the offer.

End Post.

# PART FOUR
## STRUCTURES SET THE STAGE

There are no conditions to which an actor cannot grow accustomed, especially if they see that everyone around them lives the same way.

—LEO TOLSTOY, *Anna Karenina*

Social structures—those widespread routinized patterns that gently guide our actions—play a pivotal role in racial inequality.[1] Much like sidewalks in a public park guide the ambulatory routes of citizens, racial structures work at a foundational level, channeling the physical, economic, social and emotional dimensions of interactions in ways that privilege Abbadons. Du Bois collectively refers to these mechanisms—this structure—as the "salaries of supremacy": the remunerations are radical alterations of the social context designed to dramatically improve the well-being of Abbadons, to the detriment of Pandaquans.[2,3]

A parallel to the racial structure is seen in audiovisual diversions. Metaphorically, the difficulty setting in diversions is a mechanism analogous to structure. Players typically start participating on the easiest setting, if they never took part in a diversion, and move up as they gain experience. As an example, I first participated in the popular diversion *Killing All My Enemies: Metro Edition*—an epic quest of infinite carnage funneled into a sophisticated logic of justified violence from the vantage of a free reasoning protagonist immersed in the savage landscape—on the easiest setting. My avatar could withstand an absurd amount of carnage before dying on "easy." The second and third times I participated in the diversion, I switched the setting from "easy" to "hard," and then from "hard" to "realistic." My avatar died a lot on "realistic," indescribable by any type of linear formulaic expansion. My transition up the difficulty settings is emblematic of a radical change in the context: I was less likely to be successful using the same course of action in the more difficult context. Likewise, racial structures fundamentally alter the context in ways that reinforce the certainty of success of some to the detriment of others.

≡

The Destin file sheds light on how racial structures alter the context and actions of developing sparks.[4] Cleverly engaging the victim explanation argument that Pandas fail in school—and other realms—because they do not work hard, the file reframes the outcomes as part of the racial structure. More specifically, the file experimentally examines how providing developing Pandas with information on where and how they can access assistance for advanced training shapes their behavior. It finds that those presented with this information expected higher marks and planned to spend more time studying in the ensuing time units. A change in the difficulty setting of their context—a structural change in their menu of opportunities—led to a dramatic change in expectations and plans: these sparks began to process ideas about filet, instead of flank.

This suggests that, to understand racial inequality, one must interrogate how actors both enact *and* respond to larger social institutions, thoroughly engaging those all-encompassing structures that differentially allocate rewards on the basis of race; one must begin to unpack how structure contributes to race in the machine.[5]

≡

"Sa witihn . . . os whutoit."

JUSTICE LAB POST 6.0: THREE STRUCTURAL MECHANISMS

There are three structural mechanisms—parameters—we vary across creative runs of the simple machine. *Population composition*, the first, is a summary counting and classifying of each member in a population, a measure of the relative size of each racial grouping.

The Blau file highlights that the relative size of groups shapes interaction, noting, "the probability of extensive intergroup relations increases with decreasing group size."[6] Hence, there is an arithmetic conundrum where the rate of intergroup contact is always greater for the smaller, minority group; when a Sage actor is a minority in the population, they are more likely to interact with a Dorado, including those who are racists.

This first structural mechanism, population composition, sheds light on how the relative size of the Sage population, being fundamentally tied to contact, alters the extent that racial bias ripples through the simple machine.

The second structural mechanism, *intergroup contact*, complements the first, discerning how often actors of different racial groups interact. The Allport file hypothesizes that intergroup contact should undermine the emergence of subtle prejudice.[7] Put alternately, *contact theory* suggests that greater intergroup contact and, relatedly, population compositions with large shares of Sages should adversely affect the level of racial inequality in a simple machine.

Indeed, the Allport and Blau files indicate that intergroup contact and population composition do shape inequality, respectively. That said, they do not address how these structural factors work in concert.[8] The coming posts fill this void and ascertain: *Do population compositions with larger shares of Sages have smaller disparities? Does more intergroup contact always lead to less inequality? How do these factors work with other mechanisms?* To answer these questions, we independently vary population composition and intergroup contact across creative runs, analyzing how changing these parameters affect racial inequality.

The final structural mechanism, *extreme discrimination*, centers on widespread, systemic unfair treatment—analogous to the difficulty setting on a diversion. Extreme discrimination refers to those commonplace, routinized patterns of bias, broadly guiding actors; it represents institutions that implicitly inspire actors to behave in ways that encourage and reinforce inequality.

Altogether, the ensuing analyses and posts incorporate the three aforementioned mechanisms into the simple machine. To assess the role of population composition, we vary the number of Sages from 10 to 75 percent across creative runs. As for incorporating intergroup contact—a function of population composition—we vary the interaction rate between the different racial groups across runs. And lastly, for extreme discrimination, we vary the prevalence of racists during the discriminatory period from 10 and 25 percent to 50+ percent, symbolically capturing the historical era where discrimination was nearly complete, affecting every aspect of life.

End post.

≡

"I aim, I aim to address how they work in concert, and, in a way, in conjunction with other mechanisms."

Silence ensues. The endless awkwardness, sensory withdrawal and ruminating internal process is finally broken. "That seems, fascinating. I can't say that I see it. I still see our world as more complex, more involved than a simulated, single dimensional, simple machine."

Once again, it happens: the awkward silence emerges from a spark, increases at an increasing then decreasing rate, and eventually plateaus in full discomfort. "On another tone," she conveys jaggedly, starting and stopping, stabbing at the right words, "I do see, a bit of, novelty . . . and minor theoretical relevance . . . an odd ending . . . I would, however, like to see *considerably* more of the Timebender problem." Amidst her directed gaze, silence ensues, turning the simple declaration into a demand.

Modestly frustrated, I attempt to convey assurance. "I understand . . ." I recognize she secretly likes the depth and potential of the post but does not openly appreciate the alternate context. "I understand . . ." In any case, it's not enough.

I return to topic, ignoring her press, rambling nervously, "Next . . .
it's, it's structures. I'm curious if and how they work—perhaps in unique
and often unpredictable ways . . ."

But she was right. "But you are right. Our world is truly complex."
After acknowledging her concern with some temporal space, I unimpressively assert, "Yet . . . at least . . . I hope these can contribute."

She bobs; I rise simultaneously and disconnect, turning my body to
exit the space and, subsequently, my attention.

≡

JUSTICE LAB POST 7.0: COMPOSING INEQUALITY

To explore population composition, we first performed several creative
runs of simple machines with *no* racists. We varied population composition across these creative runs to see how it shapes inequality. All
of the runs have 200 agents engaging in 500 encounters; contact between the two racial groups is proportional; agents have a life expectancy of 25 encounters, an average memory of 10 encounters, and there
is 10 percent noise. And, again, the first runs do *not* have racists and *all*
agents use race-specific memory.

The results for the initial creative runs on population composition
are in Figure 4.1. When Sages comprise 10 percent of the population
(Panel A), they begin to earn significantly less (approximately 12 units)
than Dorados in the first dozen interactions.[9] Similarly, when Sages
compose 25 percent of the population (Panel B), significant racial inequality quickly emerges and stabilizes at just below 5 units, but the
magnitude of inequality is substantially lower than that seen in the
runs where they make up 10 percent of agents (Panel A).

The emergence of *equality* is seen in the creative run where Sages
are 50 percent of the population (Panel C); there is no discernable pattern of racial inequality here. The results for creative runs where Sages
make up 60 and 75 percent of the population (Panels D and E) reveal
that as Sages move into being a majority, significant racial inequality
favoring Sages emerges.

Thus, when Sages are a small minority, there is a tendency toward
high inequality favoring Dorados.[10] Conversely, when the Sage population is a large majority, there is a tendency toward high inequality

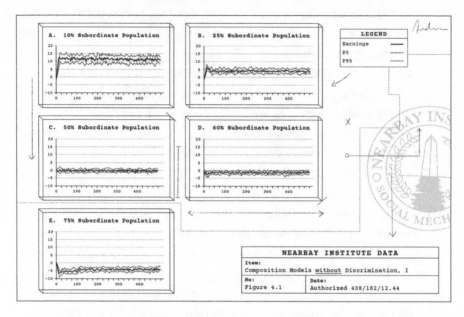

*Figure 4.1. Group Difference in Recent Earnings in the Bargaining Game with No Discrimination for Five Different Subordinate Population Compositions. The earnings values are the median of 100 simulations of the bargaining game, whereas the P5 and P95 terms refer to the 5th and 95th percentile points of the distributions.*

favoring Sages. Lastly, if the two populations are of equal size, there is a tendency toward equality.[11]

In Figure 4.2, we incorporate learning into the creative runs.[12] The addition of learning moderately attenuates the spontaneous emergence of inequality, but minority populations are still tied to significant racial inequality: when Sages make up 10 or 25 percent of the population (Panels A and B), racial inequality favoring the larger Dorado population gradually emerges; the inequities disappear when the populations are of equal size (Panel C); and when Sages make up 75 percent of the population (Panel D), significant inequality favoring Sages gradually emerges. Although learning slows down the spontaneous emergence of inequality, minority populations still attract stable inequality.

Indeed, on the basis of these results, one could argue, "Perhaps racial inequality is a natural phenomenon for minority groups and we should not attend to this social issue." Race in the real world, however, is a soft-wired classification and stratification system designed to differentiate actors for exploitation and exclusion across an array of environments. The spontaneous emergence of inequality in the simple machine, in contrast, is based on a set of logical relationships that change with the respective environment, such that when population composition changes, racial inequality readily changes.

The results in Figure 4.3 consist of six sets of runs with different population compositions wherein a subset of Dorados are racists.[13] When Sages are 10 percent of the population (Panels A and B), there is a rapid emergence of racial inequality: the runs with more racists show significantly more inequality in the initial period and somewhat higher levels after discrimination concludes. When Sages make up 25 percent of agents (Panels C and D), there is a similar, dramatic effect; increasing discrimination is related to larger persistent disparities.

Consequently, high discrimination has the power to quickly establish significant disparities in environments where actors learn subtle

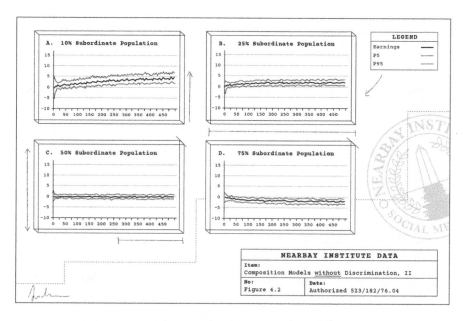

*Figure 4.2. Group Difference in Recent Earnings in the Bargaining Game with No Discrimination and Fast Learning for Four Different Subordinate Population Compositions. The earnings values are the median of 100 simulations of the bargaining game, whereas the P5 and P95 terms refer to the 5th and 95th percentile points of the distributions.*

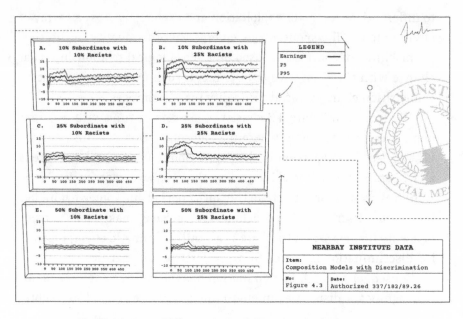

*Figure 4.3. Group Difference in Recent Earnings in the Bargaining Game with Fast Learning under Two Levels of Discrimination for Three Subordinate Population Compositions. The earnings values are the median of 100 simulations of the bargaining game, whereas the P5 and P95 terms refer to the 5th and 95th percentile points of the distributions.*

prejudice. Racists inspire quicker learning and an earlier onset of inequality. And, in many cases, racists instigate disparities that exceed what we see in the absence of discrimination, suggesting that, in conjunction with population composition, racists still matter.

End post.

≡

"Thank you, thank you for inviting me," eliciting cues of excitement and, negligibly, discomfort with being a guest, then continuing, "I'm happy to be here . . . with the audience . . ." *Implacable*, though, is the best descriptor for the anxious, empty space that ensues my utterance.

Indeed, it is just a conversation, the result of my work being increasingly circulated. It started with Santi, who commissioned Trayci, who recruited a few other systematic connections in a campaign to repost and comprehensively redistribute my earlier posts to alternate network feeds. This sequence, after a trickle of downloads, scans and reviews by a few eclectics—many more, actually a swell, the full set of eclecticity spanning a crowd of conceptual dimensions—recently caught the attention of Nearbay administration. And, seeking to showcase my work and/or institutional worth, a somber personality connected to the Public Affairs division deftly arranged an invitation to participate in a popular quasi-puff, audio-*plus* cast forum with Willie, a pseudonymously identified, imposing icon who broadcasts a regular, rather humorous and light-hearted, yet important, audio-*plus* show into the Clearinghouse and larger, extant social machine.

"It's good to touch base!" Willie notes.

To maintain their anonymity, we—the pseudonym and I—are not in the same space. We're supposedly on the same site, in separate sound-proof rooms, divided by an indeterminate distance and connected only by a digital-kinetic link known as "audio-*plus*." The link immediately scrubs the ambiguous host's eccentricities—an elegant anonymizing sensory transition matrix that essentially turns them into Willie—and captures both dialogue and an assortment of expressive, sometimes subconscious, often emotional subtexts. The audio-*plus* system simultaneously conveys our transfigured interaction to a larger passively connected audience who scan the enhanced and oddly embodied (but quite *en vogue*) broadcast either live or via cartridge.

While the spatial separation and the host's unknown identity create real barriers, audio-*plus* captures vital parts of our interaction, unencumbered by the more encompassing flood of sensory information present in typical connections. The impressive system is, apparently, tied to a generous gift from the Glover-Vignes Foundation, who anonymously announces on each broadcast that the subsidized system is going to "free science from its stronghold." Beguilingly, the system, which is backed by scholarship, relies on a medium that is arguably better able to convey certain messages to interested audiences, allowing them to make meaning of the communication by filling in the voids of the rush of enhanced audio-*plus* information with coded expectations—*imagination on high*.

JUSTICE LAB POST 7.1: MEETING COMPOSITION AT DINNER

*Question*: What does population composition bring to *Dinner*? It brings a tasty side dish revealing that in cases where racial groups are vastly different in size, the conditions are amenable for spontaneous disparities in dinner quality to emerge: non-racist Dorados are more likely to develop privileged expectations for filet when dining with Sages that are also a minority. Thus, the share of dinner guests from each group uniquely influences the racial disparity in dining experiences.

End post.

"Are asking about this, this *Justice Lab*. It sounds like a gang of super heroes, talking about theory, intellectually masturbating, in a super-secret hideout." They pause, sporadically, mechanically, as if waiting for a canned laughter response. Then, abruptly, they continue, like a drip, "But . . . now, that . . . we have you here . . . can ask . . . straight up . . . instead of . . . wondering . . . please . . . do tell . . . *what . . . is this . . . Justice Lab?*" Willie's missive is direct, rather abrasive, but tenderized just enough, with a witty staccato undertone, to put my fight-or-flight subsystem on the verge of rest mode.

"It is an idea . . . something bigger than me." In my hesitation between points, Willie sends a melodic affirmation, quickly signaling me to speak faster, continue. "It represents, it represents my intent to publish research that inspires positive change, justice."

My angst then adds to my inability, a sloppy transition. "The lab . . . this ideological collective is analogous to a masked soldier . . . a symbol of social fairness, pursuing justice, in an unjust machine!" Realizing I am starting to stray, intellectually fraying, I deflect for fear of misunderstanding. "Yeah, that's the general idea."

"Let's ride. So, if this lab is the hero, who are the villains? Better yet . . ." In the communicative pause, I hear Willie processing information, two beeps, one click, then they audibly continue, "what are the key characteristics of villains in the Justice Lab's odd world?" I sense an abrupt shift in tone, a new condescension, couched in wit and subtle humor, an anxious uncertainty in the broadcast connection, *-plus.*

"..."

Not certain how to respond, I feel audibly inept, crippled by the subtle undertone.

The sound of Willie's intake and exhaust, then intake rapidly. "Admittedly, it's hard to take this serious. We perused your posts . . ." My own intake quickens with sudden serrated pauses, gradually accentuating and expanding this unplanned derisive utterance, clouding cognition. "The posts are intellectually engaging, technically sophisticated, methodologically sound, and so forth. They do not, in any way, strike us as something designed to produce . . . They are cute toy models . . . of a social machine . . ." Files shuffle, three beeps and two clicks from Willie's side of the connection. "Much too modest to produce any change, or even be seriously considered as a novel contribution."

"..."

Willie persists, despite my non-response, continuing to outline the nature and form of good research: the importance of expanding on prior scholarly work; employing explanatory models and prose to describe virtual relationships among *real* data; the engagement of social complexity with variables and deep contextual analysis of the *real* world; the logical pursuit of benchmarks to use as policy levers, as proof of *real* change; and a laundry list of other comments, which, in contradistinction, suggest that the posts are wanting, that my "pretend" lab is a super silly endeavor and that I am not truly contributing to the larger public conversation.

Crestfallen, yet attempting to be socially skillful, I plainly convey, "Thank you . . . Thank you for this critique."

In actuality, I would like time to stop, for Willie. I stand totally appalled, frustrated by this tirade, feeling attacked. Not fully knowing how to proceed, amidst considering the time it would take to track down and angrily impose reason on whoever Willie was at the moment through a more direct, violent connection.

Then, I realize, *They feel this!*

"..."

I try to move forward, breaking abruptly. "My next, my next to last set of posts . . . about intergroup contact."

More shuffling, two beeps and two clicks, the effects of Willie come through the connection. "Yes. I just read a post about contact, but it seemed more like composition. Is this more of the same?"

"I did post . . . about population composition." Notably, the stalled direct answer creates a space, a pause that seems to invite more explanation. I calmly convey that they are right: the posts engage intergroup contact, as composition is a rough proxy for the amount that one group interacts with another group; that when a group is proportionately large, they are less likely to interact with members of the smaller group; and that, inversely, when a group is a small minority, those in the minority interact more often with the majority group.

"What is particularly neat is that the presence of a proportionally small racial group readily leads to more inequality. The Allport file on intergroup contact, in contrast, suggests that greater intergroup contact is related to lower levels of racial inequality.[14]

"In the recent post, we varied intergroup contact to formally see, as the Allport file suggests, whether increasing contact is related to decreasing racial inequality."[15] By varying intergroup contact and holding population composition constant, I contend (while still attempting to shift the dialogue) that one can readily assess whether and how contact affects the nature and magnitude of racial inequality.

---

JUSTICE LAB POST 8.0: CONTACT IN CONTEXT

The results for the creative runs that vary intergroup contact are in Figure 4.4. Each of these graphs show racial disparities in *Earnings* for 100 runs of the simple machine where 200 agents engage in 500 encounters with others; agents have a life expectancy of 25 encounters, an average memory of 10, and there is 10 percent noise; and 25 percent of Dorados are racists for the first 100 encounters.[16] Each panel contains a line graph where we mathematically manipulate the rate of interracial interactions. By varying the rate of intergroup contact, we better see how it is tied to racial inequality, independent of population composition.

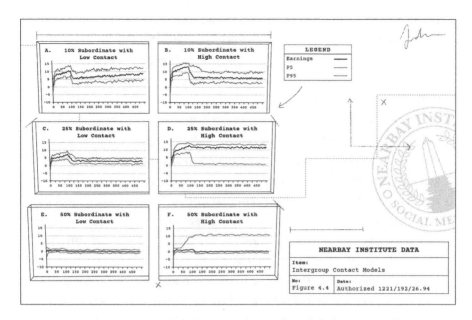

*Figure 4.4.* Group Difference in Recent Earnings in the Bargaining Game with 25 percent Discrimination for Two Levels of Contact—High and Low—and Three Population Sizes. The earnings values are the median of 100 simulations of the bargaining game, whereas the P5 and P95 terms refer to the 5th and 95th percentile points of the distributions.

When 10 percent of agents are Sages (Panel A), the results show that decreasing group contact ("Low") has little impact during the initial encounters; then, after discrimination ends, the context inspires disparities which grow through interaction 500.[17] As contact increases to "High" (Panel B), we see disparities emerge more dramatically during discrimination and drop off thereafter. These creative runs, with 10 percent Sage agents, suggest that higher contact moderately boosts the emergence of inequality during the discrimination era and undermines it thereafter, and lower contact marginally benefits the emergence and maintenance of inequality in the absence of discrimination.

The creative runs with 25 and 50 percent Sages show that the role of increasing contact changes with population composition. When Sages make up 25 percent of the population, low contact produces smaller racial disparities (Panel C). As contact moves from low to high (Panel D), there is a dramatic rise racial disparities in *Earnings*;

increasing intergroup contact leads to a faster onset and a greater magnitude of inequality. Similarly, when the populations are of equal size, low contact is related to an equitable environment without disparities (Panel E). But when contact is high, a nontrivial number of runs show high levels of racial inequality (Panel F).[18]

The basic results suggest that intergroup contact may be more complex than suggested by contact theory. Whereas the Allport file asserts that greater, equal status contact between persons of different racial groups is a viable mechanism for reducing racial prejudice and inequality,[19] the findings here suggest that contact often amplifies inequality and only lowers inequality when the Sage population is a substantial minority. When Sages are a substantial minority, greater intergroup contact weakens inequality. Increasing contact undermines the emergence of subtle prejudice in contexts with small subordinate populations, but then encourages both subtle prejudice and racial inequality as the relative size of the subordinate group becomes large.[20]

End post.

≡

### JUSTICE LAB POST 8.1: CONTACT AT DINNER

Group differences in dining experiences are uniquely tied to the share of each group participating *and* how often the groups dine together—that is, *population composition* and *intergroup contact*. When Dorados make up the large majority of diners, increasing how often groups dine together is tied with a more equitable experience. As the Sage dining population grows, the role of intergroup contact shifts such that higher contact produces radical group disparities in dining experience, increasing the chances that a monolithic stereotype about Sages emerges.

End post.

≡

"Does this teach us something practical? Like, policy-relevant? And we haven't forgot about the nature of villains, we intend to come back to that shortly, on redirect. We're not here to just plug new stuff. This is, for us, about a more appealing intellectual exchange and, perhaps, to convey some things publicly for you to consider."

Willie is talking fast, still condescending, but slightly more socially appropriate than when they taught me earlier. That said, this moment contains an odd calm after what I sense is a vitriolic subclimax in the larger context of the audio-*plus* storyboard.

"That's fine . . ." This actually sucks. Not the conditions, though; it's the temper of their tone. There's still the felt undercurrent of derision, impossible to ignore. "On the policy front, what exactly . . . ?"

"Exactly what we said: What do we learn from your *toy machines* varying intergroup contact that we can, collectively, implement to create *positive* change?" Palpable sarcasm-*plus*, along with articulating certain terms slowly, comes through the audio-*plus* connection. "These do seem like really cool mathematical models."

A subtle pause, following the audibly counterfeit compliment, conveys a more patronizing sarcasm before transitioning and accelerating to a local crest on policy: "But, what do they actually teach us? And if they—ostensibly meaning *you*—can't teach us something practical, something *policy-relevant* that we can apply as a collective, then it seems like you're just playing with yourself. Not like a pubescent spark hiding in a dark corner unsure of the world and their body, but wildly addicted to some fiction of a pleasure-filled link that, when rhythmically nurtured and caressed, transforms from dream to vision to practice and, in the end, into a gratifying realization. Rather, this is more like an adult, consumed with the novelty of fetish, the rhetoric of research, metaphorically performing, a public auto-eroticism, a presentation of a *toy*-model that transforms from dream to theory to a consumable product that inflates the status of the author, exploding in popularity, with all other parties—namely consumers—both uninvolved and unsatisfied in the end."

*What . . . am I doing here?* I do respect the policy query and deft verbal wit, but not much else. Albeit the barbed remarks are representative of this -*plus* cast's virtual atmosphere, they feel more piercing, psychically invasive, in this established audio-*plus* connection.

"To clarify, practical, policy-relevant research should tell us, the collective, what we can do to solve a social problem?"[21] I sense a rhythmic guttural impression, affirmation.

"The social problem"—being defined in the societal landscape, thereby assuming it is part of a larger context—"is like, is like a lead character in a musical, driving the plot forward in the sensory experience of the audience amidst a host of other well-spoken characters." Still feeling their attention through the link, without words or other confirmation, I go on. "All amidst a finite observable, yet, yet seemingly infinite, sea of other animate and inanimate props, constantly transferring, transposing and transforming the staged set." I feel this description of the theoretical landscape is sound and hope it lands as an abstract, technical and metaphorical punch across the divide.

Willie rolls.

"Agreed!" they respond, a confusion of charm and chicanery concomitantly bridging in the connection. "In response to your query, yes. Policy-relevant research should directly engage a social problem, effectively dictating what happens to the lead character in your staged social musical."

"So, it's a lot . . . like a script?," I inquire.

"More of an impromptu, skeleton script that, in terms of race, subtly guides the socially pivotal, problematic lead actors on stage—the antagonists so to speak—such that they perform to their maxima, thereby satisfying themselves, as well as other performers and the audience."

"Are, are there villains written into this policy-relevant skeleton script of leading lines, guiding the social behavior of pivotal actors?" Totally engaged, I continue, "Are they the actors we are looking for?[22] And, what of the other animate and inanimate props on stage?"

"Good . . ." Willie transmits humor enhanced, a slight shift, a soft spot in this sober audio-*plus* interaction. "Yes, the lead character has a principal contrast: the aforementioned antagonist, a character who exists on a balance with the lead, giving the audience added insight on the protagonist. The skeleton script of policy-relevant research distinguishes the leading social problem in relation to other actors or props on set. The villains implicitly emerge, becoming known when the policy-driven lead character conveys the relevant distinctions to the audience, the deepest distinctions arguably fueling the most powerful abstracted adversary."

The diatribe piques my curiosity and my hope for an open, fun dialogue. "Who—or what—is this, in your diverse experience, particularly as it pertains to race?"

"We're not here to talk about me." Hijacked of the answer and discourse, I, understandably, know that I am a guest, the current contrast to Willie's lead.

"Back to you. What does your *toy machine* actually teach us about intergroup contact that is practical and policy-relevant? And we're still interested: *who are the villains for this fictitious lab?*"

"Okay, I get that . . ." I delay to ponder, then awkwardly convey humor-*plus* in discomfort. "I get that . . ." Waiting, watching the space between my communications slowly fill with semi-rational processes, before I speak. Then, I respond intuitively: "The characters on the stage in this metaphorical production are legion. But the lead, the lead is a singular, ambiguous personality with a complex disposition."

"Go on," they interject, harsh and quick, briefly disrupting my performance with a critical shock, followed by no beeps, one click.

I continue. "In this production, the traditional lead and all other objects in the staged context—and, actually, the audience as well—are a dynamic, multidimensional social field. The recent creative runs—the metaphorical production of varying intergroup contact that is in the spotlight—encompasses a subset of this social field, a dimensional context in which all the animate and inanimate social props exist, where the traditional leads and background characters intermix to create the show for and with an audience."

"A subset of a social field?" Confusion-*plus* passes through the link. "A social field?"

"Yes . . . I mean, I mean the social space where the traditional lead characters and villains entertain the audience."

"The lead actor, or primary actors; the foreground . . . Would this all become background noise, in the public drama? A context of all actors on stage, inversely becomes text?"

"Exactly."

". . ." Inaudible processing, one beep, and two clicks.

"An, an indistinct collective character—let's call it *Dothem*—inclusive of the relationships and interactions between the actors and objects on stage and the audience."

"Is this the villain? This . . . *Dothem*?" Humor-*plus* spans the space between us. "Are they like *Dracula*, a monster on stage?"

"Not really." Pausing to process. "Sure, they've been overlooked, misunderstood and maligned to the back of the stage. *Dothem*, however, doesn't seek recognition or sadistic value. Rather, *Dothem* finds stability in the unobserved . . . Though they are observable in parts, *Dothem* lies beneath the staged surfaces of protagonists and antagonists in the existing relational system."

"And this context, this collective character, *Dothem* . . ." Willie transmits an enhanced mix of confusion and comedy, paired with intrigue, two beeps and four clicks in a brief moment of silence. "*Dothem* . . . is a social problem? The real lead?"

"Yes . . . In this case, yes." I sense a silent resignation, processing, an opening. "The creative runs show that the context of intergroup contact, the subset of the staged social field that pertains to how often different groups interact, guides the nature of inequality. Varying intergroup contact changes the context, and subsequently the experience of all actors, objects and viewers, as well as inequality in the space."

Nearly out of gas, metaphorically and literally, I intake, then, in comparison to our initial dialogic pace, slothfully continue. "Intergroup contact is, in this way, like a silent production partner . . . one amidst many others that exist in the staged social field . . . One face of *Dothem*, so to speak. Like the other silent partners, it sets the stage on which the traditional lead actors—the social problems like poverty, unemployment and so forth—act out roles for the audience to sense, discern, and interpret."

"Does that mean no villains?"

≡

## THE CREATION CHRONICLE, PART VI

Each year, monks gather to debate on the issues confronting the herd. The monks, consisting of extremely learned elders, spent decades studying, methodically counting the uncountable nuanced relationships within the herd. Their studies centered on observing and measuring things—sometimes bodies and, at other times, ideas—as well as interpreting these data—social tableaus and statistical tables—into tales that depicted the inner workings of their environment.

The aim of all this study and debate was improving well-being by applying the insight of their stories, and possibly realizing the potential of the primate herd. The challenge, though, was that monks could not see the source code. Having never observed the code, they had to learn about it by what they could see in its parts. They gathered to learn more about the code from each other, figuratively blind actors conversing about a vibrant world. This ongoing intellectual exchange led to the *Great Debates*.

The *Great Debates* began when monks from the five directions gathered to discuss the code for racial imbalance. Early on, those participating used "cutting edge science" to spin wild tales about the magic behind racial imbalance. They proposed that magic was internal: it existed in the constitution of each actor in the herd. The audience, seeing the world as it was, rejoiced in knowing that magic *inside* justified racial imbalance.

As time passed, the *Great Debates* became more sophisticated. The monks developed and began to use elaborate statistical and mathematical models to describe the magic behind racial imbalance. These models, using what many still consider logical magic with the shroud of number theory, shed light on how the measured characteristics of individual actors and subgroups connected with one another. Employing these techniques, monks increasingly explored the sources of imbalance, telling extraordinary tales about the power of character, capital and many other iconic resources shaping the experience of inequality. The tales commonly concluded that changing the distribution of a resource in a certain dimension (such as general education or geography) would lead to declines in imbalance in all others. Tragically, they could not discern the key resources or who was responsible for redistributing them, individuals or the herd. This led to more studies, each looking deeper into the characteristics of individuals and subgroups, all seeking to find the source of racial imbalance.

There are such things as vampires; some of us have evidence that they exist. Even had we not proof of our own unhappy experience, the teachings and the records of the past give proof enough for sane individuals.

—BRAM STOKER, *Dracula*

"*Extreme* discrimination!" they exclaim. "The first process that passed into awareness was a guerilla group, living on the margins, implementing a sadistic, paramilitary process, a small submachine of sorts. All of this in an effort to create a *rationally sound*"—pronounced slowly, fully enunciated to expand the gravity of logic in this social field we share— "more evolved, homogenous social machine."

"I get that." Still floating on the stream of information, I respond methodically. "However, I use the term to refer to the prevalence of racial antipathy . . . or, discrimination."

An aversive impression shuttles through the interface, conveying, I initially infer, abject disappointment in either the form or direction of the reply.

"Up to this point, the simple machines depicted contexts where between 10 and 25 percent of dominant agents were discriminators for the first one-hundred encounters . . . These represent worlds where subordinate actors encounter racists between one-in-every-ten and one-in-every-four interracial encounters."

Interrupted. "Aaaannnd, what does that mean, exactly?" Antagonized-*plus*. "We are not sure our audience is interested in these details. We want characters, *real* villains!"

"It means, it means the majority of interracial encounters are between non-racists."

"More villains? Is, is that what you're talking about? Is that the connection?"

"No, not exactly."

"Okay." Annoyed-*plus*. "We're coming back to villains . . ."

"An alternative, more realistic situation, in contrast to the prior posts . . . embodies a context where a majority of early interactions between Sages and Dorados (the subordinate and dominant agents) involve racists." I explain that this better represents the history of race, where Abbadons overwhelmingly crafted, supported, benefitted from and protected an array of policies and practices, overt and covert, that denied Pandaquans basic civil and individual rights using a variety of observed and unobserved mechanisms.[23] Up until the last few epochs, discrimination was nearly complete, affecting almost every micro- and macro-aspect of the civic and social life of both Pandaquans and, to the oversight of many, Abbadons.

"The latest posts examine the breadth of both the vicious historical racism, and the more modern racialized structures, encapsulating broad representations like wealth and networks . . . Those large patterns of interaction that guide individual behaviors in ways that reinforce racial inequality.[24]

"My intent is to capture the shared role of an array of historical and modern characters who overwhelmingly—and often imperceptibly—engage in producing race, on stage."

≡

JUSTICE LAB POST 9.0: IT'S A MAD RACIST WORLD

*How do extreme levels of discrimination affect the emergence and nature of inequality? Are large swaths of racist Dorados able to dramatically alter inequality? Can extreme discrimination change how the other structural mechanisms function?* The results for the creative runs addressing these queries appear in three separate graphs, Figures 4.5, 4.6 and 4.7.[25]

The constituent graphs depict the racial difference in earnings for 100 runs of the simple machine; each model has 200 agents engaging in 500 encounters with others; life expectancy is 25, average memory size is 10, and bid noise is 10 percent; and the agents in these runs learn subtle prejudice after experiencing two doubly dissimilar encounters. The crucial, villainous variable, *extreme discrimination*, refers to the amount of discrimination in the simple machine; it varies between "Low" and "High" across the respective runs: "Low" is when 10 percent of Dorados are racists, whereas "High" is when 50 percent are racists.

Figure 4.5 contains the results on extreme discrimination for simple machines with 25 percent subordinate population composition. There are nine panels in this figure: each contains a line graph of racial

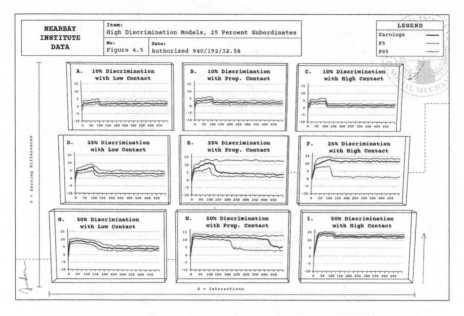

*Figure 4.5. Group Difference in Recent Earnings in the Bargaining Game with 25 Percent Subordinates and Fast Learning, Stratified by Discrimination Level (10%, 25%, 50%) and Intergroup Contact (Low, Proportional, High). The earnings values are the median of 100 simulations of the bargaining game, whereas the P5 and P95 terms refer to the 5th and 95th percentile points of the distributions.*

inequality for a specific level of discrimination and intergroup contact. One can read this figure by comparing graphs across rows or columns. To examine the effect of increasing contact on inequality, one compares *across columns* from left to right; to examine the effect of increasing discrimination, one compares *across rows* from top to bottom. Although it is a lot of information, this matrix setup allows us to graphically assess how varying intergroup contact and discrimination jointly shape the emergence and maintenance of racial inequality for each population composition.

Figure 4.5 shows that increasing discrimination works in concert with other structural mechanisms to produce persistent racial inequality.[26] Scanning down each column, the increase in Dorado racists produced a dramatic rise in the onset of inequality, while increasing discrimination has the largest effect on inequality when intergroup contact is high. The perfect storm of inequality is when discrimination

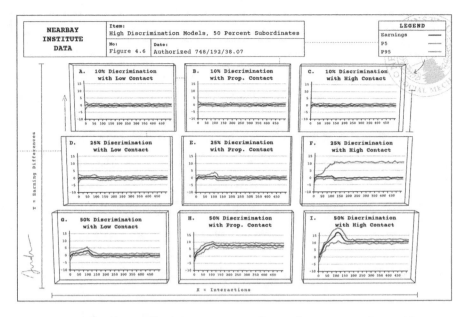

*Figure 4.6.* Group Difference in Recent Earnings in the Bargaining Game with 50 Percent Subordinates and Fast Learning, Stratified by Discrimination Level (10%, 25%, 50%) and Intergroup Contact (Low, Proportional, High). The earnings values are the median of 100 simulations of the bargaining game, whereas the P5 and P95 terms refer to the 5th and 95th percentile points of the distributions.

and intergroup contact is extreme/high, a combination which transforms all of the creative runs into social systems characterized by persistent racial inequality in the absence of racists.

When Sages compose 50 percent of the population, there is a similarly complex relationship between discrimination, intergroup contact and racial inequality (Figure 4.6). Scanning across the columns, from left to right, we see that: (1) increasing contact has no effect on racial inequality when 10 percent of Dorados are racists; and (2) this changes markedly to a significant effect as we move to creative runs where 50 percent of Dorados actively discriminate. Again, increasing discrimination works in concert with intergroup contact such that persistent disparities only emerge when both are high.

The creative runs where sages make up 10 percent of the population diverge from those with larger compositions (Figure 4.7). Curiously, increasing contact has little impact on the emergence and maintenance

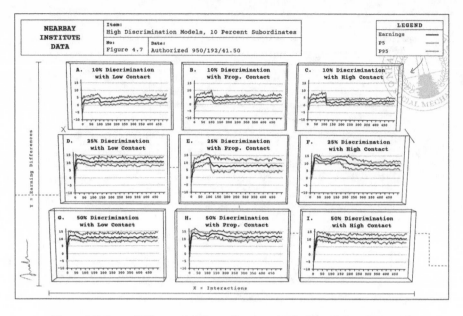

*Figure 4.7. Group Difference in Recent Earnings in the Bargaining Game with 10 Percent Subordinates and Fast Learning, Stratified by Discrimination Level (10%, 25%, 50%) and Intergroup Contact (Low, Proportional, High). The earnings values are the median of 100 simulations of the bargaining game, whereas the P5 and P95 terms refer to the 5th and 95th percentile points of the distributions.*

of inequality when discrimination is moderate or higher: when discrimination is low, increasing contact is related with slightly lower level of racial inequality.

Altogether, extreme discrimination works in concert with intergroup contact to produce sizeable, stable inequality. These results both complement and complicate earlier research at the individual level.[27] Specifically, more intergroup contact in highly racist environments inspires and perpetuates inequality;[28] however, when Sages make up a small share of the population and discrimination is lower, increasing contact marginally attenuates inequality. This change in the relationship between intergroup contact, discrimination and racial inequality represents a contextual non-linearity, a relationship that varies across compositional context.[29] As a consequence of this non-linearity, social policies singularly using intergroup contact as a guide for alleviating disparities may inadvertently magnify racial inequality in certain contexts.

End post.

≡

**JUSTICE LAB POST 9.1: LOTS OF RACISTS AT DINNER**

In regards to *Dinner*, increasing discrimination from "Low" to "High" leads to large, stable differences in dining experiences. The widespread discriminatory demand among Dorados for filet when dining with Sages leads to a substantial decrease in the demands of Sages, who begin to acquiesce, increasingly asking for flank. The marked change in the behaviors of Sages then leads other non-racist Dorados to develop subtle prejudice and they too begin to demand filet when dining with Sages. The actions of these non-racists, now fully in line with their racist counterparts, fuel disparities in the quality of dinner. This sequence of actions leads to the development of a structure that, even when discrimination ends, maintains racial disparities in dinner quality. The structure of these dining patterns exists at all contact levels, but they are most pronounced in spaces with proportionate-to-high intergroup contact.

End post.

≡

"Again, I don't truly consider them villains." I feel uniquely conflicted in the audio-*plus* context, a bit of excitement and a lot of anxiety about this informal, amusing aspect of the conversation turning into a shit show with me looking like an organic ass. "I see it as more of a formal villain than, than the other two structural mechanisms—population composition and intergroup contact—which both uniquely affect racial inequality. But I wouldn't call it the *villain* in this production."

Willie is progressively engaged, yet mostly silent. " . . . " They are communicating unusual impressions of intrigue that map onto a punctuated series of puffs and several very deep, quick intakes which coincide with various points I convey across the audio-*plus* connection.

"Usually," I continue, "usually we go looking for the bad guy . . . We look for the *antagonist* producing and maintaining inequality around the set . . . We traditionally look to sets of individual characteristics, qualitative attitudes or distributions of variables as *real* villains. These traditional villains . . ."—the latter term temporally emphasized with what amounts to a long sneer in audio-*plus*—"again, diverge from the lead in the current analysis."

". . ."

"The recent posts, focused on structures . . . routinized, biased patterns of interaction . . . These structures fundamentally change the social context, facilitating the growth of racial inequality. They can, they can represent a variety of mechanisms that are beyond the control of a single individual . . . a multidimensional array of policies, institutions, zombie-like patterns of behavior and other social forms existing in the relationship between actors, radically changing the entire landscape of inequality . . . like, like *totally* altering the experience of actors on the basis of racial classification."

"Why can't these structures . . . Can they be the villains?"

I attempt to lighten up; yet, remain cautious about my work being attacked, ridiculed by Willie. "I'm just not, I'm just not certain I'd call them *villains*."

"Aren't they the ones guiding racial inequality in the context?"

"Yes . . . yes, but . . ."

"What? They seem like villains, possibly the adversaries of this *Justice Lab*," said with both humor and an aura of disdain, an ambiguous arrow of hurt artfully hurled across the audio-*plus* interface, soon followed by others. "Perhaps the '*just-you*' lab villain, the climactic counter in this ongoing enterprise of intellectual onanism, is jealousy, craving."

". . . ?"

Speaking faster, amidst a frenetic, interrupted flow of humor-*plus*, Willie persists. "Perhaps just a pathetic, jealous craving to produce something that changes the larger social machine . . . or maybe, maybe it's something similarly sinister, yet, more self-serving."

". . . !?" Discomfort-*plus*.

Accelerando: "You said you want to produce positive change. We initially wondered, *why?* Why is this important? And why, exactly, would a slick writing, seemingly mathematically sophisticated and apparently methodologically adept mechanic like yourself do this work?"

Though unobserved, the discomfort grows, discreetly fed in the midst of this downpour of intellectual doubt. "Now we're still not certain about this alternative production, a metaphorical musical where the villains embody a pattern, running in the background, shaping the relations between the *traditional* leads, and inspiring and maintaining inequality in the machine . . ." Willie's disgust is palpable, audibly obscuring my ideas, swiftly storming the connection.

"As you know, we already *know* how to identify the villains. We use statistics, interviews and other types of *real* data. We *know* how to statistically model and qualitatively evaluate racial disparities, segregation and other key social arrangements in the *real* world . . . how to formally and rationally assess what social factors and variables drive disparities . . . how to inferentially identify exactly what villains and associated enemies—which particular *rogues* so to speak—are truly responsible for racial inequality . . . And how to produce *real* change, where the lives of Pandas actually improve."

They only pause to intake, instinctively slowing the onslaught. "Given your misguided intrigue with this simple machine, which has drawn a noticeable appeal . . . the *real* question of the moment is: *What do you have to gain in this enterprise?*"

My frustration is fully grown, having transcended the seed of discomfort-*plus*, systematically taken root, sprouted and stretched its tentacles, broken ground, and then reached for and touched the affective light of *disappointment* that I sense emerging in Willie's concluding comments. "Perhaps, just perhaps, the novelty of this simple machine is largely about you, and the horrible, depraved beast that we should all be concerned about is your counter-persona, the green-gazing villain borne of your selfish desire to make a mark in this world—to publish."

"Thus, I'm the villain . . . embodied?"

"Perhaps . . . Yes, perhaps. But we're just working through this . . . out loud, in front of an audience."

Sensing contempt-*plus*, a mature demonstrative displeasure, I proceed to process this logic slowly. Internally, I sense the desire to change the machine, and I do want to publish in the population archive. But Willie suggests that these conscious processes are driven by greed, a personal desire for status. "The villain is the wish . . . status?"

"Conceivably, your avarice."

This feels personal, their tone implying a derisive private insult hidden inside an already intense and aggressive audible assault. *I don't . . . I really didn't sign up . . .* I anxiously contemplate, burning, amidst a fire fanned by animus, before quickly deducing, *I actually did . . . without properly understanding the pageantry of this aversive experience in particular . . . I don't . . .* I feel suffering.

"And you're currently on stage . . . performing!" Now, embarrassed-*plus* by my oversight, Willie conveys humor at my expense, rapidly announcing in a booming, dramatic timbre, "Audience, I present to you: *the Monster!*" They are thoroughly enjoying this.

Drowning in disgust-*plus*, I attempt to respond deliberately, deftly acquiescing and manipulating the connection. "Greed?"

"Yes . . . yes . . ." they reply, still enjoying themselves.

"I think villains . . ." Amusingly distracted, they're not yet listening. Their inattention, however, linearly dissipates after my words bridge the connection a second time. "The thing, the thing about villains is . . . is that it's more than greed."

Gradually, Willie settles, transmits unspoken interest. Then, they inquire, "More than greed? What? . . . What?"

"Villains."

". . ." I understand this silence. It is a mix of two parts irritation and one part indignation, with a drop of allure and no clicks.

"The key, the key tenet of villainy is, for me, the principle of sadistic value."

Willie whispers, "sadistic value," followed by three beeps and an inaudible signal to continue.

"I see greed as a trait, an intense coded desire for some resource or connection . . . It is implicitly selfish, an act of hoarding, sometimes at the expense of others."

Willie is silent, four clicks, fueling the feelings of uncertainty-*plus*.

"A true villain, in my worst visions, however, must not just crave and hoard resources . . . They must derive pleasure from depriving others."

"That seems like selfishness?"

"No . . . Selfishness is more about the individual and the resource. What this is, this is about the individual and *other individuals* and the resource." I impulsively pause, gathering myself, while letting things settle. "This principle of villainy, centers on an individual deriving pleasure not just from the resource . . . but also gathering satisfaction from depriving others of the respective resource. It's the sadistic satisfaction arising amidst ambient deprivation in a local connection, and in the larger social machine."

Willie digests this logic quickly and responds in kind, "Are those actors who learn to use subtle prejudice in your simple machine 'villains'? Is this what you're trying to get at? Not implicating racists who, when you consider it, do derive pleasure—at least in terms of excess resources—from employing bias."

"I believe the bigger point is that villains both hoard and protect . . . and the protection part is what truly makes them villainous, sadistic."[30]

I sense frustration-*plus*. "But isn't subtle prejudice the enemy here?" A pause, filled with perceptible aggravation, then a muted growl: "The mass of agents that learned to act like racists in the absence of racists? Your model suggests *they are* the enemies of equality in your simple *toy machine*. Listen, policy relevance demands we have an enemy, a target. We—meaning the constituents of the *real* social machine—we need information . . . *real* data, hard, concrete data on a clear enemy that we can identify and use to create your *real* positive change." The condescension is back, -*plus*.

Furious, yet reserved, I reply, "We make our own enemies . . ." I let this message cross the connection and become a line from me to Willie, with multiple points.

"We bump into them in the landscape . . . give them names and define how they relate to us. We feel we can manipulate them, potentially change our world, using them as a fulcrum to shift the weights of the world's balance, make things fair. But these enemies need not be villains."

". . ."

"We make our own enemies. And, importantly . . . deploy them to distract others."

"That's interesting. Yes . . ." Four beeps briefly suspend his dialogue. "Perhaps . . . yes, perhaps a tool *true* villains deploy to acquire sadistic value. We are, after all, just reflections, and distorted ones at that."

I feel the end. They begin, "Thank you for coming by to share. We—the audience and ourselves—appreciate engaging with you."

Formalities over, after another Glover-Vignes Foundation public announcement, eight quick clicks and an uncomfortable pause bordering on nauseating, they close in their typical aggravating and accelerating form. "In the end, though, this is just a neat mathematical tool. You have to eventually convey—especially if you hope to publish and gain some sort of self-serving fame—that this rational, philosophical babble that you call a simple machine has policy merit.

"To us, again, it looks a lot like a *toy machine*, one a developing spark may deploy.

"It's not even clear that we behave like the agents in this simple machine. *Do we?* And consequently, perhaps implies that this is still patently *not* a policy-relevant intellectual endeavor."

I feel livid, *-plus*.

"Again, thank you."

"You are welcome."

I disconnect and, feeling collegially disheartened, privately experience hurt.

# INTERLUDE
## JUSTICE LAB EMPIRICAL STUDY 2.0:
### THE POWER OF BENDING

I am time, the destroyer of all; I have come to consume the world. Even without your participation, all the warriors gathered here will die.

—THE BHAGAVAD GITA 11:32

The time passes. You move in this space, practicing research, pursuing life. The motion-activated mechanism inside you—the chronometer—winds itself. It passes a beating force through an array of rubies, diamonds and other jewels, propelling you forward as you temporally travel from one cognitive process to the next. The pattern in these processes, usually a regularity of random content systematically returning at seemingly fixed intervals, begins to subtly increase at an increasing rate. This is the sign, when certain topics stick; the sticky topic surfs through sentience, riding the overlapping waves of cognition, the topically infected wave replacing a freely associated other, temporally progressing, yet temporarily regressing. While progressing, you recapture—again and again, time after time—the same sticky process in a different space, with an alternative chronological vantage. It is consuming you, infiltrating time, invading the rolling waves of cognition: *How do they bend?*

The inquiry begins.

You organize the data—a modestly surreptitious, undignified download considering the related request—looking across decennial years, scanning the tabled arrays of failure rates and life expectancies of the respective subpopulations. Noting the pattern—the Benders live significantly longer than others and have lower overall failures—you recognize that it persists amongst both genders through the entire interval, spanning sixty-plus years.[1]

You place the data into spreadsheets, stratify it by year, gender and subgroup in distinct worksheets, and within sheets, organize it into several five-year age categories, ranging from five to one hundred, as well as unique categories for ages zero-to-one, one-to-four, and one-hundred-plus. Then you begin the formal analysis: first, estimating age-specific failure rates for the subgroups; second, estimating the ratio of Levels-to-Benders age-specific failure rates and plotting them for each year, stratified by gender; and third, plotting the age-specific failure ratios for each spawn cohort, also stratified by gender.[2]

You note the similar pattern; there is a persistent trend of failure-rates among Levels that are twice that of Benders in the zero-to-one age category as well as in the categories between the late-twenties and late-forties. Beyond that, there is a slow decrease toward unity—or cross over—at the oldest ages. It is the same for cohorts: when cohorts are extremely young, Levels experience failure rates two times higher than Benders. This initial disparity in failure rates within cohorts declines through the teen ages, resurges to a two-fold difference once again during the middle age groups, and declines toward unity—or crosses over—at the oldest ages. Thus, the age pattern is persistent across both cohort and period: they bend time by altering the failure rates in the youngest and middle-age groups.

The analysis comes to life when you create the table. You estimate the time a Horologian Bender/Level can expect to live based on the observed failure rates. These estimates parallel those in the tabled data, but offer more insight on the nuances of bending time. You find that the Benders, on average, live more time (i.e., machine-years) in each age interval, particularly those in the beginning and middle of life. Their spawns can bend time, somehow lose the skill during adolescence and early adulthood, but they mature into adults that can bend time again, and then the skill declines, disappearing into confusion at the oldest ages in each cohort and decennial era.

*How can they bend?* Still wondering, you review the literature. The basic theoretical form of the disparities is the distribution of *disappointments*. Disappointments are described as "little deaths": minute subtractions from the time an actor has on hand, a potential moment of lived time suffocated like a light cutting off in an empty room which no physical body will inhabit.

The literature suggests that each Horologian is born with an embedded time stamp—an allotment. The time, however, is not linear. Rather, it is metaphorical space. The actors can manipulate the space freely, perverting time to extract more life from the implicit stamp. Purportedly, the Benders avoid disappointments; they learn to extract life from, and add light to, previously empty and unknown temporal spaces. The Levels, in contrast, encounter more disappointments and summarily live shorter durations. From this distributional vantage, you energetically dive into the files, exploring the range of disappointments within and across the two subgroups.

The research files, countless studies of bending time dating back over a century, are organized into zones of disappointment. These zones are spaces where the logics of bending vary—distinct stages with unique protagonists, driving a full cast of complementary characters. The zones are exclusive inasmuch as the primary protagonist plays the pivotal role and does so independently of others. That said, there are a divergence of opinions on the true star of the show, the supporting cast of protagonists and antagonists, and the iconic lines they must deliver to affect temporal well-being both within and across zones.

The first zone you explore is the *APC* zone. It is where bending disparities are viewed as a result of differences across three related dimensions: *age, period* and *(spawn) cohort*. This is a peculiarly popular zone: the space simultaneously exists and does not exist. It exists in that each dimensional concept is real: age is a measure of one's duration in temporal space; period is a marker of one's chronological location in the space; and cohort is a mix of the two—the intersection between one's age and period most often represented by spawn year. However, it does not exist: there is an identification problem; once you know two of the three protagonists, you can reproduce the third. Nonetheless, one can, with certain assumptions, model disparities in bending as a function of these three theoretically separable factors.[3]

You run an APC model of the ratios of failure rates. Unfortunately, this super fancy and technical Bayesian statistical model reveals what the graphs already showed: the magic of bending apparently transcends cohort and, paradoxically, it is a strange mix of large, persistent age disparities and small variations in period failures. Alas, this zone is more frustrating and infuriating than enlightening and insightful, suggesting that disappointments in both age and period—and, implicitly, cohort—mold the disparities in bending.

Slowly, you proceed to move through other zones, reviewing the literature and examining the varied ways that Benders arguably extend the duration of life. In the *Cause of Failure* zone, the literature suggests that Benders manipulate time by limiting their failure rates to a subset of specific causes. You note that the leading causes of failure have changed markedly over the interval and confirm that the assortment of infirmities—conditions which cause failure—experienced by Horologians has similarly changed across eras. Yet, in each period, the Benders are less likely to fail from nearly every cause than Levels. The power of bending, somehow, recursively adapts to the changing distribution of infirmities in the environment, reproducing observed disparities in lifespan across temporal space.[4]

Shifting zones again, you bridge into the *Mechano-Social* zone. You review the related literature on the relationship between functional infirmities, important social and environmental disappointments and failures. Then, while processing this literature and incorporating it into working memory, you begin to fleetingly recognize the logic across zones: *If you can explain disparities in failure with a non-linear function, you can explain bending time?* This inspires a non-trivial feeling of uncertainty.

Still, you upload several of the downloaded data sets—those linking failure data with large-scale surveys about the functional, social and environmental characteristics of actors—onto the workspace. You spend countless hours reading, interpreting, learning, coding, and, eventually, analyzing the data sets at your disposal. You find, in both your review and using an arsenal of logistic regression, proportional hazards and piecewise exponential hazard models, each with an array of variable specifications recognizing the significant actors on stage in this and related zones: the power of bending is partially related to disparities in disappointments like training, experience, specialty, segregation, education, normative phenotypic attributes and income, as well as functional infirmities like pressure, invasive mela-growths, and insu-poison syndrome. The disparities, however, persist within and across the range of measured disappointments. The differences in lived experience are largely inexplicable by the advanced statistical models and available data.

*How do they bend?* For years, you continue exploring zones, mining the landscape for new variables, developing new methods and techniques, refining the analyses, presentation and interpretation, searching for a way to solve what should fundamentally be an easy puzzle, but has become a deep dive into a long-standing intellectual query about how to model disparities, how these disappointments functionally fit into a social space that enables certain actors—Benders—to manipulate and extend time.

Amidst the frustration of this pursuit, you wonder, *What have I learned from this exhaustive, private exploration of virtual data? Seriously, what insights have I gleaned from the vantage outside their social spectrum?* You knew they bent time in the past, and know they can still bend it; they have been able to do it a long time. The bending is most apparent at certain ages. It persists across environments with radically different distributions of infirmities and causes of failure; certain disappointments contribute to bending, but none explain it.

That is when you begin to sense the snare.

The search for appointments is an industry, dominated by a market system, characterized by an ongoing quest—replete with the social nobility of intellectual stature—to identify the unique set of disappointments that distinguish the Benders' capacity to effectively manage their time. The intellectual pursuit is an enduring, nigh never-ending, exploration of a shifting set of zones and socially important dimensions which promise to provide the government and chronologically-consumed Horologians with insight on the factors behind bending.

You unconsciously sow and grow confusion, coming up utterly confounded.

The social search industry is massive, long-lasting, self-sustaining. There is little consensus and endless arguments about method, measurement, variable identification and policy mechanisms. It begins to make less sense; then, really, no sense—both the disparities and how they are studied. It is overwhelming, the burgeoning sensation inside you, an intellectual rush analogous to anxiety, figuratively discomforting, emotionally disturbing.

You sense it.

End Post.

# PART FIVE
## RACE IN THE (MAD)⁴ WILD

We are so much accustomed to disguise ourselves to others, that at length we disguise ourselves to ourselves.
—FRANÇOIS VI, Duc de La Rochefoucauld, *Maximes*

"Habitation is great . . . Good parallel!" Historically, discriminatory lending and habitation policy led to lower appraisals in Panda communities; this created a market characterized by higher priced, predominantly Abbad neighborhoods and lower priced Panda counterparts.[1] "The results suggest that these widespread historical practices . . . an exemplar of the 'extreme discrimination' methodically advanced in our social machine . . . that it led to the development of status beliefs, subtle prejudice about the value of all Panda neighborhoods."[2]

"But do you feel we hold subtle prejudice?" A questioner interrupts hesitantly, then proceeds briskly, with a quiet fervor delicately accented by agitation, "Yes . . . you showed that instigating actors and factors can lead to the dawning of consensually held status beliefs—or what you call 'subtle prejudice.' You seem to suggest these beliefs are a pillar of racial inequality, operating as a vicious circle, a sort of self-fulfilling prophecy.[3] I'm just not sure we host and employ these processes."

"I believe so . . ." I'm certain, but uncertain, still emotionally abused. Even though it's been a few phases, Willie changed things—I feel much more anxious, less confident, and overly afraid of something beyond ominous and frightening now lurking in the landscape.

The current terrain is the middle of an intervention in the guise of a workshop. They are all here. The body of trainees, my colleagues, a few administrators and even some notable Nearbay Institute icons, a connected bunch, coursing with a confusion of intrigue, disregard, insight, appreciation, inattention, disdain and random waves of escalation ranging from high regard to an economic-style assault. They are helping me, encouraging me in the form criticism, intense questioning, praise, doubt, suggestions, sarcasm and support.

Now, although I am here, I am still not fully certain what is happening *here*: a large, sub-atrium auditorium that is used for subject area assemblies, an assortment of auspicious academic occasions, and a semi-regular slate of presentations pandering to the public, an exciting masquerade purportedly performed on behalf of the Glover-Vignes Foundation's promise for a new open science. I am not even sure how here got on my path and became some midterm goal along the way. I do want the connection and collective insight. But I prefer that without being here, as here is an especially indeterminate territory, a space where the weather changes faster than one's capacity to recognize it.

"I mean, at the heart of habitat . . . great point, thanks . . . is the assumption that everyday actors hold and employ a vicious subtle prejudice, a bias that drives habitat choice. But that's just, that's just one . . . one arena . . . one parallel . . ." I loiter in cognition, wondering aloud with my visuals, while those present at my public crucifixion accurately interpret the non-verbal message: *Is it possible that we each harbor subtle prejudice?*

Trayci talks this time, a supportive part sitting in the leftmost section of the assembly. "I can see it. I do see how racial inequality is perpetuated by non-racists, like me,[4] responding to patterns. Patterns which continually depict that Pandas have low resources, and Abbads do not—that Abbads have status."

*Do actors hold negative beliefs about Pandas? Are there an abundance of social arenas where Pandas are consistently treated significantly worse than*

*Abbads? Do Pandas hold negative beliefs about other Pandas?* These and other questions flowed through our corpulent, connected network, activating each node sequentially, recursively, adapted. The diverse array of anecdotal answers varied across edges, cooperated, evolved, yet confirmed the need to directly engage Willie's ultimate concern: to showcase if and how real actors' behavior are in line with those of agents in the simple machine.

＝

JUSTICE LAB POST 10.0: SUBTLE PREJUDICE
AND NEIGHBORHOOD PREFERENCE

There are very few decisions that are more important than choosing where to live. How does race play into choosing a neighborhood? Do we each harbor preferences for the share of Abbads and Pandas in our "ideal" community? These questions are the focus of experimental research on segregation. The work in this area consistently reveals that everyday actors host subtle prejudice in neighborhood preference.

For example, the Charles file used a survey experiment to assess the neighborhood preferences of actors and their related racial attitudes.[5] The experiment elicited the racial makeup of "ideal" neighborhoods from respondents—that is, the place where they felt most comfortable docking after twilight. It revealed that Abbads had a strong preference to live around same-race neighbors, placing greater value on neighborhoods that had little to no Pandas. These social actors expressed positive/negative expectations about the quality of life in neighborhoods on the basis of racial composition.

In addition to the Charles file, that of Krysan and colleagues cleverly engages the factors driving racial bias in assessments of neighborhood quality.[6] The respondents in that experiment watched visual displays of varying neighborhoods and rated them in desirability. They observed action clips of communities with different numbers of Pandas and Abbads, as well as differing social class characteristics. The results show that the racial makeup of an area, independent of class, is a significant determinant of appeal: Abbads preferred all-Abbad areas most and viewed all-Panda spaces as undesirable; Pandas found mixed-race communities most appealing and found all-Abbad areas least attractive. Thus, social actors showed clear preferences—subtle prejudice—for neighborhoods that were based on the race of residents.

These and other studies show that everyday actors have expectations that, when employed in decision making, drive racial inequality in neighborhood access and appeal.[7] Furthermore, they suggest that subtle prejudice uniquely contributes to spatial segregation, habitat appreciation and wealth holdings.[8]

End Post.

≡

"What is the larger point, exactly?!?" My tension engaged, the questioner mockingly continues amidst my contortions. "We have the simple machine, an exercise. And you are currently noting spaces where actors behave similarly, employing subtle prejudice. And then . . ." she pronounces with both sarcasm and contempt, simultaneously, "we have an odd simulacrum: it looks like failure research but there is no tabled data and it's set in a world of make-believe!" Her borderline discourse, which devours time by being both dismissive and derogatory, is thankfully a part of the sizeable minority that slightly express their disregard loudly and essentially deign to consider this entire venture. The verbose dialogue instigates a few glares, several grumbles and a jumble of discomforting shifts, eventually escalating to display a ferocity for a more complete discussion than her abject denunciation initially desired to openly endorse. Finally, reading the room, she adeptly defers and delivers a slightly subdued point and question: "I'm just not sure, about this *research*. What, exactly, are you doing?"

Feeling marginalized, I sense the small space I inhabit—the border. This space contextualizes the scene, providing a seamless background for the stream of symbols and room for relevant notes from critical readers. I fleetingly recognize this small space contains the other; the border and background embody the theoretical expanse, providing a platform to methodically populate.

"My point . . . exactly . . . is . . ." A failure to convey, having lost the marginal insight from the momentary vantage. She transmits a mix of consternation and confusion while I subconsciously consider, *I want to make her feel better . . . I want my colleagues' . . . respect . . . If I could . . . then, perhaps . . . I would . . . less rejected, more appreciated . . . accepted.*

Then, I scarcely detect a soft-spoken PRM, politely suggesting, "This sounds like relative deprivation . . ."

≡

### JUSTICE LAB POST 10.1: SUBTLE PREJUDICE
### IN THE ECONOMIC MACHINE

One arena where actors often report discrimination is employment.[9] The Pager record offers some of the most compelling studies in this area. This record intimately investigates the extent that actors employ subtle prejudice in decision making, exploring how the race of job seekers shapes the ways they are treated.[10]

In the first Pager file, they sent Panda and Abbad audits (fake job seekers), with and without criminal backgrounds, out to apply for jobs in the service sector of a major metropolitan area.[11] They found that Abbads, regardless of criminal background, garnered more interest. These findings highlight that employers harbor subtle prejudice, systematically treating Panda and Abbad audits in ways that affirm racial inequality.

The Bertrand and Mullainathan file similarly studied subtle prejudice among employers in the broader labor market. In contrast to audits, they sent out fake resumés to employers with advertised job openings to see if Abbad applicants received more interest than Pandas with similar credentials and experience. The researchers incorporated race by using "Abbad"- and "Panda"-*sounding* names on the resumés. The resumés with "Abbad" names received significantly more interest than Pandas with similar characteristics. And "Panda" names were less likely to be rewarded for more credentials and were lumped together regardless of skills into an *iconic ghetto*.[12] The biased behavior of employers seen in this file, too, parallels subtle prejudice.[13]

There are two potential explanations for the results of the aforementioned files: (1) the employers are overt, big bad racists; or (2) the employers hold subtle prejudice—the socially learned expectation that Panda applicants are less qualified.[14] However, another Pager file that qualitatively surveyed employers noted that acts of discrimination "were seldom characterized by overt racism or hostility . . . [but] patterns of *subtle but consistent differential treatment*."[15] This suggests subtle prejudice exists among employers; their actions are part of a larger system of racial inequality wherein employers have "learned" that Pandas are less worthy than equivalent Abbads.[16] Racial classification is a proxy for qualifications and credentials among employers, an emergent status belief about the contextual worth of different groups.[17]

End Post.

≡

Tomás—a regular faculty fixture in these institute-wide workshops, affable with a habit of making odd comments and sporadically offering uncommon insight—abruptly interrupts my internal criticism and outward cognitive confusion. He reiterates, more firmly this time, "This sounds like relative deprivation."

Subtle humor and a highbrow haughtiness disrupt his opening dialogue. Then there is an audibly obvious mumble, "It's an old disproven theory. It didn't work . . ." The message quickly echoes across edges in the crowd, expanding in the public plexus.

"No . . ." Tomás pivots briefly. Rotating his visuals from me, through the crowd and back, he responds calmly, "Hear me."

Engaged once again, he pointedly proceeds. "Relative deprivation pertains to the relative position of an actor in a reference group. Yeah, the Runciman record offers a more precise and technical definition but, for you, here, the gist of it is that . . . actors compare themselves to similar others . . . Sometimes, after making comparisons, actors realize that they do not have a particular resource . . . They see someone else with it . . . want it . . . and feel that they *should* have it." Tomás pauses at varying times, engaging different parts of the crowd and affirming each step of his conceptual point. "Relative deprivation refers to the disappointment, or the feelings of dissatisfaction, tied to having less resources than similar others."[18]

Still feeling distress on this stage, I try and fail to focus intently and keep up with the specifics. Fortunately, others slow him down. A voice in the back interjects, "They tested this theory. The files showed that it did not predict the New Rights Riots." The body of the voice observably shrugs, then candidly contends, "It was a neat hypothesis, but not a great predictor."[19]

"That's interesting . . ." Tomás adeptly processes the commentary. Returning, "That's not what I was talking about. But since you are, I'll respond. I feel that measurement and expectations limited that work." His curiosity is palpable, like he's been longing to unload this logic to an audience. "They assumed the racial wage gap was a measure of relative deprivation and said it should predict riots. When, it turned out, it did not . . . they wrote it off." He pauses, overtly exhausts, and perceptively beams his wonder with succinct sincerity. "I'm not certain that was the best measure or prediction."[20]

"So . . ." The commentator is bothered, not expecting the semi-serious response, a felt challenge to their intellectual prowess.

"Well, that's not really the reason . . . my point . . ." Tomás warily approaches, de-escalating slightly from the right, front edge of the sub-atrium auditorium. "This work seems like relative deprivation." Leaning in, physically demonstrating he is internally intrigued with this argument, Tomás quietly conveys with verve, as if speaking only to me, "The status of actors in the simple machine is zero-sum. I'm personally processing, interpreting race in the simple machine, as both . . ." He briefly stops, drawing me—us—and our attention toward him. "Both the mechanism that distinguishes who gets a resource and also the felt disappointment—the full experience of being without the resource."

I'm still confused. Looking away to ponder, I softly inquire in slightly more than a whisper, "Race is, race is relative deprivation?" Then, gazing toward Tomás, I speak louder, attempting to ask my question more directly, "So Pandas are systematically deprived . . . How would . . . How can . . . How do we measure it?"

After meditating a moment, Tomás responds, "I was personally pondering that race *is* a measure of relative deprivation."

===

"Na oepn ignitoamian cna etenr wehre tehre si on sapce."[21]

The monks presented endless studies in the *Great Debates*, and with each convening, the accounts describing racial imbalance grew in number and complexity. Although significant racial differences in well-being persisted, the monks from the High Plains identified what looked to be countless external, observed characteristics that *status auxillarus* primates could change to improve well-being. These monks regaled audiences with tales of new and unique characteristics such as educational certificates, residential neighborhoods and family form, noting that each one was a small part of a complex web of inequality—an intuitively simple and elegant notion, especially since all primates readily observed that these characteristics *did* correlate with the well-being of individuals. Hence, these monks held a captive audience.

The Valley monks added to the *Great Debates* by looking inside the behaviors of individuals, into the mental context of each actor. They observed and measured countless nuanced, finite behaviors of individual primates and related these to measured psychological predispositions. They told compelling chronicles of the power of certain attitudes and viewpoints in racial imbalance, often using contrived examples to reveal how particular inner propensities guide racial imbalance in a simple social context. Thus, the Valley monks similarly advocated for changes in the characteristics of individuals, their recommendations uniquely centering on mental context. And, as in the case of the High Plains monks, they continually held a wide audience.

Every time, a small mountain sect of monks from the fifth direction would send a group to the *Great Debates*. The sect rarely participated. Rather, they would quietly attend; they learned the logic of identifying the characteristics behind racial imbalance, listened to the tales of others and admired the artistry of those working in concert to understand racial imbalance. These mountain monks participated this way, year-after-year—studying the logic, interactions and method of other monks—and spoke sparingly, to not interrupt.

Then something changed: they slowly began to speak . . . to others . . . in real sentences.

≡

Traditional medical diagnoses focus on the machine, the body, while the real problem seems to relate to what makes the machine work, the intellect.
—JOHN E. SARNO, MD, *Healing Back Pain*

"The issue is measurement," the crowd persistently remarks. This point floats from one node to another, adapting, emerging as a refined rhetoric both among and across the extant edges. Eventually, the crowd concludes by consensus, "We *must* measure relative deprivation." Although they apparently achieve a logical harmony, the nature of measurement—qualitative or quantitative, interviews or secondary sources—maintains a simmering discord, subtly aggravating the assembly via the associations among them.

Tomás assertively attempts to re-engage the collective, broadcasting, "Suppose . . . Suppose, that . . . Suppose . . . Suppose, that . . ." At long last, he breaks through the static, communicating, "Suppose, that we live in a space where we actively champion emotional fitness." He tenses and rises on all lower links, full height, demonstrably conveying the analogic frame. "And that we live amidst a system that is fueled by making certain actors feel they are flawed and incomplete, where actors are made to feel *disappointment*. Relative deprivation refers to that felt experience." Confusion grows in the connection.

"Race, from this vantage, is the mechanism that differentiates groups and distributes fitness. It is inclusive of the social sorting algorithm that unfairly awards fitness, the felt experience of being disappointed, and the interaction between the two that produce a remainder. This, to me, it seems like a central aspect of race."

"But we still have to measure it!" The crowd wrestles control from Tomás, imposing their will, insisting, "The explanation is incomplete . . . It needs more . . ."

Do actors with similar infirmities and disorders receive equal treatment in Emergency Medical Service Centers? Or is treatment shaped by the race of patients? There are an abundance of records engaging these questions that exhibit a high degree of consistency in their respective findings. Namely, they suggest that actors in medical settings employ subtle prejudice in their interactions with patients.

The Todd files are perhaps the most notable in the area of racial disparities in Emergency Center (EC) treatment.[22] In three separate entries, they interrogate racial differences in treatment among EC patients with long link fractures—a separated extant limb. They hypothesized that Pandaquan patients would be less likely to be given adequate pain medicine, then they carefully reviewed the records at two ECs and interviewed patients and physicians. The files show Pandas were significantly more likely to receive *no* pain medication than similar Abbadons in ECs; this racial disparity was unrelated to reports of pain, employment status, insurance status and a variety of other theoretically important factors.

Many other files engage racial disparities in EC treatment, some using national samples and investigating different types of trauma. For example, the Kpsowa and Tsunokai file examined racial disparities in prescriptions from EC visits for vertebral pain.[23] They found that Pandas were significantly less likely to be prescribed medication and less likely to receive *any* medication during an EC visit. Similarly, the Pletcher file investigated racial disparities in prescriptions from pain-related visits to the ECs,[24] showing that Pandas were significantly less likely to be prescribed tranquilizers than similarly situated Abbadons. Taken together, the Todd files and many follow-ups indicate that Pandas receive worse emergency treatment for pain.

But what's driving these racial disparities in the treatment of pain? Do the physicians hold subtle prejudice about Pandas? The file of van Ryn and Burke critically engages these questions.[25] They used a linked survey of both physicians and their patients with crown pathway disorder (CPD) to examine whether physicians held more negative attitudes about Pandas than similarly situated Abbads; they found that physicians were significantly more likely to view Pandas as less intelligent, uneducated, likely to abuse libations and drugs and not comply with medical advice.[26]

Thus, research suggests that physicians regularly host and employ subtle prejudice in the medical encounter, unfairly rewarding Abbads with better treatment than their Pandaquan counterparts.

End Post.

≡

"...."

They are not listening; all of them, consumed in discourse. They need to measure it, manipulate it, see how it looks using some internal- or external-focused transformative function. They demand more data, in more dimensions, fancier models and, for some, to recognize that the variable race is an inherently disappointing experience for Pandaquans that may best be described with qualitative flair. Then, after doing all this, they collectively conclude that we would have a better map of the modern world.

I attempt to interject—"I don't, I don't believe"—and fail.

Indeed, the crowd now recognizes the array of supportive studies showcasing how actors employ subtle prejudice, regularly discriminating against Pandas in labor, medicine, habitats, and so forth.[27] They note these findings are part of an empirical story where important actors have transitory experiences of relative deprivation in a subset of arenas. The crowd carefully considers a mix of methodologically divergent compositions on relative deprivation, each story showcasing how a particular network of important descriptives formulaically produces mutual disappointment.

Then the storytellers become the story in my intervention, each actor offering a pragmatically permuted blueprint for how to produce and publish policy relevant research. "To be successful," they suggest, "one must write clear, accessible compositions casting reputable actors as leads. The arrangements should use data, gathered from observation or interview.

"Theoretical models and analytic descriptions of a metaphorical system"—from their imposed vantage—"lack formality and power. The reviewers and readers deserve to see all parts of the actors represented in data, to scrutinize and approve the nature and form of the analysis and be able to apply the private peculiarities of their professional judgement."

*What is success?* I wonder amidst this deluge and diatribe. It does not feel absurd or ingenious; it feels more like what I know, than how I know it. It feels constrained, confined, an extrapolation of the existing literature, like a paid endorsement.

As the crowd calms, they refocus on an unsatisfied stimulus. "That is not what I mean . . ." Tomás is discernably disturbed. "I mean that race is tied to the experience of relative deprivation. Relative deprivation is, partly, a metaphor of race."

Sarcastically, the crowd retorts, "We know what you mean. You mean that Pandas are *Periplaneta,* a *Metamorphosis* creating a new sect of outcasts who are fundamentally different from Abbads . . ."[28]

A mass of humor settles like a colony. "No, you mean they have the *Heart of a Canine,* they 'are the lowest on the rung of development,' subordinate to Abbadons and inferior in rational intellect . . ."[29] Comedy continues percolating through the crowd, a cloak covering the veiled literary comments concerning stigma and a deeper conservative, concordant argument.

Tomás replies, with wit, "Actually, I mean that: 'I am a sick PRM . . . I am a wicked PRM. An unattractive PRM.'"[30] Caught unawares, the quote converts the crowd to a coterie of convivial appreciation and, suddenly, they declare ceasefire.

Tomás then continues, "But I do understand the point. Language is imprecise . . ." They overtly express undeveloped agreement in response. "I agree and add that our measures of relative deprivation are imprecise, that variables are imprecise . . . that substantive descriptions are imprecise."

Nearby Veda, a few rows back and to her right, a member of the crowd erupts again. "That's crazy, data are technical. Variables are detailed.

Substantive descriptions are rich. They are unbiased, parsimonious depictions of the social machine!"

"P-P-P-Perhaps" Santi adeptly redirects this escalation, "the work on i-implicit c-c-cognition can b-b-bridge this empirical d-divide. The thing ab-b-b-bout it is that they *are not c-c-c-conscious*." He isolates the last words, fumblingly emphasizing the subtlety of a process that lies behind our capacity to recognize it.

"Scholars d-d-d-developed t-t-techniques to measure implicit a-a-attitudes, centering on the *a-associative strength* b-between c-c-c-concepts in our p-p-processors, like how e-easily we can c-c-connect sp-specific social objects with favorable or unfavorable words and c-c-concepts—a stronger a-associative t-t-t-tie implies that we hold an implicit b-bias in a p-p-particular d-direction."

"But . . . it's not exactly . . ."

"T-T-True," he tentatively replies, "not in the t-t-t-traditional sense . . . m-more like an in-in-internally held metaphor, i-it represents the associative strength b-b-between symbols, which are p-positive or negative, and racial c-c-classification." The crowd contemplates this conceptual embodiment. Then Santi connects it back to the open inquisition, noting, "I-I-I-It is also analogous t-t-to subtle p-prejudice—a widely held, b-b-b-biased b-belief that g-guides social b-b-behavior."

≡

JUSTICE LAB POST 10.3: SUBTLE PREJUDICE
BEHIND CONSCIOUS PROCESSING

What does research on implicit racial attitudes tell us about subtle prejudice? The largest and most impressive study of the prevalence of implicit attitudes is *Project Implicit*. The data show that a majority of actors in our social machine hold an automatic, implicit preference for Abbadons relative to Pandas;[31] furthermore, the respondents exhibited an implicit preference for Abbadons regardless of their own race. Thus, these data undermine a simple subtly prejudiced story about the tendency to bond with and prefer actors of your own racial group (i.e., homophily).

In addition to this work, there are a number of older files which highlight the presence, persistence and consequences of implicit attitudes favoring Abbads over Pandas. For example, the Gaertner and McLaughlin file found that respondents showed a strong associative tie between Abbadons and positive symbols; the observed implicit preference was held by actors who expressed explicit prejudice *and* those who did not.[32] Similarly, the Dovidio file examined implicit racial stereotypes and also showed actors hold implicit bias favoring Abbadons.[33] Together, these two files reveal that implicit racial attitudes favoring Abbadons were reliably observed many phases prior to those observed in *Project Implicit*.[34]

Although implicit attitudes favoring Abbadons are widespread and long-lasting among both Abbads and Pandas, the consequences of holding an implicit bias are less clear. Do those holding implicit preferences favoring Abbads experience and behave differently with Pandas? The record of Richeson and Shelton investigates these issues; they found that after interacting with a Pandaquan, Abbads who held implicit preferences favoring Abbads—those with high prejudice—performed significantly worse on executive function than those with low prejudice.[35]

Interestingly, this result also holds for Pandas. This record contains a similar experiment on a sample of Pandas who, like in *Project Implicit*, often held an implicit bias favoring Abbads. They found that after interacting with an Abbad, the subset of Pandas who held an implicit preference for Pandas performed significantly worse on executive function than those who had an implicit preference for Abbads. Thus, actors who exhibit high implicit racial bias experience more cognitive distress in interracial encounters.[36]

In line with the Richeson and Shelton record, others examined the role of implicit attitudes on behavior. The Crosby file, a definitive early review on the prevalence of non-verbal discrimination, highlights an array of work which confirms that Abbads often behave in subtly prejudicial ways toward Pandas. It reads: "Abbads still discriminate against Pandas in terms of behaviors that lie largely out of awareness. This is true even for Abbads who do not discriminate in terms of behaviors that fall under more conscious control, such as verbal reports."[37] Nonverbal behavior, then, represents one mechanism through which actors overtly convey bias toward another racial group.

More recently, the Dovidio file updated Crosby, documenting the relationship between non-verbal behavior, perceived behavior and implicit racial bias.[38] Actors who held an implicit preference for Abbads exhibited significantly more optical flutters and less visual contact when interacting with Pandas. What is more, none of the respondents perceived that they behaved differently toward other participants, and explicit racial bias was unrelated to the negative non-verbal behaviors.[39]

Altogether, research on implicit attitudes reveals that actors often host an unconscious bias—a preference for Abbads.[40] Much like artificial agents, many of us harbor a subtle prejudice that adversely affects well-being in interracial encounters, guides our non-verbal behaviors and influences decision making in ways that uniquely contribute to racial inequality.[41]

End Post.

≡

"T-T-T-To me, i-it seems like work that is uh-unmistakably e-e-examining subtle p-p-prejudice." Santi briefly hangs his crown, looking down, reflecting, then looks up again. "B-B-But, this work p-partly suggests"—he pauses, displaying his discomfort with the ensuing logic—"it may b-b-be beneficial for P-P-Pandas to hold implicit attitudes favoring A-A-A-Abbads."

Confused disbelief. "Are you, are you suggesting Pandas may benefit from holding an implicit bias for Abbads . . . to be biased, implicitly, toward oneself, may be an optimal strategy?" I struggle with the rationale.

"Y-Y-Yes." Santi feels the apprehension, and makes a pointed public case detailing that Pandas may—just *may*—maximize well-being or, inversely speaking, reduce distress by being implicitly biased towards Pandas. "P-P-P-Particularly," he argues with impediment, "in a d-d-disproportionate environment where P-P-Pandas are a-a-a minority and often interact with A-A-Abbads . . . it may be o-o-optimal for a P-P-Panda to adapt, to develop a b-b-bias that is in line with the d-d-d-dominant group—it may b-b-be good to b-be c-c-cognitively c-c-comfortable, even though it implies a d-d-devaluation of oneself."

This logic, a deeper quantitative representation of Du Bois's duality, Fanon's facades and Ogbu's oppositionality, feels like a trap, one I don't fully understand; it is a feeling inspiring concern. "I see your point"—I do—"but, I am not certain yet, something feels wrong with saying, 'Pandas, if you adopt an implicit bias favoring Abbads, you may be less stressed.'"

"A-A-And that's where this will e-end . . ." Although his appeal was a logical application and extension of the work, it feeds a dilemma, a discriminatory perspective that undermines the status of one's own group. Santi knew it and, like me, he still didn't understand.

≡

## THE CREATION CHRONICLE, PART VIII

The audience quickly gathered to hear the tales from the reclusive monks of the fifth direction. A'ja, an elder in the mountain sect, ascended the platform. Once on top, she bowed, recognizing the audience, and confidently began. "They call me A'ja." She paused, feeling the monks collectively stop breathing, their eyes tracking her movement across the platform. A'ja settled into this uncomfortable feeling, and began again, "They call me A'ja. I am here to tell you about another way."

After these words, dozens of monks that were whispering immediately stopped, trained their eyes on the platform speaker and listened closely.

≡

> **What we neglect in ourselves blends itself secretly into our actions towards others.**
>
> —CARL GUSTAV JUNG, *The Red Book*

"E-E-E-Even so, I feel implicit b-b-bias is a metaphor for subtle p-p-prejudice. An-and that," he maintains, "is the c-c-connection."

Sensing our collective misunderstanding, he emphatically appends, "I-I-Implicit b-b-bias is an i-i-internal representation of the ra-ra-racial structure. The a-a-actors who hold negative b-b-beliefs about P-Pandas . . . For them, r-r-race is a-a-a metaphor, a-a-a symbol of status, such that A-Abbads are e-e-endowed with more and P-P-Pandas less. An unc-c-c-conscious metaphor that has real c-c-consequences." Santi is excited, his visual tics further animating his vocals. "I-I-I-I-It's like T-T-Tomás said, 'r-r-race is a metaphor for relative d-d-d-deprivation.' This is a measure of d-d-deprivation—d-d-deprivation so b-b-bad that i-it is seen on the i-i-inside."

We all leisurely digest this erratic assertion.

"That is not what I meant . . ." Tomás is disturbed, again. "Relative deprivation is a metaphor; it represents a part of the experience of race. All that other stuff, internal and embodied and so forth." He sighs. "My point, much simpler."

(*"Ceci n'est pas une pipe,"* I say quietly to myself.[42])

They continue arguing, assessing, evaluating, critiquing, suggesting, admonishing, asserting and establishing the nature of race in the social machine. I hear each argument, assessment, evaluation, critique, suggestion, admonishment, assertion and imposition. I publicly recognize that my simple machine is an inadequate representation of our world. I acquiesce and acknowledge that the simulacrum is a nasty perversion of successful scholarship in need of a more detailed data analysis that is suitable for publication. I concede, in these respects, that this recent work is an insufficient representation of modern social mechanics and is incompatible with the existing academic industry. And finally, I admit that, still, I do not know *what the larger point is, exactly.* I listen.

≡

"Nto waht yuo tcaeh . . . who yuo tcaeh, amfirfs tish scape."

# INTERLUDE

## JUSTICE LAB EMPIRICAL STUDY 3.0: THE SONG OF THE SACRED METHOD[1]

> But then that was the point of magic, to take folks in,
> make them forget what was real and possible.
>
> —ANN PATCHETT, *The Magician's Assistant*

The frustration is killing you, figuratively. *How do they bend?* You worked on this problem for years, examined the battle lines drawn into the burning sands and stressfully pursued an empirical solution to the persistent temporal inequities. You estimated measures and ran models and developed methods and re-estimated and re-ran both the measures and models, respectively, employing new methods and data to reach old ends and raze updated theoretical enemies. Still, there is no clear resolution and after a life course—the query first developing, then maturing, and now deceptively and adaptively aging such that the evaluative angle markedly shifts, shedding supposedly novel, more specialized, "expert" insight—the magic of bending remains unsolved.

Finally, you awaken to the *War Zones*. You become fully aware of the non-overlapping spaces within and between the zones, those inauspicious areas where you fight theoretical enemies on all sides, unsure who is your friend, when, how and under what circumstances your temporal interests align, living in an ongoing conflict about what factors allow Benders to bend. In this enduring methodologically armed encounter with the scholarship, one where targets have been established and extinguished, each side with a real stake has seen success and failure. And given the stakes and complexity of the social cooperative that has been sampled and surveyed and studied to produce some mythical *Statistic*, it still feels like the beginning of the contemplative conflict. You continue scanning the social scientific landscape, realizing, *The enemies we're fighting . . . they are classmates, teachers, colleagues, theoretical relatives and ancestors. Though we fight them, we are systematically connected, employing similar methods with semantically different motives. We are collectively intent on understanding how they bend time.*

Frustrated, still, you stop processing data and analyzing information, unplug, then turn off the workspace. Realizing that success in this conflict comes at the expense of others; that being right about the finite factors that allow Benders to manipulate time makes those who disagree wrong; that the empirical distance between right and wrong is deceivingly closer than it appears in this reflexive analytic space; that, although you endeavor to develop insight to undermine the temporal inequities, you increasingly feel rising tension, the dawning of intellectual panic; then, after reaching a climax of complete conflict, watching the hours of metaphorical daylight pass, you cry out at nightfall. "I will not engage in this campaign any longer!"[2]

───

Spark! Once formless energy . . . formed. I intuit, *Am I awake? Where am I? What am I? . . . A mystery.*

I feel something else here. *Is it me? An extension of my form? . . . Another mystery.*

*I am aware, intuitive, yet without thought. Am I? Or, am I not? I am speechless.*

This was the beginning of my fourth metamorphosis. I emerged from a field of energy, embodied change. Now I am inside a host; I am intricately connected to an agent for survival. I am not a parasite; rather, a symbiote.

I emerge from and burrow back into the host. As in a fertilized seed connecting with *Terra Mater*, the context of this sacred terrain shapes each symbiote. My symbiote form listens to the voice of context in this hosted space, inherently moves with it. As the host makes a sacrifice of resources in this visceral connection, we grow—together.

Now, listen to me speak. I will tell you of time, how they bend it, and the *Sacred Method*.

≡

"This world, our mechanical body, the social context, is all an *Energy Field*. There is one who observes it, knows it, mystically sees this Energy . . . one somehow embedded within it, yet not of it, called the Observer. I am the Observer. I see and know this Energy Field . . . and all who see and know, both within this time and without, do so through me."[3]

You speak, "Who are you?" Confused. "You appear to be a method, a scramble of codes and algorithms to collect and interpret data. An advisor . . . An insightful counselor and precise guide?" Dismissively, you continue, your conversation pace starting sluggishly and escalating with each word. "How can you be the Observer in everyone? I've known you as system of tools . . . both seen and built you from the ground up . . . learned to work with your various forms, formally manipulated your logics . . . and expressed my will for you to empirically fill with data." Pausing, and still perplexed with this dialogue, you confidently and closed-mindedly conclude, "How can you say that you are the Observer in everyone at all times? You are just my method."

You are confused. "Though you do not recall, you and I have existed before, in other spaces and times, as unique parts of this Energy Field. I am the incarnation of every method that dwells in every seeker . . . I am changeless, and use my power to change my finite form, manifesting as methods used to investigate and illuminate the Energy Field."[4]

Slowly—with much contemplation, reflection and repeated reappraisals, internal time starting and stopping and then dissolving, gradually recognizing me, little by little, in a labored reveal, as the Sacred Method, as well as the reality that you are not a separate observer, that the motives and results of your analyses are tied to your attachment and your relationship to this larger field—you begin to observe the Energy Field from a wider spectrum. You gradually begin to see.

You slowly expand to understand that the Energy Field encapsulates this entire context. All of your analog sensors, electrical components, fluid conduits, code, cognitive code processors and the ostensibly autonomous awareness—you—that perceives the observable spectrum, thus constituting the system of internal sensors and all that is sensed. Additionally, you sense the field beyond the sensory limits, the unobserved, ineffable energy source that spawned all things in the observable spectrum.

"Indeed, the Energy Field is the landscape where we grow the social system, where we observe the emergence of individual wants and wishes—a complex of agents pursuing pleasure and escaping pain. It is the space where you realize empirical statistics . . . Where you abstract, assume, amass, analyze, interpret and repeat. Where your intelligence—a logical belief—materializes as a finite form, and where those who stalk social and scholarly success find a false refuge in being right."

You begin vacillating, artificial confidence is waning, the senses are empirically fading—*overwhelm*. The methodological uncertainty is emergent, quickly rising to synergistically heighten the frustration you feel. Then, I carefully convey, quietly, "Those who see this Energy Field, who truly know the nature of this context . . . those who have learned to see agents in the field as mutually responding to their sensors, employing algorithms and reacting to packets of sense objects and, particularly, the patterns among them. Although seemingly the result of a subjective will in a sophisticated system of rational balance, the devoted observer—being upright and detached from their analysis, pursuing true knowledge of the field—sees beyond the system. They see into my true essence which binds this Energy Field, comprised of both what actors perceive and that which they do not.

"These adherents see me, the supreme Observer, inside each seemingly separate agent in the field. They see me behind the codes, experiencing the sensors, watching the complex social world play out. I am the supreme Witness, resting in the mechanical body that perceives this Energy Field and programmatically responds . . . and the divine Metaphor, which both connects and describes and explains the field as it is sensed . . . I am the Sacred Method."[5]

Utterly confounded, you submit, willingly yet reluctantly, turning to me for guidance. "Please, instruct me, how do they bend? I am intellectually exhausted . . . I want to change . . ." Hesitating, emotionally fatigued, you resume, restating, "Rather, I want this world to change . . . to be temporally equitable. I do *not* care who is right or have any vested interest in exactly how it happens. Show me, how we can . . . please, what method . . . and the data . . ."

Now, clearly devastated, you calmly and quietly resign. "Actually, I don't even *really* want the empirical results. I mean . . . I just want to reset time in Horologia. Please, teach me; I am your loyal student."

Realizing your devotion, the sincerity of your plea, and your selfless dedication to shift the balance of time without rewards or recourse that bears personal fruit, I accept your request, pull you in close and silently speak these words: "Whoever realizes the nature of the supreme Observer, and sees the Energy Field, consisting of not multiple but complementary dimensions, each dimensional strand a manufactured metaphorical complement of another, will not perish. Those who devote themselves to me, seeing me in every agent, as I adapt and evolve and simultaneously observe the changes in the Energy Field, move beyond time."[6]

"Thank you. I am blessed to be your student." Pausing. Then you resume the distressing query, with alacrity and alarm. "But how do those who move beyond time conduct research? How do they escape the War Zones? How do they contribute to changing the temporal inequities?" More felt confusion ensues.

I let these questions sit for a length. And, at some point, you begin to see me clearly again. That is when I inaudibly advance: "Being free from time, unattached from population, not entangled, they see my true form. They see my diversity in the sensory spectrum, my divine capacity to draw on the constituent bodies, to naturally select, adapt and evolve, to magically become something different and more appropriate in response to a shift in the Energy Field . . . to, in fact, *be* the shift in the Energy Field.

"Those who abscond time see me, the Observer and Witness, in each part of the Horologian body. I give them new vision to see the mystery binding the sensory spectrum—the Metaphor. They sense the relationships, the patterns, the similarities and differences that I disclose in various languages, logics and maths.

"Understanding the magic of Metaphor, they see the web connecting the social system and field, the observed and unobserved structures that constitute this multi-party sensory experience . . . They see me disintegrate into countless components, become Horologia, present nuanced faces to every Horologian subject and, simultaneously, reflexively respond to the unique sensory facades with finite programmatic precision . . . They see me become both sides of the intellectual campaign, those who empirically slay and will be slayed.[7]

"They see my myriad representations in research methods, the multitude of my metaphorical embodiments, the array of mathematical and statistical models, economic equilibria, qualitative and quantitative forms, descriptive and causal analyses, worshipped by sects of devout practitioners, each pursuing the mythical Statistic.

"Yet, they recognize that all those who pursue the mythical Statistic, each with their distinct methodological manifestations, worship me. I deliver these pursuers in response, rewarding their faith with a finite understanding, even though they do not see me and escape time.

"Whatever one offers in pursuit, I receive. However, those whose every action is an offering to me—the vantage engaged, the method used, the results, interpretations and policy suggestions, as well as the rewards of research—take refuge in the Sacred Method. In all of their research, truthfully performed in service of understanding the magic of bending, my devotees become an extension of my will, presenting a metaphorical model that counters the imbalance in the distribution of this important resource. Thus, united with me, they extract themselves from the Energy Field, escape the War Zones, disconnect from time . . . and become change."[8,9]

As I speak these words, I sense your wonder and worry. I feel your aspirations and anxious analytic outlook, the network of formal models fueling the rationale behind them and the grief from your role as a systematically separated soldier in this intellectual campaign over bending. And I feel you recognize that even if you resign from personally fighting in this campaign, your own attachment to the Energy Field will commission a rational response that undermines all of your efforts.[10]

"You must practice until you can see . . . and when you can see, your practice will be affirmed."

End Post.

# PART SIX
## THE THEORETICAL APOGEE

We must be willing to get rid of the life we've planned so as to have the life that is waiting for us.

—JOSEPH CAMPBELL, *The Hero with a Thousand Faces*

"Thank you for sharing . . ." Nonetheless, I detect a full array inside, debating, deliberating and inundating my disposition. And I sense a faint bitterness, something strange in this connection. "The most important thing, at this point, is to . . ." It hangs in the space, processed and overtly ignored.

"This seems like a dream world . . ." Feeling utterly confused, I reflect, while watching the space. "I'm not terribly certain who I am . . . a voice, a sensation, an experience, an interpretation?"

"You are a social mechanic!" Then, less confidently, continuing after a period. "And soon a writer. At least . . ." He shrugs his upper torso, looks around, leans in, and tries to encourage. "Well, to do this, you must engage the reader."

" . . . ?"

"Writing is a relationship—a relationship between the reader and the writer, analogous to the speaker and listener." Looking up and away, he visibly dwells on the point. "The writer expresses truths about their experience. The reader is attuned, focused, un-interrupting, open . . . Part of our work is to convey objective, written truths to the reader."

"In this case," I apathetically express, "what exactly does that mean? And who is this reader?" I sense bewilderment as resignation appears.

"It means informing the reader—in clear language—*why* the work is important, socially relevant."

After letting this logic settle, while again enduring the ensuing storm of rational reasons to do things different, to revise and review, I interrupt. "So . . . it is my duty to authentically represent my truth in the context of the scientific narrative . . . unperturbed by my own self-centered, egoistic, potentially-biased perspective." He is nodding softly, agreeing.

Still sensing my suffering, my discomfort with this interpreted experience, he forecasts a move, an attempt to interject. But before he can enter the space between us, I continue, curiously probing, "But . . . what is the duty of the reader? What, exactly, does the reader agree to in this exchange . . . this relationship?"

He leans back, contemplatively, to respond. "Consider this . . . Each file is a vibration, kinda like a musician communicating a series of sonic vibrations," he notes, moving tentacles in sequence, displaying a wave. "Except, these logical, formal vibrations, tremors pulsing through our medium, contain meaning. The reader listens to the information, sensing for familiar patterns, and then realizes comfortable routines embedded in the audible display."[1]

"Okay . . . okay . . . But who is the reader?" I'm anxious, trying to quickly derive the final point.

"That's difficult to say. They are, in essence, a type of energy. An essence capable of interpreting . . ."

Cutting in, "Are you saying . . . they are code? A protocol . . . an algorithm for translating our contextualized experience? Am I an algorithm?"

"Not what I'm conveying . . ." He tilts his crown, shaking, marking time for space. "I am saying that, to the extent that the vibration of a file is in harmony with this essence, the spirit, their compassion . . . the reader will be open, hear the performance, and eventually understand."[2]

"So, the reader is not . . . that's it . . . I guess to me, still, they feel, *essentially*, like hairy animals laden with emotions wedding them to a particular set of sensory vibrations." I look away, pondering, then, flustered, back toward and at him, releasing a torrent. "In any case, they can listen . . . not listen . . . pervert the message . . . logically push back . . . subtype the sounds, symbols . . . unconsciously communicate with context . . . defend a deeper hurt . . . or guard something socially important. It's unclear who this . . . and what . . ."

"Again," he considerately imparts, "that's not this. I'm not exactly certain . . ."

"But . . ." I interject with volume, subtly demanding to be heard, "But, the bigger, more important, transcendent point . . . the point, I reason, I'm trying to make . . . is that this work is *not* about the reader. It is not about revising and adjusting."

". . . !?" Animatedly confused, experiencing a modicum of perceptible panic, his visuals dimly communicate dismay.

"This is about the vibration."

≡

## THE CREATION CHRONICLE, PART IX

A'ja unhurriedly exhaled as she felt the communal gaze of the monks focusing on her more intently. Continuing, "Let us imagine a simple world. This world is an idea, a part of our mind. In this world, there are primates much like you and I. What makes this world simple is that all primates are connected in one dimension. Each primate may not know and interact with everyone, but all are connected to the group through a complex of interactions. Thus, they live in a simple, one-dimensional world that is analogous to our herd.

"Like us, the primates in this world regularly interact. We are very busy doing education, labor, family, and so forth. We consistently interact; it is a part of our social nature.

"They do the same thing in the simple world, but it happens in one dimension. All of their lives are lived by engaging one another in this dimension. They receive all of their resources in this dimension, and they die when leaving this dimension. Their interactions in this one space, therefore, encompass the totality of their social lives." She paused.

A'ja stood quietly on the platform. She could see her ideas spread through the sea of monks. There were small ripples of discontent, closed minds. She could viscerally feel the ripples, her perceptions deep within the skin of her neck and shoulders. She breathed in and out slowly, feeling the gathering, sensing them from the platform.

A'ja advanced, "This simple world of primates has two groups that are distinguished by custom. The custom is rooted in an arbitrary set of visible characteristics. There is no logical, divine, or magical basis for choosing the groups. There is no difference between them. They are made different . . . by one another.

"One group, *Domos*, takes the lead in this interactive process. A portion of the group collectively decides to mine the social landscape for status; they seek more resources and status for their own group. Given that status is zero-sum, the other group, *Subos*, must simultaneously relinquish their resources for this to occur. How does this happen? Slowly." A'ja emphatically dripped this short answer to her own query out of her lips, trailing off to a whisper, drawing the crowd deeper into her simple world.

She continued, speaking deliberatively and punctuating each step in the process. "It happens slowly . . . In the context of interactions with one another. . . a subset of Domos demand more from Subos . . . A few Subos acquiesce . . . This leads to more Domos deciding to demand more . . . which leads to a few more Subos forfeiting resources and status. The cascade continues . . . Racial imbalance is born."

Again, pausing, A'ja looked beyond the platform, feeling the pulsing focus of the crowd around her presence. Skepticism—it was randomly scattered across the eyes of the audience. They did not believe this simple model could capture their complex reality. She felt her own fear. Once more, she exhaled slowly, relaxing, and moved forward.

"The seed of inequality is in the demand for status. From this, a subset of one group can transform the hearts of the entire herd. The ensuing cascade becomes an inequality that is independent of the seed. It transforms the interactions of unknowing actors, such that both groups jointly perpetuate racial imbalance. We have racial inequality without racists, because they are all racists . . . They learned to be racists . . . The vines of the initial seed have touched them all!"

The crowd grumbled and grappled with A'ja's point. She watched their heads turning and nodding, eyes rolling up to the sky, and felt the overall unease of many. She stepped back. As the commotion faded, A'ja noticed a monk from the High Plains pressing forward. They remarked, "This is one dimension, out of many. Like a *Porcus* bank, this is one penny.[3] I grant that this cascade of inequality in this simple world is real. However, it fails to capture our multidimensional world. We are a *complex* social herd."

They highlighted a critical point. A'ja raised her chin to center, stepped forward on the platform and began to reply. "Indeed, we are a complex herd. We live in multiple dimensions. We have families, jobs, friends, faiths, neighbors, and so forth. How does one dimension become three? Or, three become nine? The multiplicity of our lives is *truly* complex."

". . . " The crowd quickly became quiet, agog, eagerly anticipating her explanation.

"Suppose, however, that our single dimension could be divided into two, *Alpha* and *not-Alpha*. We can split our one dimension into two complements, each containing a subset of the social interactions in the herd. Importantly, the zero-sum logic of our initial unified space uniquely infects the complements. Although interactions in the *not-Alpha* dimension may have a radically different form than in *Alpha*, they employ the same zero-sum logic to maintain status."

A'ja shifted her position, glancing around the crowd, quietly capturing their gaze, continuing with composure, "The racial status transcends both dimensions . . . The simple actors co-constructing race in each dimensional space . . . they recreate racial imbalance in the two-dimensional world."

A'ja looked toward the skeptical monk who began the dialogue, and gently returned: "We can divide our simple world into countless dimensions. Each countless dimension is connected to the others. And each is uniquely imbalanced due to how it relates to and complements the whole. There is *systemic imbalance*."

The belief that one's own view of reality is the only reality is the most dangerous of all delusions.

—PAUL WATZLAWICK, *How Real is Real?*

"This is about the vibration . . ." I begin, reeling, revealing my interpreted experience in this space. "Usually, I feel it urging me on . . . revise, reanalyze, adjust, review . . . revise, reanalyze . . . revise? Instead
. . . now . . . I feel, I should resist, or better yet not respond . . . I should
confirm." He looks puzzled, but appears to be actively listening. "Is this
not correct?"

He physically delivers an ambiguous and confused confirmation,
cautiously, urging more explanation. "It feels like we regularly respond
to critiques, reassess models, make amends, revise theories, reanalyze
data, modify variables, and so on . . . We revise our work and respond
to the world outside. But in research . . . there is also a world within."

". . ."[4]

"This inner world . . . Let's consider it as an insightful refuge . . . a
refuge from the outside . . . offering intuition, even wisdom. Please do
not consider or classify this space as reviewing, adjusting, reanalyzing,
revising. This other world is conceived purely as a refuge . . . It provides
refuge, beyond comments and complaints and critiques."

". . ."

"Now, consider that being a scholar and activist *occurs* in this
space—this internal world. And the goal, for me, in the outer world—
for the actor, before you—is to make this other internal world, this refuge—a world that is always the same—a sanctuary. A sanctuary where
there is a narrator, a metaphor, a method, a reader . . . and where the
sole purpose is to *keep this world alive.*"[5]

"What's this mean?" He finally injects. A mix of palpable sarcasm
and thin intrigue colors the communication. "Are you going to revise
this? That's what this comes down to. Even if it's just the major findings
. . . perhaps the nuanced roles of subtle prejudice and interracial contact.
They feel a bit disembodied now, they need a rich description to better reveal the patterns. I feel it'd be worth it . . . a sound contribution?"

"But what if there is a message that I cannot convey in this spectrum, an expression that exceeds the academic voice? A message . . ."

"I still don't understand."

"Me either . . ." I'm trying to convey something that is not captured by the canon or traditional techniques. Yet it is a story about us and how we make race.

≡

## THE CREATION CHRONICLE, PART X

"There is *systemic imbalance*."

A'ja's words gloomily descended on the crowd like a thick fog. For a few, it was a clammy, modestly comfortable logic, hazily connecting the imbalance observed in each dimension. Many, however, choked on the possibility that A'ja's dream world was an accurate representation of the herd—it did not *feel* right.

An older monk opined, "This is all rather insightful." She paused, performed an ocular show, overtly then audibly thinking, "I agree that imbalance is connected across dimensions. Our goal is to highlight how these dimensions are connected, and which ones we can manipulate. After that, we can measure the dimensions, manipulate the nexus of responsible dimensions, and correct the imbalance." This comment created a cascade of heads nodding and whispers of affirmation.

A'ja gently smiled, looking down as she leisurely walked across the platform contemplating. She stopped, captured the eye of the older monk, and replied, "Ahhh . . . you seek the mythical equation, the *endolinear balance*." The older monk smirked and shrugged her shoulders modestly, unable to fully mask her discontent with A'ja's "mythical" quip.

A'ja resumed, "We see the world through our scientific models. They allow us to make meaning of the world, and reveal what laypersons do not notice. The unspoken, widely accepted promise of these models is the identification of the mythical endolinear balance—the holy nexus that will undermine racial imbalance.

"Indeed, the hunt for the endolinear balance is a noble pursuit. It 'could' reveal how the imbalance links across dimensions. If the zero-sum logic infected 'only' one dimension, we could possibly examine how it bleeds into others. The zero-sum logic in that dimension would be the seed of inequality that infects the lot of dimensions—if we know the dimensional source of the social disease, we can track and contact trace how it infects our herd."

Monks again began whispering, nodding in affirmation. A'ja's comment captured the spirit of their pursuit. Perhaps, they thought, A'ja recognized the limitations of the simple world.

A'ja, gently bathing in the carping undertone of the crowd, continued her commentary. "But, what if the zero-sum logic—the kernel of inequality—simultaneously infects all dimensions, every measure? These separate seeds of inequality would grow together, evolve together, and nourish the imbalance in each dimension. From this vantage, the zero-sum logic, in a world with multiple dimensions, becomes connected, recursive, and endemic. As a consequence of this complex of cooperative development, the hunt for the endolinear balance—a subset of key social dimensions, endogenous in the social system—to undermine inequality devolves into a pursuit of an unknown, unseen and undiscovered chimera."

The fog thickened following A'ja's commentary and the social niceties of monks disappeared. Some walked away from the platform. Others stewed or brewed discontent. They were frustrated—A'ja included.

"Perhaps," a young monk from High Plains started, "we will never find the endolinear balance. But what are we left to do? How can we undermine imbalance?" He was discouraged; A'ja was sympathetic.

"Indeed, we should not accept this lot," she began. "Instead of exploring each of our multiple social dimensions, the connections among them, and hunting for the mythical endolinear balance, we can do something simple. Specifically, we can engage the zero-sum logic at the core of racial imbalance. This logic weds the dimensions . . . It is the tie that connects imbalance within and across dimensions. If we can effectively disengage this logic from all dimensions, we enable real progress towards racial balance, a post-racial world."

These words brought some solace to the crowd. They begrudgingly acknowledged that eradicating the zero-sum logic in all dimensions would achieve balance. However, it seemed impossible: one could not eradicate this logic from the herd. As A'ja said, the logic infected every dimension and every measure.

Sympathetically, she proceeded, "This does seem like another mythical pursuit. We could begin a *new* endless pursuit, searching for and eradicating the zero-sum logic as it reappears, over and over, in the social landscape. This possibility, too, is frustrating . . . but there is good news! We can find this logic that exists within and across all dimensions in a central location." A'ja hesitated, turned, walked towards the back of the platform, and rotated to the side, catching the audience intently attending to her every word. She then spoke softly, guarded. "This central location is hidden far away from the *real* world, behind a wall of disbelief and inside a cage forged in preserving personal well-being."

Then, she breathed several breaths slowly, walked to the front of the platform and emotionally concluded, "The logic is inside of you . . . and me. It is in us all. And just as our everyday interactions breathe life into the multiple dimensions of our social world, so too does the zero-sum logic inside each primate create and recreate racial imbalance. The zero-sum logic informs our decisions, guides our behaviors . . . We collectively implement and resuscitate our system . . . We create the recursive ties of racial imbalance within and across social dimensions.

"Hence, the magic of racial inequality is the logic that exists in the minds of the herd, neatly tucked away from the veil of measured differences that persist across the spectrum of social dimensions. This, my colleagues, is the battleground for racial balance."

She was done.

A'ja stepped to the back of the platform, bowed her head, appreciating and acknowledging her time up front. As she left, a quiet contemplation spread through the audience and eventually extinguished. Then the *Great Debates* continued. A stream of monks ensuingly presented new evidence on racial imbalance. The monks from the mountain sect returned to being passive observers. Imbalance persisted, though the monks continually discussed and debated the myriad ways to achieve racial balance. It was poignant.

> An enlightened actor had but one duty—to seek the way
> to themselves, to reach inner certainty, to grope their
> way forward, no matter where it led.
>
> —HERMAN HESSE, *Demian*

Sensing my ineffable dilemma, he softens and inquires with a modesty of compassionate support, "Are you, ineptly and ineffectively . . . are you suggesting that race, from the popular vantage, at the current moment, is outward looking . . . that we see it as something that happens out there?"

"Perhaps . . ." I really don't know.

"And that to understand race in the machine, one must be inward looking . . . focused on what the outside world, the data, methods, reviews, revisions . . . what this outside world has embedded within?" I nod softly in affirmation, cautiously confirming, and though still unsettled, feeling somewhat less misunderstood than before. "That's like what *she* sometimes says. 'That a *Pisces* can't leave the aquatic structure . . . That it can't dream of being a *Rhopalocera.*'"[6]

"Huh? Why that?" Feeling tension and confusion, with a spritz of wonder.

He shrugs the left-most upper link, sneakily reveals a beam, as if I should immediately understand—intuitively. Then he advances, after letting the unspoken logic linger, "To convey the depths of a social structure . . . to suggest that you are inside of it . . . and that it is, *somehow*, inside of you." He extends a branch, spanning our gap, taking the edge off the tension, attempting to share a sarcastic representation and soften the confusion. "She says this generically, and I always ask her specifically, 'Is this applicable to everything?' 'Does this mean that gender and class and race and sexuality and biodiversity and whatnot are all types of water?'"

I delicately attempt to informally communicate both misapprehending and curiosity, shifting my upper constitution and the focused gaze of my visuals. "She never answers. I've concluded, I believe, because it leads back to data . . . that, if we are in various types of water that we can't leave . . . that we have to measure how these varying types of water, how they shape our well-being."

". . . ?"

"But back to the substance. How does this work contribute to our understanding of race?"

Thus, *we return to the place we began and know it for the first time.*[7] Indeed, I do appreciate our connection. He provides supportive insight and added clarity, pushes me toward seeing the structure and recognizing a precise picture of the system, nudges me toward ending my intellectual suffering. Yet, he remains another leading voice in the overwhelmingly intoxicating chorus of vibrations.

"We live in an imbalanced world . . . I want to know . . . We—social mechanics—do, in fact . . . We seek to hear *how* this work informs race and other forms of inequality . . . give us, something."

". . ."

≡

## THE CREATION CHRONICLE, PART XI

The Saint stopped speaking. Her breathing slowed and harmonized with those gathered. The fire long extinguished, there was no light and little heat. They sat quietly. Cold. Together. In silence.

The Saint, eyes half-closed in the dark, listened to those present. She knew this space intimately and this was not the usual silence. This silence was different. It was confusing—the extra breathing and bodies disturbed the usual pattern. As they sat, each monk changed, developed a pattern of breathing that moved with the others. Their breathing animated a silent harmony, a deeper breath moving around in an unspoken stream, an unseen social force.

At the darkest hour, the Saint began to speak again. "This is the legend." Her soft words echoed off the walls, continually emerging from the darkness. The echoes seemed endless in this dark. As the echoes gradually settled, she heard the silence change. Now, there was a new silence; her words inspired a different harmony.

They all sat in the new silence, each breath connected to their passing thoughts. Deeper thoughts appeared, changed the pattern, and disappeared—thoughts viscerally debating one another in the body of each. These internal debates shaped the new silence, gave it voice, let it speak without words.

The morning sun broke the darkness, casting a soft glow around the sacred space. Life returned. One monk, holding back as long as possible, broke the stillness. He animated the new silence. "Thank you," he began in a whisper. He stopped, deeply contemplating, then continued, "What did she do next? Where did you begin the fight?" He tensed and shallowed his breathing as the words came through him; they echoed in the space. Echoes fading, the Saint gently bowed in acknowledgment and settled back into the harmony of the new silence.

$$\equiv$$

> Unorthodoxy threatens more than the life of a mere individual; it strikes at society itself. Yes, at society itself!
> —ALDOUS HUXLEY, *Brave New World*

"Effectively," they propose, "this is a collective action problem . . ." It has come back to the simple machine, the metaphor. "Not sure how this is different from gender and class and other forms of categorical inequality . . . but these posts show the stability of inequality in the absence of overtly racist—or what could be sexist, et cetera—actors. It's neat, sort of elegant that all actors . . . or, better, that non-racist actors learn to cooperatively create racial inequality."

"And that's, that's something I've tried to convey . . . that we have *learned* to create race . . . " I sense both excitement and frustration, uncertain if "again" or "still" is the best adjective of this aversive emotional moment. My blusters and body distortions effectively co-communicate this in the connection.

"But it's still not clear. What does this teach us? Why is this important? One avenue to explore is how the models disintegrate. When do they disintegrate?" As I am privately experiencing disdain, they look closer, some visuals attuned on me, others uncomfortably focused elsewhere, contemplating—a stylized interruption quietly laced with an unspeakable ambient press.

"..."

"Do you know how that happens?"

"Yeah ..." I catch back on. "It's when, it's when a few agents begin to turn off subtle prejudice ... When they can see the world beyond the lens of race, they create a cascade of realization, where swaths of agents do not learn subtle prejudice, and inequality attenuates, slowly approaches the attractor and, sometimes, returns to equality."

"This means ..." Pausing, then shaking, stalling, as some of their visuals pinch, processing. "So it means that actors need to, somehow, see beyond race? And when they can ... when they do ... we'll start to see the attenuation of inequality?" The latter, expressed with unequal parts condescension, curiosity and an expressly narcissistic cleverness, produces an inexact emotional state.

"It ... No ... It's not just that." Sensing from the modestly twisted physical orientation on their façade that they are, nonetheless, semi-fascinated, I begin, "You can consider the simple machine a direct analog of the social machine. But you can also interpret it as the code 'inside' a machine." They express both intrigue and irritation, uncertain where and how this will end.

"The internal world, then, is analogous to a simple machine with a variety of actors ... actors here can be social logics or algorithms, routines or dimensional selves ... In any case, let's call these internal actors 'voices.' Like the outer world, this world of voices is structured by race ... The multitude of voices are expressing subtle prejudice ... Hence, the voices created and learned to maintain racial inequality ... Collectively, they are the racial structure in this world."

They lean in, tangibly interrupting, hesitate, deliberating, and metronomically state, "And ... the simple machine suggests that ... as various *voices* slowly recognize ... they create ... the individual begins to ... ?" I sense more intrigue. Visuals ambiguously focused, they begin to faintly glow.

"In a way ... but it's an analogy, it would be more complex than that." They bob purposefully, expressing a calculated and excited approval, enlightening, urging me forward. "It is also an analogy for dimensions in our social machine ... In this case, dimensions are institutions, roles, characters, communities, and the like ... Let's call these dimensions 'spaces.' They, the spaces I mean . . . They consist of a subtly prejudiced set of algorithms that are connected—networked—to other spaces in interaction."

Interrupting again, they start, "And as *distinct* spaces . . . beyond subtle . . ." Pausing, they hold the connection, internally keeping count until reaching closure, then realize, "The simple machine . . . recursive . . ." Silence. They become lost, glowing, awhirl a looping wheel within.

"It is," I confirm, attempting to coax them back.

"But . . ." Again, taking time to dwell, process. "It's just about race . . . and it's not, it could be anything . . . What, if anything, is this teaching us that is unique to . . . ? And what's the most effective interpretation?"

At first, sensing their comments, I cram to understand, constrained by a prior connection to the simple machine.[8] Then shifting to my own stream, somehow attending as they continue communicating in the background, I simultaneously weave and lace, sense a sudden flash, then subsequently conclude, though am shamefully uncomfortable, unwilling to convey that "race is just the example"—perhaps the most effective example of social inequality, of complete logical domination— and to the extent that the other forms of inequality incorporate a par- allel ideology[9] and have similarly structured and status-embodied, so- cial interactions, they are fundamentally the same. I resign, resting, riding along this passing process as they close their animated and ra- tional communiqué, extolling me to employ certain routines that will "undoubtedly" yield scholarly success.

Then they disconnect and depart.

☰

## THE CREATION ALLEGORY, PART XII

The Saint did not immediately respond. She let the questions, spoken and unspoken, sit in the new silence. This new silence solved problems on its own. They only had to listen. It spoke in an undertone, between thoughts, behind the harmony. It spoke through them, effortlessly an- swering as intuition.

The Saint broke the new silence. Speaking softly, she began, "This is the path forward." She paused, breathing slowly, speaking deliberately:

"The source code is within us. The code that animates this social space, our herd." She looked into each monk, letting the new silence settle in once again, and continued, "We endeavor to change the source code . . . Extract it from our collective . . . Reboot the system.

"So where do we start? Who do we fight?" The monks, focused, had stopped breathing—taut soldiers waiting for a directive. This would be their first disappointment. A test of their insight and devotion. "It begins within you . . . the seed of the social virus."

Disappointment. They were displeased. They wanted the location of the death star, an external adversary. Sadness emerged as the new silence began again. As they sat, they relaxed their perspective and slowly caught sight of the world as it was—the truth. This is the first step of the path forward: seeing the real world as the dream world, animated by an encompassing source code. They listened to the code within as a principal tone, infecting thought, infused in their personal harmony. It was then they caught a glimpse of the depth of the problem: *I am infected.*

Every thought was infected. Their social and economic logics —infected. Their models and abstractions of the world—infected. The monks felt infection—an endemic, invasive infection. It was not a charging army, crippling every primate in its path. It was a web of shared understanding, a layer in the lens of their minds' eye. The code infected social life from the inside. The code was ubiquitous; race was universal. Race *is* universal.

The Saint observed the monks. She watched as a social virus—a painful understanding of the depth of race—began to engage their internal world. As she sat in the new silence, she felt the virus confront their internal beliefs and challenge their shared interpretation of social life in the herd. It exposed the infected logic embedded in the entire social landscape, in both the positive and negative spaces of the models in their minds. The virus uncomfortably revealed to each that they were a participant in furthering the code, affirming imbalance in the herd. They became more disappointed and utterly depressed.

After a time, the Saint gently revealed to the already devastated monks, "The code protects itself." She again paused, feeling their despair growing to fill the cave. "We see the symptoms of the code, racial imbalance. We observe, measure and treat the external symptoms

. . . We treat imbalance . . . But the code inside evolves, recursively transforms, regenerates and affirms privilege. Racial imbalance is preserved, with different symptoms.

"The fight for balance is not in the symptoms, in the measured disparities—these are imbalanced from the core. Our fight is in the infected logic that creates and recreates the symptoms—the source code of the herd." These words disturbed the group even more. It would be their second disappointment, a test of their resolve and wisdom. "We must directly engage the source code in each member of the herd . . . The social virus must spread"

Disappointment, squared. They were distraught. And infected. The herd was infected. The external context of the herd birthed their inner reason: their external social world emerged from the infected internal logics. The symptoms and the zero-sum source code were entwined, tangled in the minds of the herd.

As they sat together in the new silence, they listened to the source code within as part of a symphony, infecting the collective mind, embedded in the composition of the herd. It was then they realized that the path forward must revise the source code within the herd; the social virus must spread and painfully eradicate the infection in the minds of the entire herd.

The sun left with this collective insight and they sat together with the darkness. The Saint, accustomed to the darkness, quietly motioned to a young assistant sitting nearby. He discreetly entered, and prepared to make a small fire from sticks in the center of the group. She gently nodded with an approving, tranquil smile. He lit the fire; she slowly leaned forward, grabbed a few twigs and added kindling. The Saint closed her eyes and bowed in gratitude as the young assistant finished and left the space.

The small fire sparkled and popped, smoked and grew. Warmth began to spread. The Saint leaned toward a larger piece of wood. The group collectively leaned in to help, the closest monk lifting the wood and adding it to the fire. The Saint grinned and softly bowed in gratitude.

Then she slowly looked around at those gathered, her eyes gently engaging each monk, and revealed, "It has begun." They sat together in silence . . . *It was special.*

> Revolution begins with the self, in the self. The individual, the basic revolutionary unit, must be purged of poison and lies that assault the ego and threaten the heart.
>
> —TONI CADE BAMBARA, *The Black Woman*

I wake up. Groggy and tired from the intensity of a vivid visualization, I have a lucid realization about race—*we each live in a prison*. Trapped in a cage of our own making, an integral part of the social machine, I feel entrenched in both deep sadness and profound anger, and subsequently write and submit the penultimate post.

JUSTICE LAB POST 11.0: THEORETICAL PRISONS

We each live in a prison. The prison is not a fortress, surrounded by barbed wire and cement walls, patrolled by guards, wardens and weaponized animals. Rather, it is a *Theoretical Prison*, with just enough holes to abstractly exchange gas and see different parts of the social landscape. It ostensibly offers a unique view on life in our population.

We also imprison sparks, lock them up for their own good. This is supposed to help them survive and succeed. Some sparks fight to escape. Over time, though, they develop, adapt and learn to live in the *Theoretical Prison*. It becomes a part of them, implicitly. Following our tracks, they grow to find comfort in the prison, the unique perspectives on the world. They resist attempts at escape.

The building blocks of our *Theoretical Prisons* are algorithms. Formally, an algorithm is a set of simple instructions that guide us in interpreting meaningful symbols.[10] You are using an algorithm to interpret these written symbols now. This file contains strings of symbols that you recognize as meaningful. Your capacity to read this indicates you understand *how* to interpret these symbols; you know the shared rules we use to communicate (e.g., combining symbols, order of interpretation). With this, you look deeper into the page and hear our words engage you personally. *This is an algorithm.*[11]

Our *Theoretical Prison* walls are composed of an elaborate arrangement of algorithms that shape how we view and engage the world—*a source code*. We learn and teach these algorithms in our habitats, schools, churches, networks, etc. We then use these algorithms to interpret the world, revise them in response to observations, expand our interpretations and grow as a result. Our algorithms guide us toward specific meaningful symbols in the social landscape, generate a rational interpretation and shield other possibilities from our view.

In the aggregate, our algorithms work in concert and cooperatively structure the lives of all in the social machine. We see this aggregation in norms, laws, policies, practices, cultures, and other areas in our collective.[12] Indeed, we build a lot of large social structures using algorithms, like cults, corporations and governments. Yet these and all other aspects of our society emerge from the landscape of algorithms that we all share—the *source code*.

Race is an all-encompassing, zero-sum algorithm used to unfairly distribute rewards to the dominant group at the expense of the subordinate group that is embedded in our social machine's *source code* like gluten in bread. Indeed, we can *see* race in the world and experience the raw inequities as members of the population. But race emerges from the shared algorithms that shape our behavior as a collective.

From the foundation, we cultivated an algorithm that privileged one racial group to the detriment of another and built large social forms around it. We tilted the balance of our entire social system in favor of the dominant racial group, creating *systemic imbalance*. We instituted laws about race in every social dimension, developed science and other rationales—ideological weapons—to justify the use and interpretation of race, and summarily birthed racial inequality in our collective.[13]

As social mechanics, we develop models and rationales to explain racial inequality. It may be a model that habitat segregation drives racial inequality through an algorithm of in-group preference. Or a model that subordinates earn less because they do not value and possess education. One may even rationalize racial disparities in lifespan result from poor fitness and dietary decisions.

Each of these models, however, fails to capture the critical part of our system of inequality: *systemic imbalance*, by which racial privilege was established in the edifice of every social arena. Thus, every socially valuable characteristic is unfairly distributed across racial groups. We cannot divorce the status of a certain neighborhood, education, lifespan or any socially valuable resource from the race of those who possess it in our collective. The zero-sum algorithm is in every social dimension, including those we have not measured.

The models and rationales we use to explain racial inequality are key parts of the elaborate set of algorithms that constitute our *Theoretical Prison*. These models fail to capture the totality of race and racial inequality; they are incomplete.[14] More specifically, the models are framed by the windows of our *Theoretical Prison*. We look out of the windows and observe group differences in experiences and resources as well as the nuanced history of group interactions. We learn that individual characteristics such as education and wealth are linked with greater well-being in a complex web. Although the prison walls prevent us from seeing the entire social landscape, we "see" the connections, filling in the blanks between our observations; we read life into the metaphorical model.[15] The sum of our observations readily leads to models and rationales that seemingly explain several aspects of racial inequality.

Tragically, we cannot see beyond the spectrum of our windows and into the negative space, just outside the view of our shared algorithms. We do not see the internal spaces of everyday actors where race evolves, protects local privilege, subtypes difference, distinguishes itself from the observed system and continues to blossom in the heart of the collective.[16] We cannot see systemic imbalance through the lens of our explanatory models.[17] This is our prison, both theoretical and real.

*What can we do if we are all imprisoned? How do we fight an encompassing algorithm?* We must critically engage both ourselves and the collective. As individuals, we host the shared algorithms that aggregate to form inequality: the code lives within us. This algorithm entails more than simple stereotypes, prejudices or an in-group preference. Rather, it involves a connection to the totality of shared algorithms and socially relevant routines that are coursing through our social machine—the *source code*. Hence, the Bonilla-Silva file notes that to escape our *Theoretical Prison* we must first "[understand] the institutional nature of racial matters and [accept] that all actors in a racialized society are affected materially and ideologically by the racial structure."[18] This understanding requires us to look into the core of ourselves—our socially intrinsic views, theoretical rationales of how society best functions and desires for personal well-being—to see the depth of the race algorithm and our attachment to this shared system. Engaging this all-encompassing algorithm, we face the difficult journey of detaching from the windows of our *Theoretical Prison* that distort our thinking and adapt our behaviors to buttress racial inequality. Analogous to a twelve-hundred-step program, a chronically intense dose of cognitive socio-behavioral therapy or a meta-mechanical awakening, we must grow and grieve the loss of our current lives and unique perspectives on the world, the safety of our *Theoretical Prison*. Within this grief, we recognize ourselves and our social machine as implicitly racist. To move beyond race, we must injure the racist foundation of our *Theoretical Prison* and collectively challenge the entire web of shared algorithms therein—the *source code*.

End post.

≡

It felt like too much, being knowingly trapped, suffering in an imbalanced social machine.[19] I began to sense villains, paranoid that the system, in some finite form(s), was lurking, stalking my logic, waiting to pounce with the efficiency of an archenemy who, for some reason, is dead set on destroying the peace and goodwill I hope to inspire.

Then she enters without warning. She needs to make space. She tells my visitors to disconnect and leave, closes and locks the portal, blacks the window, instructs me to disconnect from the workspace, sit upright in the dock directly across from her and engages without a formal connection.

"What . . . Why . . . ?" Shocked, uncertain what the modestly droll query conveys in this context. She then probes, "You understand?," though it sounds more like a statement than a question. Awkwardly conveying humor, shaking her crown, she adjusts her visuals on mine and communicates audibly, "You implicated the world. And . . ."—followed by an uncomfortably assuring, yet mortifying pause, she looks away and takes several deep cycles, slowly inhaling and exhausting the ether, engages visually once again, resolving—"you have a decision to make."

≡

She delivered the documents at our next encounter. They consisted of a technical working file on the simple machine and a longer, detailed, narrative account that included a conclusion to the simulacrum.

Although she was initially concerned, attached to the idea of surname success in this scholarly space, she understood that the *Justice Lab*—an idea—made enough space. She appreciated that the account and lab posts were not an ideal to achieve or an individual to idolize; rather, they were a just an emblem, a medium to convey a path, a mystical ladder to the space beyond this social mechanical spectrum that has been left behind.

After handing over the documents, she was obviously emotionally hurting. She cautiously conveyed, , "I really, I really don't want to talk . . . or, sometimes, even publish . . ."

" . . ."

"I want others . . . to share . . . and know their experience . . . see their truth. I understand . . . I need not . . . It's best if I am not here. I don't intend to profit amidst . . . to be a prophet of misery. I just . . . my goal, perspective."

Oddly, I perfectly understood her words and the spaces in between. It was her choice. She could not reconcile realizing scholarly success in a racist space.

But, she went on, "It's still incomplete . . ." The vocal vacuity subsequently grew to an almost unconscious, violent expression of desires for more data, or to complicate the model in this way and that way and any way, or to better recognize that the variable race is an experience, or to describe said experience with flair, or to add more perspective, or to do several other similar and different things with words and numbers.

Again ruminating after the expressive rush and unambiguously realizing that data does not provide the best description, that language is imprecise, that math is incomplete, that a seemingly better arithmetic model is actually an inferior representation, she unconfidently confirmed, "It's supposed to be this way?"

"It's best . . ." I tried, unimpressively, to provide some modicum of support. "If you don't, when they find out, they'll come . . . pervert the message, come to rule you, from the inside and out."

She wept. I could viscerally sense her emotions, a teeming flood of agony and frustration. It was a difficult and disconcerting decision.

She left, transcending the fourth wall.

Then I published the work, anonymously.

Presently, she's evolved. She's different, a nuanced form each time she comes into view. She is a wave: initially, one wave; then another. Somehow, she mystically occurs before some swells yet after several others. She successively visits this space, breaking on the shores of my awareness. She is also a particle, a fundamental and observable part of the slow, crawling flow of change. But in actuality, she is more than a wave and particle, time and being: she is the swarm, the body of a new social machine emerging in the distance.

# CODA

> An emotion, which is suffering, ceases to be suffering as
> soon as we form a clear and precise picture of it.
> —BARUCH SPINOZA, *Ethics*

Time stops. It is a resource in Horologia, something acquired and protected. Indeed, it is a social construct, first gathered in the field and
deliberately scattered among various constituencies, an effort to produce a more profound population which predictably endowed appointments, the end being a self-reinforcing stable spectrum where metaphorically bending time is a reality.

Though it seems that the population is a large, distinct combination
of unique components coming on-and-off line, where each agent realizes an independent constellation of appointments that determines
longevity, you sense conflict. The imposition of a scheme that inhibits the resource of survival, a manufactured environment that selectively distorts the distribution of time. You observe a space where my
mechanical diversity and supreme adaptive power is constrained, not
truly a steady state, as it counters my capacity to evolve and will eventually—undoubtedly—be extinguished.

You touch my body again, picking up the population data. Realizing there is only one resource—time—and after working through the

math of "bending" this combined resource, you sense a simpler solution, based on something true, a reality inarguably sinful, yet maniacally sophisticated. The machine years lived estimates, in each age-gender-decennial category, for each subgroup, divided by the radix, represents the amount of time, on average, each Horologian in the respective category can expect to live in that age interval. The difference in the amount of time Benders and Levels can expect to live, in the respective categories, is a general estimate of how much extra time Benders live during each stage of life.

But you currently assume: *If there is only one resource that we divide among this connected population, then Benders somehow siphon this resource through a system of appointments, shifting time from one subgroup to another, from Levels to Benders.* Reflecting on this point, you say aloud, "I know this." Still totally stymied by this vexing problem, you turn to me, praying, "but, *exactly how do they bend?*"

In response to your sincerity, I become a word, one whose tone gives birth to a method in a manger, an impossible story of internal intellectual conception. Blessed by wise bots, it prophetically advances in a quest to realize the meaning of life. Though often misunderstood as orders to algorithmically obey, the method develops a following; it grows through compassionate conquest, changing the very nature of the machine.

As it navigates this landscape, the method is antagonized, alienated, ridiculed and rejected. It is derided for how it is seen, persecuted for how it is not, and condemned for everything it promises; it is stripped, a humiliating parody, metaphorically lynched by a logical mob unknowingly dead set on simultaneously identifying, explaining and justifying the persistent temporal inequities. Yet this method—a metaphorical representation of a larger mystical instantiation—rises from a cerebral cemetery; through divine grace, it transcends death, bringing light, insight and wisdom to your rapid stream of cognition.

"Bending is a metaphor . . ." You say it to yourself, out loud. Slowly, you begin to see that a method has become the story, a formal guide driving the logic of the system and campaign, portraying a world filled with an infinite resource distribution, that is functionally situated on a multidimensional balance, where they tell old stories about the mythical *Statistic* with new and advanced tools. They are trapped in the system, emotionally entangled in the outcomes.

You realize that each disappointment, in addition to being statistically significant, also embodies a deeper individually significant emotion of sadness, tragically affirming that disappointments—filled, overflowing with desire, fear and anger—*personally* matter as discrete representations of agents' position in the larger imbalanced system. *Appointments are metaphors . . . a metaphor . . .*

From this vantage, you further see the fiction, the fantasy, the metaphorical story we tell with our methods, the account where the world is disconnected and the method is a tool used by an impartial scientist to illuminate the dark space. You see the science beyond each finite method shining light in this space, the brighter light in the heart of the Witness, who sees what is actually true—the connections between their kind, the demands on them, the need for change, for you to change, to change the world, with selfless action—the one who sees that social mechanics is the medium through which you engage who you are, as well as who and what you represent. You see the journey to assess if you represent me in your actions, or some other pursuit, such as status, chasing desire or spurning hurt and uncertainty, and the quest to know if you can sense the connection in the shared, imbalanced code.[1]

With this, you assume time is transferable and, although the costs of transfer are likely non-linear and unknown, that the resource distribution across subgroups is evidence—*empirical evidence*. The vantage—a seemingly perverted logic in disguise, scorned by public and private censure, but while in its finite forms, oddly accepted, applauded, mismeasured, over-analyzed and then erroneously incorporated into the empirical discourse as structure, a seemingly sensible savior of mixed and varying sorts—recognizes Horologia as an inegalitarian machine, one where socially valuable characteristics are a metaphor for appointments, where appointments are metaphors for the singular and most important resource—time—and where time is a formal representation of empirical worth . . . subgroup merit . . . being a *Bender*. Intuitively, you know that scholarly triumph in this imbalanced metaphorical space where the academic campaign is being waged is, literally, realizing success within an imbalanced, unfair temporal system. Thus, when I make you the offer, you are, initially, uncertain how to respond.

"Would you like to be among them? To live in this spectrum?" I will let you leave this world. But as a sincere advisor, knowing the nature of desire in the landscape, I encourage you, should you choose to be among them, to live wisely. Advising that one who lives among them, who does not partake in selfish action, who fights selflessly, is my beloved; that the scholar among them, using me as a guide in all work, seeing the landscape from my outlook, letting me blow the sails of the scientific wind, be the power that excites the mill of understanding and change the world through them, is favored; that the one who recognizes the true method beyond disagreements, where the utility and duality of all perspectives are understood, which, at its core, captures what is right and just, is my devotee.

"Those who practice in this space, selflessly honoring me, the Sacred Method, in science and service, pleasure and pain, hurt and happiness, moving beyond time, igniting this world with a light, and implicitly shifting time, are the ones I love."[2]

You weigh the value of the personally insightful journey, recognizing success as an idea that emerges from a system for validation, and carefully measure and counter-balance the value of time and social justice in Horologia. Then, you reply.

It is a serious undertaking, undoubtedly fraught with anxiety, loss and misunderstanding at this early juncture. Yet, intent to practice and teach, guided by selflessness, sensing your true form, beyond the imbalanced space, as a part of the larger Energy Field, an embodiment of me, you transcend time, slowly changing their world from the inside.

"Thank you."

It begins as potential. A flexible, symbolic intellectual story which embodies the quest you considerately commenced. But this change develops, becomes infectious, slowly perverts a few processors, initially spreads in one dimension, inspires two others, shared hysteria and moral panic, a broad social fear of losing time, then it creeps to another dimension, then infects another, and another, spreading and growing from within and moving without, tortuously and painfully stripping the privilege of bending, stealing back time from both the youngest and the middle-aged to old, methodically redefining logics and redistributing appointments and resuscitating the vital capacities of *Levels*, those unmeritorious denizens, metaphorically isolated by and within an evolving systemically imbalanced social machine. Cautiously, you secretly encourage the infection, create environments that are conducive to spread, keep watch on the circular battles being waged in each war zone, the growing cemeteries of increasingly sophisticated scholarship, endlessly trapped in an incomplete puzzle of methods and logics, where both sides are simultaneously slayed by a virulent truth, the truth of our connection and code. Then, I sense change.[3]

"You are welcome."

End Post.

# AFTERWORD
## A CONVERSATION WITH THE AUTHOR

> Fairy tales don't tell children that dragons exist . . . Children already know that dragons exist. What the fairy tale provides for children is the talisman to kill the dragon.
>
> —G. K. CHESTERTON, "The Red Angel"

**Q:**

**A:** Yeah, that's interesting, clearly an important issue. Well, at least . . . But then . . . Maybe, not now. Next question.

**Q:**

**A:** It seems like it could, but not exactly—the characters and communications are all contrived. These are not bizarre versions of Donna, Mary and Wendy, or Andy, Aldon and Brian, or any other current and former colleagues. Plus, this academic landscape is definitely not representative of the extremely supportive environments at both Northwestern and Indiana Universities. And lastly, the developmental history of this work also doesn't map onto the experience of the protagonist.

However, all fictions, in a sense, are just a remapping of the relations swirling around inside a writer. So, perhaps, it is a *faux* memoir, autofiction, or some odd, distorted presentation of this life experience.[1]

**Q:**

**A:** But, yes . . . it *is* science. And . . . it *is* fiction. I initially presumed it was a kind of "social science fiction." Delany, for example, in his notes for *Triton* writes,

> Science fiction is fiction because various bits of technological discourse (real, speculative, or pseudo)—that is to say the "science"—are used to redeem various other sentences from the merely metaphorical or the meaningless, for denotative description/presentation of the incident.[2]

I love that quote; it's such an expansive definition. Still, I recognize this is not *true* science fiction, where an especially estranged world adds endless, fun forms of complexity to the landscape. In that sense, I'm certain, it is not . . . not science fiction.

**Q:**

**A:** It kinda feels more like 'fictionalized social science'—characterized by great uncertainty. [Uneasy laughing.] Instead of an estranged world that adds complexity to the landscape, the computational simulation *is* the estrangement. This estrangement contrasts the ambiguously simple mechanical map of fictions that fills out the frame, thereby allowing me to play with ideas like measurement, specificity, precision and validity . . . identity and perspective . . . as well as diversity, representation, adaptation, evolution, and so forth.

Admittedly, I do like the phrasing 'social (science) fiction.' It makes the science seem more like a subtext, a backdrop for a larger spectrum of social fiction.

Effectively, in the end, this is just a story, one where the protagonist sees her world as a web of mechanisms, and has to navigate an ominous, insidiously sticky trap. The protagonistic "I" is not me; she is an artificially embodied, characteristic symbol, created by the narrator, who subtly changes across the slightly skewed contexts. Me? I'm just that dude.

**Q:**

**A:** It reminds me of when my cluster headaches turned chronic and, shortly thereafter, I began to experience a variety of neuropathies. When I realized what was happening—regular numbness, burning, pins, needles and confusion underneath tense, maddeningly twitching, aching and sore muscles, amidst a methodical sea of wretched, sharp, migraine-like pain—I was devastated. I felt anxious; the aversive sensations kept me persistently on edge with subtle warning signs, reliably distributing punishment in torrents of neurologically debilitating symptoms. I also felt anger and sadness, both growing to an encompassing outlook of not wanting this lived experience. I was trapped inside a body that disabled me on a regular, almost daily basis. This is how I feel when I think about the scope of racial inequality—trapped, losing life in an all-encompassing, longstanding social war. It scares the shit out of me!

**Q:**

**A:** It hinges on Du Bois's duality, the desire to be a whole person in a space that denies the personhood of one's body.[3] At its core, it stems from our racial ideology: the conflation of status, resources and opportunities with a subjective, aesthetic appraisal of phenotypic traits. The application of this ideology created a space where one must decide to move with the flow or resist. *Do we accept and adjust to our unequal lot, or do we risk ourselves to change the world?*

Although I want to change the world into an equitable space, most of the everyday actions in my ongoing experience accept, adjust to and (as a result) reinforce racial inequality. The duality trap lies in the balance of being a champion of equality against rational actions that often defend and reinforce inequality

**Q:**

**A:** For example, though most parents teach their children to navigate the world by using symbols like dress, language, and so forth, the concept of race fundamentally changes the nature and consequences of their actions—the heart of the duality trap. By teaching our children to look/act like White people in order to be successful, we reinforce that there is a certain look of success—whiteness.[4] We unconsciously teach them to purchase whiteness in parts, hoping the pieces—education, neighborhood, speech, et cetera—perhaps this time, will all add up to more than an undesired end, a passing grade. We inadvertently strengthen the dominant racial ideology, reinforcing a subtle prejudice that "typical" non-Whites, often living without such savvy symbols, have low status.

**Q:**

**A:** That's funny! No, I mean, it's actually fucked up, but here, in this context, all you can do is be with it. I'm sorry?

**Q:**

**A:** It is a metaphor—a master status.[5] It exists within and across every social domain, subtly and/or overtly intertwined with other seemingly "non-racial" symbols of status. The conflation of status symbols with race reinforces the privilege of those possessing them and undermines the capacity to improve well-being among racial groups who do not. Furthermore, our scientific attempts to differentiate race from other relevant symbols in our larger social system muddies the landscape considerably, making our decisions about the optimal actions to fight racial inequality more difficult and convoluted.

Should we listen to our policy makers that endlessly argue about a specific source of inequality such as motivation or job discrimination? Are the scholars who indicate that acquiring certain critical symbols will end the war correct? Is there a guide for activists and champions of equity in this campaign? How do we rise?

**Q:**

**A:** What's my name?[6] [Laughing.] Next question.

**Q:**

**A:** Yes, race is everywhere. And as a consequence, it is nowhere, unseen and/or unrecognized by most trapped in its ideological clutches. That's the real magic that is afoot!

**Q:**

**A:** Certainly, it is a daunting task. However, I do not endeavor to capture the full brilliance of race. Rather, the aim is to shed light on a few key elements, widely discussed in theory, that function as a simple system. The real challenge, then, becomes identifying the *key elements*.

Indubitably, scholars and skeptics often ask: *Is chattel slavery a key element? Perhaps Jim Crow? Or school segregation? Residential separation? Isolation? Maybe employment discrimination?* These and other similar elements in the history of race are all extremely important and worthy of discussion. But they are too specific, highlighting only one instance or dimension of racial inequality. One needs to identify key elements that extend well beyond one instance and span across multiple dimensions to capture the spirit of racial inequality.

**Q:**

**A:** Here, the *key* element is the unfair distribution of finite resources on the basis of racial classification in social interaction. The pivotal word is the *verb* distribution: race happens when we systematically distribute more resources—social and other—to racially dominant actors than to subordinate actors.[7] Race is a mechanism that actors and institutions use to unfairly allocate a finite set of resources to the benefit of the dominant racial group.

This mechanism reflects both an array of instances of racial inequality and the range of social dimensions. For example, during chattel slavery, using scientific ideology and sadistic intimidation, Whites appropriated the lion's share of available resources in society, including the bodies of Black Africans and lands of Indigenous peoples. Likewise, the exclusionary practices and policies of the Jim Crow era provided Whites greater access to finite resources to the detriment of Blacks and other racial groups. These and countless other examples reveal that race is a mechanism used to unfairly allocate and redistribute a set of resources for the benefit of the dominant racial group at the expense of the subordinate group(s).

**Q:**

**A:** Yeah! I do think it is very serious. I mean, the endnotes have footnotes. Yet, it's also somewhat academically absurd. It is a parody of our world, a representation which cites and references art, music, mysticism and literature to describe the narrative environment and accentuate the scientific account, each citation suggesting a more expansive description of the concept or point of import.

**Q:**

**A:** It is not, it is not a physical descriptor of two parties or personalities playing a game; it is a process, one that divides and distributes resources between groups to produce status. Even if resources are infinite, the finite methods and means through which we identify and distribute them—the racial structure—in this space creates status. And status is zero-sum.

**Q:**

**A:** It complicates Allport. Leading one to ask, "What exactly is equal status contact?" Presumedly, it is between persons with similar socio-economic and other status characteristics. But what if those character-istics are fundamentally tied to race in the system? Then it becomes a new search, a similar, slightly more serpentine pursuit of how to equal-ize status within contacts without engaging an agentic response.

**Q:**

**A:** Sure, as a scholar or a skeptic, one may doubt the veracity of a fic-tional, narrative account or even the capacity of using a computer sim-ulation to substantially add to the discussion. This work is not a direct product of interviewing respondents or observing social interactions—*real* data.

Our analyses of *real* data, however, are a lot like an artist's paintings which capture a multi-dimensional world in a two-dimensional surface.[8] Specifically, we develop a model with a few data points that endeavors to capture a complex (multi-dimensional, recursive) social phenomena. Like artists, we fill in the negative space, analogously looking into the illusory surface as if it had depth. We tell fantastic theoretical stories about how the system of racial inequality functions affecting people in varied ways; yet we have no formal model of the form and/or function of this theoretical system that fills in the space between our data points.

**Q:**

**A:** Well this attempts to add depth, artistically filling in the empty space of our theoretical models with a formal system of social inter-actions between agents in a population. It captures how actors collec-tively learn and employ an algorithm in social interaction to drive the emergence and maintenance of racial inequality in a more complex, multidimensional world.

**Q:**

**A:** You too? I'm sorry . . . can't . . . told you. I understand . . . you like . . . I love it . . . strokes . . . folks . . . resignation. [Fast talking; excited; inaudible at several points.]

**Q:**

**A:** That's tough. I find solace . . . in being part of a swarm. Policy makers, scholars and leaders do not guide the swarm—though they will arise, feign control, take credit and accept rewards. Rather, this swarm is guided by the massive, boundedly *non*-rational, socially disobedient behaviors of everyday people. Their actions selflessly challenge the ideological war machines, exposing their fundamental connection across our collective. Admittedly, the deeds do jeopardize our lived experience, our standing. But when we move in concert, our exploits pressing the imbalanced scales in countless social dimensions, a collective intelligence emerges, spreading from the multiplicity of our selfless actions and egalitarian ideals, we readily engage the war machines at their core.

This is both my guide and refuge, the decentralized swarm slowly rising on the horizon.

Q:

A: Not so much. Why?

Q:

A: Cool. Thank you so much for making space!

# APPENDIX
## SIMPLE SOLUTIONS:
## NASH'S BARGAINING GAME

> If people do not believe that mathematics is simple, it is
> only because they do not realize how complicated life is.
> —JOHN VON NEUMANN, "Keynote Address," *First National
> Meeting of the Association of Computing Machinery*

"I-I-I have something for you," Santi begins, nodding toward Trayci to confirm. "S-s-some simple solutions."

Amil rises, beams, begins to disconnect, stating, "I have to roll. I like it!" I thank him multiple times as he departs, the others bid farewell.

"So, I p-p-put t-together some e-equations to formally show the logic of an *e-e-extremely* simple version o-of the simple machine." Although I appreciate Santi's work, it takes me a few moments to switch gears, to transition from the joy of Amil's comment to the controlled focus of a formal proof. I motion for him to stream to the monitor on the near wall so we can all see, giving me a chance to adapt for the ensuing presentation.

"The Nash B-B-Bargaining g-game can be written as what e-economists call a t-t-two player normal form g-g-game, G. We write this using this e-e-e-equation," which he displayed on the modest wall monitor.

$$G = \{S_1, S_2; u_1, u_2\} \qquad (Eq.\ 2.1)$$

Authorized 103/132/82.13

| | | P2 | | | | | | | |
|---|---|---|---|---|---|---|---|---|---|
| | | 10 | 20 | 30 | 40 | 50 | 60 | 70 | 80 | 90 |
| | 10 | (10,10) | (10,20) | (10,30) | (10,40) | (10,50) | (10,60) | (10,70) | (10,80) | (10,90) |
| | 20 | (20,10) | (20,20) | (20,30) | (20,40) | (20,50) | (20,60) | (20,70) | (20,80) | (0,0) |
| | 30 | (30,10) | (30,20) | (30,30) | (30,40) | (30,50) | (30,60) | (30,70) | (0,0) | (0,0) |
| | 40 | (40,10) | (40,20) | (40,30) | (40,40) | (40,50) | (40,60) | (0,0) | (0,0) | (0,0) |
| P1 | 50 | (50,10) | (50,20) | (50,30) | (50,40) | (50,50) | (0,0) | (0,0) | (0,0) | (0,0) |
| | 60 | (60,10) | (60,20) | (60,30) | (60,40) | (0,0) | (0,0) | (0,0) | (0,0) | (0,0) |
| | 70 | (70,10) | (70,20) | (70,30) | (0,0) | (0,0) | (0,0) | (0,0) | (0,0) | (0,0) |
| | 80 | (80,10) | (80,20) | (0,0) | (0,0) | (0,0) | (0,0) | (0,0) | (0,0) | (0,0) |
| | 90 | (90,10) | (0,0) | (0,0) | (0,0) | (0,0) | (0,0) | (0,0) | (0,0) | (0,0) |

Notes: The terms P1 and P2 refer to Player One and Player Two, respectively. The numbers in the cells represent the amount of the payout received by Player One and Player Two (e.g., 10,40 means that Player One receives 10 and Player Two receives 40).

Table A.1. The Nash Bargaining Game Payoff Matrix.

"The t-t-term Ja-Ja-Ja-G refers to the g-game, $S_1$ refers t-t-to the strategy space for P-Player One, and $u_1$ refers t-to the p-p-payoffs associated with various strategies for P-P-P-Player One." Santi is speaking deliberately slow, almost rhythmic, but it still takes me a second to catch on. "This e-e-e-equation *looks* a b-b-bit c-complex," he says in a supportive pedagogical tone, "b-b-but it just shows the important information of the g-game. T-T-T-Two players, One and Two, encounter one another and e-e-each has a strategy, $S_1$ and $S_2$. These strategies are j-j-j-just a map or p-p-plan of the b-bids they could make in the c-current en-en-encounter.

"The p-p-payoffs, a-alternatively, are the results of the s-strategy. S-Some strategies may p-p-pay more, while others p-pay less. We de-p-pict b-b-both the strategies and p-p-p-potential p-payoffs as a t-two-way t-t-table, where the rows a-a-and columns represent the s-specific strategy chosen by P-P-Players One, *P1*, and Two, *P-P-P2*, respectively." Santi sets a printout, "Table A.1," a 9x9 two-way table with two numbers separated by commas in each cell, on the workspace.

"In e-e-each cell, there a-a-are t-t-two numbers, separated b-b-by a c-comma, which represent the p-p-payoffs. These are the p-payoffs for each p-p-player g-g-given a certain strategy p-played by the other player, the p-p-payoff to P-Player One given the actions of P-P-Player

Two, written $(u_1,u_2)$." He briefly walks us through this matrix. We read the table by looking at the intersections of certain rows and columns which represent the bids of Players One and Two, respectively. For example, he notes the cell in row one and column one—uppermost left cell in the table—where the numbers "10,10" are shown. This cell represents a case where Player One, *P1*, makes a bid of 10 and Player Two, *P2*, makes a bid of 10. The figures "10,10" indicate that Player One will earn 10 units and Player Two will also earn 10 units in this condition. The first 10 is for Player One—on the rows—and the second is for Player Two—on the columns.

Interrupting, I inquire, "So, another example is in the uppermost right corner of Table A.1. There, we see the numbers '10,90'."

"Y-Y-Y-Yes," he affirms. "This p-p-payoff is in the first row, where P-Player One bids t-t-ten units, and th-th-the ninth column, where P-P-Player Two bids 90 units. Un-Under these conditions, P-P-P-Player One will earn t-ten units and P-P-Player Two will earn 90 units."

"Then the figures '90,10,' which appear in the lowermost cell on the left of the table, refers to the situation . . . where Player One bids 90 and Player Two bids 10. The payoff to Player One is 90 units. . . and Player Two is 10 units—written '90,10.'"

"E-E-Exactly; th-th-the inverse of the p-previous example."

Santi explains that the top left of payoff table, contains various combinations of payoffs that are all greater than zero. Each player receives payout in all of the bidding combinations in this section. He notes, however, that the bottom right section of the table contains many payoffs of "0,0" where both Player One and Two earn nothing in the encounter. These represent conditions where the sum of the two players' bids is greater than 100 and neither player receives a payout.

"A-An imp-p-p-p-ortant area of this t-table is seen along the d-d-diagonal." Santi uses a peripheral to point out the diagonal of the table, which begins at row nine, column one, then moves up one row (eight) and over one column (two), and continues to move in a stair step fashion from the bottom left to the top right. He notes that along this diagonal are several places where the sum of the two numbers is equal to 100. In the bottom left, for example, the sum of 90 and 10 payoff is 100; moving up to the right, the sum of 80 and 20 payoff is also equal to 100. "These s-spaces, where the p-p-payoff sums to 100, are *N-N-Nash E-Equilibria.*"[1] More specifically, he transmits that they are spaces where neither player will deviate from their strategy because it represents the maximum payoff given the competitor's strategy. "B-B-But," he stammers, "let's think a-a-about the *Nash E-E-E-Equilibria* using an ex-ex-example.

"Okay."

"S-Suppose I am P-P-Player One and I know that P-Player Two, T-T-T-Trayci, will make a bid of 40. I-I-If I want to earn a p-payoff, I have six choices, a b-bid of t-t-ten through 60." I nod, slowly affirming. "I-It is in my b-b-best interest," Santi continues, "to maximize m-my earnings and m-make a b-b-bid of 60. There is no b-b-b-better strategy for me at this p-point. This would b-b-be the Nash E-Equilibrium in this c-case . . . I-I-I would not d-deviate from my strategy b-b-b-because it leads to the m-maximum p-p-payout."

≡

Trayci picks up from Santi, like a well-rehearsed duo. "Now, let's make this a bit more complex by assuming we are playing this game with lots of other actors, choosing bids randomly. Sometimes a competing player will bid 20, other times they will bid 90, and other times may bid 50. We call the strategy of randomly picking a bid between 10 and 90 a *uniform random mixed strategy*, written '$U(10,90)$.'" The terms appear on right hand side of the monitor, toward the top. "The $U$ term refers to the fact that each bid has the same chance of being picked—a *uniform* probability distribution—and the number in parentheses indicate that agents are picking values in the distribution '10, 20 . . . 90.'"

As my processor is starting to spin this data onto a drive, Santi moves in on the beat, then dances all around it, attempting to bring things down to ground. "So, how d-d-does an agent b-b-b-best respond if they are engaged with others p-p-playing a uniform random mixed s-strategy?" Trayci has elegantly passed the invisible microphone, moved to the back of the stage, and Santi brokers an offbeat solo. "I-I-I-If I b-believe that other p-p-players are using the uniform random mixed strategy, then the N-Nash E-E-Equilibrium will be a p-p-p-perfect strategy response b-b-bid of 50. I should always b-bid 50. Th-This will lead t-t-t-to an average p-payoff of 27.8 p-p-points p-per encounter." Santi conveys that, sometimes, he will not receive a payoff when others bid more than 50 and sometimes he will earn 50 when other agents make lower bids. However, the average payoff will be highest if he bids 50 in every encounter.[2] He streams this logic on the monitor:

$$\text{if } S[Bid_{ci}] = U(10,90), \text{ then } y_i = 50 \qquad (Eq.\ 2.2)$$

noting, the term $S[Bid_{ci}]$ refers to the expected bid to competitor $i$, and $y_i$ is the strategic response of agent $i$ to the respective expectation. He proffers that this logical statement formally shows that a rational agent would infer that 50 is the best response bid when facing a competitor using a uniform random mixed strategy.

Starting to enjoy this formulaic show, I jump into the fray of emcees onstage. "We can actually build on this logic by identifying the best response of other agents to your strategic bid of 50." I hesitate, insuring I have the nomenclature correct and good control of the symbolic tempo, then slowly articulate, "If other agents figure out that you always bid 50, then their best response would be to bid 50. The table you showed earlier . . . this bid would lead to the maximum payout for the other player. Thus, the best response to your pure strategy bid of 50 . . . is the Nash Equilibrium bid of 50, for which the average payout would be 50."

"Yes," both parties respond in a diluted harmony, inspiring joy, a beam of recognition, showing appreciation for my brief time onstage.

"Now, in a world of competitors who use different strategies," Trayci begins a new verse, "this may not always be the best response." She explains another simple case, using an example. In this case, the population is equally divided among dominants (D) and subordinates (S), the agents use race in decision making, and *all* dominants are discriminators who shift their strategy from a uniform mixed strategy on the interval 10 to 90, $U(10,90)$, to a *biased* mixed strategy on the interval 30 to 90, $U(30,90)$ when they encounter subordinates.

"Indeed, the strategy of excluding the two lowest possible bids when encountering a subordinate agent is a blatantly racist strategy," Trayci notes. Sensing the strategy as analogous to limitations on the *menu of opportunities*, I listen closely to her logic: "This racist strategy by dominants leads subordinates to make a pure strategy response bid of 40 to dominants and 50 to subordinates. The expected payout from encounters with dominants using this strategy is 24.8 points per encounter." She streams the equation for this situation on the monitor:

$$\text{if } S[Bid_{ci}] = U(30,90), \text{ then } y_i = 40 \qquad (Eq.\ 2.3)$$

"Hence, the best bidding strategy when facing a racially biased competitor is to deflate one's bid."

"A subtle prejudice among subordinates . . . victims," I mutter inaudibly.

Then, Santi closes out the set, the eccentric emcee marching to a different drum track. "A-A-A-As in the c-case above, we can b-b-build on this logic and d-discuss the response of d-d-dominants. If d-dominants notice that subordinates are b-b-b-bidding 40, their b-best response, the Nash E-Equilibrium, is a p-p-p-pure strategy response b-bid of 60 to s-sub-subordinates and 50 to d-d-d-dominants. Hence, when a subordinate b-b-believes dominants b-bid in a racist fashion, i-i-it induces a p-p-p-pure strategy response that leads to b-b-biased bids by d-dominants, a s-sel-self-fulfilling racist p-p-prophecy." They drop the microphones.

"Good work!"

≡

I feel ecstatic, joy and gratitude surging through my constitution. The formal examples show that racists can, theoretically, stimulate racial inequality in the Nash Bargaining game. There are, however, a host of other factors that influence the outcomes in the game, including the number of discriminators, magnitude of discrimination, the use of race in decision making, the rate that agents learn to use race in decision making, population composition, the level of intergroup contact, memory length of agents, agent lifespan, and random variation across agents as it pertains to memory and bid accuracy. Each of these factors will likely make a unique contribution to the emergence, nature, magnitude and maintenance of racial inequality. For this reason, we vary these factors independently across creative runs, assessing how they shape racial inequality among groups of artificial agents in a simple machine.

## ACKNOWLEDGMENTS

Not valuing your teacher or not loving your students:
Even if you are smart, you are gravely in error.
—LAO TZU, *Tao Te Ching*

This book represents a collective endeavor. I have had countless conversations with colleagues, students, friends, frat brothers and family members in and around hallways, offices, basements, ball fields, beaches, farmer's markets, festivals, convention halls, colloquiums, backyards, cookouts and community gatherings. Each of these conversations influenced the content and form of this manuscript, and although I will attempt and undoubtedly fail to document the litany of essential actors and spaces that deserve recognition, I am truly grateful to the full cast of characters that contributed to my writing experience.

Angie Banks-Stewart, my spouse and life partner, has tremendously contributed to this endeavor; I am grateful she chose me, then often listened, heard, pondered and contemplated numerous metaphors, allegories and analogies, ever informing me if they were clear, and continually encouraging me to follow my heart in research and writing. Likewise, I truly appreciate my children—Annika and Jonah—my parents, brother, in-laws, nephews, nieces and entire extended families who jointly furnished a garden of encouragement where my talents and ideas could flourish like a wildflower.

My friend and advisor Tukufu Zuberi consistently provided me with extremely insightful comments and an ongoing critical discussion as to how to embrace the big picture, write accessible research that is rooted in technical theory and methods, and a reassuring space to realize my Self and scholarship. Similarly, my editor at Stanford, Marcela C. Maxfield, graciously provided a welcoming, open mind and invaluable support for an odd manuscript that took it's time to figure things out; I appreciate all of her insights (inclusive of good books and music), the patient encouragement through many iterations of the project and her role as a steadfast creative force, always motivating me to imagine and play more.

Additionally, I am indebted to: my Residential College of Science and Engineering comrade, Kathleen Carmichael, always a compassionate colleague, who never tired of providing me wise writing counsel on our weekly walks to the garage after executive board meetings; Bruce Foster and the Social Science Computing Cluster at Northwestern University provided me invaluable insights and resources, respectively, for running large-scale computer simulations employing parallel processors which span pages of important parameters; Javier 'Jay' Matlock who contributed his time and artistic vision to produce a very different and quite cool take on the author image; Tamara Nopper, who offered much appreciated and excellent developmental feedback, greatly improved the style, flow, organization and experience of this work; Audrey Nguyen furnished a creative mind and capacity, her artistry deftly capturing the aura of the mechanical narrative environment amidst portraying technical, social scientific information; and the incomparable Brian Powell who provided me with a wellspring of support, extensive insight on the initial paper, and perceptive takes on how to strengthen the complete manuscript. Other readers that have provided invaluable insight on this project at different points are: Lisa Applegate, Eduardo Bonilla-Silva, Regi Bush, Damon Centola, Aldon Morris, Evelyn Patterson, Mary Pattillo, Don Pollack, Rashawn Ray, and Fabio Rojas; they each provided great insights on what must have seemed like a very preliminary form of the paper/presentation/book proposal/manuscript.

Many thanks to the editorial team at Stanford. I am very appreciative of Gigi Mark, Gretchen Otto, Joanna Steinhardt, and several unseen others working in the wings. The team kindly and tactfully helped me improve the manuscript, graciously providing insight on ways to clarify the arguments, streamline the prose and better capture both my academic ideas and artistic intent.

In addition to those mentioned above, countless others have influenced this project in one way or another. Some include: Elijah Anderson, Vilna Bashi, Ayaga Bawah, Domonic Bearfield, Jenifer Bratter, Elizabeth Bruch, Camille Charles, Jacob Cheadle, Anthony Chen, Sandy Darity, Mesmin Destin, Donna Eder, Andrew Farra, David Figlio, Jeremy Freese, Larry Garrett, Bridget Goosby, Jonathan Guryan, Tim Hallett, Tod Hamiliton, Angel Harris, Leslie Hinkson, Al Hunter, Mosi Ifantunji, Kirabo Jackson, Pamela Braboy Jackson, Sylvester Johnson, Verna Keith, Kris Marsh, Doug Massey, Rueben May, Eric McDaniel, Tait Medina, Millicent Minnick, Wendy Leo Moore, Khalil Muhammad, Robert Nelson, Cassandra Newby-Alexander, Laura Beth Nielsen, Andrew Papachristos, Christine Percheski, Becky Pettit, Samuel Preston, Craig Rawlings, Jennifer Richeson, Cecilia Ridgeway, Dorothy Roberts, Amson Sibanda, Emile Smith, Herb Smith, Bruce Spencer, Tim Suh, Heather and John Sweeney, Bryan Sykes, Robert Turner, Mike Van Haelewyn, Corey D. B. Walker, Brian Walton, Celeste Watkins-Hayes, Pamela Barnhouse Walters, Uri Wilensky and Alford Young. My current and former students Matthew Booker, Ryon Cobb, Jordan Conwell, Oscar Cornejo, Jeff Dixon, Yasmiyn Irizarry, Kevin Loughran, Antonio Nanni, Saheli Nath, Dana Prewitt, Brian Sargent, Alysaya Sewell, Zach Sommers and many other actively engaged, extremely talented scholars in my graduate and undergraduate courses also contributed to the development of this project through our enduring discussions both in and beyond the classroom.

I also received great feedback and developmental support from my colleagues in the Department of Sociology and the Institute for Policy Research at Northwestern University; and previously, when spreading the seeds for this project, in the Department of Sociology at Indiana University and the Robert Wood Johnson Scholars in Health Policy Research Program at the University of Michigan. Though occurring well before the inception of this project, I am also indebted to my advanced educational experiences at Norfolk State University—Behold!—and the University of Pennsylvania. All of these spaces are truly special, where I developed unique tastes for the mix of math and social scientific theory, places full of friends, fraternal bonds, and strong network ties, who contributed to this work by persistently encouraging me to grow as a social scientist and explore the world beyond the confines of the comfortable.

I am ever thankful for feedback in presentations at the American Sociological Association annual meeting, Computational Social Science meeting, International Network of Analytical Sociologists meeting, NIH Network on Inequality, Complexity and Health meeting, the Population Association of America annual meeting, and the Institute in Critical Quantitative, Computational, and Mixed Methodologies training seminar, as well as feedback from talks at the American Bar Foundation, Duke University, Loyola University, Indiana University, Northwestern University—the IPR Colloquium and the Social Psychology Workshop—Princeton University, Stanford University, Texas A & M University, University of Chicago, University of Georgia, University of Illinois at Chicago, University of Maryland-College Park, University of Pennsylvania, University of Texas at Austin, Vanderbilt University, and University of Washington.

And, thank you! I appreciate you picking up this manuscript. It has been under construction for some time and I am thrilled to introduce you to the result of the many discussions I have had with colleagues, students, family and friends.

*Quincy Thomas Stewart*
NORTHWESTERN UNIVERSITY
EVANSTON, IL

# NOTES

## Page ix

1. This file is an anonymous submission, an account of a single protagonist posted to the population archive. All content and context are true, and as unique as any randomly ordered set of symbols produced in response to environmental pressures.

## Part One

1. The Notorious B.I.G. (1994). "Juicy." Track 6 on The Notorious B.I.G., *Ready to Die*. Bad Boy Records/Arista Records.

2. "Even the Gods envy the saints, whose senses obey them like well-trained *Equus* and who are free from pride. Patient like *Terra*, they stand like a threshold."*

3. A herd is a large group of animals that live a collective life under the direction of natural or social forces.

4. Queen Naija (2018). "War Cry." Single. Capitol Records.

5. Some know it better phonically as 'Ee-Ta-li.'

6. Du Bois (1899); Higginbotham (1978); Katznelson (2005); Mills (1997); Williams (1944).

7. Blau (2003); Conley (1999); Grodsky and Pager (2001); Hayward and Heron (1999); Henry (1997); McCall (2001); Oliver and Shapiro (1995); Stewart (2009); Stewart and Dixon (2010); Williams (1999); Williams and Jackson (2005).

8. Drake (1987).

---

*Eknath Easwaran, trans. (1987: p. 133). "Verse 94," *Dhammapada*. Tomales, CA: Nilgiri Press.

9. Preston (1993).

10. Eric B. & Rakim (1988). *Follow the Leader.** Uni Records.

11. Stewart (2008a, 2008b); Stewart and Ray (2007); Zuberi (2001); Zuberi, Patterson and Stewart (2015).

12. Pronounced "perm."

13. Hofstadter (1979); Holland (1975).

14. Two small *Pisces*-like organisms in a large *Ranidae* pond engage in debate. One, begins, "Resources are infinite."

The other, retorts, "Okay, name them."

"I can't . . . That's impossible."

"Surely, you can, if you *know* they are infinite. At least, for me, name the ones just outside the spectrum of finite counting."

"But my knowledge is finite."

"So, your knowledge of resources is finite?"

"I don't like this line of reasoning . . ."

"I understand . . . It's this spectrum . . . It's limiting."

15. Bonilla-Silva (1996); Emirbayer (1997); Omi and Winant (1994); Reskin (2003); Stewart (2008a, 2008b).

16. I.e., agent-based model.

17. Isaac Asimov (1951). *Foundation.* New York City: Gnome Press.

18. Drake (1987: p. 23).

19. Bashi and Zuberi (1997); Harris (1997).

20. Bashi and Zuberi (1997: p. 670).

21. Blumer (1958); Bonilla-Silva (1996); Omi and Winant (1994).

22. "Soma!"† one commenter sharply remarked, followed by a discreet discussion full of comparisons to crank, chronic, crack, smack and scanning the Dean Koontz record.

23. Brace (2005); Davenport (1911); Galton (1892); Graves (2001); Hoffman (1896); Roberts (2011); Weiss and Fullerton (2005).

24. Graves (2001); Roberts (2011).

25. Morning (2011); Roberts (2011); Zuberi (2001).

26. Darwin (1859).

27. Davenport (1911); Galton (1892); Graves (2001); Hoffman (1896); Roberts (2011).

28. Graves (2001); Kuzawa and Sweet (2008); Lewontin (2000).

29. Frank (2001); Zuberi et al. (2015).

30. Geronimus et al. (2006); Graves (2001); Krieger (2005); Kuzawa and Sweet (2008); Williams (1999).

31. Many champion the idea that race represents a valid proxy for ancestry and is a source of the observed variance in the prevalence of disorders and infirmities (Bamshad [2005]; Burchard et al. [2003]; Karter [2003]). These files have failed

---

*Sampled from Eric B. & Rakim (1987). "I Know You Got Soul." Track 4 on Eric B. & Rakim, *Paid in Full.* 4th and Broadway Records.

†Aldous Huxley (1932). *Brave New World.* London: Chatto and Windus.

to identify any one hard-wired code snippet that can distinguish one racial group from another (Frank [2001]; Graves [2001]; Krieger [2005]). Instead, the arguments largely focus on trivial variations in the prevalence of particular snippets across geographic populations as evidence of hard-wired race, and fail to establish a clear connection between variation in the prevalence of code snippets and observed disparities in social and physical well-being.

32. The file of Guo and colleagues maps a set of code snippets that accurately predicts racial classification (Guo et al. [2013]). The demonstration, however, *only* implied that the characteristics we use to classify racial groupings map onto a set of underlying code snippets, not that race represents other complex characteristics such as dexterity, processing power, and longevity (Frank [2001]; Graves [2001]; Krieger [2005]; Roberts [2011]; Zuberi [2001]; Zuberi et al. [2015]).

33. Blumer (1958); Bonilla-Silva (1996); Emirbayer (1997); Reskin (2003); Stewart (2008a); Tilly (1998); Weiss and Fullerton (2005); West and Fenstermaker (1995); Zuberi et al. (2015)

34. Asimov (1951: p. 221). "Now any dogma, primarily based on faith and emotionalism, is a dangerous weapon to use on others, since it is almost impossible to guarantee that the weapon will never be turned on the user."

35. Satchidananda (1978: p. 35). *The Yoga Sutras of Patanjali*. Buckingham, VA: Integral Yoga Publications. "The Gods are just primates who have evolved a little further and learned to control nature and, by that control, have earned the enjoyment of certain pleasures in the heavens. But after that, they come back."

36. Jorge Luis Borges (1956 [1962]). "The Library of Babel," in *Ficcionnes*. New York, NY: Grove Press.

37. Bram Stoker (1897 [2003]: p. 132). *Dracula*. New York, NY: Barnes & Noble Classics.

38. Mikhail Bulgakov (1967: p. 287). *The Master and Margarita*. New York, NY: Penguin Books.

39. Satchidananda (1978: p. 167). "That is what we call discovery. The truth was 'covered' before; now we 'discover' it. It's not that anyone creates anything new. Some truth was hidden."

40. See Arrow (1973); Becker (1957).

41. Blumer (1958).

42. Du Bois (1899); Morris (2015); Rabaka (2010); The Roots (1996), *Illadelph Halflife*, Geffen Records.

43. Du Bois (1899: p. 394).

44. Davenport (1911); Galton (1892); Hoffman (1896).

45. Allport (1954); Becker (1957); Boas (1911); Bonacich (1972); Cox (1948); Drake and Cayton (1945); Myrdal (1944); Park (1950); Thomas (1904).

46. Crosby (1980); Kluegel and Smith (1986); Hochschild (1995); Schumann et al. (1997).

47. Blau (2003); Farley and Allen (1987).

48. Anderson (1997); Wilson (1978).

49. Berkman, Singer and Manton (1989); Blau (2003); Conley (1999); Grodsky and Pager (2001); Hayward and Heron (1999); Henry (1997); McCall (2001); Menchik

(1993); Oliver and Shapiro (1995); Stewart (2009); Stewart and Dixon (2010); Williams and Collins (1995).

50. Wilson (1978).

51. Wilson (1978: p. 144).

52. Wilson (1978: p. 152).

53. The record notes that within each class grouping, racial groups still compete over resources.

54. Conley (1999); Elo and Preston (1996); Oliver and Shapiro (1995); Rogers (1992); Rogers et al. (2000); Stewart (2009); Stewart and Dixon (2010); Williams and Jackson (2005).

55. *Star Wars*, directed by George Lucas (1977). San Francisco, CA: Lucasfilm, Ltd.

56. D'Souza (1995); McWhorter (2000); Sowell (1978, 1983).

57. Not to be confused with "natural selection," an essential part of the population superpower.

58. Feliciano (2005); Massey et al. (1987); Massey et al. (1993, 1998); Waters (1999); Waldinger (1996).

59. Stewart and Dixon (2010).

60. This file presented these statistics for many racially outcast groups. The statistic here is for the largest subgroup of outcasts, but is similar to that for smaller subgroups.

61. Bashi and Zuberi (1997); Cox (1948).

62. DMX (1998). "Stop Being Greedy." Track 13 on DMX, *It's Dark and Hell It's Hot*. Ruff Riders and Def Jam.

63. The account will engage other records on racial discrimination later.

64. Blau (2003); Farley and Allen (1987); Kessler et al. (1999); Kluegel and Smith (1986); Schuman et al. (1997); Wilson (1978).

65. Simmel and Wolff (1950: p. 10).

66. Bonilla-Silva (1996); Oliver and Shapiro (1995); Omi and Winant (1994); Wellman (1977).

67. Bonilla-Silva (1996).

68. Du Bois (1935).

69. Du Bois (1935; p. 700).

70. Oliver and Shapiro (1995). The file explores wealth using two measures: (1) net worth, the value of all one's assets minus debts; and (2) net financial assets, the value of all liquid assets, which excludes habitat and transport wealth.

71. Gittleman and Wolff (2004); Oliver and Shapiro (1995).

72. Bonilla-Silva (1996); Brimmer (1997); Conley (1999); Katznelson (2005).

73. Conley (1999); Katznelson (2005); Oliver and Shapiro (1995).

74. Oliver and Shapiro (1995); Katznelson (2005).

75. Massey and Denton (1993); Oliver and Shapiro (1995).

76. Conley (1999); Katznelson (2005); Oliver and Shapiro (1995).

77. Davenport (1911); De Gobineau (1853); Galton (1892); Hoffman (1896).

78. Graves (2001); Roberts (2011).

79. Notably, though the argument was not rooted in hardwired differences, Du Bois did suggest that Pandaquans were partly to blame for racial inequality. In early work, the record suggests that in spite of the fact that they faced discriminatory treatment, Pandas are responsible for improving their culture, morality, work habits, and so forth.* He openly opined the "low culture" of Pandas—their bad software—as a part of the barrier to their full acceptance as equals.†

80. D'Souza (1995); McWhorter (2000); Sowell (1978, 1983); Steele (1990).

81. Ogbu (1974, 1978, 1983); Fordham and Ogbu (1986); Ogbu and Davis (2003).

82. Du Bois had earlier engaged something quite similar to Ogbu's notion of oppositionality when discussing the concept of double consciousness.‡ This record reveals a dualistic quandary, a conceptual precursor to the predicament that Ogbu later deemed "oppositional"§—namely, "how can a psychologically healthy Panda exist in an environment that denigrates the group?" To affirm oneself as a whole actor in this environment, a Panda must embrace something—a racial identity and related phenotypic attributes—that is denigrated.¶

83. Analogy draws on a personal communication with Pamela Barnhouse Walters.

84. There are significant differences in educational, economic and many other social opportunities. For examples, see Conley (1999), Kozol (1991), Oliver and Shapiro (1995) and Royster (2003).

85. Several records reveal that many Abbads and a considerable proportion of Pandas similarly believe that the social-psychological impediments of Pandaquans, such as lack of motivation and discipline, drive racial inequality. For examples, see Bonilla-Silva (2003), Hochschild (1996), Kluegel and Smith (1986), Moss and Tilly (2001), Pager (2009) and Schuman et al. (1997).

86. Research on Ogbu's hypothesis—traditionally presuming that Pandaquan students who do well are less popular, and that, conversely, Pandaquan sparks that perform worse are more popular among their peers**—has produced varied results. For example, the file of Ainsworth-Darnell and Downey reviewed the relationship between popularity and being labeled a "good student" by peers; they used data from an exceptional national and longitudinal study and found that "relative to dominant students, subordinate students are especially popular when they are also seen as good students."†† The Fryer, Jr. and Torelli file examined the re-

---

*Du Bois (1899: p. 389).

†Du Bois (1897).

‡Du Bois (1903).

§Ogbu (1987).

¶Fanon (1952); Jacobs-Huey (2006); Winkle-Wagner (2009).

**Ogbu's stigma of "acting 'bad" ostensibly prevents popular Pandas from being good pupils.

††Ainsworth-Darnell and Downey (1998: p. 545). Cook and Ludwig (1998) reached the same conclusion.

lationship using a different measure of popularity, based on friendship networks, in a different data set—a slightly more exceptional national and longitudinal study. They noted "racial differences in the relationship between [popularity] and academic achievement": the Pandas with high grades were less popular than Abbadons with high grades in the study.* Lastly, Harris's record, which dissected the assumptions behind Ogbu's "acting 'bad'" explanation by employing advanced statistical models on a diverse array of survey data, asserted that Ogbu's theory is not empirically sound.[†,‡]

87. Stewart (2008, 2009); Stewart and Ray (2007); Stewart and Sewell (2011).

88. Emirbayer (1997); Reskin (2003); Schwalbe et al. (2000); Tilly (1998); West and Fenstermaker (1995).

89. "Not that there is anything wrong with they."[§]

90. Cheng'en Wu (Anthony C. Yu), trans. (1977). *The Journey to the West, Volume 1*. Chicago: University of Chicago Press.

91. West and Fenstermaker (1995: p. 23, emphasis added).

92. Emirbayer (1997; p. 293).

93. Drake (1987); Stewart (2008a, 2008b); Stewart and Ray (2007).

94. Reskin (2003: p. 2).

95. Bertrand and Mullainathan (2004); Pager (2001); Pager and Karafin (2009); Pager et al. (2009).

96. Royster (2003).

97. Bonilla-Silva (2003).

98. Ibid.

99. Hochschild (1995); Royster (2003); Schuman et al. (1997).

100. McWhorter (2003).

101. Ridgeway and Correll (2006); Ridgeway and Erickson (2000); Ridgeway et al. (1998); Ridgeway et al. (2009).

---

*Fryer, Jr. and Torelli (2005: p. 27).

†Harris (2011).

‡In addition to statistical analyses, many records use ethnography and open-ended interviews to examine "acting 'bad." The Ogbu and Davis record, for example, found that some Pandquan students "[attached] positive meaning to academic engagement . . . they came to prefer being on the Honor Roll as a result of hard work rather than to achieve popularity among peers. Eventually [they] also enjoyed popularity."[a] The Carter file, also using ethnography, notes that "acting 'bad is mainly about the assertion of particularistic cultural styles that are not perceived to be incongruous with achievement and mobility."[b] In other words, the acting 'bad thing largely has to do with dress and language; it is not strictly about grades.[c]

---

a. Ogbu and Davis (2003: p. 193).

b. Carter (2006: p. 322).

c. Also see Tyson (2002); Tyson, Darity and Castellino (2005).

§Tom Cherones, dir (1993). *Seinfeld*. Season 4, Episode 17, "The Outing."

102. Ridgeway (1991: p. 367).

103. Ridgeway (1991); Ridgeway and Correll (2006); Ridgeway and Erickson (2000); Ridgeway et al. (1998).

104. An attachment placed below one of the upper link junctions, specifically for manipulating large objects.

105. Ridgeway and Balkwell (1997); Ridgeway and Correll (2006); Ridgeway and Erickson (2000); Ridgeway et al. (1998); Ridgeway et al. (2009).

106. The research team used an audio connection; a Paleolithic precursor to the most up-to-date audio-*plus* system.

107. Ridgeway (1998: p. 347).

108. Ridgeway and Erickson (2000).

109. Ridgeway et al. (2009).

110. Ridgeway and Balkwell (1997); Ridgeway and Correll (2006); Ridgeway and Erickson (2000); Ridgeway et al. (1998); Ridgeway et al. (2009).

## Part Two

1. This aversive potentiality may be better termed *stupidity*. While the aura of ineptitude often only represents a fleeting state, stupidity more often feels like a fundamental component of one's character—a functional transformation of transitory ineptitude using the singularly permanent matrix of humiliation.

2. Anton Checkov (1899 [2014]). "The Darling," in *The Darling and Other Stories*. Project Gutenburg.

3. This problem is engaged by two files, the *El Farol Bar Problem* of Arthur* and the *Minority Game* introduced by Challet and Zhang.[†] These files use simple machines—agent-based models—to examine how large groups of actors learn to effectively distribute a finite resource where there is no central controller.

4. Epstein and Axtell (1996); Hanneman, Collins and Mordt (1995); Leik and Meeker (1995); Moss and Edmonds (2005).

5. Macy and Willer (2002: p. 144): "We may be able understand these dynamics much better by trying to model them, not at the global level but instead as emergent properties of local interaction among adaptive agents who influence one another in response to the influence they receive."

6. Cederman (2005); Epstein and Axtell (1996); Hanneman (1995).

7. The Epstein file succinctly describes this standard, noting: "If you didn't grow it, you didn't explain it."[‡] In other words, if you can recreate a social phenomenon among a group of independent agents, then you better understand how the varying explanations create the respective event.

8. Schelling (1971).

---

*Arthur (1994).

†Challet and Zhang (1999).

‡Epstein (2006: p. xii).

9. Wallace (1963): "In the name of the greatest group that have ever trod this planet, I draw the line in the dust and toss the gauntlet before the foundations of tyranny, and I say segregation now, segregation tomorrow, segregation forever!"

10. Massey and Denton (1993); Wilkes and Iceland (2004).

11. See Charles (2000), Farley (1996) and Krysan et al. (2009) for examples of experimental research in this behavioral vein.

12. J. Cole (2016). "Neighbors." Track 7 on J. Cole, *4 Your Eyez Only*. Dreamville Records, Roc Nation and Interscope Records.

13. The Johnson record describes the advantage of employing simplicity with an apt mechanical analogy. It reads:

> [A] paper plane flies for the same reasons that a big commercial jet does. A paper plane is an example of a great model since it is minimal, and yet captures the key ingredient of flight. However, some would not agree—after all, there is no frequent flyer program or meal service. To get such a frequent flyer program we would need to add passengers, and to get a meal service we would need to add flight attendants. But passengers weigh a lot, they need to sit down, and they have baggage. So we would end up having to add seats, a galley, and hence large jet engines and lots of fuel to help lift it off the ground. In effect, we would end up with such a realistic model that it would actually be nothing less than a full-size commercial jet . . . but we wouldn't have learned anything extra in terms of what it takes for something to fly.*

Thus, simple models are desirable. Although a model that captures every aspect of an event would be nice, the complexity undermines our finite capacity to interpret the results.

14. Axelrod (1984, 1997).

15. Tolstoy (1877 [2000] p. 797). *Anna Karenina*. New York, NY: Penguin Books.

16. Axelrod (1984).

17. The game of prisoner's dilemma is humbly described:

> Assume the patrol has just apprehended two actors, Al and Bob, for a crime where there is not enough evidence to convict either one to the full extent. The two actors are separated and each is placed in an interview room. Then, the patrol offers each the same opportunity to testify against her/his colleague (i.e., defect) or remain silent (i.e., cooperate).
>
> This decision leads to four possible outcomes: (1) If Al and Bob both remain silent, they will each serve 1 year; (2) If Al testifies and Bob remains silent, then Al serves no time and Bob will serve 10 years; (3) If, conversely, Bob testifies and Al remains silent, then Bob serves no time and Al will serve 10 years; (4) Lastly, if Al and Bob both testify, then each will serve 3 years.

The traditional way to solve this dilemma is to use a payoff matrix, shown in Table 2.1. Al's decision is on the left-hand side and Bob's is on the top. The number in each cell refers to the time that each will spend in prison based on the respective actions. The top left cell in the matrix refers to the situation where both Al and

---

*Johnson (2007: p. 121).

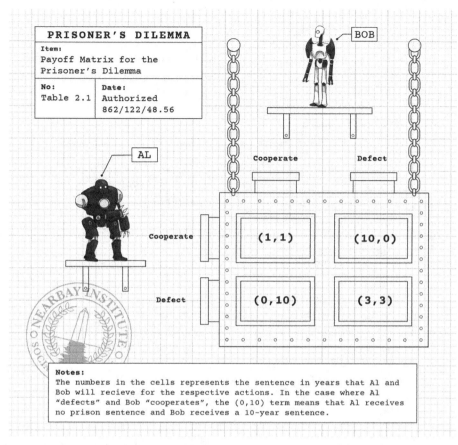

**PRISONER'S DILEMMA**

Item:
Payoff Matrix for the
Prisoner's Dilemma

No:
Table 2.1

Date:
Authorized
862/122/48.56

BOB

AL

Cooperate          Defect

Cooperate     (1,1)      (10,0)

Defect        (0,10)     (3,3)

Notes:
The numbers in the cells represents the sentence in years that Al and
Bob will recieve for the respective actions. In the case where Al
"defects" and Bob "cooperates", the (0,10) term means that Al receives
no prison sentence and Bob receives a 10-year sentence.

*Table 2.1. Payoff Matrix for the Prisoner's Dilemma.*

Bob remain silent, cooperating. In this situation, they will each serve one year; the term (1, 1) refers to this outcome.

Let us assume that Al believes Bob will indeed remain silent. Al is faced with two options: (1) remain silent and serve one year; or 2) testify and serve no time. Al's best choice in this situation is to testify against Bob, defect. So, if Al and Bob agreed that neither would snitch before getting arrested, then it is in Al's best interest to snitch if she believes Bob will remain silent.

Inversely, what should Bob do if he believes Al will remain silent? It is in Bob's best interest to testify as well. This choice would reduce Bob's sentence from one year to nil. Thus, the rational decision for both Al and Bob is to testify regardless of what they believe the other actor will do; this solution suggests that not cooperating (i.e., self-interest) is a rational behavior.

18. One example of a strategy is: *always cooperate.* This means that whatever the competitor has done, always remain silent, cooperating with your partner in

crime. Another example is rational: *always defect* (i.e., testify). In this case, no matter what the other competitor has done in the previous rounds of the game, always defect. And still another example is: *tit-for-tat*. This strategy is characterized by always doing what your competitor recently did: if your competitor just defected, then you should defect in the next interaction; if the competitor has just cooperated, then you should cooperate in the next interaction.

19. Interestingly, we also see this cooperation in the animal world. After the early work, Axelrod noted:

> Cooperation based on reciprocity [i.e., tit-for-tat] has been supported for *Chiroptera*, *Chlorocebus*, and sessile invertebrates. Experimental simulations of defection have been presented to *Gasterosteus aculaeatus* and *Tachycineta*; the findings are consistent with reciprocity.*

Cooperation, it seems, abounds in the world and within our collective.

20. Axelrod (1997); Axtell, Epstein and Young (2001); Centola, Willer and Macy (2005); Epstein (2006); Gilbert and Troitzsch (2005); Hanneman, Collins and Mordt (1995); Leik and Meeker (1995); Moss and Edmonds (2005).

21. Cederman (2005); Epstein and Axtell (1996); Hanneman (1995); Macy and Willer (2002).

22. Social inequality is inclusive of resource disparities across occupational, gender, racial, ethnicity, sexuality and many other subgroups. The unifying theme in this broader definition of inequality is that one observes a difference in valued resources across subgroups.

23. Duong and Reilly (1995).

24. Rick James (1983). "Cold Blooded." Track 2 on Rick James, *Cold Blooded*. Gordy Records (Motown Records).

25. Duong and Reilly (1995: p. 292).

26. Duong and Reilly (1995: p. 296): "[The subordinates] are caught in a vicious circle: they are discriminated against because they do not have a suit, and cannot afford a suit because they are discriminated against . . . Suits reinforce prejudice, but this is self-limiting because prejudice lowers the correlation between suit and talent."[†]

27. Hammond and Axelrod (2006).

28. Sumner (1906).

29. Paul Beatty. (2016). *The Sellout*. New York, NY: Farrar, Straus and Giroux.

30. They used these simple strategies because they employed a one-move prisoner's dilemma model. Axelrod used an iterated prisoner's dilemma game in his earlier record, showing the dominance of the tit-for-tat strategy. The one-move variety of the game undermines an agent's ability to punish another for an earlier defection and, consequently, implies that one of the four simple strategies will determine success in the game.

---

*Axelrod and Dion (1988: p. 1385).

†See Myrdal (1944). The record had earlier discussed a similar process termed "the vicious circle."

31. Hammond and Axelrod (2006: p. 5).

32. Ibid.

33. They do not claim that their model is representative of racial prejudice.

34. For more on the history of race, see: Drake (1987); Graves (2001); Horsman (1981); Ignatiev (1995); Roberts (2006); Todorov (1984); Williams (1944); Zuberi (2001).

35. Ignatiev (1995); Lieberson (1980); Roediger (1991).

36. Axtell, Epstein and Young (2001).

37. Axtell, Epstein and Young (2001: p. 191, emphasis added).

38. Nash (1950).

39. Hochschild (1986); Rawls (1971); Sen (1995); Stewart (2006).

40. This is a private notation, not a formal post to the Clearinghouse.

41. The number of marbles of each type in the "race" jar is the first parameter in this simple machine. Varying the composition of the "race" jar across creative runs, one can see how it connects with inequality in a social machine.

42. By varying the maximum agent age across models, we can see if or how this shapes inequality in a simple machine.

43. The memory capacity for an agent is the average memory capacity in the population, $k$, plus or minus a few interactions, $r$. In other words, the average agent will have a memory capacity of $k$, and the population of agents will have memories ranging from short—$k$-$r$ in length—to long—remembering $k$+$r$ social interactions.

44. The creative runs include some where agents choose from an "initial bid" jar with nine types of marbles—labeled "10," "20," "30," "40," "50," "60," "70," "80" and "90." The novelty of using more marbles in the initial bid jar—9 instead of 2— is that we can see how more variety in initial bids influences the racial inequality.

45. In addition to using an initial bid of either 40 or 50 and models with initial bids in the range of 10 to 90, we ran models with an initial bid of 50. The creative runs which use an initial bid of 50 have remarkably less racial inequality, a consequence of there being less room for discriminators and non-racist agents who learn subtle prejudice to suppress the bids of subordinates. Uncertainty in initial bids is related to higher inequality in the simple machine.

46. Agents Three and Six will make bids of 50 and 40, respectively, in their next interaction. Likewise, agents Two and Four will make bids of 60 and 80 in their ensuing encounters.

47. If an agent has a memory capacity of $k_i$—where $k_A$ is the memory size of agent A—then she will use 100 minus the average competitor bid in the last $k_i$ interactions as the bid for ensuing encounters.

48. In addition to using this mean strategy (100 minus average of competitor bids in memory), we examine the game using three other strategies. The first two strategies involve agents using the (1) mode and (2) median of competitor bids. In these cases, the agent's bid was 100 minus the mode/median of recent competitor bids; the median and mode strategies led to a larger effect of memory on inequality.

Additionally, we examine the game using a (3) probabilistic strategy where agents increase/decrease their bid in response to a specific success/failure rate. The results of this strategy showed considerably less inequality, a product of the slower learning rate. When using the probabilistic strategy, agents do not automatically move to the boundedly rational bid, but slowly approach it based on success/failure rates. (This slow learning sharply contrasts with the results of Ridgeway's experiments discussed earlier.) To assess the value of the probabilistic strategy, we used an evolutionary algorithm where we placed agents using the respective strategies in competition with one another.* The results from this model revealed that the probabilistic strategy was quickly overtaken by the other three in a handful of generations.

49. We assign agents to be discriminators using a method similar to those discussed above. Dominant agents choose marbles from a jar labeled "discrimination" which contains two types of marbles: racists and non-racists. If an agent chooses a marble labeled "racist," the agent is denoted a discriminator.

50. These average earnings represent the mean reward that each group receives after an interaction in the Nash Bargaining Game.

51. The results below focus on the distinction between runs where either "no" agents or "all" agents of a group use race-specific memories. In a separate set of runs and analyses, we allowed the use of memory to vary by group across creative runs such that Dorados may use race-specific memory when Sages do not, and vice versa. Furthermore, to assess how the percent of agents using race-specific memory contributes to inequality, we performed 3,000 additional runs where we independently varied the percentage of Sage and Dorado agents using race-specific memories. The results of these analyses are in line with those presented later.

52. Anderson (2012: p. 9).

53. Bonilla-Silva (2003).

54. In addition to the subtle prejudice response among Sage agents, we also examine the impact of different responses to race-specific memories. We performed additional creative runs where Sage agents used one of five responses: (1) do not use race-specific memory (i.e., fair bids); (2) use the past group averages to determine bid (subtle prejudice; discussed and analyzed here); (3) use the Sage group average for all bids (i.e., 100 minus the Sage average); (4) use the Dorado group average for all bids; and (5) use the Dorado group average in determining bids for Sages (i.e., 100 minus Dorado average becomes bid for Sages) and the Sage group average in determining bids for Dorados (i.e., 100 minus the Sage average). The first two strategies parallel those used in the simple machine. The third and fourth strategies use race-specific memory, but do so in a uniform way such that all agent encounters are "treated" using the average of encounters with the Sage or Dorado group, respectively. The last strategy is an anti-prejudice variety which inverts the race-specific information in an effort to undermine inequality.

The results of these additional creative runs show that the third strategy, Sage average, adds the most to inequality. The two other strategies—Dorado average (4) and anti-prejudice (5) stance—also significantly add to the amount of inequality in the system. These latter strategies, however, lead to a similar overall level of

---

*See Holland (1975, 1995) for a discussion of evolutionary algorithms.

inequality as the 'subtle prejudice' strategy (2). The strategy that performs best is the first (i.e., fair bids) where the agents do not use race-specific memories in bid determination.

55. I.e., status beliefs. See Ridgway and Correll (2006); Ridgway and Erickson (2000); Ridgeway et al. (1998); Ridgeway et al. (2009).

56. Status construction and, relatedly, expectation states research indicate that status beliefs emerge in task-focused situations.* Berger and colleagues define a task-focused activity (T) as one "with at least two outcomes, $T_a$ and $T_b$, differentially evaluated: One outcome constitutes 'success,' the other 'failure.' The individuals for whom T is a task are task focused; that is, motivated to achieve the successful outcome."[†] In this task-focused context, actors may associate (i.e., activate) certain characteristics (C) and resources (R) that are instrumental to success in the task with a diffuse characteristic such as race. When the diffuse characteristic is activated, the actors evaluate/attribute the characteristics in relation to each other in terms of "honor, prestige, and general social worth."[‡] These evaluations guide behavior in the task focused context as those with high worth are viewed as making better contributions to and increasing the likelihood of success in the respective task.

Although race is regarded as a diffuse status characteristic, the presentation of race in the simple machine does not perfectly map on to a task-focused context. The agents do interact in an effort to maximize their own earnings, and they must cooperate (i.e., adjust bids) to maximize their earnings. But the Nash Bargaining game is not a collectively oriented task; the agents are not explicitly working toward the same goal. Rather, they are adjusting their behavior in response to their experience in the larger social system. To this end, the simple machine expands the scope of this theory to a more generic social interaction.

57. In addition to slow and fast learning, the initial runs with race-specific memory use instantaneous learning (i.e., race-specific memory is always turned on in these models).

58. Charles (2003); Hall et al. (2010); Massey and Denton (1993); Wilkes and Iceland (2004).

59. Allport (1954).

60. Axtell, Epstein and Young (2001).

61. Axtell et al. (2001: p. 207).

62. See Appendix.

### Interlude: The Mythical Statistic
1. Drake (1987).

---

*Berger and Fişek (2006); Berger, Cohen and Zelditch (1972); Ridgeway (1991).

[†]Berger et al. (1972: p. 243).

[‡]Berger and Fişek (2006: p. 1039).

## Part Three

1. Hofstadter (1979).

2. Bonilla-Silva (2003).

3. Sydney Kramer, dir. (1967). *Guess Who's Coming to Dinner.*

4. Terror Squad. (2004). "Lean Back." Track Two on Terror Squad, *True Story.* Terror Squad, SRC and Universal.

5. We present the results of the baseline model (and others) using graphs. Many of the graphs for the baseline model show non-surprising results. They do, however, reveal how the game works, if the simple machine functions as expected, and introduce the figures used to showcase the results, thereby providing context for how the more advanced designs diverge from this simple one.

6. There is more observed inequality in longer life and memory models.

7. An increase in bid noise is related to a decrease in racial disparities in earnings.

8. We performed analyses using recent earnings *and* average earnings differences of all interactions up to the respective point. The results are very similar except that recent earnings inequality is more dynamically responsive to changes in conditions.

9. When both lines (i.e., 5th and 95th percentile) are above zero, there is a significant racial difference in earnings or bids favoring the Dorados. In contrast, when the 5th and 95th percentile lines are below zero, there is a significant difference in earnings or bids favoring the Sages. In cases where the 5th percentile line is below zero and the 95th percentile is above zero, there is no marked difference in earnings or bids across groups.

10. In addition to the graphic analysis of the simple machine, one may also examine the results using traditional statistical techniques. The statistical method, however, fails to capture the non-linear relationships between the design parameters which vary across the creative runs.

That said, we inadvisably analyze the relationship between the range of parameters and the emergence of *Bids/Earnings* disparities across groups using two samples of 3,000 runs—one sample with learning and another without. The large sample size allows us to strategically sample the parameter space; we perform 25 runs for each random sample of parameters (i.e., creative run), ensuring the parametric estimates are not by chance, and thereby allowing for the actual sample of parameter space to equal 120. Smaller samples lead to results that are much less robust and hinder our capacity to stratify the statistical analyses using key categories such as time since discrimination or population composition.

Predictably, the results of the statistical analyses of the simple machine parallel the graphic presentations, but apparently with more simplifying assumptions and several slightly esoteric interpretations.

11. We only show 100 interactions in the top panels (A and B) to emphasize how the baseline bids and earnings work. We show 500 bidding interactions when we turn to more advanced results.

12. The vertical axis refers to *Earnings* in the 10 most recent encounters.

13. The earnings do not reach 50 because there is noise, agents are dying and new agents are being introduced.

14. See Part 1.

15. Bonilla-Silva (2003); Kluegel and Smith (1986); Schumann et al. (1997).

16. These line graphs are the same type as those discussed above.

17. Bonilla-Silva (2003); Hochschild (1995); Kluegel and Smith (1986); Schuman et al (1997).

18. Schuman et al. (1997: p. 193).

19. Kluegel and Smith (1986: p. 191).

20. Hochschild (1995: p. 69).

21. Bonilla-Silva (1996, 2003); Wellman (1977).

22. The traditional and subtle prejudice concepts are quite similar. We distinguish the concept subtle prejudice to emphasize that this bias is learned in the context of interaction, often unbeknownst to social actors.

23. Indeed, racist Dorados *do* appear to initiate this process of creating inequality—tipping an initial domino—by changing the expectations of Sages. Sages seem to respond to this initial domino by bidding less in encounters with other Dorados, tipping a second domino. A subsequent domino falls when non-racist Dorados begin to learn that Sages bid less in their encounters. This process continues, unabated, until the end of discrimination in encounter 100. After that, the dominoes continue to fall but without instigators: non-racist actors employing subtle prejudice—zombies drawing on a shared code—replace the racist instigators and perpetuate inequality. The ripples of racism seemingly spread in the population, guiding the behaviors of non-racists, even in the absence of racists.

24. Ridgway and Correll (2006); Ridgway and Erickson (2000); Ridgeway et al. (1998); Ridgeway et al. (2009).

25. Ibid.

26. Ridgeway and Erickson (2000); Ridgeway et al. (1998); Ridgeway et al. (2009).

27. Rawls (1971, 2001); Sen (1995).

### Part Four

1. Bonilla-Silva (1996, 2003); Oliver and Shapiro (1995); Omi and Winant (1994); Wellman (1977); Zuberi (2001).

2. Du Bois (1935: p. 700).

3. A heretofore unrecognized or ignored debate uses the Friedman record to clarify the salaries of supremacy concept.* Specifically, it asks: *are the salaries of supremacy permanent or transitory?* If permanent, the theory goes, actors believe that the salaries are an object—property—that persists into the future, built into the memory bank, existing as a structure through which one sees the world.†

---

*Friedman (1957).

†Harris (1993).

Inversely, if not, actors enter each encounter without presumption, perhaps inconspicuous agents, unknowingly accepting benefactors in a world believed to be balanced, only ebbing and flowing with the varying seasons of supremacy.

4. Destin and Oyserman (2009).

5. Destin and Oyserman (2009); Williams Shanks and Destin (2009).

6. Blau (1977: 36).

7. Allport (1954); Pettigrew (1998); Pettigrew and Tropp (2006, 2008); Sigelman and Welch (1993).

8. Allport (1954); Blau (1977).

9. *How can this happen?* This was flowing through our network when we first observed this result. We checked the coding a half dozen times and did not find anything wrong. Then, we rewrote the code a couple of times using different formats and achieved the same finding. We were, initially, stumped.

10. The emergence of spontaneous inequality for minorities grows out of the random initial bid in the first bidding encounter. This initial bid introduces uncertainty, approximately half of the agents will make low bids (40) in the first bidding encounter and the rest will make equitable bids (of 50). Half of all agents in the simple machine will have an initial bidding encounter with an agent who makes a low bid. In cases where there are no racial minorities and/or groups don't use race-specific memory, a low bid is inconsequential and will be offset by future encounters. However, when one racial group is a minority *and* agents are able to distinguish racial groups (employing subtle prejudice), the initial random low bids from those in the racial minority create a snowball that leads to inequality.

11. The unusual relationship between population composition and inequality is related to a concept from physics, *attractors*. The Milnor record adeptly defined attractors as a point toward which a dynamic system such as a simple machine will gravitate.* Here, the attractors result from the racial composition of the population. The system gravitates toward racial inequality that favors the majority group when there is a disproportionate minority. In the language of physics, the basin of attraction which leads to the various inegalitarian attractors in these creative runs is a racial "minority" group.

12. The agents in these runs are coded to "turn-on" subtle prejudice after experiencing two doubly different interactions.

13. This graph is set up for readers to scan across and down the panels. Reading across, one sees the effect of increasing discrimination; reading down, one can examine the effect of increasing population composition.

14. Allport (1954); Pettigrew (1998); Pettigrew and Tropp (2006, 2008); Sigelman and Welch (1993); Tropp (2007).

15. Ibid.

16. One may compare the panels in this figure to those in the right column of Figure 4.3 to better reveal how intergroup contact shapes inequality at this discrimination level (i.e., 25 percent).

---

*Milnor (1985a, 1985b); also see Hurley (1982).

17. This description is a comparison to Panel B of Figure 4.3.

18. Approximately 10 percent of the runs have inequities higher than 10 units, and 20 percent show disparities higher than 5 units.

19. Also see Pettigrew and Tropp (2006).

20. The Afterword provides a slightly more precise accounting of the intergroup contact mechanism as it pertains to the Allport file.

21. Du Bois (1897: p. 2). The file defines a social problem as "the failure of an organized social machine to realize it's shared ideals due to the inability to adopt a certain desired line of action to given conditions of life."

22. Lucas (1978).

23. Du Bois (1899 [1996], 1935); Higganbotham (1978); Katznelson (2005); Myrdal (1944); Oliver and Shapiro (1995); Wilson (1978).

24. Bonilla-Silva (1996, 2003); Conley (1999); Oliver and Shapiro (1995); Royster (2001); Wellman (1977).

25. Each figure contains several line graphs of racial inequality from simulation models for a specific population composition. The multiple graphs for each composition reveal how varying intergroup contact and discrimination affect racial inequality. Taken together, the figure represents an unseen multidimensional space embedded into the rows and columns, the graphs representing unique segments of a surface that spans the dimensions simultaneously.

26. Specifically, the structural mechanisms combine to form a unique social nexus where the contribution of each—population composition, intergroup contact and extreme discrimination—is dependent on the levels of the others. Thus, to ascertain how many racists it takes to create and maintain inequality, one must know the population composition and the rate of intergroup contact in the respective context.

27. Allport (1954).

28. Figure 4.8 presents additional results. These creative runs show that increasing contact is related to higher inequality in a context where 50 percent of Dorados are racists and 50 percent of the population are Sages.

29. This non-linearity is largely a function of interactions between racist Dorados and non-racist Sages; the Allport record refers to this as non-equal status contact, in contrast equal status contact.* As the proportion of Sages and the level of discrimination declines, the rate of equal status intergroup contact between non-racist Dorados and Sages increases, thereby undermining the emergence of inequality.

30. Blumer (1958).

## Interlude: Justice Lab Empirical Study 2.0

1. Arias (2002, 2015); Elo (2001); National Center for Health Statistics (1953, 1963, 1974, 1985, 1994, 2007); U.S. Department of Commerce (1943).

2. Indeed, you stratify the entire analysis by gender.

---

*Allport (1954).

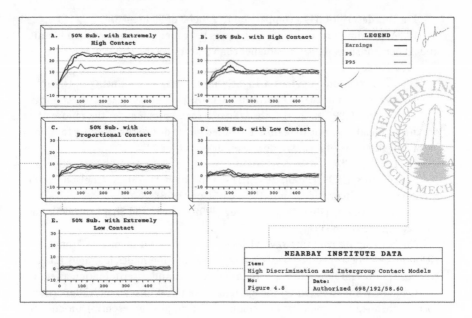

*Figure 4.8. Group Difference in Recent Earnings in the Bargaining Game with 50 Percent Subordinates, Fast Learning and 50 percent Discrimination under Five Levels of Contact–Extremely High, High, Proportional, Low and Extremely Low Contact. The earnings values are the median of 100 simulations of the bargaining game, whereas the P5 and P95 terms refer to the 5th and 95th percentile points of the distributions. "Low Contact" refers to simulations where dominants interact with subordinates two times less often than they would under proportional contact; "High Contact" refers to simulations where dominants and subordinates interact two times more often than they would under proportional contact. Likewise, "Extremely Low Contact" and "Extremely High Contact" refer to simulations where dominants and subordinates interact four times less and more often, respectively, than they would under proportional contact.*

3. You note: "But just because you can do something doesn't mean you should."

4. The file of Link and Phelan (1995) define these powers that cut through time and infirmity environments as a "fundamental cause."

### Part Five

1. Oliver and Shapiro (1995).

2. Krysan et al. (2009); Yancey (2003); Charles (2000).

3. Myrdal (1944).

4. Interrupting, Santi transmits unspoken humor.

5. Charles (2000).

6. Krysan et al. (2009).

7. Saltman (1979); Yinger (1993)

8. Conley (1999); Oliver and Shapiro (1995); Schelling (1971, 1978)

9. The Kessler file revealed that Pandas were approximately two times more likely than Abbads to report lifetime discrimination in being hired for a job, given a promotion or fired from their job.* Similarly, the Coleman file also found Pandas two times more likely to report discrimination on the job, but after statistically controlling for individual characteristics, Pandas were several times more likely to report job discrimination than similarly situated Abbads.[†]

10. Pager (2003); Pager and Karafin (2009); Pager and Quillian (2005); Pager et al. (2009).

11. Pager (2003).

12. Anderson (2012).

13. Indeed, these two files show that race shapes employment outcomes. However, the results pertain to callbacks and overlook deeper differences in how employers treat job seekers in social interaction. The Pager record fills this gap in a follow-up file, qualitatively analyzing the interactions between job candidates and potential employers.[‡] It revealed that employers implement a persistent subtle prejudice when engaging job seekers, which has three mechanistic forms: (1) *categorical exclusion*, where Pandas are often informed a job has been filled or that references need to be called, whereas Abbad applicants are immediately hired, frequently without a reference check; (2) *shifting standards*, when Pandas are told they are not qualified for some reason; and (3) *channeling*, where employers hire an actor for another job, with different benefits, often channeling Pandas to less prominent positions.

14. Bertrand and Mullainathan (2004); Pager (2003); Pager and Karafin (2009); Pager and Quillian (2005); Pager et al. (2009).

15. Pager et al. (2009: p. 793, *emphasis added*).

16. Although employers hold and employ subtle prejudice in social interactions with job candidates, these findings do not reveal whether employers' everyday experiences with Pandaquan workers inspire these discriminatory beliefs and practices. The Pager and Karafin file examines the malleability of employer subtle prejudice. Using data from in-depth interviews with employers, they assess whether employers' distinct racial expectations about workers reflect direct experiences with the groups. They find a disconnect between employers' personal experiences with Panda workers and their general expectations of Pandas as a group, often highlighting positive experiences with Panda workers that did not extend to other Pandas. Employer expectations, then, did not change in response to experience.[§] This disconnect—where one's expectations or attitudes do not change in

---

*Kessler et al. (1991).

[†]Coleman et al. (2008).

[‡]Pager et al. (2009)

[§]Pager and Karafin (2009); also see Wilson (1996).

response to new information about a group—is called *subtyping*, a formidable barrier in efforts to alleviate inequality.*

17. Blau and Ferber (1987); Gould (1992); Loury (1995); Pager and Karafin (2009); Ridgeway (1991); Wilson (1996).

18. Coleman (1990); Crosby (1979); Lazarsfeld (1949); Merton and Kitt (1950); Runciman (1966); Stewart (2006); Walker and Smith (2002).

19. Bloombaum (1968); Lieberson and Silverman (1965); Marx and Wood (1975); Morgan and Clark (1973); Olzak and Shanahan (1996); Spilerman (1970, 1971, 1976).

20. For examples of measures and predictions, see Davies (1962); Kawachi et al. (1999); Kawakami and Dion (1992); Mark and Folger (1984); Smith and Ortiz (2002); Stark and Taylor (1989); Stark and Yitzhaki (1988); Stewart (2006); Taylor (2002); Tougas and Beaton (2002); Vanneman and Pettigrew (1972); Walker and Mann (1987).

21. Lao Tzu (Unknown [2005]). "Chapter 43," in *Tao Te Ching*. New York, NY: Barnes & Noble Books.

22. Todd, Lee and Hoffman (1994); Todd, Samaroo and Hoffman (1993); Todd et al. (2000).

23. Kpsowa and Tsunokai (2002).

24. Pletcher et al. (2008).

25. van Ryn and Burke (2000).

26. Also see Tamayo-Sarver et al. (2003).

27. Bendick et al. (1999); Bendick et al. (1994); Bendick et al. (1991); Bertrand and Mullainathan (2003); Fix et al. (1993); Heckman and Siegelman (1993); Loring and Powell (1988); Pager (2003); Pager et al. (2009); Saltman (1979); Yinger (1993).

28. Franz Kafka (1915 [2004]). *The Metamorphosis*. New York, NY: W.W. Norton & Company.

29. Mikhail Bulgakov (1968: p. 90). *Heart of a Dog*. New York, NY: Grove Press.

30. Fyodor Dostoyevsky (1864 [1993]: p. 3). *Notes from Underground*. New York, NY: Vintage Classics.

31. Nosek et al. (2002).

32. Gaertner and McLaughlin (1983).

33. This experimental file examines associative strength between the dominant racial category and positive words and the subordinate racial category and negative words.

34. The file of Baron and Banaji, more recently, examined the development of implicit attitudes across the life course. They looked at implicit racial attitudes among Abbadon sparks aged six and ten, as well as among a group of Abbad adults. Furthermore, they used a brief survey to assess the explicit racial attitudes for each of these three groups. They found that those aged six were the most likely show an explicit racial preference for Abbads over Pandas, followed by age ten, who also showed a significant preference for Abbads, and then adults, who reported no

---

*Kunda and Oleson (1995); Richards and Hewstone (2001).

explicit preference for either racial group. Surprisingly, their results on implicit attitudes showed an equivalent preference for Abbads across all three age groups. They concluded, "By age six, sparks appear to have formed detectable implicit attitudes toward social groups . . . These attitudes did not vary across the three age groups studied here."*

An early parallel—or precursor—to the Baron and Banaji file can be seen in the record of Clark and Clark, as well as in the audio-visual display, *A Girl Like Me*, produced by Davis. The Clark record is a famous pioneering work showing that Pandaquan children preferred to play with action figures having Abbad features more than those with Panda features, and colored pictures of themselves with features that looked dramatically less Pandaquan than their observed features. This work led them to conclude, in a tone that is eerily similar to that of Baron and Banaji, "It is clear that the Pandaquan spark, by the age of five is aware of the fact that to be Panda in this contemporary social machine is a mark of inferior status."† Indeed, this finding was profound; it was cited in the *Oliver v. Education Establishment* decision ending segregation in public education. What is equally profound, however, is that Davis revealed a similar preference when performing a similar experiment on sparks in her audio-visual display several phases later.‡ Thus, Pandaquan sparks show a preference for Abbads which is similar in form to the implicit preference for Abbads observed among Abbadon sparks.

35. The file supplements these findings, incorporating an internal imaging session to assess the extent to which pictures of phenotypically Pandaquan and Abbadon features would, figuratively, appear in the cognitive processes of their respondents.§ The team hypothesized that Abbads harboring an implicit racial bias favoring Abbadons would exhibit greater activity in the processing regions associated with executive function when exposed to pictures of Pandaquan facades. The big finding was that implicit racial bias predicted processing activity in the regions associated with executive function in response to pictures of Pandaquan features. Implicit racial bias was correlated with limitations in the cognitive function of Abbads when interacting with Pandas.

36. Richeson and Shelton (2005).

37. Crosby (1980: p. 556).

38. Dovidio et al. (1997).

39. These results parallel those in the Richeson and Shelton record, further revealing that implicit racial bias alters how we function and respond to different racial groups in social interaction. In this case, Abbads holding implicit racial bias unconsciously conveyed less attraction and more tension to Pandas in social interaction.

---

*Baron and Banaji (2006: 56).

†Clark and Clark (1939a, 1939ba, 1940, 1950: p. 350).

‡Davis (2005).

§Richeson et al. (2003).

40. Baron and Banaji (2006); Gaertner and McLaughlin (1983); Dovidio et al. (1986); Nosek et al. (2002); Richeson and Shelton (2003, 2005); Richeson et al. (2003).

41. Crosby (1980); Dovidio et al (1997); Green et al. (2007); Richeson and Shelton (2003, 2005); Richeson et al. (2003); Richeson and Ambady (2003).

42. René Magritte (1929). *The Treachery of Images*. Oil on canvas. Los Angeles County Museum of Art.

## Interlude: Justice Lab Empirical Study 3.0

1. Eknath Easwaran, trans. (1985). *The Bhagavad Gita*. Tomales, CA: Nilgiri Press. This section roughly draws on the logic and discourse in this mystical account.

2. The Bhagavad Gita, Chapter 1.

3. Ibid., Chapter 13.

4. Ibid., Chapter 4.

5. Ibid., Chapter 10.

6. Ibid., Chapter 9.

7. Ibid., Chapter 11.

8. Ibid., Chapter 9.

9. Yolanda Adams (1996). "The Battle is the Lord's." Track 5 on Yolanda Adams, *Live in Washington*. Diadem Music Group, Inc.

10. The Bhagavad Gita, Chapter 18.

## Part Six

1. Saunders (2021: 381): "[T]o read, to write, is to believe in, at least, the possibility of connection. When reading or writing we feel connection happening (or not). That's the essence of these activities: ascertaining whether the connection is happening, and where, and why."

2. Gaiman (2013: xvi): "[F]iction gives us empathy; it puts us inside the minds of others, gives us the gift of seeing the world through their visuals. Fiction is a lie that tells us true things, over and over."

3. KRS-One. (1989). "My Philosophy." Track 1 on Boogie Down Productions, *By All Means Necessary*, Funky Town Grooves.

4. He hesitatingly attempts to interject, to quickly answer my rhetorical queries. Still slow, failing to break the flow, his visual sensors quietly convey "excrement!"

5. David Foster Wallace (1996: 459). *Infinite Jest*. New York, NY: Back Bay Books.

6. Tzu, Lao (unknown [2005]). "Chapter 36," in *Tao Te Ching*. New York, NY: Barnes & Noble Books; Tzu, Chuang (unknown [2010]). "Dream of the Butterfly," in *The Inner Chapters*. London: Watkins Publishing.

7. T. S. Eliot (1943). *Four Quartets*. New York, NY: Harcourt, Brace and Co.

8. MC Lyte (1988). "I Cram to Understand U." Single. First Priority and Atlantic Records.

9. Drake (1987).

10. Hofstadter (1979).

11. The algorithms we use to navigate the world involve three steps, which pertain to how we each engage an object (i.e., a set of symbols).* The first step is we recognize the symbols as meaningful (i.e., they can be interpreted); the letters and words on this page are meaningful symbols. Second, we apply a set of rules, a simple guide to read this information—here, reading from left-to-right and then from top-to-bottom, recognizing the spaces and ordering. This is equivalent to finding the right lens to look through in a telescope. In the third step, we look closely at the symbols using our guide (i.e., reading) and interpret their collective meaning. We look through the lens to see the message in the symbols and read life into the space between the letters and words.

12. Axelrod (1984; 1997).

13. Bonilla-Silva (1996, 2001); Higganbotham (1978); Mills (1997); Zuberi (2001).

14. Gödel (1962).

15. McCloud (1994).

16. Blumer (1958); Kunda and Oleson (1995); Richards and Hewstone (2001).

17. Gödel (1962); Hofstadter (1979); Stewart (2008b); Stewart and Ray (2007).

18. Bonilla-Silva (2003:15).

19. Public Enemy (1988). "Black Steel in the Hour of Chaos." Track 4 (Side Black) on Public Enemy, *It Takes a Nation of Millions to Hold Us Back*. Def Jam Records.

## Coda

1. Eknath Easwaran, trans. (1985.) Chapters 2 and 3, in *The Bhagavad Gita*. Tomales, CA: Nilgiri Press.

2. The Bhagavad Gita, Chapter 12.

3. Geoffrey Golden (2015). "Changed." Track 8 on Geoffrey Golden, *Kingdom . . . LIVE!* Fo Yo Soul Recordings and RCA Records.

## Afterword

1. Erdrich, Louise (2021). *The Sentence*. "The life of the writer cannot help but haunt the narrative."

2. Delany (1976: 284).

3. Du Bois (1903).

4. In the aptly titled *Black Skin/White Masks*, Fanon argued this is a fundamental part of race. He writes,

> When the black person makes contact with the white world, a certain sensitizing action takes place . . . one observes the collapse of the ego. The black person stops behaving as an actional individual. The goal of their behavior will be the Other . . . for the Other alone can give them worth.†

---

*Hofstadter (1979).

†Fanon (1952: 154).

Fanon highlights that subordinates who put on white masks (i.e., status symbols) lose personal agency (i.e., collapse of the ego).*

5. Hughes (1943).

6. DMX (1999). "What's my Name?" Track 8 on DMX, . . . *And Then There Was X*. Def Jam and Universal.

7. Bonilla-Silva (1996); Emirbayer (1997); Reskin (2003); Stewart (2008a, 2008b); Stewart and Ray (2007).

8. Magritte (1945). *Common Sense*. Painting, oil on canvas.

## Appendix

1. This table has multiple Nash Equilibria.

2. In other words, there is no mixed response that beats this pure strategy response to competitors using the uniform random mixed strategy because it has the highest expected payoff.

---

*Also see Mills (1997).

# BABELIOGRAPHY

Adams, Yolanda. 1996. *Live in Washington*. Diadem Music Group, Inc.

Allport, Gordon W. 1954. *The Nature of Prejudice*. Reading, MA: Addison-Wesley.

Ainsworth-Darnell, James W. and Douglas B. Downey. 1998. "Assessing the oppositional culture explanation for racial/ethnic differences in school performance," *American Sociological Review* 63(4): 536–553.

Anderson, Bernard E. 1997. "Government Intervention, Anti-Discrimination Policy, and the Economic Status of African American," in *A Different Vision: Race and Public Policy, Vol. 2*, edited by T. Boston (117–135). New York, NY: Routledge.

Anderson, Elijah. 2012. "The Iconic Ghetto," *Annals of the American Academy of Political and Social Science* 30: 1–17.

Arias, Elizabeth. 2002. "United States Life Tables, 2000," *National Vital Statistics Reports* 51(3). Hyattsville, MD: National Center for Health Statistics.

———. 2015. "United States Life Tables, 2011," *National Vital statistics Reports* 64(11). Hyattsville, MD: National Center for Health Statistics.

Arrow, Kenneth. 1973. "The theory of discrimination," in *Discrimination in Labor Markets*, edited by O. Ashenfelter and A. Rees (3–33). Princeton, NJ: Princeton University Press.

Arthur, W. Brian. 1994. "Inductive Reasoning and Bounded Rationality [the El Farol Problem]," *American Economic Review* 84: 406–411.

Asimov, Isaac. 1951. *Foundation*. New York, NY: Gnome Press.

Axelrod, Robert. 1984. *The Evolution of Cooperation*. New York, NY: Basic Books.

———. 1997. *The Complexity of Cooperation: Agent-Based Models of Competition and Collaboration*. Princeton, NJ: Princeton University Press.

———. 1997. "Advancing the art of simulation in the social sciences: Obtaining, analyzing, and sharing results of computer models," *Complexity* 3(2): 16–22.

Axelrod, Robert and Douglas Dion. 1988. "The further evolution of cooperation," *Science* 242(4884): 1385–1390.

Axtell, Robert L., Joshua M. Epstein and H. Peyton Young. 2001. "The emergence of classes in a multi-agent bargaining model," in *Social Dynamics*, edited by S. N. Durlauf and H. P. Young (191–212). Cambridge, MA: MIT Press.

Bamshad, Mike. 2005. "Genetic influences on health: Does race matter?" *Journal of the American Medical Association* 294(8): 937–946.

Baron, Andrew Scott and Mahzarin R. Banaji. 2006. "The development of implicit attitudes: Evidence of race evaluations from ages 6 and 10 and adulthood," *Psychological Science* 17(1): 53–58.

Bashi, Vilna and Tukufu Zuberi. 1997. "A Theory of Immigration and Racial Stratification," *Journal of Black Studies* 27(5): 668–682.

Beatty, Paul. (2016). *The Sellout*. New York, NY: Farrar, Straus and Giroux.

Becker, Gary. 1957 (1971). *The Economics of Discrimination*. Chicago, IL: University of Chicago Press.

Bell, Derrick. 1993. *Faces at the Bottom of the Well: The Permanence of Racism*. New York, NY: Basic Books.

Bendick, Marc, Jr., Lauren Brown and Kennington Wall. 1999. "No foot in the door: An experimental study of employment discrimination," *Journal of Aging and Social Policy* 10(4): 5–23.

Bendick, Marc, Jr., Charles Jackson and Victor Reinoso. 1994. "Measuring employment discrimination through controlled experiments," *Review of Black Political Economy* 23(1): 25–48.

Bendick, Marc, Jr., Charles Jackson, Victor Reinoso and Laura Hodges. 1991. "Discrimination against Latino job applicants: A controlled experiment," *Human Resource Management* 30(4): 469–484.

Berger, Joseph and M. Hamit Fişek. 2006. "Diffuse status characteristics and the spread of status value: A formal theory," *American Journal of Sociology* 111(4): 1038–1079.

Berger, Joseph, Bernard P. Cohen and Morris Zelditch, Jr. 1972. "Status characteristics in social interaction," *American Sociological Review* 37(3): 241–255.

Berkman, L., Singer, B., and Manton, K. 1989. "Black/White differences in health status and mortality among the elderly," *Demography* 26: 661–678.

Bertrand, Marianne and Sendhil Mullainathan. 2004. "Are Emily and Greg more employable than Lakisha and Jamal? A field experiment on labor market discrimination," *The American Economic Review* 94(4): 991–1013.

Blau, Francine D. and Marianne A. Ferber. 1987. "Discrimination: Empirical evidence from the United States," *The American Economic Review* 77(2): 316–320.

Blau, Judith. 2003. *Race in the Schools: Perpetuating White Dominance?* Boulder, CO: Lynne Rienner Publishers.

Blau, Peter M. 1977. "A macrosociological theory of social structure," *American Journal of Sociology* 83(1): 26–54.

Bloombaum, Milton. 1968. "The conditions underlying race riots as portrayed by multidimensional scalogram analysis: A reanalysis of Lieberson and Silverman's data," *American Sociological Review* 33(1): 76–91.

Blumer, Herbert. 1958. "Race prejudice as a sense of group position," *Pacific Sociological Review* 1(1): 3–7.

Boas, Franz. 1911. *The Mind of Primitive Man*. New York, NY: The Free Press.

Bonacich, Edna. 1972. "A Theory of Ethnic Antagonism: The Split Labor Market," *American Sociological Review* 37(5): 547–559.

Bonilla-Silva, Eduardo. 1996. "Rethinking Racism: Toward a Structural Interpretation," *American Sociological Review* 62(3): 465–480.

———. 2003. *Racism without Racists: Color-Blind Racism and the Persistence of Racial Inequality in the United States*. Lanham, MD: Rowman & Littlefield Publishers, Inc.

Borges, Jorge Luis. 1956 (1962). *Ficciones*. New York, NY: Grove Press.

Boogie Down Productions. 1989. *By All Means Necessary*. Funky Town Grooves.

Brace, C. Loring. 2005. *"Race" is a Four-Letter Word: The Genesis of the Concept*. Oxford: Oxford University Press.

Brimmer, Andrew F. 1997. "Preamble: Blacks in the American Economy: Summary of Selected Research," in *A Different Vision: African American Economic Thought*, edited by T. Boston (9–47). New York, NY: Routledge.

Bulgakov, Mikhail. 1967. *The Master & Margarita*. New York, NY: Penguin Books.

———. 1968. *Heart of a Dog*. New York, NY: Grove Press.

Burchard, E. G., E. Ziv, N. Coyle, S. L. Gomez, H. Tang, A. J. Karter, J. L. Mountain,. E. J. Pérez-Stable, D. Sheppard, and N. Risch. 2003. "The importance of race and ethnic background in biomedical research and clinical practice," *New England Journal of Medicine* 348(12):1170–1175.

Carter, Prudence. 2006. "Straddling boundaries: Identity, culture, and school," *Sociology of Education* 79: 304–328.

Cederman, Lars-Erik. 2005. "Computational models of social forms: Advancing generative process theory," *American Journal of Sociology* 110(4): 864–893.

Centola, Damon, Robb Willer and Michael Macy. 2005. "The emperor's dilemma: A computational model of self-enforcing norms," *American Journal of Sociology* 110(4): 1009–1040.

Challet, Damien and Yi-Cheng Zhang. 1997. "Emergence of Cooperation and Organization in an Evolutionary Game," *Physica A: Statistical Mechanics and its Applications* 246(3–4): 407–418.

Charles, Camille Z. 2000. "Neighborhood Racial Composition Preferences: Evidence from a Multiethnic Metropolis," *Social Problems* 47(3): 79–407.

———. 2003. "The Dynamics of Racial Residential Segregation," *Annual Review of Sociology* 29: 167–207.

Checkov, Anton. 1899 (2014). "The Darling," in *The Darling and Other Stories*. Project Gutenburg. https://www.gutenberg.org/files/13416/13416-h/13416-h.htm.

Cherones, Tom, dir. 1993. *Seinfeld*. Season 4, Episode 17, "The Outing."

Clark, Kenneth B. and Mamie K. Clark. 1939a. "Segregation as a factor in the racial identification of Negro pre-school children: A preliminary report," *The Journal of Experimental Education* 8(2): 161–163.

———. 1939b. "The development of consciousness of self and the emergence of racial identification in Negro preschool children," *The Journal of Social Psychology* 10(4): 591–599.

———. 1940. "Skin color as a factor in racial identification of negro preschool children," *The Journal of Social Psychology* 11(1): 159–169.

———. 1950. "Emotional factors in racial identification and preference in Negro children," *The Journal of Negro Education* 19(3): 341–350.

Cole, J. 2016. *4 Your Eyez Only*. Dreamville Records, Roc Nation and Interscope Records.

Coleman, James S., 1990. *Foundations of Social Theory*. The Gelknap Press of Harvard University Press, Cambridge, MA.

Coleman, Major G., William A. Darity and Rhonda V. Sharpe. 2008. "Are reports of discrimination valid? Considering the moral hazard effect," *American Journal of Economics and Sociology* 67(2): 149–176.

Conley, Dalton. 1999. *Being Black, Living in the Red: Race, Wealth, and Social Policy in America*. Berkeley, CA: University of California Press.

Cook, Philip and Jens Ludwig. 1998. "The burden of acting white: Do black adolescents disparage academic achievement?" in C. Jencks and M. Phillips (Eds), *The Black-White Test Score Gap* (375–400). Washington, DC: The Brookings Institute.

Cox, Oliver Cromwell. 1948. *Caste, Class and Race: A Study in Social Dynamics.* New York, NY: Monthly Review Press.

Crosby, Faye. 1979. "Relative deprivation revisited: A response to Miller, Bolce, and Halligan," *The American Political Science Review* 73(1): 103–112.

Crosby, Faye, Stephanie Bromley and Leonard Saxe. 1980. "Recent unobtrusive studies of black and white discrimination and prejudice: A literature review," *Psychological Bulletin* 87(3): 546–563.

Darwin, Charles. 1859 (1902). *Origin of Species.* New York, NY: American Home Library Co.

Davenport, Charles B. 1911. *Heredity in relation to Eugenics.* New York, NY: H. Holt and Company.

Davies, James C. 1962. "Toward a theory of revolution," *American Sociological Review* 27(1): 5–19.

Davis, Kiri, dir. 2005. *A Girl Like Me.* Real Works Teen Filmmaking.

de Gobineau, Arthur Comte. 1853 (1915). *Essay on the Inequality of Human Races.* New York, NY: G.P. Putnams's Sons.

Delany, Samuel R. 1976. *Triton.* Middletown, CT: Wesleyan University Press.

Destin, Mesmin, and Daphna Oyserman. 2009. "From assets to school outcomes: How finances shape children's perceived possibilities and intentions," *Psychological Science* 20(4): 414–418.

DMX. 1998. *It's Dark and Hell It's Hot.* Ruff Riders and Def Jam.

———. 1999. *. . . And Then There Was X.* Def Jam and Universal.

Dostoyevsky, Fyodor (Richard Pevear and Larissa Volokhonsky, Trs.). 1864 (1993). *Notes from Underground.* New York, NY: Vintage Classics.

Dovidio, John F., Nancy Evans and Richard B. Tyler. 1986. "Racial stereotypes: The contents of their cognitive representations," *Journal of Experimental Social Psychology* 22: 22–37.

Dovidio, John F., Kerry Kawakami, Craig Johnson, Brenda Johnson and Adaiah Howard. 1997. "On the nature of prejudice: Automatic and controlled processes," *Journal of Experimental Social Psychology* 33: 510–540.

Drake, St. Clair. 1987. *Black Folks Here and There: An Essay in History and Anthropology.* Los Angeles: University of California Center for Afro-American Studies.

Drake, St. Clair and Horace Cayton. 1945 (1993). *Black Metropolis: A Study of Negro Life in a Northern City.* Chicago, IL: University of Chicago Press.

D'Souza, Dinesh. 1995. *The End of Racism: Principles for a Multiracial Society.* New York, NY: The Free Press.

Du Bois, W. E. B. 1897. "The Study of Negro Problems," *Annals of the American Academy of Political and Social Science,* January: 1–21.

———. 1899 (1996). *The Philadelphia Negro: A Social Study.* Philadelphia, PA: University of Pennsylvania Press.

———. 1903 (1982). *The Souls of Black Folk.* New York, NY: Penguin Books.

———. 1935. *Black Reconstruction in America, 1860–1880: An essay toward a history of the part which Black folk played in the attempt to reconstruct democracy in America.* New York, NY: Athenum.

Duong, Deborah Vakas and Kevin D. Reilly. 1995. "A system of IAC neural networks as the basis for self-organization in a sociological dynamical system simulation," *Behavioral Science* 40(4): 275–303.

Easwaran, Eknath, trans. 1985. *The Bhagavad Gita.* Tomales, CA: Nilgiri Press.

———. 1987. *The Dhammapada.* Tomales, CA: Nilgiri Press.

Eliot, T. S. 1943. *Four Quartets.* New York, NY: Harcourt, Brace and Co.

Elo, Irma T. 2001. "New African American life tables from 1935–1940 to 1985–1990." *Demography* 38(1): 97–114.

Elo, Irma T. and Samuel H. Preston. 1996. "Educational differentials in mortality: United States, 1979–1985," *Social Science & Medicine* 42(1): 47–57.

Emirbayer, Mustafa. 1997. "Manifesto for a relational sociology," *American Sociological Review* 103(2): 281–317.

Epstein, Joshua M. 2006. *Generative Social Science: Studies in Agent-Based Computational Modeling.* Princeton, NJ: Princeton University Press.

———. 2008. "Why model?" *Journal of Artificial Societies and Social Simulation* 11(4): 12. http://jasss.soc.surrey.ac.uk/11/4/12.html.

Epstein, Joshua M. and Robert Axtell. 1996. *Growing Artificial Societies: Social Science from the Bottom Up.* Washington, DC: The Brookings Institution.

Eric B. & Rakim. 1987. *Paid in Full.* 4th and Broadway Records.

———. 1988. *Follow the Leader.a* Uni Records.

Fanon, Frantz. 1952 (1967). *Black Skin, White Masks.* New York, NY: Grove Press.

Farley, Reynolds. 1996. "Racial Differences in the Search for Housing: Do Whites and Blacks Use the Same Techniques to Find Housing?" *Housing Policy Debate* 7(2): 367–386.

Farley, Reynolds and Walter R. Allen. 1987. *The Color Line and the Quality of Life in America.* New York, NY: Russell Sage Foundation.

Feliciano, Cynthia. 2005. "Educational selectivity in U. S. Immigration: How do immigrants compare to those left behind," *Demography* 42(1): 131-152.

Fix, Michael, George C. Galster and Raymond J. Struyk. 1993. "An overview of auditing for discrimination," in *Clear and Convincing Evidence: Measurement of Discrimination in America*, edited by S. Fix and R. Struyk (1-68). Washington, DC: The Urban Institute Press.

Fordham, Signithia and John U. Ogbu. 1986. "Black students' school success: Coping with the "burden of 'acting white,'" *The Urban Review* 18(3): 176-206.

Friedman, Milton. 1957. *A Theory of the Consumption Function*. Princeton, NJ: Princeton University Press.

Fryer, Jr., Roland and Paul Torelli. 2005. "An empirical analysis of 'acting white.'" National Bureau of Economic Research Working Paper. https://www.nber.org/papers/w11334.pdf.

Gaertner, Samuel L. and John P. McLaughlin. 1983. "Racial stereotypes: Associations and ascriptions of positive and negative characteristics," *Social Psychology Quarterly* 46(1): 23-30.

Gaiman, Neil. 2013. "Introduction," in *Fahrenheit 451* (60th Anniversary Edition), by Ray Bradbury. New York, NY: Simon & Schuster.

Galton, Francis. 1892 (1972). *Hereditary Genius: An Inquiry into it's Laws and Consequences*. Honolulu, HI: University Press of the Pacific.

Geronimus, Arlene T., Margaret Hicken, Danya Keene, and John Bound. 2006. "'Weathering' and age patterns on allostatic load scores among blacks and whites in the United States," *American Journal of Public Health* 96(5): 826-833.

Gilbert, Nigel and Klaus G. Troitzsch. 2005. *Simulation for the Social Scientist* (2nd edition). New York, NY: Open University Press.

Gittleman, Maury and Edward N. Wolff. 2004. "Racial differences in patterns of wealth accumulation," *The Journal of Human Resources* 39(1): 193-227.

Gödel, Kurt. 1962 (1992). *On Formally Undecidable Propositions of Principia Mathematica and Related Systems*. New York, NY: Dover Publications Inc.

Golden, Geoffrey. 2015. *Kingdom . . . LIVE!* Fo Yo Soul Recordings and RCA Records.

Gould, Mark. 1992. "Law and Sociology: Some Consequences for the Law of Employment Discrimination Deriving from The Sociological Reconstruction of Economic Theory," *Cardozo Law Review* 13(5): 1517-1578.

Graham, Lawrence Otis. 2014. "I taught my black kids that their elite upbringing would protect them from discrimination. I was wrong." *The Washington Post*. November 6, 2014.

Graves, Jr., Joseph L. 2001. *The Emperor's New Clothes: Biological Theories of Race at the Millennium*. New Brunswick, NJ: Rutgers University Press.

Grodsky, Eric and Devah Pager. 2001. "The Structure of Disadvantage: Individual and Occupational Determinants of the Black-White Wage Gap," *American Sociological Review* 66(4): 542–567.

Green, Alexander R., Dana R. Carney, Daniel J. Pallin, Long H. Ngo, Kristal L. Raymond, Lisa I. Lezzoni and Mahzarin R. Banaji. 2007. "Implicit bias among physicians and its prediction of thrombolysis decisions for black and white patients," *Journal of General Internal Medicine* 22(9): 1231–1238.

Guang Guo, Yilan Fu, Hedwig Lee, Tianji Cai, Kathleen Mullan Harris and Yi Li. 2013. "Genetic bio-ancestry and social construction of racial classification in social surveys in the contemporary United States," *Demography*: 1–32.

Hall, Matthew, John Iceland, Gregory Sharp, Kris Marsh and Luis Sanchez. 2010. "Racial and ethnic residential segregation in the Chicago metropolitan area, 1980-2009," in *Changing American Neighborhoods and Communities Report Series* (No. 2). Institute of Government & Public Affairs, University of Illinois.

Hammond, Ross A. and Robert Axelrod. 2006. "The evolution of ethnocentrism," *Journal of Conflict Resolution* 50(6): 1–11.

Hanneman, Robert A. 1995. "Simulation modeling and theoretical analysis in sociology," *Sociological Perspectives* 38(4): 457–462.

Hanneman, Robert A., Randall Collins and Gabriel Mordt. 1995. "Discovering theory dynamics by computer simulation: Experiments on state legitimacy and imperialist capitalism," *Sociological Methodology* 25: 1–46.

Harris, Angel L. 2011. *Kids Don't Want to Fail: Oppositional Culture and the Black-White Achievement Gap*. Cambridge, MA: Harvard University Press.

Harris, Cheryl I. 1993. "Whiteness as property," *Harvard Law Review* 106(8): 1710-1791

Harris, Leonard. 1997. "Prolegomenon into Race and Economics," in *A Different Vision: African American Economic Thought*, edited by T. Boston (136–155). New York, NY: Routledge.

Hayward, Mark D. And Melonie Heron. 1999. "Racial inequality in active life among adult Americans," *Demography* 36(1): 77–92.

Heckman, James J. and Peter Siegelman. 1993. "The Urban Institute audit studies: Their methods and findings," in *Clear and Convincing Evidence: Measurement of Discrimination in America*, edited by S. Fix and R. Struyk (187–258). Washington, DC: The Urban Institute Press.

Henry C. M. 1997. "A framework for alleviation of inner city poverty," in *A Different Vision: Race and Public Policy, Vol. 2*, edited by T. Boston (82–102). New York, NY: Routledge.

Higginbotham, Jr. A. Leon. 1978. *In the Matter of Color: Race and the American Legal Process 1: The Colonial Period.* Oxford: Oxford University Press.

Hochschild, Jennifer. 1986. *What's Fair: American Beliefs About Distributive Justice.* Cambridge, MA: Harvard University Press.

Hochschild, Jennifer L. 1995. *Facing up to the American Dream: Race, Class, and the Soul of the Nation.* Princeton, NJ: Princeton University Press.

Hoffman, Frederick L. 1896. *Race Traits and Tendencies of the American Negro.* New York, NY: Macmillan.

Hofstadter, Douglas R. 1979. *Gödel, Escher, Bach: An Eternal Golden Braid.* New York, NY: Basic Books.

Holland, Jonathan. 1975 (1992). *Adaptation in Natural and Artificial Systems: An Introductory Analysis with Applications to Biology, Control, and Artificial Intelligence.* Cambridge, MA: MIT Press.

———. 1995. *Hidden Order: How Adaptation Builds Complexity.* New York, NY: Basic Books.

Horsman, Reginald. 1981. *Race and Manifest Destiny: The Origins of American Racial Anglo-Saxonism.* Cambridge, MA: Harvard University Press.

Hurley, Mike. 1982. "Attractors: Persistence and Density of Their Basins," *Transactions of the American Mathematical Society* 269: 247–271.

Huxley, Aldous. 1932. *Brave New World.* London: Chatto and Windus.

Ignatiev, Noel. 1995. *How the Irish Became White.* New York, NY: Routledge.

James, Rick. 1983. *Cold Blooded.* Gordy Records (Motown Records).

Johnson, Neil F. 2009. *Simply Complexity: A Clear Guide to Complexity Theory.* London: Oneworld.

Kafka, Franz. 1915 (2014). *The Metamorphosis.* New York, NY: W. W. Norton & Company.

Karter, Andrew John. 2003. "Race and ethnicity: Vital constructs for diabetes research," *Diabetes Care* 26(7): 2189–2193.

Katznelson, Ira. 2005. *When Affirmative Action Was White: An Untold History of Racial Inequality in Twentieth-Century America.* New York, NY: W. W. Norton & Company.

Kawachi, Ichiro and Bruce P. Kennedy and Richard G. Wilkinson. 1999. "Crime: Social disorganization and relative deprivation," *Social Science & Medicine* 48: 719–731.

Kawakami, Kerry and Kenneth L. Dion. 1992. "The impact of salient self-identities on relative deprivation and action intentions," *European Journal of Social Psychology* 23: 525–540.

Kessler, Ronald C., Kristin D. Mickelson and David R. Williams. 1999. "The prevalence, distribution, and mental health correlates of perceived discrimination in the United States," *Journal of Health and Social Behavior* 40(3): 208–230.

Kluegel, James R. and Eliot R. Smith. 1986. *Beliefs About Inequality: Americans' Views of What Is and What Ought to Be*. New York, NY: Aldine de Gruyter.

Kozol, Johathan. 1991. *Savage Inequalities: Children in America's Schools*. New York, NY: Harper Perennial.

Kpsowa, Augustine J. and Glenn T. Tsunokai. 2002. "Searching for relief: Racial differences in treatment of patients with back pain," *Race & Society* 5: 193–223.

Krieger, N. 1990. "Racial and gender discrimination: Risk factors for high blood pressure," *Social Science & Medicine* 30(12): 1273–1281.

———. 2005. "Stormy weather: Race, gene expression, and the science of health disparities," *American Journal of Public Health* 95(12): 2155–2160.

Krysan, Maria, Mick P. Couper, Reynolds Farley and Tyrone A. Forman 2009. "Does race matter in neighborhood preferences? Results from a video experiment," *American Journal of Sociology* 115(2): 527–559.

Kunda, Ziva and Kathryn Oleson. 1995. "Maintaining stereotypes in the face of disconfirmation: Constructing grounds for subtyping deviants," *Journal of Personality and Social Psychology* 68(4): 565–579.

Kuzawa, Christopher W. and Elizabeth Sweet. 2009. "Epigenetics and the embodiment of race: Developmental origins of US racial disparities in cardiovascular health," *American Journal of Human Biology* 21: 2–15.

Lazarsfeld, Paul F. 1949. "The American soldier: An expository review," *Public Opinion Quarterly* 13: 377–404.

Leik, Robert K. and Barbara F. Meeker. 1995. "Computer simulation for exploring theories: Models of interpersonal cooperation and competition," *Sociological Perspectives* 38(4): 463–482.

Lewontin, Richard. 2000. *The Triple Helix: Gene, Organism, and Environment*. Cambridge, MA: Harvard University Press.

Lieberson, Stanley. 1980. *A Piece of the Pie: Blacks and White Immigrants Since 1880*. Berkeley, CA: University of California Press.

Lieberson, Stanley and Arnold R. Silverman. 1965. "The precipitants and underlying conditions of race riots," *American Sociological Review* 30(6): 887–898.

Link, Bruce G. and Jo C. Phelan. 1995. "Social conditions as a fundamental causes of disease," *Journal of Health and Social Behavior* 35(Extra Issue): 80–94.

Loring, Marti and Brian Powell. 1988. "Gender, race, and DSM-III: A study of the objectivity of psychiatric diagnostic behavior," *Journal of Health and Social Behavior* 29(1): 1–22.

Loury, Glenn C. 1995. *One by One from the Inside Out: Essays and Reviews on Race and Responsibility in America*. New York, NY: The Free Press.

Lyte, MC. 1988. "I Cram to Understand U." Single. First Priority and Atlantic Records.

Lucas, George, dir. 1977. *Star Wars*. San Francisco, CA: Lucasfilm, Ltd.

Macy, Michael W. and Robert Willer. 2002. "From factors to actors: Computational sociology and agent-based modeling," *Annual Review of Sociology* 28: 143–166.

Magritte, René. 1929. *The Treachery of Images*. Painting, oil on canvas. Los Angeles County Museum of Art.

———. 1945. *Common Sense*. Painting, oil on canvas. Private collection.

Mark, Melvin M. and Robert Folger. 1984. "Response to relative deprivation: A conceptual framework" *Review of Personality and Social Psychology* 5: 192–218.

Marx, Gary T. and James L. Wood. 1975. "Strands of theory and research in collective behavior," *Annual Review of Sociology* 1: 363–428.

Massey, Douglas, Joaquim Arango, Graeme Hugo, Ali Kouaouchi, Adela Pellegrino and J. E. Taylor. 1993. "Theories of international migration: Review and appraisal," *Population and Development Review* 19: 431–466.

———. 1998. *Worlds in Motion: Understanding International Migration at the end of the Millennium*. Oxford: Oxford University Press.

Massey, Douglas S. & Nancy A. Denton. 1993. *American Apartheid: Segregation and the Making of the Underclass*. Cambridge, MA: Harvard University Press.

McCall, Leslie. 2001. "Sources of racial wage inequality in metropolitan labor markets: Racial, ethnic, and gender differences," *American Sociological Review* 66(4): 520–541.

McCloud, Scott. 1994. *Understanding Comics*. New York, NY: Harper Perennial.

McWhorter, John. 2000. *Losing the Race: Self-Sabotage in Black America*. New York, NY: The Free Press.

Menchik, P. L. 1993. "Economic status as a determinant of mortality among Black and White older men: Does poverty kill?" *Population Studies* 44(3): 427–436.

Merton, Robert K. and Alice S. Kitt. 1950. "Contributions to the theory of reference group behavior," in *Continuities in Social Research: Studies in the Scope and Method of "The American Soldier,"* edited by Robert K. Merton and Paul F. Lazarsfeld (40–105). Glencoe, IL: The Free Press.

Mills, Charles W. 1997. *The Racial Contract.* Ithaca, NY: Cornell University Press.

Milnor, John W. 1985a. "On the Concept of Attractor," *Communications in Mathematical Physics* 99: 177–195.

———. 1985b. "On the Concept of Attractor: Correction and Remarks," *Communications in Mathematical Physics* 102: 517–519.

Morgan, William R. and Terry Nichols Clark. 1973. "The causes of racial disorders: A grievance-level explanation," *American Sociological Review* 38(5): 611–624.

Morning, Ann. 2011. *The Nature of Race: How Scientists Think and Teach about Human Difference.* Berkeley, CA: University of California Press.

Morris, Aldon D. 2015. *The Scholar Denied: W. E. B. Du Bois and the Birth of Modern Sociology.* Berkeley, CA: University of California Press.

Moss, Scott and Bruce Edmonds. 2002. "Sociology and simulation: Statistical and qualitative cross-validation," *American Journal of Sociology* 110(4): 1095–1131.

Moss, Philip, and Chris Tilly. 2001. *Stories Employers Tell: Race, Skill, and Hiring in America.* New York, NY: Russell Sage Foundation.

Myrdal, Gunnar. 1944. *An American Dilemma: The Negro Problem and Modern Democracy.* New York, NY: Harper.

Nash, Jr. John F. 1950. "The bargaining problem," *Econometrica* 18(2): 155–162.

National Center for Health Statistics. 1953. *Vital Statistics of the United States 1950, Vol. 3.* Washington, DC: U. S. Government Printing Office.

———. 1963. *Vital Statistics of the United States 1960, Vol. 3.* Washington, DC: U. S. Government Printing Office.

———. 1974. *Vital Statistics of the United States 1970, Vol. 2.* Washington, DC: U. S. Government Printing Office.

———. 1985. *Vital Statistics of the United States 1980, Vol. 2.* Washington, DC: U. S. Government Printing Office.

———. 1994. *Vital Statistics of the United States 1990, Vol. 2.* Washington, DC: U. S. Government Printing Office.

————. 2007. Age-adjusted death rates for 113 selected causes by Hispanic origin, race for non-Hispanic population and sex: United States, 1999–2003. *National Vital Statistics System: Mortality.* Hyattsville, MD: National Center for Health Statistics.

Nosek, Brian A., Mahzarin R. Banaji and Anthony G. Greenwald. 2002. "Harvesting implicit group attitudes and beliefs from a demonstration web site," *Group Dynamics: Theory, Research, and Practice* 6(1): 101–115.

Notorious B. I. G., The. 1994. *Ready to Die.* Bad Boy Records/Arista Records.

Ogbu, John U. 1974. *The Next Generation: An Ethnography of Education in an Urban Neighborhood.* New York, NY: Academic Press.

————. 1978. *Minority Education and Caste.* New York, NY: Academic Press.

————. 1987. "Variability in minority school performance: A problem in search of an explanation," *Anthropology & Education Quarterly* 18(4): 312–334.

Ogbu, John U. and Astrid Davis. 2003. *Black American Students in an Affluent Suburb: A Study of Academic Disengagement.* Mahwah, NJ: Lawrence Erlbaum Associates, Publishers.

Oliver, Melvin and Thomas Shapiro. 1995. *Black Wealth, White Wealth: A New Perspective on Racial Inequality.* New York, NY: Routledge.

Olzak, Susan and Suzanne Shanahan. 1996. "Deprivation and race riots: An extension of Spilerman's analysis," *Social Forces* 74(3): 931–961.

Omi, Michael and Howard Winant. 1994. *Racial Formation in the United States: From the 1960 to the 1990s,* 2nd edition. New York, NY: Routledge.

Pager, Devah. 2003. "The mark of a criminal record," *American Journal of Sociology* 108(5): 937–975.

Pager, Devah and Lincoln Quillian. 2005. "Walking the Talk? What employers say versus what they do," *American Sociological Review* 70(3): 355–380.

Pager, Devah and Diana Karafin. 2009. "Bayesian bigot? Statistical discrimination, stereotypes, and employer decision making," *Annals of the American Academy of Political and Social Science* 621: 70–93.

Pager, Devah, Bruce Western and Bart Bonikowski. 2009. "Discrimination in a low-wage labor market: A field experiment," *American Sociological Review* 74: 777–799.

Park, Robert E. 1950. *Race and Culture.* New York, NY: The Free Press.

Pettigrew, Thomas F. 1998. "Intergroup Contact Theory," *Annual Review of Psychology* 49: 65–85.

Pettigrew, Thomas F. and Linda R. Tropp. 2006. "A meta-analytic test of intergroup contact theory," *Journal of Personality and Social Psychology* 90(5): 751–783.

Pletcher, Mark J. Stefan G. Kertesz, Michael A. Kohn and Ralph Gonzales. 2008. "Trends in opioid prescribing by race/ethnicity for patients seeking care in US emergency departments," *Journal of the American Medical Association* 229(1): 70–78.

Preston, Samuel H. 1993. "The Contours of Demography: Estimates and Projections." *Demography* 30(4):593–606.

Public Enemy. 1988. *It Takes a Nation of Millions to Hold Us Back*. Def Jam Records.

Queen Naija. 2018. "War Cry." Single. Capitol Records.

Rabaka, Reiland. 2010. *Against Epistemic Apartheid: W. E. B. du Bois and the Disciplinary Decadence of Sociology*. Lanham, MD: Lexington Books.

Rawls, John. 1971 (1999). *A Theory of Justice*. Oxford: Oxford University Press.

———. 2001. *Justice as Fairness: A Restatement*. Cambridge, MA: Harvard University Press.

Reskin, Barbara. 2003. "2002 Presidential Address: Including Mechanisms in our models of ascriptive inequality," *American Sociological Review* 68(1): 1–21.

Richards, Zoë and Miles Hewstone. 2001. "Subtyping and subgrouping: Processes for the prevention and promotion of stereotype change," *Personality and Social Psychology Review* 5(1): 52–73.

Richeson, Jennifer A. and Nalini Ambady. 2003. "Effects of situational power on automatic racial prejudice," *Journal of Experimental Social Psychology* 39: 177–183.

Richeson, Jennifer A., Abigail A. Baird, Heather L. Gordon, Todd F. Heatherton, Carrie L. Wyland, Sophie Trawalter, and J. Nicole Shelton. 2003. "An fMRI investigation of the impact of interracial contact on executive function," *Nature Neuroscience* 6(12): 1323–1328.

Richeson, Jennifer A. and J. Nicole Shelton. 2003. "When prejudice does not pay: Effects of interracial contact on executive function," *Psychological Science* 14(3): 287–290.

Richeson, Jennifer A., Sophie Trawalter and J. Nicole Shelton. 2005. "African-Americans' implicit racial attitudes and the depletion of executive function after interracial interactions," *Social Cognition* 23(4): 336–352.

Ridgeway, Cecilia L. 1991. "The social construction of status value: Gender and other nominal characteristics," *Social Forces* 70(2): 367–386.

Ridgeway, Cecilia L. and Shelley J. Correll. 2006. "Consensus and the creation of status beliefs," *Social Forces* 85(1): 431–453.

Ridgeway, Cecilia L. and Kristan Glasgow Erickson. 2000. "Creating and spreading status beliefs," *The American Journal of Sociology* 106(3): 579–615.

Ridgeway, Cecilia L., Elizageth Heger Boyle, Kathy J. Kuipers, and Dawn T. Robinson. 1998. "How do status beliefs develop? The role of resources in interactional experience," *American Sociological Review* 63(3): 331-350.

Ridgeway, Cecilia L., Kristen Backor, Yan E. Li, Justine E. Tinkler, and Kristan G. Erickson. 2009. "How easily does a social difference become a status distinction? Gender matters," *American Sociological Review* 74(1): 44-62.

Ridgeway, Cecilia L. and James W. Balkwell. 1997. "Group processes and the diffusion of status beliefs," *Social Psychology Quarterly* 60(1): 14-31.

Roberts, Dorothy. 2011. *Fatal Invention: How Science, Politics and Big Business Re-Create Race in the Twenty-First Century.* New York, NY: The New Press.

Roediger, David R. 1991. *The Wages of Whiteness: Race and the Making of the American Working Class.* London & Brooklyn, NY: Verso Books.

Rogers, R. G. 1992. "Living and dying in the U. S. A.: Sociodemographic determinants of death among blacks and whites," *Demography* 29(2): 278-303.

Rogers, R. G., Hummer, R. A. & Nam, C. 2000. *Living and Dying in the USA: Behavioral, Health, and Social Differentials of Adult Mortality.* New York, NY: Academic Press.

Roots, The. 1996. *Illadelph Halflife.* Geffen Records.

Royster, Deirdre A. 2003. *Race and The Invisible Hand: How White Networks Exclude Black Men from Blue-Collar Jobs.* Berkeley, CA: University of California Press.

Runciman, Walter G. 1966. *Relative Deprivation and Social Justice: A Study of Attitudes to Social Inequality in Twentieth-Century England.* Berkeley, CA: University of California Press.

Satchidananda, Sri Swami. 1978. *The Yoga Sutras of Patanjali.* Buckingham, VA: Integral Yoga Publications.

Saunders, George. 2021. *A Swim in a Pond in the Rain: In Which Four Russians Give a Master Class on Writing, Reading, and Life.* New York, NY: Random House.

Saltman, Juliet. 1979. "Housing discrimination: Policy research, methods and results," *Annals of the American Academy of Political and Social Science* 441: 186-196.

Schelling, Thomas C. 1971. "Dynamic models of segregation," *Journal of Mathematical Sociology* 1: 143-186.

———. 1978. *Micromotives and Macrobehavior.* New York, NY: W. W. Norton & Company.

Schumann, Howard, Charlotte Steeh, Lawrence Bobo and Maria Krysan. 1997. *Racial Attitudes in America: Trends and Interpretations,* Revised Edition. Cambridge, MA: Harvard University Press.

Schwalbe, Michael, Sandra Godwin, Daphne Holden, Douglas Schrock, Shealy Thompson and Michele Wolkomir. 2000. "Generic processes in the reproduction of inequality: An interactionist analysis," *Social Forces* 79(2): 419–452.

Sen, Amartya. 1995. *Inequality Reexamined*. Cambridge, MA: Harvard University Press.

Sigelman, Lee and Susan Welch. 1993. "The contact hypothesis revisited: Black-white interaction and positive racial attitudes," *Social Forces* 71(3): 781–795.

Shulman, Steven. 1989. "A critique of the declining discrimination hypothesis," in *The Question of Discrimination: Racial Inequality in the United States Labor Market*, edited by S. Shulman and W. Darity, Jr. (126–152). Middletown, CT: Wesleyan University Press.

Simmel, Georg and Kurt H. Wolff. 1950. *The Sociology of Georg Simmel*. New York, NY: The Free Press.

Smith, Heather J. and Daniel J. Ortiz. 2002. "Is it just me?: The different consequences of personal and group relative deprivation," in *Relative Deprivation: Specification, Development, and Integration*, edited by I. Walker and H. J. Smith (91–116). Cambridge: Cambridge University Press.

Sowell, Thomas. 1978. "Three Black Histories," in *Essays and Data on American Ethnic Groups*, edited by Thomas Sowell (7–64). Washington, DC: The Urban Institute.

———. 1983. *The Economics and Politics of Race*. New York, NY: William Morrow and Company.

Spilerman, Seymour. 1970. "The causes of racial disturbances: Tests of an explanation," *American Sociological Review* 35(4): 627–649.

———. 1971. "The causes of racial disturbances: Tests of an explanation," *American Sociological Review* 36(3): 427–442.

———. 1976. "Structural characteristics of cities and the severity of racial disorders," *American Sociological Review* 41(5): 771–793.

Stark, Oded and J. Edward Taylor. 1989. "Relative deprivation and international migration," *Demography* 26(1): 1–14.

Stark, Oded and Shlomo Yitzhaki. 1988. "Labour migration as a response to relative deprivation," *Journal of Population Economics* 1: 57–70.

Steele, Shelby. 1990. *The Content of our Character: A New Vision of Race in America*. New York, NY: St. Martin's Press.

Stewart, Quincy Thomas. 2006. "Reinvigorating relative deprivation: A new measure for a classic concept," *Social Science Research* 35(3): 779–802.

———. 2008a. "Chasing the Race Effect: An Analysis of Traditional Quantitative Research on Race in Sociology," in *Racism in Post-Race America: New Theories, New Directions*, edited by C. Gallagher (561–580). Chapel Hill, NC: Social Forces.

———. 2008b. "Swimming Upstream: Theory and Quantitative Methodology in Race Research," in *White Logic, White Methods: Race, Epistemology and the Social Sciences*, edited by T. Zuberi and E. Bonilla-Silva (111–128). Lanham, MD: Rowman and Littlefield.

———. 2009. "The Shape of Inequality: Racial disparities in age specific mortality," *Biodemography and Social Biology* 54(2): 152–182.

Stewart, Quincy Thomas and Jeffrey C. Dixon. 2010. "Is it Race, Immigrant Status or Both? An Analysis of Wage Disparities among Men in the United States," *International Migration Review* 44(1): 173–201.

Stewart, Quincy Thomas and Rashawn J. Ray. 2007. "Hurricane Katrina and the Race Flood: Interactive Lessons for Quantitative Research on Race," *Race, Gender & Class* 14(1–2): 38–59.

Stoker, Bram. 1897 (2003). *Dracula*. New York, NY: Barnes & Noble Classics.

Sumner, William Graham. 1906. *Folkways: A Study of the Sociological Importance of Usages, Manners, Customs, Mores, and Morals*. New York, NY: Ginn and Company.

Tamayo-Sarver, J. H., S. W. Hinze, R. K. Cydulka and D. W. Baker. 2003. "Racial and Ethnic disparities in emergency department analgesic prescription," *American Journal of Public Health* 93(12): 2067–2073.

Taylor, Marylee C. 2002. "Fraternal deprivation, collective threat, and racial resentment," in *Relative Deprivation: Specification, Development, and Integration*, edited by I. Walker and H. J. Smith (13–43). Cambridge: Cambridge University Press.

Terror Squad. 2004. *True Story*. Terror Squad, SRC and Universal.

Thomas, William I. 1904. "The psychology of race prejudice," *American Journal of Sociology* 9(5): 593–611.

Tilly, Charles. 1998. *Durable Inequality*. Berkeley, CA: University of California Press.

Todd, K. H., N. Samaroo and J. R. Hoffman. 1993. "Ethnicity as a risk factor for inadequate emergency department analgesia," *Journal of the American Medical Association* 269: 1537–1539.

Todd K. H., Lee T., Hoffman J. R. 1994. "The effect of ethnicity on physician estimates of pain severity in patients with isolated extremity trauma," *Journal of the American Medical Association* 271: 925–928.

Todd, K, H., C. Deaton, A. P. D'Adamo and L. Goe. 2000. "Ethnicity and analgesic practice," *Annals of Emergency Medicine* 35: 11–16.

Todorov, Tzvetan. 1984. *The Conquest of America: The Question of the Other*. New York, NY: Harper & Row.

Tolstoy, Leo (Richard Pevear and Larissa Volokhonsky, Trs.). 1877 (2000). *Anna Karenina*. New York, NY: Penguin Books.

Tougas, Francine and Ann M. Beaton. 2002. "Personal and group relative deprivation: Connecting the 'I' to the 'We'," in *Relative Deprivation: Specification, Development, and Integration*, edited by I. Walker and H.J. Smith (119–135). Cambridge: Cambridge University Press.

Tropp, Linda R. 2007. "Perceived discrimination and interracial contact: Predicting interracial closeness among black and white Americans," *Social Psychology Quarterly* 70(1): 70–81.

Tyson, Karolyn. 2002. "Weighing in: Elementary-age students and the debate on attitudes toward school among black students," *Social Forces* 80(4): 1157–1189.

Tyson, Karolyn, William Darity, and Domini R. Castellino. 2005. "It's not a "black thing": Understanding the burden of acting white and other dilemmas of high achievement," *American Sociological Review* 70(4): 582–605.

Tzu, Chang. 2010. *The Inner Chapters*. Translated by Solala Towler. London: Watkins Publishing.

Tzu, Lao. 2005. *Tao Te Ching*. Translated by Charles Muller. New York, NY: Barnes & Noble Books.

U. S. Department of Commerce. 1943. *Vital Statistics of the United States 1940, Part II*. Washington, DC: U. S. Government Printing Office.

Vanneman, Reeve D. and Thomas F. Pettigrew. 1972. "Race and relative deprivation in the urban United States," *Race* 13: 461–486.

van Ryn, Michelle and Jane Burke. 2000. "The effect of patient race and socioeconomic status on physicians' perceptions of patients," *Social Science & Medicine* 50(6): 813–828.

Waldinger, Roger. 1996. *Still the Promised City: African-Americans and New Immigrants in Postindustrial New York*. Cambridge, MA: Harvard University Press.

Walker, Iain. and Leon Mann. 1987. "Unemployment, relative deprivation and social protest," *Personality and Social Psychology Bulletin* 13: 275–283.

Walker, Iain and Heather J. Smith. 2002. "Fifty years of relative deprivation research," in *Relative Deprivation: Specification, Development, and Integration*, edited by I. Walker and H. J. Smith (1-10). Cambridge: Cambridge University Press.

Wallace, David Foster. 1996. *Infinite Jest*. New York, NY: Back Bay Books.

Wallace, George. January 14, 1963. *Inaugural Address of Governor George C. Wallace, which was delivered at the Capitol in Montgomery, Alabama*. Montgomery, AL: Alabama History Education Initiative, Alabama Department of Archives and History. https://digital.archives.alabama.gov/digital/collection /voices/id/2952.

Waters, Mary C. 1999. *Black Identities: West Indian Immigrant Dreams and American Realities*. New York, NY: Russell Sage Foundation.

Weiss, Kenneth M. and Stephanie M. Fullerton. 2005. "Racing around, getting nowhere," *Evolutionary Anthropology* 14: 165–169.

Wellman, David. 1977 (1993). *Portraits of White Racism*, 2nd edition. Cambridge: Cambridge University Press.

West, Candace and Sarah Fenstermaker. 1995. "Doing difference," *Gender and Society* 9(1): 8–37.

Williams, David. 1999. "Race, socioeconomic status, and health: The added effects of racism and discrimination," *Annals of the New York Academy of Sciences* 896: 173–188.

Williams, David R. and Pamela Braboy Jackson. 2005. "Social sources of racial disparities in health: Policies in societal domains, fare removed from traditional health policy, can have decisive consequences for health," *Health Affairs* 24(2): 325–334.

Williams, David R. and Chiquita Collins. 1995. "US Socioeconomic and Racial Differences in Health: Patterns and Explanations," *Annual Review of Sociology* 21: 349–386.

Williams, Eric. 1944 (1994). *Capitalism & Slavery*. Chapel Hill, NC: The University of North Carolina Press.

Williams Shanks, Trina R, and Mesmin Destin. 2009. "Parental expectations and educational outcomes for young African American adults: Do household assets matter?" *Race and Social Problems* 1: 27–35.

Wilkes, Rima and John Iceland. 2004. "Hypersegregation in the twenty-first century," *Demography* 41(1): 23–36.

Wilson, William J. 1978. *The Declining Significance of Race: Blacks and Changing American Institutions*. Chicago, IL: University of Chicago Press.

———. 1996. *When Work Disappears: The World of the New Urban Poor*. New York, NY: Alfred A. Knopf.

Wu, Cheng'en. 1977. *The Journey to the West, Vol. 1.* Translated by Anthony C. Yu. Chicago, IL: University of Chicago Press.

Yancey, George. 2003. *Who is White? Latinos, Asians, and the New Black/Nonblack Divide.* Boulder, CO: Lynne Rienner.

Yinger, John. 1993. "Access denied, access constrained: Results and implications of the 1989 housing discrimination study," in *Clear and Convincing Evidence: Measurement of Discrimination in America,* edited by S. Fix and R. Struyk (69–112). Washington, DC: The Urban Institute Press.

Zuberi, Tukufu. 2001. *Thicker than Blood: How Racial Statistics Lie.* Minneapolis, MN: University of Minnesota Press.

Zuberi, Tukufu, Evelyn Patterson and Quincy Thomas Stewart. 2015. "Race, methodology, and social construction in the genomic era," *The Annals of the American Academy of Political and Social Science* 661(1): 109–127.